MISSING FOR GOOD

ALEX COOMBS

First published in Great Britain in 2020 by Boldwood Books Ltd.

Cover Design by Nick Castle Design

Cover photography: Shutterstock

A CIP catalogue record for this book is available from the British Library.

Paperback ISBN 978-1-83889-863-2

Hardback ISBN 978-1-80426-185-9

Large Print ISBN 978-1-83889-862-5

Ebook ISBN 978-1-83889-865-6

Kindle ISBN 978-1-83889-864-9

Audio CD ISBN 978-1-83889-857-1

MP3 CD ISBN 978-1-83889-858-8

Digital audio download ISBN 978-1-83889-860-1

Boldwood Books Ltd
23 Bowerdean Street
London SW6 3TN
www.boldwoodbooks.com

To Constance

1

Jamie McDonald was waiting to kill someone. He looked again at the display on the dashboard – it read 18:55 Mon 24 Jan. It didn't seem to have changed in what felt like an hour. The temperature outside was five degrees Celsius. About the same as a fridge. He was tense; time was dragging, moving so slowly.

'So who's paying for the hit?' he asked the man sitting next to him.

'What?' Jordan McKenna replied, having been lost in thought.

'I said, who's paying for the hit?' McDonald said. The two of them, he and Jordan, were parked up in a small white van by the side of the road in Howe Street in Edinburgh's New Town. It was a dark night and a fine rain was falling.

Jordan shrugged. 'Some guy,' he said in a way that made it clear he wasn't going to talk about it. 'You don't need to know.'

Bet it's Millar, thought McDonald. He looked out of the window away from Jordan and checked the side mirror. That was all he was going to get. It didn't really matter. He knew it was Millar. Jordan was Millar's man in Edinburgh.

He glanced at Jordan, medium height and build, hunched in his puffa jacket behind the wheel. The orange street light outside shone on the two of them. He was a handsome guy, thirty-five, but the years and the lifestyle were starting to catch up. In this light he looked ten years older. You could see the lines. Now he took a tobacco pouch out of his jacket pocket and started to roll a joint.

'What the fuck do you think you're doing, Jordan?' said McDonald irritably.

'What does it look like?' Jordan glared at him in an aggrieved way. 'It's only a joint, for fuck's sake.'

'Put it away.'

Jordan shook his head irritably but did as he was told. Nominally, he was in charge, but the reality was that the man sitting beside him called the shots. Jordan didn't want to offend the man he had hired – he had a terrifying capacity for violence and Jordan was frightened of him.

Numpty, thought McDonald. Here they were in Edinburgh's elegant Georgian New Town, just a short, five-minute drive along the cobbled streets from Bute House in Charlotte Square where the First Minister lived. It was quite probable that the police would be patrolling round here and what did Jordan want to do? Smoke weed. Two men in a small van. And not just two men. They looked like criminals. They were criminals. Why don't we just put a sign up saying 'up to no good'? he thought.

He put his hand in his inside pocket and felt the gun there. It felt reassuring.

McDonald was a formidable guy, his pecs visible through the dark blue jumper he was wearing. The huge muscles of his biceps bulked out his jacket. Hard, defined jail muscle. Jordan had met him at HMP Addiewell, at the time McDonald was due for release on license, eight years for a bar room stabbing.

When Jordan had been given tonight's job and heard McDonald was available for hire, he'd asked him immediately. McDonald wasn't the kind of guy to fuck up. What he hadn't factored in was McDonald's new-found tetchiness caused largely, in Jordan's opinion, by him giving up his five-gram-a-day coke habit.

'Run over again what we're going tae do?' Jordan said.

McDonald said wearily, 'When we see the girl, I get out and open the back doors. When she reaches the van, I stop her, get her in the back and off we go. You drive, I restrain her. Simple. She won't cause any trouble; she'll be too frightened.'

'And if there's someone with her?' asked Jordan. His tone was insistent. McDonald's nerves were taut, he could really do without this pointless questioning.

'One person, they get in the van with the girl. Two people...' He shook his head irritably. He was tired of this. There could be endless permutations – what if she arrived riding a camel? 'Fuck it, if there's two or more with her, we dinnae do anything.'

'OK... and then, if there's just her?' Back to the original scenario.

'We drive out to Muirhouse. I deal with the girl.' There was a yard that Jordan rented there. Even if anyone heard a gunshot in Muirhouse, they wouldn't bother too much about it. It was that kind of place. You minded your own business. McDonald carried on.

'We put her in the other van and I take her away. You torch this van. We meet up tomorrow at Morris's bar in Partick, twelve noon.'

'How are ye going to dispose of her?'

'My business.' McDonald's tone shut down any more questions.

Jordan checked his watch.

'Here she comes – guid, she's alone.'

Lit by the orange street light, her long legs striding up the steep hill towards them, she wore jeans and Ugg boots and a woollen hat with a bobble of faux fur pulled down low over her face.

'Sure?' This was her. He took a deep breath. This was the girl he was going to kill.

'Absolutely sure,' Jordan said.

Now was the moment. He got out of the van. Cold rain and a bitter wind. Now the adrenaline hit him as the coke used to. Now his heart was pounding as he psyched himself up for dealing with her. Now he felt a mix of panic and excitement and then his eyes widened in recognition.

Christ, it was her!

'Jamie!' She smiled, her eyes sparkling with delight at seeing him. His right hand tightened around the gun in his pocket.

'Hello, Aurora,' he said quietly.

2

To understand the present, we have to revisit the past. Hanlon thought of her therapist's words from eight months previously. Do we, Dr Morgan? Do we really? Speak for yourself, Doctor. I'm in the here and now.

The target appeared in the cross-hairs of the telescopic sight, the barrel of the .22 rifle resting motionless on her old folded Barbour jacket. A cold, February afternoon. The gentle chilly breeze tugged at her hair. She could smell the damp of the turf under her body, kept short by sheep grazing, and the tang of salt in the air from the sea. Clouds scudded across the hard grey Scottish skies.

Her breathing was steady, the bull's eye at the centre of the concentric rings of the target motionless in the centre of the cross-hairs. She gently squeezed the trigger, feeling the rifle kick. Hanlon glanced down at the dog beside her, waiting with good-natured patience.

She ruffled the soft fur on Wemyss's head and stood up, slinging the rifle over her shoulder, and walking over to the paper targets she'd been shooting at. She pulled them away from the old wooden fishing crate she'd gaffer-taped them to. Looking at the holes in the paper, she nodded, satisfied. It was good marksmanship. She stretched and looked down from the hillside where she was standing.

It was a spectacular view. Below her was the rocky coastline of the east side of the Argyll peninsula and the very blue waters of the Gulf of Arran. The island of Arran itself rose up majestically from the sea, its huge craggy hills dominated by the largest of the peaks, Goat Fell, its summit a crazily jagged assembly of rock, like nature attempting a futurist modern art sculpture.

Hanlon and the dog walked down the track that led to the road by the shore and the cottage she was renting. The land was frozen and cold. Dead, brown bracken, the few stunted birch trees ghostly and skeletal. About half a mile away, she could see the roofs of the village of Skipness. Even village was pushing it – there was a church, a shop, a small school and a village hall but there was just a small handful of houses there. She shook her head in wonder as she looked at it. She was a Londoner; she could never have predicted that she would end up living in such a small place.

West of the village, accessible by a rutted track, was the tumbledown one-bedroom cottage she was renting. Its main attraction for her was the isolation. That and the price. It was hers until the holiday season started in May, just a few weeks away now, then she would have to move on. She didn't mind. She had no roots.

She could access her property by a path that led up into the hills as well as by its drive that ran up from the road. She was walking down this track when she saw the car, slowly bouncing its way along the potholed road towards her house.

Hanlon immediately dropped down into the bracken so she would be hidden from view, got her binoculars out and focussed on the vehicle. The dog, obedient as ever, crouched by her side. The car was a black Audi estate. She didn't recognise it. She knew most of the cars in the village by now and it wasn't one of them.

The Audi parked in front of her cottage, the driver's door opened, and a man got out. He was tall, wearing a charcoal suit and tie, dark-haired. It wasn't someone she knew. He walked up to the door, knocked, and waited. When no one answered he calmly walked back to the car and got in. Even from this distance she could sense his self-possession. She saw him take a briefcase from the passenger seat, open it, remove some papers and start to read, making notes with a pen. He did not look threatening. Hanlon had made more than a few enemies in her life; she was always looking over her shoulder. This guy looked harmless.

She stood up and walked down the track. As she drew nearer he noticed her, put his paperwork down, opened the door and got out of the car. He looked very out of place in his suit and highly polished black Oxford brogues standing outside the grey pebble-dashed cottage in the middle of the countryside. She walked up to him. He was tall, as she had surmised from a distance, and slim. She guessed he was about forty. He had a long, saturnine face and heavy dark eyebrows.

'Hanlon?' he asked.

She nodded and watched as he ran an appraising gaze over her muddy walking boots, rifle in one hand, army surplus combat trousers, old cracked Barbour jacket. Wemyss, her dog, stood by her side, regarding the man suspiciously.

'And you are?' she said.

'My name's James Gillies.' He reached into the breast pocket of his tailored jacket and removed a business card. His suit was tailored and looked expensive. She took his card and glanced down at it.

'A lawyer.'

'A lawyer.' He gave her another appraising look. 'My employer asked me to meet you and bring you to him for a meeting.'

She frowned. 'What, right now?'

He nodded. 'Right now.'

She looked at him, perplexed. Right now? True, she wasn't the easiest person to get in touch with. But surely an e-mail wouldn't have been too difficult? He had managed to find her physical address, after all. Whoever Gillies worked for must know her name, so they could have given her some kind of advance warning.

'Who is your employer?' she asked. The tone in her voice was questioning, suspicious. Why not just call?

Gillies' face was impassive. 'He's a prominent businessman.'

Really? she thought. A prominent businessman. Does he not have a name? Do you have to be so mysterious? A buzzard wheeled lazily in the air high above them; in the distance on the grey loch, a fishing boat was visible on the horizon. She could hear the whine of a chainsaw in the wood down the road. Life was going on around them while the two of them stood like some odd still-life tableau, Gillies out of place in his sombre suit and highly polished wing tip shoes.

'OK,' she said, 'where does this prominent businessman want to meet me?'

He ignored the sarcasm in her voice. 'Near Oban,' he said.

Hanlon thought, That's going to be about a two-hour drive, north, up the Argyll coast. Two hours there, say an hour's meeting with the mystery man, then back. Five hours. She wouldn't be home until after dark.

'If you tell me what it's about, I'll consider it.' There was no way she was going on a four-hour journey without knowing why.

'His daughter's disappeared,' Gillies said.

Missing persons, she thought. That sounded good to her. She looked at Gillies; no more was going to be forthcoming. She pointed at the dog.

'He'll have to come too.'

'Fine.' Gillies didn't miss a beat.

She nodded at the rifle. 'I'll just put this away.'

'Five minutes,' Gillies said. He seemed a man of few words.

She let herself into the cottage, left her boots on the mat by the door and pulled on a pair of Air Max training shoes. Wemyss looked at her with interest and his tail swished on the floor. Training shoes meant a run and he loved running.

'Not today, boy.' She ruffled the fur on his head. 'We're going to meet a client.' The dog looked at her and she kissed his head. He sensed her excitement and wagged his tail. 'That's right, a client.' She grinned at the dog. 'Our first one!'

The two of them left the house and she locked the door. The taciturn Gillies opened the hatch and the border collie jumped inside. Hanlon got in the passenger seat and Gillies climbed in. He started the car.

'What's her name?' she asked. He turned his head and looked at her, frowning. 'The missing girl,' she prompted him, 'what's her name?'

'Aurora,' he said. 'Her name's Aurora.'

3

The black BMW 4 x 4 drove slowly towards a block of flats in Clydebank in the west side of Glasgow. From the living room window on the sixth floor, Calla Lennox looked at the car with a growing feeling of unease. Drug dealer, had to be. Nobody with money would be coming here otherwise. Especially in a car like that. Calla had been born on the estate – she knew just about everyone who lived here. Aside from a couple of years in care homes and a period across the river in Port Glasgow, it had been home for most of her life. She was dyslexic; she couldn't write the word, but she knew a vehicle like that spelled 'trouble'.

'Drew, come here,' she said to the man sitting with his feet up on the sofa. He was short and muscular with a round, pleasant face and spiky dark hair. He was wearing a Celtic away jersey and a heavy gold chain round his neck.

He looked up from his phone. 'What now?' he said in an exasperated tone. The baby had only just gone to sleep.

'Come and look at this.'

The 4 x 4 was pulling up outside their block. She stared at it with troubled eyes.

Calla's face was worried, her voice quiet. 'Bloody women,' he muttered to himself, putting his phone down.

He went over to the window.

'What?'

She pointed at the car. They exchanged looks. They were both concerned now.

Drew thought frantically. Had he had issues with anyone recently? Home, pub, small deals of Charlie and weed here and there, all local, all above board – these were some of the things running through his head. He didn't owe Frank – his supplier – any money, he hadn't cheated anyone, he was a reliable dealer, he didn't short-change customers. Maybe it was nothing. Or if it wasn't, maybe it was nothing to do with him.

Had someone fitted him up? Surely not?

The BMW parked. They stared down at it, far below, pulling up by the front door, the light glinting off its bodywork. It was like waiting for the curtain to go up before a show. Who was going to get out?

Calla and Drew watched, holding their breaths, hoping to be able to release them in relief. Then the doors opened, four doors, all in unison as if choreographed, and four men got out. Three pairs of trainers and one pair of highly polished black brogues hit the dirty tarmac outside the front doors of the tower block simultaneously. Three men in bomber jackets; the one who had been sitting in the front passenger seat wearing a tan mac. He was much taller than the others – you could see that even from up here. He pushed some of his floppy dark hair back from his forehead and lit a cigarette. He suddenly looked upwards towards them. Calla knew it was impossible for him to be looking at her directly, but that was what it felt like. He took a few drags on his cigarette and then threw it to the ground, half smoked; three of them headed inside, one stayed behind, leaning against the bonnet of the car.

'God, it's the Big Man,' Drew muttered.

Calla somehow knew they were coming for them. 'Oh, Jesus Christ, no...' she whispered.

Graeme Millar strode into the lobby of the tower block, walking with the invincible self-confidence that practised violence gave you, flanked by his minders, Big Dougie and Ray. She had heard about them from Drew, although she had never met them.

'What have you been up to, Drew?' wailed Calla. This woke the baby who started to cry. She looked in anguish at her husband, then picked up her daughter, Palmer, and held her close. 'There, there,' she said, soothing the baby.

What had Drew been up to? Surely to God nothing he could have done would have warranted Millar's presence? He simply wasn't important enough. Millar controlled the drugs trade in Dumbarton and the other towns and suburbs like Clydebank on the western fringes of Glasgow. He was the guy who Drew's dealer bought his coke from; he was top of the food chain and Ray was his second in command.

'Nothing, woman,' he snapped. He lit a cigarette. Calla looked at him with anguish. It was obvious to her that the same question that was going through her mind was going through his. The Big Man was here for a reason, but God knew what. Surely it could have nothing to do with him? He was too far down the pecking order to attract Millar's attention. But here he was, nevertheless.

Drew walked into the bedroom and came out carrying a baseball bat.

Her husband had a short fuse and Calla could see that far from being intimidated by Millar he was determined to take the initiative.

'Put it down, Drew,' Calla shouted at him. 'Don't be stupid!'

He hefted the aluminium bat; Oh, God the idiot. She could guess what he was thinking – that he'd show Millar. There was a pounding on the door.

'Drew, it's Millar, put the bat down,' she begged, starting to cry.

He shook his head. 'Nobody fucks around with me in my own place, Calla,' he said. Another couple of blows on the door.

'Go and open it,' he ordered her.

She did so and Big Dougie, about six foot four, raw boned, his long, pale face and very light blue eyes topped by fine, blond hair, shoved the door open. She didn't say anything, instead, she backed away from the door, terrified, Palmer cradled in her arms.

Now the Big Man and Ray walked into the flat and Dougie closed the door behind them and stood leaning against it. She had never met Millar, but she recognised him from descriptions. He was massive, with a hard, brutal, red face and glittering eyes. The blue two-piece suit and raincoat somehow made him seem even bigger. He always wore a suit, she'd heard that. Rumour was true, then. She felt like a small child in his presence. Drew, still holding his baseball bat, walked backwards as the two men came into the living room. What the hell did he think he was going to achieve? she thought. The idiot.

Calla followed them, clutching her daughter like a talisman. Please, God, she prayed frantically, let her be all right. Please, God, let him not hurt her. Everyone was ignoring her as if she were just a piece of the furniture – that suited her just fine. The lounge had seemed perfectly large a minute or so ago, now it seemed tiny, like a child's room, and she and Drew were the bairns and here were the grown-ups, to punish them.

Millar was so close, she could have leaned forward and touched him. He was even bigger than she had imagined. He had very black hair, thick and coarse-looking, long on the top and cut short on the sides. It was sticking up here and there as though he had pushed his fingers through it. His eyes looked crazy; she could see he was high – coke, probably.

Why not? He sold enough of it.

She shrank into the corner of the room, her arms wrapped tight around baby Palmer. The Big Man glanced at her.

'You're Calla?'

'Aye, Mr Millar,' she said, swallowing nervously. She stared at the floor; she didn't want to meet his eye.

'What do you want, Millar?' Drew said aggressively.

Shut up, you cretin, thought Calla, looking up, trying to catch Drew's eye. But that was Drew for you, he never had known when to back down. Like now – he was holding the bat in front of him, threateningly.

Millar turned to look at him. For Calla, time seemed to stop. Like when you had a car crash. Everything happened in slow motion.

'And just what the fuck do you think you're doing with that?' Millar was pointing at the baseball bat.

Drew raised the bat menacingly.

'What are you doing in my flat with these two pricks?' he said.

Calla stared at the three men. The guy with Millar, Ray, was very good-looking, about fifty, she guessed – she had thought he was young, but now, with her heightened senses, she could see the lines on his face. He had a flowery shirt under his jacket that looked expensive, blue chinos and properly good-looking trainers, not like the crap ones from the local market that Drew was wearing.

Millar's face darkened. Like lightning flickering over a stormy sky. There was a sudden blur of movement. He moved very quickly, without warning, and hit Drew in the face; Drew cried out in pain, his hands covering his nose, then Millar, grabbing the bat from him, drove the metal end hard into Drew's stomach. Drew doubled up and gasped for breath.

Millar swung the bat into Drew's head as if he were hitting a ball out of the park. The noise was horrible. She winced. Drew's legs went and he collapsed. Calla squeezed her eyes tight shut. Then she heard a couple of dull thuds. Millar had dropped the bat and was hitting Drew, his face a kind of mask of animal rage. 'Fucking threaten me, you fucking wee bastard...would you? Fuckin' would you?' The monologue was punctuated four times by his fist; now her eyes were open and she saw that there was something in his hand. Drew was face down, not moving. There was a lot of blood, so red, pooling from him, spreading out onto the carpet. Calla felt sick and black spots danced in front of her eyes. Please, God, let me not faint, she prayed. Her legs were like jelly. Blood on the hands of Millar, on his tan raincoat. Millar straightened up, breathing heavily.

He turned to Calla, his face enraged.

'Where's your fucking brother?' Millar said angrily. 'Jamie McDonald, where is he?'

She shrank into the corner of the room, pressed herself hard against the wall for support. So this hadn't been about Drew at all; it was about Jamie.

'Port Glasgow,' she whispered.

'He isnae there, we looked.' Ray said, his face stern.

'I don't know, I swear to God.' Tears were running down her face.

Millar took her chin gently but firmly in his bloody hand – Drew's blood. She could smell it. He looked into her eyes. His were hard, pitiless; they dropped down to the baby in her arms, to Palmer.

'She's very small,' he said. He put his head on one side; his eyes flickered meaningfully to the partially open window. She had no doubt he was capable of it. He was capable of anything.

'Where is he?' he demanded.

'I don't know,' she whispered. 'Please...'

Millar bent forward and leaned his head close to hers.

'I've heard you're close to Jamie… When that brother of yours calls you, you be sure to find out exactly where he is,' he said. His eyes didn't leave hers.

She swallowed nervously. 'Yes, Mr Millar.'

'Good girl,' he said approvingly. He took his hand away from her and turned away, staring down at Drew's body with a slight frown on his face.

Millar left the room. Ray came up to her. He nodded in the direction of Drew.

'I'll be round tomorrow with some cash for your expenses.'

Calla nodded. Ray didn't need to add 'for the funeral'. She understood what he meant well enough.

Ray paused at the door. 'Clean up behind us,' he ordered. 'Oh, and it goes without saying, we weren't here.'

She nodded again.

You weren't here. None of you were here.

She heard the door close behind them and her legs buckled. She slid down the wall so she was sitting on the floor and she started to cry.

'Oh, Jamie, what have you done?' she whispered.

4

It was nearly two hours after leaving Hanlon's cottage in the small village that Gillies slowed and pulled off the road. She wasn't sure exactly where they were, only that it was about a ten-minute drive north of the town of Oban.

Gillies had refused to make conversation during the journey. Hanlon had tried her best but all she'd got had been monosyllables. After a while she gave up trying to engage with him and just looked out of the window as the beautiful landscape passed by. The further north they went, the rockier and wilder the countryside became. Occasionally they would drive past a standing stone in a field, deserted, mournful and mysterious. Nobody really knew why the stones had been placed there nor what the mysterious cup and ring markings on them meant. They were just there. Puzzling.

Not unlike Gillies, she reflected.

As the road twisted its way through the rocky hills, bare and forbidding at this time of year, she thought that this potential job offer could not have come at a better time. Finding work had been a hell of a lot harder than she had anticipated.

After an hour she closed her eyes and dozed. The entire journey had been spent in more or less complete silence except for the music that had played continuously since they had left Hanlon's cottage.

After two hours she knew one thing for sure about the taciturn lawyer: he certainly had a thing for the blues. The entertainment display on the car's dash gave the name of the artist so Hanlon, who wasn't keen on music of any description, by now was well aware of what the Robert Cray Band, Muddy Waters, Bessie Smith and Etta James sounded like.

Depressing, to her way of thinking.

Etta finished and Robert Cray returned to let them know about his suspicions regarding his partner and her boss, suspicions that would inevitably lead to him moving out and living in some flophouse, drinking whiskey for breakfast, if the pattern of earlier songs held true. Nobody ever seemed to get the blues and be motivated to do anything remotely useful about the situation, Hanlon reflected. She wondered if Gillies took this defeatist mindset into work with him.

The road dropped down a hill with a view of the sea below them. It was practically dark now, the land in the distance a foreboding sable mass. The driveway they stopped at had an imposing entrance: two large stone pillars surmounted by crumbling lichen-encrusted lions and a set of double gates. The lions and pillars were old, but the gates were new. They were also large, made of metal bars surmounted by spikes disguised as ornamental and painted gold, but they looked sharp. Extremely sharp. They weren't just decorative. There was evidence of more attention to security. There were two CCTV cameras that were partly hidden by the plinths that the lions were on. On either side of the gate was a high metal mesh fence. Razor wire ran along the top. Gillies' boss obviously took security seriously, Hanlon thought. Gillies pressed a button on his key fob and the gates swung slowly inwards.

The drive was lined by tall rhododendrons, their mournful leaves funereally drab as the car slowly made its way along the meandering ribbon of tarmac. The sky above them was almost black now; it was a depressing arrival, shrouded in the darkness of the evergreen foliage on both sides and the gathering approach of night.

They rounded a corner and the house came into view.

'Kinnachan House,' said Gillies laconically. Hanlon almost jumped in her seat; it was about the only thing he'd volunteered until now.

The place wasn't unusual for the west coast of Scotland. It was late-nineteenth-century style, built of dark stone, granite, she guessed, and had the touches that Victorian Scots seemed to go for: crenellations as a castle might have running along the roof, and circular turrets at the corners, the odd leaded window.

The place was as sizeable as it was ugly. Behind it, in the darkening gloom, she could see the sea and, beyond that, indistinct hills rising up high into the sky that might have been the island of Mull or part of the mainland on the other side of the loch. They were north of Oban now and the lands surrounding them were as bleak and forbidding as they were beautiful.

Gillies pulled up in front of the large wood-panelled door. A dozen or so security lights bathed them in their harsh white illumination. She noted the alarm boxes on the walls, no less than three of them, and the security cameras. She and Gillies got out of the car; the cold salt, sea breeze whipped into their faces, wet with drizzle. The lawyer released Wemyss from the back and the dog ran to Hanlon to check all was OK and then stood patiently by her side, sniffing the air and looking around him with interest.

The door was opened by a guy, in his thirties she guessed, wearing a suit and a serious expression. He had a very short, military-style haircut and a nose whose shape had been modified by severe punishment over the years. He nodded to Gillies, gave Hanlon a cursory glance and then, ignoring her, spoke to the lawyer.

'So you're here. He's waiting in the study.'

Gillies nodded and the man suddenly turned to Hanlon with a charming smile. 'I'm sorry, I'm forgetting my manners. You must be Hanlon. I'm Andy Hampton – I work for Mr Cameron. Thank you for coming at such short notice. Please, follow me...'

The three of them walked into the house. In the lobby, Hampton paused and turned to Hanlon. 'Can I take your coat?' She nodded and removed her old Barbour jacket. He disappeared with it into a cloakroom by the door and reappeared seconds later. She looked around. She was feeling distinctly underdressed for this place.

They were in a large hall, high-ceilinged and very long. There was a wide staircase running upstairs to the left. The decor was a total contrast to the outside of the house. That was traditional, nineteenth-century baronial vernacular, inside was classic, cool modern. The hall floor had been restored to highly polished stone flagstones, a grey runner carpet ran the length of it, modern art hung on the walls. The lighting was recessed. Far away some baroque music, maybe Bach, was playing. The three of them walked in silence down the corridor, their footsteps muffled by the carpet. The dog walked slightly to one side of Hanlon, the claws on his paws clicking on the stone of the floor, the only sound above the music.

They neared the end of the entrance hall and then Hampton stopped.

'In here, please.'

He knocked on one of the tall wood-panelled doors and ushered them into a room. It was, in keeping with the house, large. There were floor-to-ceiling windows, which overlooked the loch and the hills on the other side. The view would have been spectacular if it hadn't been so dark beyond the glass. The room was carpeted; there was a fireplace at one end with a log fire burning, a desk with a computer screen at the other. More art of a minimalist nature was on the wall, maybe twenty or so paintings, modern, mostly abstract, except for one picture that stood out from the others both in subject and style. It was a large oil painting of a woman standing and leaning over a table to look at a laptop. It was a view of her painted from behind. Her face was reflected in the window of the room – it was dark outside. It was very skilfully done, hyper-realistic; she looked as if she could just step out of the frame if she wanted to. The table in the painting must have belonged to an artist, maybe the one who had made the picture; there were jars with brushes, tubes of paint, a wine bottle and glasses. She was young, blonde, you could tell she was beautiful. She was also naked.

There was a man in the room standing with his back to them, looking out at the view.

Gillies, Hanlon and the dog walked in and the door closed behind them. The man staring out at the loch was tall; his hair was short and grey, skilfully cut.

He turned around and faced them. He was not young, far from it – she guessed he was probably in his sixties – but he looked good for his years, trim and fit. No stranger to the gym and the cross-trainer. The colour of his hair matched his two-piece suit, which was beautifully cut, tailored to fit his slim figure. Like a concours vintage car, he looked expensively maintained.

'You must be Hanlon,' he said. In one hand he had a small bottle of Czech lager that he was holding almost self-consciously, like it was a prop on stage. 'Do sit down.' He gestured with an open palm at the sofa and chairs that were arranged in a semicircle facing the windows with a couple of low coffee tables in front of them. Hanlon glanced down at her worn, slightly muddy combat trousers, her old green jumper, and looked with irritation at Gillies. OK for him in his suit. She presumed she was here for a prospective job interview and she was uncomfortably aware that she was dressed like some kind of handyman.

'Can I get you a drink?' The guy's accent was educated Scottish.

'Coffee, please. Black, no sugar.' She said. He looked at Gillies, who, taciturn as ever, shook his head.

He nodded, took his phone out and tapped on the screen, then repocketed it.

'Right,' he said decisively. He sat down on a chair slightly to the side of Hanlon. He took a mouthful of beer from the bottle in his hand, 'Do you have any idea who I am?'

'No.' Hanlon didn't see any need to elaborate.

'There's no need to worry,' he said reassuringly. It didn't seem politic to tell him she wasn't worried at all. 'My name's Hamish Cameron.'

Hanlon wondered if he was going to feed her more and more snippets of information until she eventually guessed who he was. If so, they could be there some time.

He smiled. 'I'm an art dealer.'

'That's nice,' Hanlon said. She guessed that explained the pictures and the security. He looked at her expectantly.

'So how can I help you?' she asked.

'I'm also a father,' he said. 'My daughter is missing.' There was a lengthy pause. 'I want you to find her for me.'

So, there we are, she thought. She felt a brief surge of excitement. This would be her first case since she had left the police and set up as a private investigator.

'The police?' suggested Hanlon.

'She's not been gone long enough for that. They would almost certainly tell me not to worry, that young people often go away for a period without warning...' Cameron smiled ruefully '... and, of course, she's an adult, but...' he shook his head '... she's not been in her flat for a week. I know her flatmate is worried...' he drank some beer '... and I certainly am, which is the main thing as far as you're concerned.'

'Did the flatmate contact you?' she asked.

Cameron shook his head. He looked slightly embarrassed by the question, seeming to search for the right words before saying, 'No, I um, I heard that she was missing.'

'You heard that?' said Hanlon. 'And your daughter, you've called her? Texted her? E-mailed her?'

'It's not that simple.' Cameron frowned. 'Unfortunately she's not speaking to me. We had... we fell out some time ago. Her mother died...' he was wearing a wedding ring on his left hand and she noticed he twisted it unconsciously as he spoke '... and she's blamed me for her death ever since.'

Hanlon looked at him, evaluating him in his expensive but casual suit and simple but, oh, so tasteful crushed linen shirt. On his wrist was a slender gold band that was his watch; she would bet it was ultra-expensive. His shoes were loafers that he wore without socks, just a hint of tanned ankle. He was the picture of both studied elegance and restrained control.

Her mind, naturally suspicious, started speculating.

An estranged father and daughter. She wondered about the control. Was that an issue? The daughter wasn't speaking to him, he hadn't spoken to the flatmate, yet somehow he knew that the girl was missing. How could he have known? She thought of the CCTV, the alarms, the floodlights, his ex-army employee. Had he got her under surveillance too?

'How old is she?' asked Hanlon.

'Aurora's twenty-three, she's in her final year of an MA in English literature at Edinburgh University.' Cameron's eyes locked onto hers. 'She's the only child I have, my only family really, now Giulia's gone... I've lost a wife; I don't want to lose a daughter.'

'Well, as you yourself said, she's only been gone a week,' Hanlon pointed out. Shut up, you fool, she said to herself. Are you trying to talk yourself out of a job?

Cameron shrugged. 'Maybe it's nothing, but this has never happened before. I pay her credit-card bills, I get to see what she's been spending and where – there's been no activity there. OK, her debit card is her business. She has an allowance, not huge, but enough. All the same, it's very unusual for her not to use her plastic.'

Hanlon scratched her head. The whole thing smelled bad. A father who was not on speaking terms with his daughter but – admittedly, she was guessing – spied on her and tried to keep her tied to him financially.

It had a strong odour of unhappy, dysfunctional family about it. Nothing cheery was ever going to come of something like this. And she had taken a dislike to Cameron. On the other hand, she was broke. She was driving a seventeen-year-old Vauxhall Corsa. With a cassette deck as standard. And did it matter that she didn't like him, anyway? He was a customer.

'OK,' she said decisively, 'with the proviso that when I find her, if she doesn't want me to tell you where she is or what she's up to, that decision is hers and you respect it.'

Cameron made a kind of open-palmed gesture with his hands.

'Absolutely,' he said. 'I don't want anything from her. I just want to know that she's all right.'

Of course, you do, thought Hanlon cynically.

'So if I find her, and she is OK but doesn't want to talk to you or communicate with you, you'll be happy with a photo.'

He nodded. 'I guess so,' he sighed, 'she's very... well, headstrong. It wouldn't surprise me if it came to that – I want reassurance more than anything.'

'I'll tell her you're worried about her,' Hanlon said.

He smiled sadly, 'Thank you. A reunion would be nice too... but let's be realistic.'

'Good,' Hanlon nodded, 'that's settled then.'

The Corsa needed a new exhaust.

She stood up. 'I'll need information.'

Cameron nodded. 'Gillies has prepared a pack for you: pictures, bio, personal information.'

There was a silence and they looked at each other; an antique grandfather clock in the corner struck five.

'I'll pay you three hundred a day, plus reasonable expenses,' he said.

'That sounds fine,' she said. It was more than she had been expecting. She would have done it for a lot less.

'Good,' said Cameron briskly. They both stood up, he extended a hand and they shook.

'Gillies will take you home,' Cameron said, dismissing her.

Gillies stood up. 'Shall we go?'

Hanlon looked at the lawyer with amusement. All those professional qualifications to end up as a gofer for some rich guy. Maybe that was why he spoke so little. It was pent-up resentment.

Maybe that was why he played the blues.

5

Ray pulled up outside the crack house in the BMW 4 x 4 and turned the engine off.

'This the place?' asked Millar.

Ray looked at Big Dougie sitting in the passenger seat. 'Aye, this is the place.'

Millar put his hand on the baseball bat next to him on the back seat. 'Nobody fucks me around,' he said ominously.

The three of them got out of the car. They were in Muirhouse, a less than lovely suburb of Edinburgh. The crack house, a squat where you could buy and consume under the same roof, was in an area of social housing, quiet streets of two-storey grey pebble-dashed blocks of flats. As they got out of the car, a bitterly cold wind hit them. Dougie shivered. There was a burned-out car parked by the kerb opposite the house they were about to go in. The windows had been shuttered by the council to prevent break-ins, not that it had done any good. The door was metal too. A sunken-cheeked, hard faced guy in his twenties stood outside, smoking a cigarette. It was seven p.m. and dark; the street light outside the property wasn't working.

Ray noticed the man standing guard by the door was looking at the three of them making their way towards him. The guy looked nervous, as well he might. They were all big men, but Millar, who was in the lead, was huge; dark-haired, red-faced, wearing his cheap-looking blue two-piece suit, a baseball bat in one large meaty hand. Judging by the expression on the doorman's face, he didn't think Millar was holding it because he wanted a game. Ray walked up to him and looked him in the eyes, seeing the fear there. He noticed him swallow nervously. Ray could see that he was supposed to mind the door; that would usually mean chasing away the street kids and keeping an eye out for the police who occasionally drove past or checking on customers, not dealing with situations like this.

'What do you want, pal?' the doorman asked, putting out a warning hand to stop him. Ray looked him in the eyes. The guy didn't see the punch coming, but he sure as hell must have felt it. He was on his knees spluttering for breath.

'Ahh, Jesus...' he groaned.

'Go,' Ray ordered, pointing. The doorman painfully straightened up, did as he was told and walked stiffly away down the street. He was clutching his chest; Ray guessed breathing was hurting him a lot.

Ray opened the door and the three of them walked inside. Dougie closed the door and leant against it. The room was large and dimly lit by a lamp in the corner. There was a strong smell of weed, cigarette smoke, and mould. It was very hot – there was an old-fashioned coal-effect gas fire on full. There was a battered vinyl sofa patched with duct tape with a couple of junkies sitting on it who hadn't moved when the door had opened and the three of them had come in. A man wearing a leather jacket and a frown strode into the room through a doorway at the back.

'Who are youse?' he asked, his voice harsh and challenging.

'Where's Alan?' Millar demanded.

Leather jacket strode over to him, fists balled, aggression in every movement of his face and body. Millar looked steadily at him; he didn't say a word, then, without warning and with great speed, swung the baseball bat at him, mid-body. There was no avoiding it, the blow came too fast for that. But leather jacket moved quickly, he swivelled his body and took it on the shoulder. Millar was big and heavy and the force of the bat when it impacted staggered the guy. He grunted in pain but didn't go over and

Millar hit him again. This time the bat made contact with his head. There was a dull thud and he collapsed on the floor.

The junkies didn't move. Neither did leather jacket.

'What the fuck's going on?' Another man appeared from the doorway. Ray stepped forward, hit him hard and the guy cried out and bent over, clutching his damaged face.

Millar was on him, one hand hooked in his hair.

'Hello, Alan, remember me?' he snarled as he yanked upwards savagely. Alan gasped in pain. Millar pulled Alan's head close to his mouth. 'Where's Jamie McDonald?' Ray glanced around the room to check all was still in order. Dougie was still leaning against the front door of the crack den in case anyone tried to come in, watching as Millar and Ray dragged Alan inside the kitchen and slammed the door behind them.

In the room they'd just left, the junkies were still motionless; one of them was asleep, the other was gauching away, the kind of head nodding that heroin users do, and absent-mindedly scratching. He had long greasy hair and a painfully thin, lined face. Now he opened his eyes and nodded at Big Dougie, who put a warning finger to his lips. Dougie was from Edinburgh and he knew the guy vaguely, Junkie Dave. Dave took the hint and closed his eyes. The guy who Millar had hit was still on the floor; he hadn't moved.

In the kitchen Alan was sitting on a chair, Ray stood behind him and Millar faced him, leaning on the kitchen table, smoking a cigarette.

'Where's Jamie McDonald?'

'Dinnae ken.' He looked pleadingly at Millar. 'You know I wouldnae lie to you, Graeme, please...'

Millar took a deep drag on the Marlboro and narrowed his eyes thoughtfully. Alan's blood-stained face – Ray had broken his nose – looked pleadingly up at him.

'Jordan McKenna was doing a job for me a week back,' Millar said irritably. Ray glanced at his boss nervously. Millar had developed a mania about people letting him down, like Jordan, or betraying him, or just getting in the way like that moron in the leather jacket he'd just hit. He was uncontrollable if he felt that someone was trying to put one over on him.

He'd already killed one person that day and Ray was worried that it might not end there.

Millar glared at Alan. Alan shivered in fear and Millar took out his hip flask and had another hit of Bowmore. Ray watched him take a second appreciative mouthful. Then he pulled a wrap of coke out of his breast pocket, tipped some on to the back of his hand and snorted it. His eyes bulged. He inhaled some more smoke from the cigarette, looked down at Alan and continued. 'Jordan hired McDonald to help. Neither have been seen since.' He prodded Alan in the chest with the end of the bat. 'It's not like Jordan to do a runner...'

Alan tilted his head up to focus on Millar.

'Jordan's got a place near here, a wee lock-up with a wee bit yard,' Alan mumbled. His lips were cracked and bloodied. 'Have you looked there?'

'Address?' Millar said.

Relief washed over Alan as he started to speak, Ray could see it on his face. Ray thanked God he was able to give Millar something.

Jordan's yard was about five minutes' drive away from Alan's place. As they left, Dougie bent forward and slipped fifty quid into the front pocket of Junkie Dave's denim jacket.

'Nice one, Big Man,' Dave whispered.

* * *

Jordan's yard was in a quiet, semi-industrial street. On one side was a steel fabricating business, on the other a cul-de-sac with some lock-up garages. Opposite were some flats and an access road. Dougie pulled over just outside the gate and they got out of the BMW.

They walked up to the entrance. There was a high chain-link fence topped with barbed wire; access was via a metal gate padlocked shut with a heavy chain. They could see a small breeze-block garage, some wheelie bins and a white van inside the compound. They examined the padlock and chain.

Millar rattled it experimentally.

'There's bolt cutters in the back of the car,' Ray said.

'Get them,' Millar said.

He reached a hand inside his jacket and took out the hip flask. Ray smelled the perfumed whisky fumes as he unscrewed the cap and drank. Dougie returned from the car, put the jaws of the bolt cutters around the heavy links of the chain and, grunting with effort, forced the handles together. The metal parted and the chain fell open slackly with a metallic scraping sound. Ray pulled his gloves on and opened the gate; it sagged slightly on its hinges and its bottom scraped along the ground. They slipped inside and Millar led the way over to the van. Ray glanced inside; he could see it was unlocked.

They walked to the back and stood there staring at the closed doors. Ray wrinkled his nose against the smell. They looked at each other. There was a heavy odour of rotting meat. He opened the door.

There was a body wrapped in polythene sheeting, a pair of feet wearing worn trainers poking out. The smell was terrible.

Dougie put his hand to his mouth; Ray could see he was gagging slightly.

'Guard the gate, Dougie,' he said. Gratefully, Dougie moved away from the van and its terrible contents.

Millar watched him walk away from the van and turned to Ray, his slab-like face impassive. 'Go and check,' he said. 'See which one it is.'

Ray nodded, opened the driver's door and leaned in. He tugged the plastic away from the head that was just behind the front seat. He emerged, coughing, and nodded. He took a couple of deep breaths.

'It's Jordan,' he confirmed.

Millar nodded. He didn't seem surprised; he must have thought it would be the case. Jordan was a good, reliable employee, he wouldn't have walked out on him. No prizes for guessing who had put him there. Jamie McDonald.

They closed the van's door and draped the chain around the gate so it looked secure. Millar's phone vibrated and he pulled it out, frowning.

'Aye?' he said. He switched it to speakerphone so Ray could listen in.

'It's Calla.' A woman's voice.

'Who?'

'Calla Lennox, Mr Millar.' Her voice was quiet, hesitant, almost inaudible.

'Oh, yes.'

'Jamie called, Mr Millar, you said to let you know the moment he did... I have his address.'

'Good girl,' Millar said approvingly. 'Text it tae me.'

He ended the call and looked at Ray. Ray felt another lightening of the load. Both Jordan and McDonald found. A good night's work. So, there was just the girl to find now – Aurora Cameron. He knew that no one could let Millar down and get away with it, not in Millar's mindset. He hadn't the faintest idea who the Cameron girl was or what she'd done to upset Millar, but it really didn't matter. These days, just to be in Millar's way was to trigger a potentially fatal response. All sense of proportion seemed to have gone.

No exceptions.

'What now, boss?' asked Ray. He wondered if Millar could hear the relief in his voice. An angry, frustrated Millar was not a pleasant person to be spending time with.

'Drop me at the Waldorf Astoria,' the big man said. 'I'm staying there. I'll call you later with instructions.'

The three of them got into the BMW and Dougie drove them westwards to the centre of Edinburgh.

6

Hanlon and Wemyss watched as the Audi's tail lights bounced down the track. She stood a moment outside the house. She could hear the surf crashing onto the rocky beach a few hundred yards away in the darkness. It was the only sound she could hear. It was very loud. She took a deep breath and looked up at the night sky. There was hardly any light pollution here. Out on the sea she could see the green starboard light of a fishing boat and in the distance the yellow glow from a house's windows, but that was it.

She stretched, exulting in the loneliness and the silence. The wind tugged at her clothes and she turned and went inside.

She switched the lights on and lit the fire she had laid earlier in the grate in the living room. The old clock on the wall said seven o'clock. She fed Wemyss a can of dog food, opened the fridge to look for something to eat and stared at the bodies of three rabbits that sat on the lowest shelf. She'd been given them by the farmer who lived up the road. At the time she'd been delighted – he'd stopped by in his pick-up truck and offered them to her. 'If you don't like rabbit, the dog will.'

The problem was, she had no butchery skills whatsoever. She hadn't thought about that at the time. She couldn't just throw them away. She closed the door. I'll look at them in the morning, she told herself. She went upstairs, had a shower, started her laptop and inserted the memory stick Gillies had given her that contained the information on Aurora Cameron.

She hadn't eaten but she wanted to find out more about the missing girl before she did anything else.

Aurora Cameron was twenty-three. She had been born at Ross Hall Hospital in Glasgow, went to primary school in the city and then, when she reached secondary-school age, was educated at a boarding school in a town near London, Wycombe Abbey, one of the country's top girls' schools.

The folders and files on the memory stick were arranged chronologically and meticulously, as she might have expected since Gillies had compiled it. First she looked at pictures of Aurora's mother, Giulia. Italian, an ex-model from Turin. She looked like models so often do in that identikit way: tall, slender, leggy, full-lipped. Here in the photos, there were some catwalk images, but mostly the images were of her on the beach with young versions of Aurora – who was blonde like her mother – making sandcastles in a bikini, smoking a cigarette outside a bar, pulling faces at the camera.

None of Cameron. He was the man behind the lens. Hanlon had the same feeling that she'd had at his house. A man forever arranging things to his satisfaction, people, pictures, places. And, of course, the same ethos underlaid his business: he didn't make things, he arranged things. He arranged exhibitions, sales, events, careers.

She suddenly thought of Gillies, the dark, saturnine lawyer. Cameron had even arranged a legal adviser/factotum who was as silent as the grave.

She opened the folder labelled 'School'. Aurora's school reports. Languages, A grades, ditto art. Well, no surprise there. Sciences and maths, less so, sport, poor. A distinct lack of effort.

Then alarm bells rang. She had been discovered with some other girls smoking weed in the woods in the school's extensive grounds. That was post-GCSE. Her results had been good, straight As. Sixth form, more trouble with drugs; e-mails flew – Cameron certainly wasn't trying to hide stuff from her. Thinly veiled threats to the school from Cameron channelled via the lawyer. Aurora was beginning to go off the rails. Then, the summer after her first year of sixth form, the end of Year Twelve, rehab. Hanlon recognised the name, a well-known clinic.

More photos. Now Hanlon was able to recognise the girl in the painting in Cameron's study as Aurora. An older, more self-confident version, but her, nevertheless.

Aurora with Giulia, looking very much like the model that her mother had been. But a haunted look in her eyes now, no longer smiling at the man behind the camera. Honey-gold hair, honey-brown eyebrows in a perfect arc, mother and daughter both with the same nose, slightly on the large side, a feature that added a touch of humanity to what would otherwise have been a slightly unearthly beauty.

Then, post-rehab, more unhappiness. Six years ago. Aurora would have been seventeen. There was even a copy of Giulia's death certificate, cause of death – overdose. A copy of the order of funeral service; Aurora had read a poem. Photos from the funeral. And there was Aurora, stony-faced in black. A rare shot of Cameron, also in black, looking stern but composed, talking to another man, a head taller, jet-black hair. Hanlon guessed he was probably one of Giulia's relatives. Although Giulia and her mother were blonde, Hanlon associated the kind of hair this man had with Italy rather than the UK – it was very dark, like her own, a kind of Mediterranean black. There was obviously little love lost between the two men. The taller guy was frowning, caught by whoever was using the camera jabbing a finger into Cameron's chest. Tall guy looked furious.

Then her A level results, straight A stars – her drug history and the tragedy hadn't affected her studies. There was her acceptance letter from Edinburgh university. The final page in the file contained her current address – a street name and number, Howe Street, that meant nothing to Hanlon. She didn't know Edinburgh at all well.

Hanlon rubbed her eyes. Enough looking at the screen for now.

Standing up, she stretched and went over to the sink to fill the kettle. The accusatory presence of the dead rabbits in her fridge hung in the room. Glancing up, through the window of the small kitchen, she saw a car's headlights bouncing up the track to the cottage. She frowned – was this Gillies again? Had he forgotten something? Hanlon looked out of the window as the vehicle pulled up in front of the house – a Land Rover. She went over to the front door and switched on the outside lights for the forecourt.

The driver's door opened. A tall man got out, red-headed, good-looking, in his thirties. Murdo Campbell, a police detective she had met the year before on Jura, an island just off the Argyll coast. She hadn't seen him for a few months, but they'd kept in touch with the occasional text and e-mail. She'd sent him a Christmas card with her address on – 'if you're ever in the area'.

Hanlon opened the door to him.

'Hello, Murdo, what brings you here?' Her voice was friendly. She liked Campbell and was pleased to see him.

'I'm in court in Campbeltown in the morning,' he said. 'I'm staying there overnight. I thought I'd come the long way round and visit you.'

She nodded, ushering him in. Campbeltown was at the end of the long, narrow Argyll peninsula, maybe thirty or so miles from where she was staying. Here on the east side where she was, the road was a twisting, single track with passing places; it took twice as long to drive. He had come considerably out of his way to visit.

'So, how are you?' she asked. He looked tired; there were bags under his eyes. One of the disadvantages of being as pale as he was, things like that were very visible. She had a shrewd idea that she had got the Cameron job via him. She waved him to a seat. Campbell looked around with interest.

Hanlon's rented cottage was small. There was the front room that the door opened directly into; there was a kitchen through a small passageway and a staircase leading upstairs to a bedroom and bathroom. The living room was as spartan and immaculate.

'Would you like a drink?' she asked.

'Tea, please,' he said.

She nodded and turned. As he followed her into the kitchen she asked, 'Do you know how to clean rabbits?'

'I'm sorry?' The question had obviously baffled him.

She laughed and nodded at the fridge. 'I've got three rabbits in there. I was given them earlier today but then I realised I'm not sure how to gut them, or skin them, come to that.' Or cook them, she thought. How do you even do that?

Campbell laughed. 'Yes, I do know how to clean a rabbit.' He took his tie and jacket off. 'Have you got an apron?'

She did. He tied it on.

'Knife? Chopping board?' he asked. She handed them to him. He sharpened the knife on a steel that was sitting on the counter. It was the instinctive action of a man who handled food a lot. As it happened, the knives had a good edge to them. Hanlon didn't know what to do with the kitchen knives that were sitting in a wooden block on the work-surface, but she kept them sharp anyway. 'Rabbits?'

She opened the fridge.

'Here you are…'

'Thank you, and two bowls, one for the meat, one for the waste.'

He picked up the first rabbit, examined it with a critical eye and deftly inserted the knife. She looked on as Campbell expertly skinned and gutted the rabbits.

'You're very good at this, aren't you?' she said. He smiled at her, giving her a glimpse of very white, even teeth.

'I used to shoot them for my mother, and then when my sister, Ish – you've met her – got a job in a local restaurant, I used to sell them to the chef who worked there.' Ishbel Campbell, Murdo's sister, was a restaurateur who had a well-known place in Glasgow's centre.

As he worked on the rabbits, his hands slick with blood, Hanlon asked, 'Did you give my name to a lawyer called Gillies?'

Campbell looked up at her from his bloody chopping board. 'Aye, I did. Has he called you?'

'He was round this afternoon.' She told him of what had happened, her drive with the lawyer to visit Cameron. Campbell nodded.

'I had heard he worked for some wealthy businessman. I gave your card out to several people and some law firms that I thought might be interested. I think once you get known you should get a reasonable amount of work. Scotland's a relatively small pool. You should start to get recommendations. Cameron's well known in Glasgow. He eats at Ish's restaurant quite often.' He started jointing the rabbits. 'It's paintings, isn't it? That's what he does – sells them?'

Hanlon said, 'Yes, he's an art dealer.'

He resumed his work. 'Gillies, eh, so he drove you to the other side of Oban – how long did that take?'

'Long enough,' she said, smiling, thinking of the interminable, silent car journey.

'Bet you couldn't get a word in edgeways...' Campbell didn't smile a great deal, in that respect he was rather like her, but when he did, it lit up his face.

Hanlon smiled. 'Yeah, he's not exactly talkative.'

'Is he still listening to blues music?'

Hanlon shuddered. 'God, yes...'

Campbell laughed. 'He was like that as a kid. Everyone else liked Eminem or S Club 7, not him... weird.'

'Well, he hasn't changed.'

Campbell put the skinned and gutted carcasses onto the chopping board in a line and finished jointing them for her. He put the pieces in the clean bowl he hadn't used. The other was full of guts and fur. He washed the knife and his hands. 'There you are. Be careful when you eat it – there are a lot of bones in a rabbit.'

'Thanks,' Hanlon said. 'Shall we go next door?'

Campbell took the apron off and they sat in the living room with their tea. He studied Hanlon, sitting relaxed on the sofa with her dog. She was wearing old jeans and a man's white shirt, several sizes too big for her, the sleeves rolled up. She looked formidably fit.

'So where did you meet Gillies?' she asked.

'Oh, I was at school with James. He was a bright kid, did law at Glasgow then joined a firm of solicitors. He was involved mainly in corporate stuff, then he got this job with Cameron. He got in touch with me a couple of days ago to ask if I knew of any ex-police who might be interested in doing a bit of private detective work. I thought of you. What's it all about, if you don't mind me asking?'

'No, not at all.'

She told him. Campbell sipped his tea thoughtfully.

'Cameron's never come across my path professionally,' he said. 'As far as I know he's squeaky clean. High-end art deals aren't the kind of thing that the people I come across are interested in, and they wouldn't want to hide or launder money in them, too easily seized by us. POCA...'

She nodded.

'I suppose you could transport them easily though...' he mused, still thinking of stolen paintings. 'Anyway, his name's never come up. I hear he's got quite a place.'

'He sure has. It's like a castle. A pretend castle, but a castle nevertheless.'

'Gillies said that. There's a bit of a story to it. Cameron's parents used to live across the loch from that place. They were shit poor. He used to look at it, the impoverished wean, holes in his breeks, the shining mansion on the hill, and think... one day... well, that's what he told Gillies anyway.'

He put his cup down.

'And now his daughter's missing, you say.'

'And now his daughter's missing, but I'll find her.'

He looked at her. Quietly determined. Confident. The windows shook and rattled as another strong gust of wind shook them. The fire in the grate had died down to a mound of glowing red embers. Wemyss was asleep – he could see the dog's legs move as he chased something in his dreams. The room was lit by a small lamp in the corner. It was warm and cosy. He yawned.

'And how are you?' asked Hanlon. 'Busy?'

'Not especially. We've got a bit of trouble on at the moment with what I'm hoping is not a turf war. There's this guy, Graeme Millar, kind of old-school gangster, quite the psycho actually.' He tapped the side of his head for emphasis. 'He controls the west side of Glasgow and the satellite towns, Alexandria, Dumbarton. Anyway, earlier today he killed this guy, Drew Lennox, a small-time drug dealer. It was spectacularly vicious.'

'Charming,' said Hanlon.

'Well, you know how it is...'

'Will he go down for it?' she asked.

'No.' He shook his head. 'Only circumstantial evidence and a witness, the victim's wife, who denies that Millar was ever there. She's shit-scared, with good reason. She's got a young baby.'

He fell silent, thinking of Millar. Six foot five of malice in human form. The dead man's wife, Calla, and her baby, a girl, Palmer.

Calla had been shaking with fear when he'd interviewed her. She hadn't seen what had happened; the assailants' faces were masked, she'd said. She had clutched Palmer fiercely to her; she'd kept looking towards the window, her eyes flicking from the baby to the window, repeatedly. In a sudden flash of realisation, Campbell had thought Millar had probably threatened to throw the baby out. They had been seven floors up.

They both knew he would have done it. Would do it if she talked.

There was no way anyone was going to tell them what had happened. And he couldn't blame them.

'Everyone's frightened of Millar,' he said. 'Nobody on that estate will dare to come forward. It'll go nowhere.' Hanlon nodded.

He stood up and stretched. 'I'd better go. I'm nearly asleep.'

She nodded and stood up too. She fetched his coat and he put it on.

'If you ever need help with rabbits again...'

'I was thinking about moving on to deer,' she said, smiling.

'I can do deer,' he said quickly. 'I'll take you stalking.'

'I'd like that,' Hanlon said. He looked at her slightly surprised, she sounded like she meant it.

'It sounds fun,' she added.

'Well, when we get some time, I'll arrange it.' He looked at her. 'It was good to see you again, Hanlon. I'm glad you've got the job. If you need any help, unofficially...'

'Thank you,' she said. 'It was nice to see you too...'

Campbell opened the door. It had started raining since he had arrived and an icy gust of wind blew into the house together with a fine spray.

'Dreich,' he said. 'I'll see you...'

'Bye,' said Hanlon. She closed the door behind him. The Land Rover's engine started and the lights washed through the window as Campbell turned and headed off down the track.

* * *

Hanlon sat on the sofa, thinking of Aurora.

A young girl, mother gone, alienated from her father, a controlling weirdo. She could sympathise. Her grey eyes narrowed as she thought of her own past. Nobody had been around for her – well, she couldn't change that, but she could make a difference now. She knew what it was like to grow up in an unhappy family. She had been determined to do a good job anyway, but now she felt a kind of crusading zeal. She would track Aurora down, come hell or high water.

She suddenly thought of Dr Morgan, her analyst. Now, in her imagination, but as clearly as if she were in the same room, Dr Morgan said, 'So are you finally ready to engage with the world again, instead of hiding away from everyone, including me, which is what you've been doing for the past six months?'

'I've been waiting for a sign, Dr Morgan, and here it is.'

The girl was the sign she had been waiting for. Time to find Aurora Cameron; she couldn't stay missing for good.

If anyone can find her, thought Hanlon, it'll be me.

7

The Dunedin View Hotel was on the outskirts of Edinburgh. From its creaky website, comment section and images, it looked to be far from perfect, but Hanlon rather liked that. It was the kind of place that wouldn't ask questions or have a dress code, and they were certainly happy to take Wemyss. It also had a gym, which she was looking forward to. The nearest one to her where she lived in Argyll was a good hour's drive away and she missed the feeling of muscle versus heavy iron that she got from a serious weight session.

Hanlon pulled up outside in her ageing Corsa. As she parked it she reflected that when the car was new, so too was she in the police force, well, if you call three years new. She did some mental calculations, she'd have been newly promoted from uniform to traffic, incredibly exciting times. What would that girl make of the forty-year-old woman expertly reversing into the parking bay?

Well, she would have admired her self-confidence. She would have admired her toughness, her extraordinary fitness levels, her ability to handle herself in a fight. But all these things had come with a price tag. Her younger self would have been appalled at her lack of friends and social network, the absence of anything that might be construed as fun. And, of course, the lack of anything to show for the last twenty years in terms of material success. She was living, practically penniless, in a rented cottage in a village miles from anywhere, on the west coast of Scotland, with a dog for company. She laughed. It wasn't the stuff that dreams were made of.

She pulled the sun-visor down and looked at her very grey eyes in the mirror, cold, hard, watchful, set in an attractive but slightly brutal face. If you don't like it, Hanlon told her younger self, tough.

You did it, she told her younger self. You took the steps on the path that led to this. You only have yourself to blame.

Oh, well, thought Hanlon as she let Wemyss out of the back, she'd have liked the dog.

She checked in. She liked the way the hotel didn't seem to have a well-manned reception. She would be able to come and go at all hours fairly incognito. The hotel was on the outskirts of Edinburgh, near a place called Cramond. It looked to be good for walking Wemyss. The sea was fairly close by and he loved swimming. While she'd been puzzling over hotel websites it had crossed her mind how ridiculous she would have found all this fussing over an animal not that long ago; now the dog was dictating her life to a considerable, surprising, extent.

The hotel itself didn't have many facilities, other than the gym. There was a bar, which did rudimentary food – that was fine. It had a couple of function rooms; she saw that one of them was booked by the East Lothian Heating Symposium. It announced this proudly on a dark blue felt board with those stick-on magnetic letters. The place to be!

Her room was fine. It needed repainting, the skirting board was scuffed, and the bathroom was tired, but it was luxurious after the cottage she was living in. No need to go grovelling to Gillies to ask for more money for an upgrade. She lay with the dog on the bed, stroking his soft fur absent-mindedly. First stop, the university.

Time to find her target. She'd begin where Aurora studied, at the English department.

* * *

She drove into the centre of town and parked her car near Buccleuch Street, about a mile or so, she guessed, from the castle, which dominated the centre of the city. This was the hub of the arts faculty of the university, it seemed. There was a square of grey stone tenements with brass signage plaques giving the names of the various departments housed within them. Beyond that were a couple of more modern glass and concrete buildings on a small semi-landscaped campus. Students wandered around looking alternative. They seemed ridiculously young to her. Hanlon felt ambivalent towards them. She had never been to university herself and felt, maybe unfairly, she freely acknowledged, that they were looking down at her.

Is that partly why you're so aggressive? It was the voice of her therapist, rising up inside her. Compensating for low self-esteem?

No, Hanlon told the invisible Dr Morgan, who, it seemed, had taken up residence more or less permanently in her psyche. That's because generally speaking I'm surrounded by idiots or arseholes.

A friendly youth with an unconvincing beard directed her to a sixties-modernist tower block where, after a discussion with security, she went up to the floor marked English Studies. She knocked on the departmental secretary's door.

Julia Swinson, the secretary, was an intelligent-looking woman who Hanlon guessed to be more or less the same age as herself, maybe slightly older, in her forties, elegant, thin, with large and expressive eyes. Some time back, Hanlon had paid to have some business cards made. Six months ago she had imagined handing them around liberally to the throng of eager clients desperate for her assistance. The reality had been different. They had gathered dust on a shelf. This was the first time she had ever given one out. Swinson seemed slightly bemused. She examined the card carefully.

She looked warily at Hanlon and said, 'I don't think I've ever met a private investigator before now. What exactly are you wanting?'

Briefly Hanlon explained that a student's family were concerned about her. She had been missing for some time. Swinson nodded.

'What's her name?'

'Aurora Cameron.'

Swinson's face cleared and she smiled. 'Of course, I know the girl you mean.' She nodded. 'Aurora, such a lovely name... She's a very good-looking girl as well – shame about the tattoos, but that's just a personal opinion, showing my age. Fashions change.' She shook her head. Hanlon had been worried that the secretary would be close-mouthed – well, this obviously wasn't the case. Swinson kept up a continual monologue. She ran her hands over her keyboard, looking at the screen.

'Yes, here we are, I thought so. She's in Dr Griffiths' tutorial group. They're actually meeting today.' She glanced at the clock on the wall. 'They finish at twelve, so about an hour...'

Hanlon pulled a face. 'Oh, dear, my car's on a meter.'

Swinson laughed. 'Look, I shouldn't really do this, but I will. Anything for a private investigator!' She stood up and went to a metal cabinet with about a dozen shallow drawers, selected one, opened it, and took out a small piece of paper.

'What's your registration number?'

Hanlon gave her it and she wrote it down on the form and gave it to Hanlon.

'Display that so it can be seen through the windscreen – it's a visitor's permit for the staff car park. There's no barrier but it's patrolled regularly. I've given you a week so you can come and go.'

'Thank you,' Hanlon said. She meant it.

Swinson smiled. 'Perk of the job. The postcode's on that permit. OK,' she said briskly, 'go and move your car, then come back and if you go down that corridor—' she pointed '—room 3.12 is at the end. He'll be happy to speak to you – Dr Griffiths is very accessible. Tell him I said you could.'

'Thanks,' Hanlon said. Swinson could have been obstructive, unhelpful or even ordered her to leave the building, instead of which she could not have been more pleasant. Hanlon was profoundly grateful.

* * *

She went and moved her car to the small car park, which was about a ten-minute walk away. She walked across the small campus to the David Hume Tower, as the block was named, and back to the department.

Swinson wasn't at her desk so she made her way down the corridor as she'd been instructed. Standing outside the door of 3.12 was a tall, rumpled-looking man with glasses, a beard and a balding head. He was wearing chinos and a tweed jacket and staring at his phone. He looked up as Hanlon approached. He had a kind face, alert and intelligent.

'Can I help you?' he asked.

'I'm looking for Dr Griffiths.'

He smiled and put his phone away. 'I'm Dr Griffiths, how can I help?'

Hanlon felt confused. 'Shouldn't you be teaching in there?' She pointed at the door.

'You're quite right, I should.' He smiled. 'They're supposed to be debating the pros and cons of Evelyn Waugh, who they should have read by now, if only in their anthology.' He sighed. 'They didn't. Lazy sods. I'm making them read some now. Anyway, what do you want?'

She explained. His cheery manner evaporated and he looked serious.

'Aurora, eh. I was wondering what had happened to her myself. I haven't seen her for...' he frowned '... at least a week. She'd have done her homework – she always did... Look,' he said, suddenly business-like, tapping the card she'd given him, 'this is her tutorial group. Speak to them, give them each one of your cards – someone must have some idea of where she's gone.'

'Thanks,' she said, pleased by this unexpected offer of help.

'To tell you the truth, I've been worried about her for a while. We'll discuss that later. Anyway, first things first, come with me.'

He opened the door and they went inside.

In the small room were a couple of tables pushed together and a dozen plastic chairs arranged around them. Books lined the walls, together with framed photos of various men and women, famous writers presumably, and a couple of framed posters, one of *A Clockwork Orange*, the other of *Death in Venice*. It looked as if he was a film buff as well as a book lover.

Nine heads looked at them, five male, four female. It was certainly a balanced class in terms of sex. None of the glances looked terribly friendly. Maybe they just hadn't been enjoying their Evelyn Waugh, she thought.

'This is...'

'Hanlon,' she said.

If Griffiths noticed the lack of title, he didn't comment. 'Hanlon is looking for Aurora. As some of you may know, she hasn't been around for a while and her family are concerned about her. She's going to give out some business cards...'

She walked around the small room handing out cards. Everyone took one.

She addressed the students, who looked mildly rebellious. She decided to tell it how it was.

'Like Dr Griffiths said, I'm looking for Aurora Cameron. Her family are very worried about her. If you have any information could you contact me? My mobile number's on the card. Everything will be treated with the utmost confidentiality. Thank you...'

Nobody said anything. The silence lengthened. The sound of feet shuffling.

'OK,' Griffiths said, 'that'll be all for today.' Immediately, as if a spell had been broken, end-of-class hubbub broke out; they started putting books and pens away, closing laptops and tablets, starting conversations. Griffiths raised his voice over the noise. 'For next time I would like you to write five hundred words on Waugh, subject, the relevance of Waugh today...' Cue groans and rolling of eyes. 'See you next week. Don't forget Dr Fryman's lecture on "Sex and Sensibility – Erotic Currents in Post-war Literature". It's good stuff...'

The students filed out. Griffiths waved a hand at Hanlon.

'Please, take a seat...' He pointed to a visitor's chair on one side of his desk. She did so; he sat down opposite her. His phone buzzed. He looked at it and pulled a rueful face.

'I can give you ten minutes now to talk about Aurora.'

'Thanks,' said Hanlon. 'You said you'd been worried about her?'

'Yeah. On two counts.' Griffiths looked suddenly serious, and leaned forward on his desk. 'First, drug use. She was very bright, and hard-working. Her assignments were always in on time, but she was turning up to class seriously wrecked some days. Oh, and booze. Some days you could smell her coming. But she sought help and got it. I thought we were over the worst, but you never know with addicts, do you?'

'No, you don't,' Hanlon said.

'I just feel that's something you need to bear in mind when you're looking for her. She's potentially unstable – be very gentle with her.'

'How do you mean?' she asked.

Griffiths scratched his beard. 'Aurora can fly off the handle, get over-aggressive. I suppose it's a defence mechanism.' He smiled helplessly. 'I don't know, I'm not a psychologist, but she is volatile – you'd do well to remember that.'

'I understand,' Hanlon said. 'Thanks.'

'The other worry was this odd thing with her father.'

So it wasn't just me who found him odd, thought Hanlon. Her mind suddenly flashed back to the nude portrait on his study wall. Griffiths looked at her as if he didn't know exactly. 'Last term, we were looking at this text by an author who had been sexually abused by a close relation, and Aurora, well, she almost literally howled. It was such a weird noise, it threw me for a second – I'd never heard such a thing – then her face was suddenly wet with tears, like someone had thrown a bucket of water over her, and she just ran out of class.'

'What did you all do?' Hanlon asked.

Griffiths gestured helplessly. 'We were very British about it – we all kind of pretended nothing had happened. She rejoined the class half an hour later. Maybe she discussed it with friends, but I don't think she was particularly pally with anyone in the tutorial group. Aurora kind of kept herself to herself.'

'But you think that text had touched a nerve?' she asked.

Griffiths said, 'How else to explain it? I mean, obviously, I don't know, I really don't.' He shook his head, emphasising his helplessness. 'But I've never had that reaction before, not with incest. I have—' he emphasised the 'have' '—had similar reactions two or three times when violence towards women has been a theme in a text. So, I don't know, like I said, but you should be aware of it and I for one would not be at all surprised if her father turned out to be abusive.'

Hanlon nodded.

'Have you met him?'

He nodded. 'Funnily enough, yes. I obviously don't normally meet students' parents, but I was at some gallery do in Edinburgh, as a guest, and I was introduced to him. He was charming, I remember, but why wouldn't he be? He's an art dealer – he schmoozes people professionally. He didn't look like a man who would abuse his daughter but, then again, they never do, do they?'

Hanlon made a non-committal remark. In her experience over the years they had come in all shapes and sizes.

Griffiths continued. 'But if she is missing, something like that could be a contributory factor. I felt you ought to know.'

'Did you speak to her about it?' she asked.

Griffiths shook his head. 'No, I'm not getting involved with students' private lives, at least not when it's a question of sex. It's not that I don't care, it's just that things like that can be...' he hesitated '... misconstrued... There have to be boundaries,' he added hastily.

Hanlon nodded. 'What did her classmates make of her?'

Griffiths pulled a face. 'Classmates isn't really the word. They are a tutorial group; they see each other once a week. The lectures, well, there could be three hundred people there. As I said before, I don't think she had any particular friends. She was quite aloof, and then there was the beauty thing. I think it was a bit of a handicap.'

'A handicap?' Hanlon was puzzled.

'Yeah, it was intimidating. The others felt that they couldn't... that she was too good-looking to want to bother with them. And then the money. She was rich, another divide. So I think it made mixing hard. But why don't you go round to her place, speak to her flatmate, Morag McMillan?' He found the address section on his phone and she read him her number. He forwarded Aurora's details to her.

'Oh, don't tell Morag I gave you her name or the address – she really doesn't like me, at all.' Hanlon frowned. 'If my name comes up it'll distract her. I think you want her focussed on Aurora, not me. Keep me informed, please,' he said. 'I would appreciate it.' Then he glanced pointedly at the clock.

She stood up. 'Well, thank you, Dr Griffiths, for your help.'

'John, please.'

As she opened the door he called, 'Don't forget to keep in touch.'

'I won't,' she promised.

'Please don't.' He looked at her and she could see sadness in his eyes. He obviously cared deeply about Aurora. She heard a catch in his voice as he said, 'I'm worried something has happened to her. She's very fragile.'

* * *

Hanlon walked back to the car park and drove the short distance from the university to the park that surrounded Arthur's Seat, the lopsided rocky hill that dominates the Edinburgh skyline, sticking up asymmetrically above the roofs of the houses. A constant landmark and a reminder of the presence and power of nature in this urban landscape.

There was plenty of flat grassland for the dog to chase the ball that she threw for him. As she played with the dog, Hanlon thought of what Griffiths had told her. A picture of a hard-working student, still managing to hold things together despite drug and alcohol issues. While these thoughts ran through her head, Wemyss dashed back and forth. He loved the game, his muscular, athletic body a flash of black and white as he endlessly ran backwards and forwards to retrieve his ball, occasionally barking for what seemed to be the sheer pleasure of it all.

Aurora. Poor little rich girl. No friends. And what to make of Griffiths' suggestion that she had been sexually abused by her father? While Hanlon brooded about this she was watching the seemingly endless column of tourists walking in single file up the path that led to the sandstone cliffs, Salisbury Crags, and from there to the summit of Arthur's Seat. There were so many of them. From this distance they were like a parade of ants in search of food.

Hanlon frowned. She herself hadn't been physically abused but she had suffered years of mental torment as a child, she knew what inescapable unhappiness was like. Aurora had sought redemption in drink and drugs, Hanlon's salvation had been exercise and boxing, violence really, lashing out at a world that had hurt her. But they had both pushed it to the limits, another line of coke versus another set of burpees or squat jumps or press-ups or barbell curls. Another e, another left jab, straight right, left hook.

The quest for oblivion. Losing yourself.

She thought of Cameron. He was definitely controlling, but was that necessarily a bad thing? She didn't have children but if she did and they were going off the rails, and she had the resources, would she not keep them under observation? Well, he was innocent until proven guilty, but she made a mental note to herself to go and investigate Cameron's background. Abusers often come from abused families. Misery handed on like a baton in a relay race. She would find out from Murdo Campbell the name of the village that Cameron had come from, across the loch from where he now lived. There would be contemporaries of his still alive and still living there; they'd talk. In a small village, private affairs were generally public knowledge. It'd be a start.

She looked at the address for Aurora that Griffiths had given her. It tallied with the one from Cameron. It was in the New Town of Edinburgh, just a couple of miles from where she was at the moment. She called Wemyss, put him in the car and drove him back to the hotel.

* * *

Ten minutes later she was outside the flat in Howe Street in the New Town. Wide grey cobbled streets, communal gardens behind railings, tall grey stone buildings under a leaden grey sky. Edinburgh was a very gunmetal-grey city, the kind of colour that expensive London pubs had been painted a while ago – it was as if the city had been made over by Farrow and Ball.

She went up the steps of the tall grey tenement, its broad granite steps flanked by black iron railings, to the big black front door, and looked at the row of buzzers, eight of them, two each for the four floors. She found the names Cameron/McMillan and rang. No reply. Hanlon frowned and went back to her car that was parked across the street and settled in for a wait. While she did so, she looked at house prices and the cost of rentals in this area. Both were high. Edinburgh New Town was not a cheap area.

An hour later, one person had left the building, a middle-aged woman, and two had entered it, one a guy who looked to be in his thirties and an elderly man. None of them looked like a Morag McMillan, student.

Another hour passed by. Hanlon had read two newspapers on her phone and was better informed of the state of the world and increasingly bored. Then a woman on a bike slowed, stopped and secured the bicycle to the railings by the street. She took her helmet off and shook out her short dark hair. She looked about the right age; she looked as if she might be a student. She walked up the steps towards the front door and Hanlon got out of her car and ran over to her.

'Morag McMillan?'

The girl turned and stared at Hanlon. She was tall; Lycra suited her long legs. Her dark hair was cut in a geometric bob, and she was quite pretty but with thin lips that made her look judgemental and severe.

'Yes?'

Hanlon walked up the steps. Morag was taller than her and stared down on her with an unfriendly expression. Hanlon gave her one of her business cards; Morag took it and looked at it suspiciously.

'My name's Hanlon. I was wondering if I could have a word with you about Aurora Cameron.'

'What's it to you?' Morag's tone was unfriendly.

'Her family are worried about her.'

Morag glared at her. 'Her family.' Her voice was scornful. 'You mean that bastard of a father of hers.' She looked again at Hanlon's business card. 'A detective? Is that who you're working for – Hamish Cameron?'

Hanlon gave a kind of despairing shrug; it was obvious that whatever Morag had heard from Aurora, it wasn't good.

'Look.' There was no point denying it. Hanlon tried to reason with her. 'He's worried about her. That's all. I just want to make sure she's OK. If Aurora is well, just let me meet with her, and I'll go away and get out of everyone's hair. That's a promise. But if, on the other hand, she's in trouble, I can help. It's a win-win situation. I won't say anything to her father that she doesn't want me to.'

Morag, seemingly unimpressed by this, said, 'Go away,' and turned to open the door.

'Fine,' Hanlon said. She was obviously not getting anywhere. 'But if you change your mind, please call me.'

'Don't wait up,' said Morag, letting herself into the tenement, but Hanlon noticed that she slipped the card inside her pocket.

Hanlon shrugged and went back to her car. As she sat behind the wheel, Griffiths' voice returned to her memory.

I'm worried something has happened to her. She's very fragile.

* * *

Hanlon didn't notice the tall man at the café opposite who took a sip of his coffee and then picked his phone up.

'Yes, Mr Millar?' The voice on the other end was expectant.

'She's just leaving.'

* * *

Hanlon drove back into the hotel car park. She was thinking about Morag and about what she'd learnt about Aurora. The spaces near the building were occupied. She parked on the far side of the car park, which was broken up with a couple of large island beds of shrubs and trees. It was now quite dark. She got out of the driver's seat, closed the door and stretched. She was unaware of anyone behind her.

A tremendous blow hit her in the back, to the right of her spine. The force of it slammed her against the car. Despite the pain, instinct kicked in. Twenty years of ring-work – she didn't need to think. She spun round and drove a left hook into her assailant's body. Hard and fast. She only caught a glimpse of him, tall, powerful, his features unseen behind a ski-mask. He took the punch on his arm and hit her with an expert uppercut into her stomach. Textbook. It drove the wind out of her and she felt sick as she fought for air. Another blow to her gut and as she collapsed onto the wet tarmac of the car park she was manhandled upright, a hand wrapped in her thick hair.

A man's voice close to her ear. 'Stay the fuck away from Aurora Cameron.'

The hand let go of her and her legs buckled, another punch, this time to her face, and she blacked out.

8

'Well, Inspector, how's the murder on that estate looking?'

Detective Inspector Murdo Campbell looked at the DCI and said, calmly, 'Not good, quite frankly. The deceased is a man called Drew Lennox, known as "Wee Drew".' He paused. 'That wasn't ironic – he was small, about five four. Anyway, he was known to us as a small-time dealer. He'd been in trouble for assault, possession, nothing serious. So, his wife called in the attack at three p.m. on Monday. He was dead on the living-room floor...'

Mechanically he filled in the details: the head injury, the three stab wounds. The head wound had probably killed him outright, some kind of blunt instrument, probably a baseball bat, hazarded Campbell. The stab wounds were deep; the knife had been driven in with great force.

'And who did it?'

'Well, his wife says that three masked men burst in and did it, Glasgow accents. She was too frightened to do anything. They wore gloves.'

'Do you believe her?'

Murdo shook his head and said, 'Well, no, mainly because it's not true. There is CCTV in that tower, it just so happened that there was a "malfunction" just before the incident took place, but two more cameras that cover the access road to the estate show a black BMW 4 x 4 registered to a Ray Downie.'

'And who's he?' The DCI had recently transferred from the Borders, you could tell. Just about any policeman in this part of Glasgow would know Ray Downie. Or certainly someone from his extended family.

'Ray is Graeme Millar's main lieutenant, sir,' Campbell explained.

'Ah.' No need to explain who Graeme Millar was.

'Exactly, sir, Calla Lennox, the widow, is hardly going to testify that Millar killed her husband.' He shook his head. 'Nobody on that estate is going to have seen them. The janitor of the block isn't going to say that he blocked the camera.'

The DCI sighed. 'What a nuisance... You think Millar did it personally?'

'Yes, sir, I do.' He thought back to what the lab had told him. The wounds had been inflicted with incredible force – 'ferocious' was the word used. 'The ferocity of the attack, the force with which he was stabbed, it's the kind of thing Millar does. It's almost trademark – he's extremely violent. Ray Downie is from a crime family. The Downies are fairly notorious. If he had killed Lennox it would have been efficient and low-key. He wouldn't have gone to town.'

'So Millar's a headcase.'

'That he is, sir,' Campbell confirmed.

'Hmm.' The DCI scratched his head thoughtfully. 'Do you think the press are going to be all over this one, Murdo?'

Campbell shook his head. 'I don't think so. The media are wary of Millar. He was linked to the death of a journalist a couple of years ago. I doubt if this killing will get too much media coverage – everyone's scared of him. Even the press.' He added, hesitantly, 'Mrs Lennox has a three-month-old daughter...'

The DCI's eyes automatically turned to the family group in the photos on the filing cabinet.

'He wouldn't, would he?'

Campbell nodded. 'He would.'

The DCI said, 'What an animal...' He sighed. 'What a world we live in. So, we know who, how about why? Did Lennox try and rip him off? Surely he wouldn't be that stupid?'

Campbell said, 'No, he was working for Millar. When I say that, I mean indirectly. Lennox's supplier was one of Millar's men. He wouldn't dare.' He paused. 'There is one thing – Calla Lennox has a brother, James McDonald. He did seven years for GBH, lucky to have the charge reduced from attempted murder. A fight in a nightclub in Hamilton. I don't know if that has anything to do with things. I personally suspect it has.'

The DCI said, 'Well, we'll keep it as an ongoing investigation. I suppose no one's going to be busting our balls over it. We should be grateful for small mercies. Locate James McDonald, see if he can throw any light on this.'

'I'll do that. He shouldn't be too hard to find.'

'And have a word with Downie, not that it'll do much good, I suspect.'

'Very good, sir.'

The DCI stood up, as did Campbell; the meeting was over.

'Keep me informed.'

'I will, sir.'

He sighed and walked down the corridor, looking at his watch. Nearly six p.m. He thought of Hanlon; he wondered how she was getting on in Edinburgh. Better than he was here in Glasgow, almost certainly. Nobody would ever dare testify against Millar. He had spoken to the caretaker himself; he was shit-scared of Millar, as was everyone in this case.

He went back to his desk and started work on finding McDonald. First port of call, his probation officer.

9

They were in the Regent, in a room with twin beds, in a cheap hotel in Meadowbank. Meadowbank, the former stadium, was currently a vast building site and looked to be that way for some time to come. But the hotel in a run-down street nearby was fine for their purposes. Ray emerged from the bathroom, Dougie was lying on one of the beds, smoking a cigarette. Ray, his body wet from the shower, sat down on the other. He looked around him. He'd never stayed at the Waldorf Astoria, but he was willing to bet it was nicer than this.

Big Dougie was twenty-eight. He was tall, blond and raw-boned. Ray thought he looked like a Viking. Perhaps he was – there had been a lot of Viking activity in Scotland in the distant past.

He flexed the fingers of his right hand.

'Your hand OK?' Dougie asked.

It was a bit sore still from where he'd hit Hanlon's head. He'd been wearing leather gloves; his knuckles were fine. But it was a reminder that he wasn't as young as he used to be. He ought to leave hitting people to Dougie. He was younger, his bones were more robust.

He wondered if she'd heed the warning. She would if she were wise. Millar didn't like giving second chances. He rarely gave first chances, come to that.

Oh, Millar, what the hell went wrong? wondered Ray. He'd worked for Millar for over twenty-five years, but of late it was like being trapped in a marriage that had gone hideously awry. Millar was getting crazier, and increasingly violent. He was also getting more and more paranoid, convinced people were plotting against him. Ray tried to restrain his boss, but it was increasingly difficult. He tried to telepathically send a message to Hanlon: please go home, go home now, or you'll be returning there in a box.

'Did you know Jordan?' Dougie asked.

'What, the dead guy in the van? No, just that he worked for the Big Man in Edinburgh and it would appear that he's been offed by this Jamie McDonald.'

He leaned over Dougie and peered at the screen of his tablet. Computer games baffled Ray. What was the point? He just didn't get them, in fact they really irritated him, but he was wise enough to keep his mouth shut. Dougie loved them.

'What's that? What are you doing?' he asked, more to be polite than anything.

'It's a virus. I'm trying to infect the world...' Dougie said. Why? Ray wondered, but he didn't say anything.

'Well, can you pause it for a moment or two?'

Big Dougie sighed. 'OK.' He looked annoyed at being stopped; he must have been doing really well in his game.

He looked at Ray, who had returned to his bed and was looking at him with impatience. Ray could see himself in the mirror on the bedroom wall. He looked hard at his reflection, his powerful, muscular body. I'm looking good for someone on the wrong side of fifty he thought. Ray was a physical fitness nut, ran five miles a day, worked out. His silver hair was shaved close to his head in a buzz-cut. His abs were chiselled. Already Ray was missing the absence of a gym, he worked out for at least an hour a day when he could.

They had been working together now for a couple of years and Big Dougie, six three in his bare feet, was perfectly happy to let Ray make the decisions and do the thinking. Thinking was not his area of expertise.

'And?' he asked irritably.

'Tomorrow. I want to go over tomorrow,' said Ray.

'What's to go over? We go round to his flat and kill the fucker.'

Ray sighed. 'Yes, that's it, Einstein, but there are some things I'd like to think about.'

'Such as?' Dougie was puzzled; it seemed simple enough.

'How are we going to get there?' Ray asked.

'We'll drive.' He frowned, Ray could see him wondering, what was the issue here? There was the BMW outside.

'Oh, will we? Where are we going to park? That's my car out there,' Ray said, indicating the general area of the street. 'If I park that in a car park it might have number plate recognition. I don't want to be in Musselburgh officially. If I park it in a side street we might have to fuck around looking for a parking place. It's probably residents only. I don't want a ticket. I do not want my car officially parked just down the road from a killing.'

'OK, then, we'll get an Uber.'

Ray shook his head. 'We'll get the bus.'

'The bus? We're going to kill a man and we're getting a fucking bus!' Dougie was incredulous.

'Aye, what's wrong with that?'

'What's wrong?' Dougie sounded cross. 'Are you being serious?'

He leapt off the bed and stood in front of Ray, towering over him. He looked furious.

Ray's eyes didn't leave Dougie's. He suddenly hooked a leg across behind his partner's, sweeping Dougie's legs from under him. Simultaneously he sprang off the bed and pushed him hard. Dougie collapsed backwards and Ray was on top of him, pinning him to the carpet. He leaned forward, holding Dougie's wrists down against the floor, and inclined his head so their noses were nearly touching. He could smell the whisky and cigarettes on Dougie's breath.

'Ye'll dae whit youse fuckin tellt,' he said, menacingly, mimicking Dougie's accent.

Dougie started to laugh. 'Get off me, you're awfie heavy, Ray.'

Ray leaned his face closer to Dougie's. His mouth opened and their tongues met.

* * *

Afterwards they lay next to each other in bed sharing a joint.

'Why does the boss want him dead anyway?' asked Dougie.

Because he's gone crazy, would be the honest answer, thought Ray. Because in Millar's mind, fragmenting under the drugs and the booze or maybe just natural causes, McDonald was either 'out to get him' or he had 'let him down'.

Ray propped himself up on one elbow, took the joint from Dougie and inhaled deeply.

'Well, to make an example of him maybe?' He exhaled the smoke thoughtfully.

'I guess.' Dougie ran a hand across Ray's chest. His pectorals were like iron. His skin was hairless; Ray liked to wax.

'Like I said earlier,' Ray said, 'Jordan was the boss's man in Edinburgh. We've been moving a lot of gear out here these days. It's a growing market. Jordan's death has really screwed things up. Thank God, Millar's got someone else working out here too. They'll have to pick up the slack, do Jordan's work as well as theirs.'

'Whereabouts in Edinburgh?'

'I don't know. Maybe the uni.'

'Why can't they handle McDonald, then? Why us?'

'Cos they're the brains and we're the brawn. That's the way it is.'

And also, he thought, Millar trusts me more than anyone. God help me if that changes.

'Aye.' Dougie took the blunt from Ray. 'Carry on...'

'Where was I?' Post-coital relaxation and the weed were making Ray feel a bit muzzy. 'Oh, aye.' He recovered his train of thought. 'Catriona, Jordan's girl, said that Jordan was doing a hit, and he'd contracted the job to Jamie McDonald.'

'Who is McDonald anyway?' Dougie asked.

'A guy that Jordan had met inside, doing time for a stabbing.'

'So why the fuck did McDonald kill him?'

'I have absolutely no idea.' He frowned. 'But he did. Now, before we kill him, we ask him about a girl called Aurora Cameron. Millar wants to find her, and don't ask me why, or who she is, because I don't know. But he wants her, that's the important thing.'

Probably she was someone else who'd 'let him down' or had been 'taking liberties', both capital offences now seemingly. Fleetingly, he wondered again what she'd done to attract Millar's fury. None of his business.

'Have you got that?'

Dougie rolled on his back and stared at the ceiling. 'Yes, yes, yes. Subdue him, question him then kill him. Millar wants a message sending out. Nobody messes with his employees unless they want a real fucking shit-storm. We're the message.'

Incoming call. Ray picked up his mobile and glanced at it.

'Speak of the devil,' he said to Dougie. 'Aye, boss... mmhm... sure, can you text me the details? Sure, tomorrow lunchtime... aye, will do... we'll be there, bye the now.'

He put his phone down.

'Well?' asked Dougie.

'He's just checking that we're OK for tomorrow. He says he'll meet with us afterwards at lunchtime.' He rolled his eyes – well, that was just great. That was lunch ruined. They'd better not cock things up, or Millar would want to know why.

'Jesus,' said Dougie, 'it's going to be a busy day.' He yawned.

'Tired?' asked Ray.

'Knackered,' said Dougie.

He pulled the duvet over himself but just before he closed his eyes, he checked his phone.

'Ha!' he said.

'Ha, what?' Ray said.

'It's my virus, look, Ray, it's successfully mutated.'

'That's just great,' replied Ray, wearily, 'now can we get some sleep.'

'Humanity's dead.' Dougie was triumphant.

'Well,' Ray said, rolling over, 'let's hope McDonald will be as easy to kill. Good night.'

10

Hanlon woke up at seven. She lay in the dark, checking in with her body. She had three main areas of pain: her face, her back and her ribs. She ran her fingers gently over her face. Tender to the touch, but it did not feel too bad. God alone knew what it looked like though. She slid out of bed and went into the bathroom. Under the harsh white light, she stripped off and checked her body and face.

Her right eye was swollen and discoloured. She was lucky that she had been moving downwards when she'd been hit in the face; the blow hadn't been as hard as it could have been. Where she'd been hit in the back she had a large purplish bruise and there was more bruising to her ribs. But nothing felt broken. She breathed in deeply, experimentally. No sharp pains – hopefully that meant her ribs were intact. She touched her face. Her nose and left cheekbone were sore and the swollen flesh felt hot to the touch. Luckily, her mouth seemed undamaged. It was nothing she couldn't live with. Hanlon had been beaten up before, both inside and outside a boxing ring, for sport and in the course of her job. She knew her body and she felt that these injuries were mainly cosmetic. The violence had been mainly designed to frighten, not to hurt her. It could have been a lot worse. A hell of a lot worse.

She hadn't bothered calling the police. The men who had done this were pros. There would be nothing on the car park CCTV – either they would have obscured their number plate, or they would have used a false one. Besides, she didn't want the hassle. Or the inevitable lecture about leaving things to the appropriate authorities.

She went back into the room, made a cup of tea and got back into bed; she wanted to think. Wemyss shook himself, the metal of his name tag clinking against his collar. He stood up and nuzzled her. 'Yes, we'll go out soon,' she said.

She tried to piece together what had happened, what she could remember of the attack in the car park. First, the voice. A man's voice, deep, the accent Scottish. Surprise, surprise. She was well aware from the little time that she had spent in Scotland that there were all sorts of accents, but she was fairly ignorant of them. As a rule of thumb, west coast seemed quite gentle. This wasn't, this was harsh. Glasgow?

What else? He was tall, about six foot, and, boy, could he punch. So, a trained fighter and also someone with experience of violence. There had been no hesitation, he'd known exactly what he was doing. A professional. That was about it, that and she would be able to recognise his trainers. When she'd collapsed onto the tarmac of the car park she had seen his shoes, two-tone black and white, chunky soles and on the tongue of the shoe was a logo she didn't know. Hanlon hung around a lot in gyms, she was clued up on gym-wear. Not to mention the relentless targeting that she experienced online by sportswear companies. The shoes she remembered weren't from one of the big companies. They were niche, they had to be expensive. They were distinctive and slightly unusual. Whoever had attacked her had an eye for style. Not a style she liked, but style nevertheless. The important thing though was that she knew if she saw them again, she'd recognise them.

One other thing: he'd been wearing quite a lot of aftershave. He had certainly gone to town on it. This had to be habitual. Surely no one went out to beat someone up thinking, better make sure I smell good? His aftershave had a distinctive smell, unusually heavy and flowery for a man. She'd remember that smell for a long time. So she was dealing with a thug who took pride in his appearance.

Well, so much for that. It wasn't a great deal. She lay in bed, staring at the ceiling. She was annoyed with herself – she felt that she should have been able to fight back more effectively; how she could have done this, she wasn't sure. Then she laughed grimly. Well, at least she didn't feel intimidated. She had no intention whatsoever of backing down.

How had he known how to find her? Actually, it was more than likely there had been at least two, she thought, one for the muscle and one as a lookout/driver/help. A professional would need back-up. The attack had gone to plan, like clockwork, but things like that rarely did. So, how had they known where she was staying?

Who knew? She had told Gillies and she had told Morag. That in turn meant Cameron knew, or could have found out. Well, speculation was useless and why would Cameron want his hired help scared off anyway?

Had Gillies deliberately tipped someone off? You couldn't imagine him running his mouth off down the pub.

Morag? Surely not.

Had she mentioned where she was staying to Dr Griffiths? She really couldn't remember.

She thought some more of Cameron. If someone wanted to hurt Cameron – and he was successful and rich, of course he would have enemies – then harming his daughter made a great deal of sense. She was easy to get at, for a start, and Cameron, with his security system and staff, would be much harder. And he certainly cared about Aurora.

Whatever the truth of the abuse allegations, he was obsessed, either understandably (an overprotective father whose wife had died tragically young) or unhealthily (sexual abuse) with Aurora. And then, if that were the case, maybe someone had an informant within Cameron's organisation.

Well, speculation was proving to be a dead end. What she could do was maintain her fitness so that if she met up with her attacker again, she'd be ready.

She got out of bed, swallowed a couple of painkillers and did a hundred press-ups, four sets of twenty-five. Then her abs, abs that had just a few hours ago protected her from the worst of the body blows. Sit-ups, crunches, Russian twists and plank. Then ten minutes of yoga to ease those cramped and achingly bruised muscles.

She checked her phone – nothing. She'd been hoping for at least one call about Aurora from the students she'd spoken to in Griffiths' tutorial or from Morag.

She pulled a tracksuit on and led Wemyss out to the car park. It was still dark and much colder than the west coast. A chill north wind was blowing.

She selected a playlist on her phone, keyed in 6 km as her distance on her running app, put her earphones in, the dog on his lead and set off at a brisk jog.

The first five minutes hurt like hell, then, as her body warmed up the pain lessened, and she found her natural rhythm, her heavy hair bouncing as she ran, her strong legs carrying her effortlessly through the deserted streets. After ten minutes she opened up, her strides long and graceful, her breathing deep and rhythmic.

As she ran through the darkness, she could feel the power in her legs and the muscles in her body stretching, and she started to smile with the sheer pleasure of her fitness. Now the black night was gradually giving way to light, she thought how odd it seemed to be running through the outskirts of a city, along pavements, her way lit by street lights. She'd been living in the countryside of Argyll for six months now; running had been on deserted roads by the sea and in the hills. Although she had lived all her life in London, she was beginning to find the presence of houses and traffic alien, claustrophobic.

She was worried about Aurora. She thought of the girl's face, seen only in photos. Beautiful and serious. The attack on Hanlon to scare her off showed one thing for sure: that Aurora was involved with professional criminals. There could be no doubt about that whatsoever. Until the attack the night before, she had just assumed the girl had gone off the rails, drugs, boyfriend, stress, something like that. That was not to minimise the gravity of the situation. She was no psychologist. She thought of Dr Morgan; she could visualise the doctor laughing at the thought of Hanlon as a mental health professional – if anyone was mildly fucked up it was her, and she knew it. But with the girl's history – dead mother, estranged controlling father, who, whether or not he had been abusing her, was certainly a far from normal parent, drug and alcohol abuse and lack of a framework of friends – she had to be high risk for potential self-harm. It was quite a list and it all added up to a potent cocktail.

But organised crime? She hadn't been expecting that.

The flatmate seemed best placed to give her the information she needed. OK, so the first approach hadn't gone well; she'd give Morag another twenty-four hours and then go and see her again, try to be either a bit more forceful or a bit more pleading depending upon what seemed best. In the interim, she'd go and have another look round the university.

They got back to the hotel, she gave Wemyss his breakfast, a can of dog food, showered and went down for breakfast. As she closed the hotel door the dog looked at her imploringly.

'OK,' she promised, 'I'll steal you a couple of sausages from the buffet.'

The door clicked behind her.

* * *

Several miles away on the other side of Edinburgh, Big Dougie and Ray were walking down a dark side street in Musselburgh, a seaside town that abutted the capital.

Ray was silent and preoccupied, but he was far more worried about Millar. He glanced at Dougie next to him, he too looked tense, doubtless he was thinking about McDonald. Ray remembered, God, when was it? Two years ago probably, a similar scenario, him, Millar and the late unlamented Mickey D, dead now of a smack overdose. They'd smashed a door down in a tenement in Nitshill in Glasgow, on the Paisley borders. Looking for the name of an informant. The guy, shoulders held down by Ray, feet by Mickey D. Millar had found a pair of kitchen scissors in a drawer. The guy bucking for all he was worth, pants round his knees, eyes popping out of his head, mouth gagged with a tea-towel stuffed in it. The blood, the smell, as Millar got to work with the scissors. Ray had nearly collapsed himself. Millar was crazy. And Ray had the misfortune to work for him. This wasn't what he'd signed up for. But there was no retirement policy and he was too scared to resign.

At the back of his mind was the unspoken thought; you could well be next.

He pushed the thought of Millar away. Let's concentrate on the job at hand.

It was tenements again. Musselburgh had been gentrified since he had last been there but Kincardine Close, the address Millar had given them, had been spared the hand of redevelopment. It was a poor street in a poor neighbourhood. Gates sagged, hedges were overgrown. They got to number fifteen. Most of the windows were still dark; people were still asleep. Dougie had a backpack over his shoulder with a crowbar and a short-handled heavy club hammer inside. The communal door was a worry, Ray didn't want to be battering it down at seven a.m., waking up God knew how many people.

They walked up the short path to the property in the darkness; there was no security light and no street lights in the close. There was a communal wheelie bin and a scrubby bush on either side of the flagstones.

'Fucking dump,' said Dougie, sotto voce to Ray.

Ray had a small pistol in his coat pocket, a Makarov that Millar had given him. Guns. They'd never needed guns in the old days. But McDonald was probably armed, after all.

Millar had shown him how to take the safety off; that was easy enough. 'There's five bullets in it,' said Millar. 'That should be more than enough. If you do get nicked with it, this gun's never been used in a crime, it's clean. Bring it back though, OK.'

Ray had only ever used a gun once in his life; he'd shot a drug dealer in the thigh. A warning. It had been easy enough. But that, compared to killing somebody, seemed almost light-hearted. He had never killed anyone before. Ray was Millar's minder, occasionally he beat people up, but generally he didn't need to. The look of quiet confidence in his eyes that came from seven years of jail time and more than a few fights was usually enough. And when he wasn't doing strong-arm stuff, Ray was running Millar's empire, a safe, efficient pair of hands. He didn't want to be doing this. Part of him wanted something to go wrong, something beyond their control so they could abandon the job and not lose face.

The anticipated problem with the shared front door never materialised. It was unlocked. They looked at each other and grinned. It was a good omen.

'First floor,' Dougie said.

They walked up the grey granite steps, their feet echoing in the stairwell. There were two doors on the first floor; one had a pram outside and two pairs of wellingtons, one pink, the other red with ladybirds on. Not that one, then. They looked at the other door opposite, went over to it. It was blue, scuffed and there was the name McDonald written in biro on a piece of card and taped to the wood.

Ray rapped loudly on the door. 'Police!'

They looked at each other. Big Dougie took out a fake Police Scotland warrant card and held it up to the fish-eye spy hole in the door. They heard footsteps, silence as presumably McDonald scrutinised the card holder, then the door opened.

It was the first time Ray had ever seen his target, the man he was supposed to kill, the man who had almost certainly killed Jordan McKenna. McDonald was medium height, dark-skinned with very black stubble. His hair was quite long and glossy black. He must have been an early riser because he was dressed. Ray felt a stab of disappointment. He would have much preferred a yawning, bleary-eyed guy in a dressing gown. He was wearing jeans and trainers and a green jumper. Ray noticed the biceps bulging through the wool, jail-time muscle he guessed, contraband steroids and hundreds and hundreds of push-ups in the cell. Endless push-ups. He'd been there.

McDonald looked at the two large, unsmiling men in front of him. 'Police eh?' he said and yawned, putting his left hand up to his mouth. 'Sorry, I'm not really awake...'

Big Dougie nodded, started to step forward, and as he did so McDonald, with no warning, with incredible speed, hit him in the face with his right hand and slammed the door shut. The punch had been lightning fast and very hard. Dougie moaned with pain, sank to his knees, hands cupped across his shattered nose; blood pooled out between his fingers and dripped on the floor.

'Jesus,' he groaned.

'Fuck it,' Ray said angrily. 'Come on, you big numpty.' He pulled a wad of tissues out of his coat pocket and handed them to Dougie and the two of them retreated down the stairs and out into the street.

In the cold, dark air Dougie tilted his head back, pressing the sodden tissue to his nose and said, indistinctly, 'Let's go back and kill the cunt.'

'Let's not, Dougie,' said Ray, shaking his head. Talk about leaving a calling card, Dougie's blood on the floor as clear as day to the police forensics team who would arrive to the crime scene of a gangland killing. He might as well leave his driving licence behind while he was at it, speed the whole process of his arrest up, save everyone time.

'Come on…' He shook his head; he really wasn't looking forward to explaining this fiasco to Millar.

* * *

From his hiding place at the end of the close, behind another of the ubiquitous wheelie bins, McDonald watched the two men walk away.

'Thank fuck for that,' he breathed.

He'd been expecting something along these lines ever since he'd killed Jordan – he'd taken to sleeping fully clothed.

He had recognised Ray immediately, thank God. Millar's enforcer. He'd had him pointed out in a nightclub in Hamilton one time. There weren't many avowedly gay hoodlums; Ray was a bit of an oddity. But they'd nearly fooled him with the fake ID. He had come within a whisker of letting them in. If he had, he would be dead by now. As soon as that door had slammed shut he had run to the window at the back of the flat and, hanging by his fingertips, dropped down to the garden at the back. There was an alley, like a service road, that ran along the back fence, over which he'd climbed and run along to where it joined the close. There, he had hidden for three or four minutes and observed the door until the men Millar had sent had emerged and made their way back down the street.

Millar. If Ray Downie was after him, that meant Millar had sent him. That meant Millar knew where he was living. Until now, there had been some measure of hope – maybe Jordan had been working for someone else who had wanted Aurora killed. Jordan had worked for Millar, but he could have been freelancing. But now McDonald had seen Ray, well, that was that. If Ray came calling then he had definitely fallen foul of Millar. Shit, thought McDonald, of all the people to have made an enemy of. Graeme Millar, that psycho. He had a very uncomfortable feeling that he was a dead man walking.

Now that the coast was clear, he couldn't see those two returning. If something goes badly wrong when you're psyched up to kill someone you're not going to go and have a coffee and a cigarette and wander back for a second bite of the cherry. He walked back into the building and up to his flat. Outside the door he saw the bloodstains and guessed what had run through Ray's mind. Too much DNA evidence. Thank God for small mercies. He wondered how they had tracked him down here. Calla, he guessed. He had only spoken to her once since he'd killed Jordan. He'd mentioned that he was in Musselburgh. Millar must have questioned her. She wouldn't have given him up without a struggle; growing up in the slum part of Port Glasgow, she'd adored him, Jamie, her protector. They'd both grown up in the care system, after they'd been taken from their home on the state for various periods of time. Their parents were hopeless junkies. They weren't bad people, just entirely unsuited to bringing up children. He didn't blame Calla for giving Millar his address. He hoped she was OK – Millar was unforgiving.

He let himself back into the flat and grabbed a sports bag into which he hurriedly stuffed some clothes. He went into the kitchen, got a knife out of the cutlery drawer and lay on the floor. He prised the panel from the base of one of the kitchen units off and reached his arm in under the shelving unit. He pulled out a couple of freezer bags full of cash, then another freezer bag, a handgun, a Makarov. He didn't know it, but it was virtually identical to the one that Ray had been carrying. Millar had bought six of them as a job lot. The other four were at a safe house in Bearsden owned by a retired schoolteacher, a pillar of the community, who the police would never suspect of such a thing. The teacher's junkie son owed Millar quite a lot of money.

The gun and the five K went into the sports bag. He added a knife too, a razor-sharp, slim-bladed chef's boning knife.

He drummed his fingers on the counter and said aloud, 'Fuck it, why not?' It's not every day you get to survive a murder attempt. Wave goodbye to six months of clean time, Jamie.

He ran his fingers under the base of one of the wall-cupboards that were above the faux-stone of the work-surface. His fingertips found the wrap he had promised himself he had given up. He pulled it free of the

Scotch tape, and stood up, looking at the folded piece of paper in his hand, five grams of prime coke.

He stared at it for some time. As if it were a hand grenade about to explode. Which, for a heavy duty coke addict like him, it was. Part of him wanted to just flush it down the toilet. Half a year of no coke, no drugs. Aurora had got him off the drugs – she had been his saviour. It was her he had phoned in the early days when the desire to score had been almost uncontrollable; it had been Aurora who had talked him out of relapsing dozens of times.

Jamie had developed a five-gram-a-day habit, and she had helped to free him from coke dependency. So doing a line wasn't just a relapse, it would be a betrayal of her. But then again, he had saved her life. So they were quits; he owed her nothing. The bullets meant for her had wound up in Jordan instead. God knows why Jordan had wanted her dead, but right now that wasn't the issue.

As he stared at the paper containing the drug, it struck him that he had only been pretending to Aurora and to himself that he had given up. If he'd been serious he wouldn't have hung onto the gear as he had. He could have flushed it down the loo, instead he'd carefully taped it under a cupboard where he could find it easily.

Well, now wasn't the time for introspection, he told himself.

He carefully unfolded the paper wrap and, using a credit card from his wallet, pushed out a generous line of coke.

He stared at it hungrily, a man in the desert staring at an oasis. Coke had fucked his life up before – Christ alone knew how much money he had spent on it. And now look, he was back at it. Big difference, thought McDonald, is that my days on this earth are now probably very much numbered. Not much point being clean and sober while Millar's after me. He resealed the wrap and put both it and his card back in his wallet. He stared at the coke again for quite a while. He shrugged his muscular shoulders. Might as well be hung for a sheep as a lamb, he thought.

He had a bottle of vodka at the back of a cupboard and he poured himself a generous measure in a whisky glass.

He shotted the vodka; it burned its way down. God, that felt good. He took a Clydesdale Bank twenty-pound note from his wallet, rolled it up into a tube and then leaned forward and did the coke. Just like old times, just as if he had never stopped. Getting back on the roller coaster for one last ride. One nostril closed, folded twenty up the other. Snort. WHOAAAH! He steadied himself for a moment and grinned.

'Fuck, fuck, fuck... Welcome back,' he said out loud, then, 'Let the good times roll.'

He picked up the sports bag and headed out into the freezing darkness of a bitterly cold February East Lothian morning.

11

Hanlon headed back to the centre of town. The dog was in the back, looking attentively out of the window. It was rush hour on Thursday morning and the traffic was heavy. Edinburgh seemed to be being dug up whichever way you went. Other drivers gave her a wide berth. The great thing about driving an ancient, battered cheap car like the Corsa, she reflected, was that fellow motorists were a lot more polite than when she'd had a top-of-the-range Audi. It was either because they felt sorry for her – obviously poor – or nervous in case, as a member of the underclass, probably uninsured, potentially violent, she might drive either carelessly or aggressively. Whatever the reason, people waved her out at junctions, didn't sound their horn when she aggressively cut across them if she had to make an unexpected turn. It made for relaxing driving.

Her phone rang. The car had no Bluetooth so she pulled over. It was Morag.

'I'd like to meet with you,' she said. She sounded worried, a completely different tone from the previous day. 'I think we need to talk.'

Hanlon tried to hide the elation in her voice as she replied.

'I'd love that,' she said. 'Shall I come over to you?'

'No,' Morag said, 'I'd rather meet somewhere else. Do you know the Gallery of Modern Art? That's not far away from me.'

'No, but I can find it.' She glanced down at her phone.

'OK, well,' Morag added, 'the museum is housed in two separate buildings. I'll meet you in the main gallery – there's a coffee shop in there.'

'Fine,' Hanlon said. 'When?'

'It opens at ten – let's say ten-thirty.'

'I'll be there,' Hanlon promised.

The phone went dead. She keyed in the destination to the maps on her phone and drove off.

Twenty minutes later Hanlon was pulling into the car park behind the dark grey stained stone of the gallery, which was a long, narrow two-storey building set in a large grassy park. She could see its twin, the second gallery, just down the hill.

She walked in, nodding politely to the uniformed guard. The gallery was practically empty, except for some tourists and a couple of very obvious art students wearing art-studenty clothes. She found the cafeteria. Morag was waiting for her, sitting facing the door. She was wearing a long baggy grey jumper, a very short blue denim skirt and black tights with motorcycle-style boots. She too looked, suitably enough, very art student. Her face was pale and the only flash of real colour about her was a pair of chunky red earrings. She didn't notice Hanlon; she was staring into space lost in thought.

* * *

Mentally, Morag wasn't at the museum. In her mind she was where they made Desert Island Discs, the radio programme in which famous people choose their favourite music to accompany them on a lonely stay on a desert island. She was at the BBC, she'd been staying at the Langham Hotel, nearby. In a suite. 'Today,' said Lauren Laverne, the presenter, 'we have as our castaway the well-known writer…' No… she rewound her fantasy in her head. 'Today,' said Lauren Laverne, 'we have as our castaway the uber-famous writer and influential thinker, who has been described by *The Guardian* as "the voice of our times", Morag McMillan. Hello, Morag.'

'Hello, Lauren,' she said. Laverne was obviously nervous. Morag smiled reassuringly at her; she was always gracious.

'And what is your first piece of music?'

'Well, Lauren,' she said judiciously, 'I know all about art and I was forever, when I lived in Edinburgh, before locating to New York where I now live, hanging around the Gallery of Modern Art... As most people know, I just love art...'

* * *

'Hello,' said Hanlon.

Morag jumped slightly, she must have been miles away, thought Hanlon. 'Oh, my God! What's happened to your face? You look awful!' Morag looked shocked.

Hanlon pursed her lips irritably. 'Someone doesn't want me poking my nose in. It's a professional hazard, Morag, it's really not as bad as it looks.'

'If you say so.' Morag looked at her dubiously.

'I do.' Hanlon's voice was firm, shutting down debate.

'Well, thank you for coming,' Morag said, staring at Hanlon with what looked like horrified fascination. 'I'm so sorry I was rude to you yesterday.'

'That's OK.' Hanlon picked up her coffee and blew on it. 'Now, how can I help you?'

'So...' Morag repeated herself. 'So, I last saw Aurora over a week ago, nearly a fortnight actually. She came back from an NA meeting...'

'NA?' asked Hanlon, 'Narcotics Anonymous?'

'Narcotics Anonymous,' confirmed Morag. 'She'd given up coke a year ago and started going then. Normally she's really happy when she gets back from a meeting, recharged, but that night...' there was a faraway look in her eye and Hanlon guessed she was reliving it in her memory '... she was in a real state, panic-stricken. I went into her room and she was flinging clothes into a suitcase.'

She drank some coffee. Hanlon could see the bags under her eyes that make-up couldn't hide.

'Did you ask what had happened?'

'Yes, of course I did.' Morag looked at her irritably. 'I said something stupid like, did someone say something to upset you at the meeting?' She rolled her eyes in annoyance at herself. 'Obviously it was far worse than that. Something huge had gone down and she said, "Look, get out of my face, this is really serious," and then she left the flat. She was terrified, shaking, like... in a state of shock.'

'Do you have any idea what might have happened?' Hanlon asked.

Morag shook her head. 'None whatsoever. She was refusing to discuss it.'

'I see,' Hanlon said. 'And this was which day?'

Morag thought. 'It was a Monday, not this Monday just gone, the week before, so about ten days, nearly a fortnight.'

Some time ago, thought Hanlon. And nobody has heard from or seen her since. That is worrying. Particularly when someone has tried to warn me off by beating me up. Aurora is obviously in deep trouble.

'Do you know where she went? Do you have any ideas? Any friends, places that you can think of?' she asked.

'No idea.' Morag appeared to think hard, hesitating. 'I'm guessing somewhere in Edinburgh. I mean, the city's big enough to hide in, she would never have gone home and as far as I know she hadn't really got any friends in Scotland she could stay with... I do know that wherever she went it wasn't abroad.'

'Why's that?' asked Hanlon.

'She keeps her passport in a box-file that's in a cupboard in the lounge, so she doesn't mislay it, together with the official papers that relate to the flat – the lease is in her name. I was looking for the TV licence the other day and I saw it in there. She hadn't taken it.'

Hanlon nodded – so, not abroad, and probably still in Edinburgh.

'Do you think whatever she was running from might have anything to do with any of her classmates? How were her studies going?'

Morag shook her head. 'Aurora loved her subject, loved her studies. There were no problems there. But like I said, I don't know what had upset her.'

Silence fell. It was very quiet in the café, the only sound the hissing of the coffee machine.

'What do you study, Morag, if you don't mind me asking?' Hanlon was curious.

The girl shook her head. 'No, I don't mind. I graduated in Eng Lit last summer. I'm doing a Master's in Creative Writing now. Paul Wyre is the course tutor.' She paused. 'Do you know him?'

Hanlon shook her head. 'Should I?'

Morag looked at her pityingly, a look that was meant to be noticed. 'He's a well-known writer,' she said. 'Anyway, I know Griffiths, Aurora's tutor.' She looked challengingly at Hanlon. 'Of course, she didn't get on with him.' She emphasised the word him. 'That man is an evil bastard.'

Hanlon frowned, slightly puzzled. Really? Griffiths certainly hadn't come across that way. She recalled what he had said about Morag not liking him. Well, that was certainly true.

'What's so bad about him?' she asked.

Morag gave a tight little smile; it was slightly infuriating. I'm so superior, it said, and you're an idiot. Morag's pitying looks were beginning to get to Hanlon. Condescending bitch, she thought.

In the back of her mind, Dr Morgan said, warningly, 'Don't lose your temper. You're rushing to judgements as usual.'

Morag said, 'Do you know *Othello*?'

'The board game?' She'd never played it; it had been around in her youth.

'No, not the board game.' Morag shook her head in a condescending way. (See, Doctor, look at that! It's not my imagination at all!) 'The play, the Shakespeare play.'

With her maddeningly superior air, she said, 'It's got a character called Iago in it.'

'Whatever.' Hanlon shrugged. She had no interest in English literature whatsoever.

'You should read more,' said Morag accusingly.

'There's lots of things I should do, believe me,' said Hanlon wearily. 'I'll put Shakespeare on the list.'

'Never mind, you'll find out soon enough about Griffiths,' Morag said smugly. 'I know him well – he was my tutor for a year. He'll get his comeuppance.'

'What do you mean by that?' asked Hanlon, puzzled.

'I'm going to expose him, show the world what he really is like—' Morag smiled '—and make my name doing so. Revenge will be sweet.'

Hanlon wondered if she was planning some kind of exposé in the student newspaper. 'So what's he been doing, some sort of "sex for good marks" type of thing?'

'No.' Morag shook her head. 'Other lecturers do that.' She smiled rather sadly. 'Hello, Mr Wyre... No, he's far more subtle, far more devious. Anyway...' she patted her laptop '... it's all on here. My novel will be a media sensation when it's published. It's explosive. Everybody says so.'

'Hello, fame and fortune,' Hanlon said.

'You bet, it's being published by Grassmarket Books,' she said with a boastful air, then, slightly bitterly, 'Some of us are born with a silver spoon like Aurora, others have to graft for it.'

'Did she have reason to be afraid of Griffiths?' asked Hanlon.

Morag nodded. 'Griffiths likes to hurt people. I'd look into that if I were you.'

'Could you be a bit more specific?' asked Hanlon.

She shook her head. 'No, I won't say any more. It's in my book, fictionalised. He doesn't do things himself, he's like Iago. Griffiths isn't a violent man, not directly, he's not going to turn up at our flat and shoot someone. He's subtle, and, please, don't drop me in it when you speak to him. He doesn't know that I know anything. I'm just Aurora's flatmate as far as he's concerned.'

'So you think Griffiths has something to do with her disappearance?'

'Not directly, I told you, that's not how he works.' She shook her head. 'Aurora was physically frightened, I think, and Griffiths isn't physically frightening. He'd have hired someone, obviously. Like you would a plumber to unblock a drain, you wouldn't do it yourself.'

So Griffiths was a suspect in Morag's eyes. Hanlon thought about the hiring of professional muscle. She thought of the night before. Were they the metaphorical plumbers? Griffiths' attempt to forestall any investigation? He certainly knew she was looking into Aurora's affairs.

Hanlon continued, 'What else can you tell me about Aurora that might be relevant to her disappearance? Boyfriend?'

Morag nodded. 'Luke Bastien, he's an artist. They were close. She wanted to be closer but he's one of these, "oh, no, I'm married to my art" types. I don't know if they're still an item – she didn't like discussing her love life.'

She made it sound like it was a character failing. That you should be very open about it. Hanlon thought, I really can't think of anything worse than hearing about other people's sex lives. But maybe I'm old-fashioned.

Hanlon wondered for some reason if Bastien was one of those artists that you hear about who seem to prey on women, historically more than a few, Modigliani, Picasso, Eric Gill all sprang to mind.

'How old is Luke?' she asked.

The question seemed to take Morag by surprise, 'I'm not sure, Aurora's age, I guess, twenty-three? Why?'

'Oh, no particular reason,' Hanlon said. Then, 'Have you got his mobile number and an address for him?'

Morag nodded. 'He lives just down the road from here, in fact, in Dean Village.' She got her phone out and forwarded the relevant information to Hanlon.

'In a shared house?' Hanlon asked.

Morag laughed. 'No, he's an artist, he lives in a garret, on very little money, on baked beans and dreams. I know him well. Aurora was his meal ticket, if you ask me. And, well, that's just about everything I know.'

'Thanks, anything else that you can think of that's relevant?'

Morag shook her head. 'No, if anything else occurs to me I'll call you, but look into Griffiths. He'll be behind this.' She sounded very confident about it.

'Thank you very much for your help. I'll keep you informed, and, like you mentioned, if there's anything else you think of...'

Morag nodded. 'Sure, I'll call you. Oh,' she said, 'there is one thing.' She looked down at the table top and traced a pattern with her forefinger on the dark surface. Her tone was worried. 'I think I might be being stalked.'

'Really?' Hanlon was concerned. 'Who by?'

Morag shrugged and raised her head, looking directly at Hanlon. 'I don't know. I've seen him several times – he's quite unmissable.'

'What does he look like?' Hanlon asked.

'He's a big guy, looks like he might have been in prison, dark hair.'

'Does he follow you?' Hanlon asked.

Morag shook her head. 'No, I've only seen him outside the flat.'

'OK, let me know the next time you see him,' Hanlon said. 'If I'm in the area I can follow him. He won't know me. Failing that, try to get a picture of him. Will you do that?'

'I sure will. Maybe he's why Aurora ran away.'

'Maybe he is.' Hanlon wanted to know more. 'I certainly want to trace him. A picture would be invaluable. But be careful, OK, no heroics. Don't open your door to anyone you don't know and vary your routine – do that much until we know more.'

'OK, I will. Where are you staying anyway?' Morag asked. 'Is it nearby?'

'At the Dunedin View Hotel in Cramond, not far away. I'm booked in for a week there, but I'll probably make it two.'

Morag stood up. 'OK, then. Well, since you're here anyway, I'd go and have a look around this place if I were you. It's a great little gallery.'

'I will,' lied Hanlon.

Morag swung her laptop in its rucksack over her shoulder and left the café. Hanlon gave her five minutes and followed suit. She didn't feel like looking at pictures – she wanted to go and talk to Luke Bastien.

* * *

She left the building and stood on the terrace outside the door staring at an exhibit that stood in the grounds of the gallery, neon lettering on scaffolding that read, 'THERE WILL BE NO MIRACLES HERE'. Her eyes were drawn by a man, who was sitting on a bench nearby smoking a cigarette and looking balefully in her direction. Some weirdo, she thought. She passed by and he stood up and strode off down the path to the front entrance.

She went round the back to the car park, got into her car and the dog bounded around in the back seat. Wemyss had obviously had enough of sitting around. Hanlon rolled her eyes and, sitting in the passenger seat, took her trainers off and pulled a pair of walking boots on. Wemyss's constant desire for exercise was fine when there was nothing to do, it matched her own, although the dog was probably not driven by an inner psychological restlessness – he was a dog. But right now, it was a nuisance.

She looked at her phone and discovered a public footpath that ran alongside a river, the Water of Leith, nearby.

They walked up a path that hugged the narrow, fast-flowing waterway and headed upstream, Wemyss trotting ahead, his tail erect, snuffling the air and the occasional vertical object, a tree, a post, a bench, with a connoisseur's interest. It was an enjoyable walk, the path running through the centre of a great city, a part of it, yet very separate from it, a reminder of how things used to be before the houses and people came, and how things would be after them.

While they walked she thought of what Morag had told her. Aurora trying to go clean. Well, good for her. Drugs had killed her mother. So she had been to an NA group meeting, fellow addicts trying to lead a normal life, and something had happened there that had freaked her out, panicked her.

Fine before the meeting, not fine after it.

Whatever it was had to be a direct threat to her, some form of violence. Something extreme to provoke flight. In Aurora's case who was it? Who was she running from? Her ex-dealer? Almost certainly not. Even if she hadn't given up Charlie, all she needed to do was call her father – he'd settle up any outstanding bills. Undoubtedly with strings attached, but still...

Someone from NA? Their meetings were open to anyone who identified as an addict – could be one of the attendees was a crazy, violent person.

What about her father? Again, possible but unlikely. That reminded her, she had been thinking about going back to his village, finding out what kind of a person he had been. The child is father to the man. Would she find rumours of violence or child abuse in Cameron's family background?

Then what to make of these claims that Griffiths was up to no good? Morag was studying Creative Writing; if anyone was likely to make a mountain out of a molehill it was probably an aspiring writer with an overactive imagination. It was difficult to imagine Griffiths as anything other than what he seemed to be. A perfectly pleasant guy, who seemed worried about Aurora.

And this man that Morag claimed was stalking her. Was he connected to Aurora's disappearance?

And what to make of Morag's claim that her own tutor, Paul Wyre, was involved in some MeToo scenario? Then there was the boyfriend. Luke Bastien. Well, he was an unknown quantity. Hopefully not for long. She'd call him in a minute.

She whistled for the dog and turned around. They had been going for about twenty minutes; the round trip by the time they got back to the car would have eaten about an hour out of their day. Wemyss ran up to her and she scratched the soft fur on the top of his head. 'You're very time-consuming, Wemyss,' she said to him. The dog gave her a wolfish grin.

They got back to the car and she put the dog in the back and phoned Luke.

To her surprise he picked up almost immediately.

'Hello?'

A pleasant voice, English; he sounded upper-class, posh. If Luke was starving in a garret it was probably by choice, not necessity.

'Hello, my name's Hanlon. I'm a private investigator.' She was getting used to saying these words, so much less convincing than 'police'. 'Police' opened doors; private investigator, the reaction seemed to be bemusement. She thought of Julia Swinson, who had seemed so excited to have met one, and smiled.

She carried on, 'I'm looking for Aurora Cameron. I was wondering if I could speak to you about her.'

'Sure, that's no problem.' A pause. 'What can I help you with, specifically?'

'We'll talk about this when I see you,' she said. 'What's the address?'

He gave it. It was the same as the one Morag had given her. I've got such a suspicious mind, she thought. I can't seem to believe anyone about anything.

'I'll see you in half an hour.'

* * *

Back in the Howe Street flat, Morag had seen the man she thought was following her again. There was a small café opposite her building and there he was, sitting outside at a table, despite the cold temperature, wearing a pea jacket and a beanie hat. A big guy, with a tough-looking face. It was giving her the creeps. She looked at him through the camera on her phone. He was too far away for a picture.

Morag moved away from the window. She was more worried than she liked to admit. To take her mind off him she looked at her laptop and thought of her novel. It was obsessing her. To be honest, it was not going as well as she had led Hanlon to believe. She had poured her life into it, including all the stuff that was going on at university that would create a furore when it was published. Paul Wyre, sleeping with his students, and Griffiths, that devious pervert. In fact the whole department was a nest of vipers.

She closed her eyes and indulged in another mini-fantasy. She was spending a lot of time daydreaming these days.

'So, Morag,' the presenter for BBC Arts Scotland said, 'and when your bestseller provoked a *Panorama* special, how did it make you feel?'

'I've always believed in the truth, Kirsty,' she replied. 'I felt vindicated... but it's not about me.' She lowered the pitch of her voice and put on her caring face. 'It's about the others. As a famous writer I have a voice. I'm speaking for the voiceless, for the dispossessed and powerless...'

A while later she opened her eyes. Then there was all the stuff about Aurora and her family – it was so explosive.

She had lied to Hanlon. Grassmarket had passed on her novel. More fools them. It was a blip. Nothing else. There were plenty more publishers. They'd live to regret it. She glanced at the massive five-hundred-page manuscript. Then at her laptop. She went back to the window; the man had gone. What if he broke in here and took it? And took her laptop? It wasn't backed up to the cloud – she'd have lost it forever.

She texted Hanlon, told her he was gone. Morag didn't know what had happened to make Aurora run and she was scared. Maybe it was this guy. Or maybe he was someone that Wyre had sent, some criminal from his past that he knew, dispatched to break in and steal her manuscript. A lot of people would be affected when the book was published. She was uncomfortably aware that she had talked about the book a lot, maybe too much.

She had of course saved the file onto a memory stick, but what if the hypothetical burglar, now only too real to her, took that too? You can't be too careful, she thought. I should hide this.

She went into the kitchen, cling-filmed the memory stick that contained the back-up of the novel and took out a Tupperware container of green lentils from the cupboard. She tipped them out into a pint glass, dropped the stick into the bottom of the Tupperware, replaced the lentils and put them back in the cupboard. Well, that was done. Nobody would find it there, would they? Morag strongly believed in her destiny; she was convinced that she was going to be a famous writer.

Would she remember where she'd hidden it? It seemed a ridiculous question but wasn't. She'd already lost one memory stick with the manuscript on, and that wasn't all. Lots of things had got lost over time.

Somewhere hidden in the flat was her mother's front door key, which she had put somewhere safe and promptly forgotten. Aurora had lost five grams of coke that she had hidden when she was using. Admittedly she had been trollied at the time, but there were precedents. Back-up for a back-up. She would write down exactly where she'd hidden it.

At her laptop she opened a new document in Word and tapped away. Morag's fingers flew over the keys; she could touch-type pretty much flawlessly. She was a fast writer and she put together the semblance of a poem with a confident facility. She smiled to herself as she typed, inserting the camouflage text around the keywords.

Save as: 'Poem for Aurora – apologies to e e cummings – Grace a Jean Lescure.'

There we are, she thought. The clue is in the title.

Another couple of minutes and she had uploaded the poem to her website, MoragMac97writer.

She got her phone and texted Hanlon.

Hi, been thinking about what you said. That man who was out there right now, in the café opposite, unfortunately he was too far away for my camera phone… If I fall under a bus, you can find where I've put my manuscript in Poem for Aurora on my website. Speak soon.

Send.

12

Millar strode along Rose Street, well known for its many bars and restaurants, towards the Crown, the pub he had chosen to meet up with Ray and Dougie. Millar was wearing one of his trademark two-piece blue suits and his habitual scowl. People took one look and moved out of his way on the pavements.

Halfway along, the cobbled street was blocked by a council road-sweeping vehicle. The small machine with its rotating brushes spinning around cleaning the rubbish out of the gutter was moving at a snail's pace. Just as Millar drew level with it, a bicycle from a food-delivery chain mounted the pavement, to skirt the machine, and headed directly towards him. The cyclist wasn't going to give way, neither was Millar. Millar altered his position slightly to occupy the centre of the pavement; the cyclist rang his bell. Millar's face flushed a deeper red. Who did this arsehole think he was, Bradley fucking Wiggins? He moved to one side, ostensibly to let the cyclist pass between him and the wall, and as the cyclist did so Millar slammed his elbow sideways into the guy's Lycraed body with all the weight of his powerful six-feet-five frame behind it.

It must have been like being hit by a sledgehammer in the ribs. The cyclist fell sideways, his feet caught in the pedals, his head, protected by his helmet, hitting the wall of the building. Millar lifted his leg and stamped viciously down on the cyclist's leg, crushing it against the metal frame of the bicycle. His victim shouted in pain, outrage and fear. He was now on the pavement, one leg under his bike, the other still held in the pedals by the foot clips. He was trapped. Millar bent over him and he looked up in terror at Millar's coarse, maddened features and coke crazy eyes. The few pedestrians around watched nervously. No one was going to intervene.

'You cunt,' Millar screamed at him. 'Keep off the fucking pavement.' He then stood up, straightened his jacket and continued down the road. Jesus Christ, he thought angrily, some fucking people. No manners.

* * *

The Crown was a small bar just off Rose Street with a stained wooden floor and wooden tables and chairs. It was a very basic pub, dark and dingy. Dougie was drinking lager, and Ray, Guinness. Ray could see that the barman was eyeing them warily; he guessed they looked like trouble, particularly Dougie, a big blond guy with a damaged face, the strip of sticking plaster on the bridge of his nose emphasising the swelling round his eyes.

Ray was feeling sick with nerves. He was getting increasingly scared of Millar. These days you didn't know the Millar you were going to meet. This obsession with people betraying him was getting well out of hand. That had included Jordan; when he had initially disappeared Millar had taken it as a personal slight and threatened he'd hack him into wee pieces. Now it appeared McDonald had killed him, Jordan had been forgiven.

Maybe he had gone insane, Ray sometimes wondered. But what could he do?

He was particularly concerned about his own safety and that of Dougie. He had been close to Millar and he was aware that Millar was particularly vengeful if he felt he'd been let down by someone he'd once loved or trusted. When Millar had threatened to throw Calla's bairn out of the window, Ray knew he had been perfectly serious. It was becoming a nightmare. He never knew what the day would bring.

The door opened and Millar walked in, blocking the light momentarily. Ray's heart sank. He glanced at the guy behind the bar who had noticeably grimaced. Millar had that effect on people. No prizes for guessing what he was thinking, Another one of them – what was this place today, gangster central? Millar walked over to their table and Ray and Dougie jumped to their feet like squaddies when a general appears. There would be no prizes for guessing who was in charge.

They had a brief muttered conversation then Millar approached the bar. Ray noticed the exaggerated deference in the body language of the guy serving, you didn't have to work for Millar to notice how dangerous he was. Millar's eyes were particularly glittery today God knows how much coke he'd had, Ray thought.

'Large Grouse, half of Tennent's.' The barman nodded and poured the drinks. Millar gave him a twenty, downed the Grouse in one. 'Another of those and keep the change,' he said. 'Where's the toilet?'

'Thank you, sir. Back there,' he said, pointing.

Millar disappeared for a few minutes then returned, sniffing loudly and rubbing his nostril, collected his drinks and went over to the table. Ray caught sight of the expression on Dougie's face. Extreme worry covered it, maybe poorly disguised terror.

'So, you let him get away?' said Millar after he sat down.

'We didn't...' Dougie began. Ray kicked him under the table.

'Sorry about that,' Ray said. Millar wouldn't want to hear any excuses. If anything, they might provoke one of his rages. He seemed in quite a good mood at the moment, Ray thought, but you never knew with Millar. He was very volatile; he could fly off the handle over nothing.

Ray said, 'I've put the word out that there's a one K reward for a phone call telling me where he is.'

'Double it,' Millar said, without elaboration.

Ray nodded. 'Will do.'

'We beat the woman up like you wanted,' Dougie said brightly.

Millar pressed his lips together and turned a baleful glare on Dougie. Shit, thought Ray, what's gone wrong?

'Oh, did you?' he said, heavy on the sarcasm.

'Aye, we did.' Dougie looked puzzled, a trifle hurt.

'The beating up was only part of it,' Millar explained, as if to a backward child. 'You were supposed to scare her off – that was the object of the exercise.'

'Aye.'

'Well, you didn't.' Silence. Ray and Dougie looked at each other. Millar continued, 'An hour ago she was having coffee at that art place with Morag McMillan, Aurora Cameron's flatmate. And I don't think they were discussing fuckin' Picasso.'

'Oh,' said Ray.

'Yes,' hissed Millar, his crazy eyes boring into them. 'Oh, indeed. That's two jobs you've cocked up in just a few hours. What are you going to do as an encore?'

'What can I say?' said Ray, slightly desperately.

'Well, you can say, "I won't fuck up the next job I get given."'

'I won't fuck up the next job I get given,' repeated Ray.

'Right, good,' said Millar, partly mollified, 'I sincerely hope for your sake that's the case.' He took a big drink of lager and sniffed loudly. 'Now, this is what I want you to do.'

Millar explained slowly and patiently what their task for the day was. When he was finished, Ray asked him, 'And what about Hanlon?'

'What about her?'

'Do you want us to take her out?' Ray asked.

Millar considered the question. 'No, not for now,' he said thoughtfully. 'Later, certainly, but not just yet. She can't do any harm. Besides, she might lead us to Aurora Cameron – that's what I'm hoping for anyway. She's certainly resourceful, she obviously doesn't scare easy and people will tell her things they wouldn't tell us.'

He stood up.

'Now, let's see if you can manage this simple task. If not—' he looked down at them from his great height '—nobody is indispensable.'

* * *

Half an hour later Dougie pressed the intercom marked Cameron/McMillan. He heard the receiver being lifted.

'Police,' he said. The door buzzed and he glanced at Ray as he opened it with his gloved hand. Ray nodded at him and grinned. This was going to be so much easier than this morning.

13

Luke may or may not live in a garret, thought Hanlon as she walked through the chi-chi charm of Dean Village, but if he does it's in a really nice area. Dean Village was like her idea of what a small Swiss or Austrian town might be like. It was so incongruous, in this grey, cold, northern city. The narrow streets, the cobbles, the omnipresent roar of the Water of Leith in the gorge that it ran through, the occasional wood-framed or timbered building. It didn't look like her idea of Scotland at all, and certainly not the kind of place where painters went to suffer for their art.

Hanlon found the address without too much trouble. As she suspected, it was no penniless artist's hovel. Far from it. It was a three-storey stone building with a couple of turrets overlooking the river. She was reminded of Cameron's Gothic pseudo-castle. They did seem to like turrets in Scotland. She put architecture from her mind and frowned. From what Morag had said about Luke she had been expecting a dilettante student, not someone obviously doing well through his art.

Once again, there was a disturbing question mark between a Morag version of events and reality. *He lives in a garret, on very little money, on baked beans and dreams... Aurora was his meal ticket, if you ask me.* Those had been Morag's words. Luke did not look like a man in need of a meal ticket. How much can I trust what you say, Morag? she thought. She found his name on the intercom, L Bastien, and she was buzzed in.

She walked up the stairs to the top flat; light poured in through narrow windows on the staircase. On the second floor the door was open, and a slim youth dressed in a paint-splattered shirt over a T-shirt and jeans, worn espadrilles on his bare feet, was standing in the doorway.

'Are you Hanlon?' he said.

'Yeah.'

'Do come in...'

Luke Bastien was twenty-three – Morag had said that he was Aurora's age – but looked about seventeen, absurdly young. He had dark curly hair, ringlets, not too dissimilar to her own, but her hair was quite coarse and his looked fine. He had long dark eyelashes, the kind that many women would kill for, and high cheekbones with full lips. He was extraordinarily good-looking in a feminine way. Hanlon somehow doubted he'd been captain of the rugby team at school.

The door from the stairs into his flat gave onto a small hall with three doors. She could see a bathroom to the left, a closed door in front of them and, through an open door, a living room. He led her into this.

It was a large space. It had a kitchen area at one end and a kind of breakfast bar separated it from a small sitting area with a sofa and a couple of chairs.

'Have a seat.' He gestured at the chairs. She sat down on one and Luke kicked off his espadrilles and sat cross-legged on the sofa. He pushed a hand through his dark curls; he had several silver bracelets on his slim arm that slid back and clattered as he moved.

'So, Aurora...' he said.

'She's gone missing,' said Hanlon, 'or hadn't you heard?' She studied his face for signs of guilt or worry. Luke showed none of these.

Luke sighed. 'I had heard, yes, but I'm sure she'll turn up. Aurora's strong.'

'When was the last time you spoke to her?' she asked.

'I'm not sure, a while ago.' He looked meaningfully at her. 'You do know we've split up, don't you?'

'I didn't. I'm sorry.'

'No, it's fine, one of those things...' He smiled. 'It was amicable. We're still good friends.'

Luke certainly didn't seem heartbroken.

'So when was the last time you saw Aurora?' she asked.

'I really don't know... let me check my phone.'

He looked at the screen and frowned. 'Not for a couple of weeks. I guess I haven't heard anything from her since we split up. That was a Sunday.'

A couple of weeks ago, a Sunday. That was just before the night that she came back from the meeting, thought Hanlon. She looked at Luke. How amicable was it really? Had he been dumped for another man? She couldn't imagine that he would be any danger to anyone. It would be hard to imagine Aurora fleeing in terror from Luke, but stranger things had happened.

'Why did you split up, if you don't mind me asking?' she asked.

Luke scratched his head, and sighed. 'The classic reason: selfishness. I'm an artist, Hanlon – if you're in my life you play second fiddle to painting. She'd want to go out, to a club or to a restaurant or to see people. I'd just want to work. You can't blame her. I certainly didn't.'

It certainly sounded plausible. She also really could not see Luke as the kind of man to terrify anyone, and Aurora had been seriously frightened, according to Morag, when she disappeared. Although, and this was beginning to worry Hanlon, she only had Morag's word for that.

'Aurora was terrified when she left her flat, according to her flatmate. Do you know what could have caused that?'

Luke frowned. 'I would take anything Morag said with a pinch of salt if I were you.'

'How do you mean?'

Luke said thoughtfully, 'She's given to exaggeration, but, more to the point, everything she says or does is based on what she can get out of it. She's very self-centred, sly even, so...'

Hanlon nodded. She could see that Luke was a shrewd judge of character, or appeared to be.

'Did Aurora have any enemies that you knew of? Anyone she was afraid of?'

He shook his head. 'Only herself.'

'How do you mean?' she asked.

'She had a very self-destructive side to her,' he said, 'and that went with a monumental temper too. Sometimes she directed it inwards and hurt herself, sometimes she'd lash out...' He sighed. 'She was unbalanced. It wouldn't surprise me to learn she had enemies.'

'But you liked her?'

Luke laughed. 'Opposites attract. I'm quite calm. She liked that. We got on well.'

Luke fell silent, then, 'Do you want to see a painting of her? How I saw her?'

Hanlon was intrigued. 'I'd love to.'

He uncoiled himself from the settee and stood up, motioning her to follow. They went into the hall and then he opened the door that had been closed and he motioned to her to go in.

'My studio.' More than a hint of pride in his voice.

She went inside. 'Wow,' she said.

The studio was large and lit by natural light flooding in through the floor-to-ceiling windows. There was a spectacular view over the village and the Water of Leith below. The studio was located in one of the turrets that she had noticed from the street.

The first impression was of disorderly, painterly clutter. There were canvases stacked against the walls. There were two canvases on easels, a table covered in artist's paraphernalia – she had a chaotic impression of tubes of oil paint, brushes and rags. The two canvases were pictures of Aurora, one of her getting out of a bath, the other in her underwear sitting on an untidy bed, playing with her phone. Hanlon hadn't realised that Aurora was so tattooed. They ran across her shoulders, her arms, her pubis.

'She could get this picture tattooed on her,' she suggested. 'It'd be like infinite regression.'

Luke laughed. 'Yeah, like mirrors reflecting mirrors.'

She moved closer to the easels. The paintings captivated her. They were hyper-realistic; she knew little about art but there was obviously tremendous technical skill in the pictures as well as an intense quality of feeling. In the painting of her in the bath she looked relaxed, the water dripping down her skin unbelievably realistic. In the one with the phone there was an almost palpable feeling of tension and anger. The pictures also looked strangely familiar and not just because she had seen a fair few photos of the girl. She suddenly recalled Hamish Cameron, Aurora's father, had one very similar hanging on the wall. Aurora's back must be relatively tattoo free. Now she could see that the table in front of her was the same table that she had seen in the painting on the wall in Cameron's study. Luke must have painted it. It seemed bad enough to have a picture of your daughter naked – to know it had been painted by her boyfriend of the time, Hanlon thought it a bit creepy.

'I like painting her,' Luke commented. 'She's very paintable.'

'She's very good-looking,' was Hanlon's comment.

Luke shrugged. 'Sure, but so's the girl who works in the pub across the road and I don't want her to model for me. I need more than looks. It's character that's important, and Aurora certainly has that.'

There were some other canvases on the floor, turned to face the wall. 'Want to see a few more?'

She nodded and he turned three of the canvases around. Luke wasn't restricted to painting people; there were a couple of almost impressionist pictures of Edinburgh street scenes. The same attention to detail and the same unsettling ability to convey the character of a place. They weren't the attractive touristy parts, like Dean Village or the area round the castle; these were tough, mean places. In one of them there were three street kids, feral, thin-faced. You could feel the air of menace and violence hanging over them. She knew the type, in trouble since they could go to school, brought up in foster homes or with negligent, junkie parents in rancid social housing. They would have an almost family connection with a local firm of solicitors. Juvenile prisons then the adult version.

'Kids from Muirhouse and Pilton,' he said, 'couple of miles that way—' he pointed '—but a whole world away in terms of life.'

'Do you know them?' she asked. It seemed odd to think of Luke hanging out with these street kids. They could eat him for breakfast.

'Mmhm, they let me draw them, I buy them cider and Super strength lager in return.' He grinned. 'They think it's hilarious that I could make a living painting. They like patronising me, like I'm some kind of oddity. But I think they're a bit flattered too.' He looked sad suddenly. 'I suppose I'm the only person who's ever shown any interest in them, other than the police and social services.'

She decided to bring up the painting on Cameron's wall. 'Do you know Aurora's dad, professionally?' she asked.

Luke nodded. 'Hamish, yes. I've met him a few times. He wanted me to sign on as one of his artists. I said no.'

'Why did you do that?' Hanlon asked. 'Isn't he one of Britain's top dealers?'

'Oh, yes.' He smiled, a man with a keen sense of his own worth, 'But he wants too much in commission. That's fine if you need your career boosting. There's a lot of shit art out there and if you're on Cameron's books, people will buy you. Regardless. He's got the kind of clout that can make markets.'

'But you don't need that?'

He shook his head. 'I've got talent.' He smiled; she was suddenly aware of Luke's self-confidence. He might look like a slightly ditsy kid but there was a rock-hard adult sensibility underneath. She could see what had attracted Aurora to him. 'I'll let you see my cuttings file – I'm a genius, seemingly. According to *Apollo* magazine and *The Spectator*. But seriously, I'm doing OK. And I've got an agent. And I'm his biggest artist. With Hamish, I'd only be, what...' he screwed his face up '... maybe number nine, maybe lower.' He laughed. 'Much higher in terms of ability, but not sales. One of these—' he pointed at Aurora '—will currently set you back ten grand, and it'll be twice that next year.' He shrugged. 'So it goes... Also, she'd have gone mad if I'd signed up with her dad. She hates him.'

'Do you know why?'

Luke frowned. 'She blames him for her mother's death – they were close. She would have left me if I'd gone with Cameron. She feels very strongly about him.'

'How did he react when you turned him down?'

'He wasn't that happy, but he's a pragmatist.'

'Did he know you were going out with Aurora?' she asked.

Luke pointed to the pictures: Aurora naked, Aurora in her underwear.

'I guess he maybe had his suspicions,' he said drily.

Well, Cameron's relations with his daughter and Luke were secondary to her main purpose here.

'Do you have any idea at all why she might be in hiding?' asked Hanlon.

'Not that I know of,' he said, 'but I guess she must have some kind of reason if she ran off like that. I can't fathom it out myself. I'll ask around, see if anyone I know has any ideas, although I'm not that optimistic.'

'Do you know anyone that she might be staying with?'

Again he shook his head. 'No, but maybe she's not in Edinburgh any more. If someone's after you, why not just get on a plane?'

'Because her passport's still here.' Again, we only have Morag's word for it, she thought.

'OK, then.' Luke shrugged. 'Why not London or Glasgow? Tunbridge Wells, to pick a place at random? Llandudno? She could be anywhere.'

'It's a good point,' said Hanlon, 'but people usually run to places they know. I'm here now in Edinburgh. I've got a few other leads to follow. I'll be in touch.'

He nodded. 'Do.' He hesitated. 'Look, I know I sounded a bit callous, but I do like Aurora a lot, and she is a strong woman, believe me. I mean, God knows she's got her faults – she's got one hell of a nasty temper, and she can be physically violent.' He shook his head. 'I've seen it – it's quite frightening. So she's no pushover physically, and she's strong mentally. She managed to give up drugs, she managed to somehow do enough work to be doing well on that MA course, her tutors love her, she managed to survive quite a lot of shit in her life, she'll survive this. Of that I'm sure. But please, come and see me whenever you want.'

Hanlon nodded. 'I'll take you up on that.'

'Please do.' He looked at her speculatively. 'I'd like to paint you, if you have time.'

'Really?' That was unexpected. 'Why?'

He looked at her seriously. 'Because you've got an interesting face.'

She grimaced and touched her black eye. 'Because of this?'

He smiled. 'I don't know you, Hanlon, but I can guess that it's not the first time you've been in a fight.'

'That's true,' she said. He was a good judge of character, she thought.

'I'm an artist, I notice things,' he said. 'So will you sit for me?'

'I'll give it some thought,' she promised. I wonder if it's flattering to be told you have an interesting face? she wondered. As a compliment it sounded a bit double-edged.

She left the flat and walked slowly back to her car.

14

The following day, Hanlon was up at six-thirty. A forty-minute run with Wemyss bounding along effortlessly beside her, then forty-five minutes in the gym where the other two fitness fanatics in the hotel watched her uneasily from the corners of their eyes. She was a startling sight. A muscular woman with a battered face, her left eye practically shut, a huge livid bruise on her cheekbone and another one visible on her lower back below the crop top she was wearing. Bicep curls, hammer curls, single-handed preacher curls, bench press and some leg work. Hanlon attacked the weights with a practised, vicious, single-minded intensity. Every curl of her muscles was done with revenge foremost in her mind.

The gym had a single heavy boxing bag hanging from a chain and a selection of rather tired-looking gloves in a box. You could help yourself. The two men watched surreptitiously in abashed awe as Hanlon pulled on a pair of sixteen-ounce sparring gloves and did two three-minute rounds, slamming combinations, jab, straight right, left hook, into the hard leather. The bag creaked and swung on its hinges as she saw, not a black cylindrical piece of stuffed leather, but the masked face of her assailant. The sweat poured down her face and her eyes gleamed with bloodlust. I'm so going to hurt you.

I'm going to find you, Mr Aftershave, and kick your bollocks till they shoot out of your nose, she vowed.

Then breakfast, more smuggled sausages for Wemyss, who devoured them greedily. He seemed to be developing a taste for staying in hotels. It had gone half eight. She texted Morag, no reply. Still asleep, she guessed. Her phone pinged, a message from Hamish Cameron. He was staying at the George Hotel, his usual suite, could she call round before ten?

Yes, she could. The George Hotel was just up the road in the New Town from where Morag and Aurora lived.

Hanlon put the dog in her car and drove into town.

'My usual suite...' How much arrogance was crammed into those three words? It was so much more than a statement of spatial location. It signified wealth, power, privilege. What it said to her was, I don't stay in a room, I stay in a suite. I often stay in a suite (my usual suite), I'm that kind of guy. They all know me there. I'm a valued customer.

God, what a prick.

It was Friday morning and the traffic was practically gridlocked.

She drove through the suburbs whose names meant nothing to her and she was now in the prosperous New Town with its wide cobbled streets and high grey tenements. The shops were those of the wealthy Scottish bourgeoisie: cheese shops, delis and expensive children's boutiques. There were hipster places, a Swedish bakery, bicycle shops and plenty of restaurants. Then suddenly she came to an abrupt halt.

There were three police cars and an ambulance outside the tenement building where Morag lived. She stared at it in shock, thinking, It can't be, I must have got the wrong street, but she knew she hadn't. There was the landmark church with the big dome at the bottom of the road; there was the café where Morag claimed to have seen her stalker. There was... The car behind Hanlon angrily honked its horn and she swore irritably, resisting the urge to give the guy behind her the finger, put the car in gear and drove past the police activity. She was thoroughly alarmed now, she prayed to a God she had no faith in that Morag was all right.

Maybe it's nothing to do with Morag, she thought, but she didn't believe it. She turned left into the next road and parked. She walked back towards Howe Street down a broad interconnecting street, the grey cobbles of the road slick with rain. A small knot of people was on the pavement outside. Local residents wondering what was going on.

'Excuse me,' Hanlon said to a grey-haired woman in a dressing gown and Crocs. 'Do you know what's happening? A friend of mine lives in there.'

The elderly woman said, 'Aye, dear, a young girl's dead.'

Hanlon's heart sank. It was what she had been dreading but was hoping was not going to happen.

'Do you happen to know her name?'

'McMillan, dear, Morag McMillan.'

15

The George Hotel was a large, imposing grey building in a very wide street flanked by large imposing grey buildings. It was a solid testament to comfortable, unostentatious wealth.

Hanlon went into the hotel up to Reception and asked where Cameron's suite was. She was politely given directions to an upstairs floor. She got into the lift, barely noticing her surroundings. She was still in a state of shock over what had happened to Morag. It was hard to believe that someone so young, so confident, someone with the world at her feet, was gone. Who the hell could have done it and why?

And with that thought came rage, that someone, maybe the men who had beaten her up, probably the men who had beaten her up, had so casually taken a girl's life. She silently vowed to herself to bring them to justice.

She walked down the corridor and knocked on the door. Cameron opened it. He was wearing a dark blue, two-piece suit and a plain white T-shirt. His stomach was flat beneath the fabric; he looked good for a man of his age. He was every inch the confident, successful businessman.

'My God, what's happened to your face?' He was visibly shocked.

'Someone tried to warn me off looking for Aurora,' Hanlon said grimly.

'Shit, I'm sorry.' Then he realised that she was still in the corridor. 'Do come in...'

He ushered her into the suite. He had a view over George Street; the room was flooded with the cold grey Edinburgh light. He waved her to a seat, and sat down on a settee opposite. She looked around. Cameron had a sitting room, a small kitchen area and through one door she could see his bedroom; opposite was a closed door, presumably the bathroom. It was a far cry from her dingy room at the Dunedin. She wondered if the George took dogs – probably not. Then again, if you had money, most things were possible.

She briefly described what had happened in the car park of the hotel.

'I'm so sorry...' He shook his head regretfully. He seemed to assume it was somehow his fault.

'Don't be,' she said dismissively. 'In some ways it's quite encouraging – it shows maybe I'm headed in the right direction. I've certainly rattled somebody's cage.'

Cameron nodded. 'So, have you found anything out about Aurora?'

She gave him a brief synopsis of what had been happening: that Aurora was happy at university, well regarded by her tutors; that something had frightened her; that she was in hiding, probably in Edinburgh; she didn't have her passport – tactfully leaving out Griffiths' theory that Cameron was an incestuous paedophile.

'Drugs?' he asked, an agonised expression on his face.

Hanlon shook her head. 'She's been clean for a while.'

'Thank God,' Cameron said with relief. 'It's just that I lost Giulia to drugs. I know Aurora's had problems in the past. I don't want to lose her to them too, and it's so easily done. One batch of heroin that's purer than you're used to... or, I forget the statistic but you're several times more likely to suicide if you're high. So, thank God for small mercies.'

'Indeed. But just before I arrived here,' she said, 'I passed by Aurora's flat. Her flatmate—'

'Morag, Morag McMillan.' His lip curled contemptuously. There was no mistaking the venom in his voice.

'You know her?' asked Hanlon. It seemed unlikely.

'I know of her,' he said, pulling a face.

'You don't like her?'

'I've got nothing against her,' he said.

Hanlon raised her eyebrows. Let's wait for the qualification, she thought.

'But...'

'But?' She raised an eyebrow.

'I know David Carmichael quite well,' Cameron said. Hanlon looked blank. 'Grassmarket Books, one of Scotland's premier publishers, mainly literary fiction. Morag sent them a manuscript – she knows one of the editors, seemingly.'

'Is this to do with Morag's book?' she said.

'She told you about it?' he asked.

'She did,' Hanlon confirmed.

'Anyway,' he carried on, giving her a suspicious look, 'Carmichael got in touch with me. I featured prominently in the novel, and not, may I add, in a flattering way.'

'In what respects?' she asked.

'Well, I was a wife-murderer with a thing for under-age girls.'

'Under-age girls? Anything else?' She was really curious to know if Morag had claimed he was having sex with his daughter, Aurora.

'What do you mean, anything else?' he said irritably. 'Isn't that bad enough?' He frowned.

Maybe not, then, thought Hanlon.

'I suppose it could have been worse,' he admitted.

You betcha, thought Hanlon.

'It wasn't like they were children – I mean, we're talking teens, not tots,' he hastened to add. She stared at him. 'These under-aged girls I'm alleged to be involved with,' he clarified.

She was fascinated by his all-round creepiness. The morning was not turning out brilliantly. Morag dead. Cameron airily discussing sex with barely pubescent girls.

She was beginning to feel that she wanted to have a shower after this conversation had finished. Cameron took a mouthful of coffee. Hanlon had a sudden vision of the diligent Gillies wading through Morag's book with a highlighter, loyally marking up any passage that might be libellous and sending threatening letters to any would-be publisher.

'Anyway, Carmichael rejected the manuscript, and warned me about it.

And I was just one of the players in it. I never read it, but there were seemingly descriptions of people that he guessed were very much not drawn from imagination.'

My novel will be a media sensation. She remembered Morag's words. She might well have been right. Most Scots wouldn't have a clue who Cameron was, or care, come to that, but journalists would. He might not be well known but he was a big fish in a small pond and wealthy men pressuring vulnerable young girls into sex was currently news for once.

Maybe too, Hanlon thought, you didn't want the police alerted to what you've been up to. Maybe you don't want your computer seized and its contents examined. The acronym came back to her: PTHC, pre-teen hard core – maybe that's what you don't want dragged into the public domain.

'Trouble is,' he said bitterly, 'there'd be nothing I could do about it. It's too good a lie to deny. People would want to believe it – everywhere I went people would be sniggering at me behind my back. Look, there's the child-fucking wife-murderer. Well, hope the bitch never gets it published. Trouble is, these days, she could do it herself.'

'Well, Morag won't be doing that,' Hanlon said.

'Why not? What makes you so sure?' He looked puzzled.

'She's dead.'

16

Hanlon sat down in the hotel lobby and ordered a coffee. She thought about what Cameron had just told her about Morag. The first thing that struck her was that this anti-Morag rant could be some kind of elaborate smokescreen, a double bluff, so that she would think he couldn't be implicated in her death, not after revealing how much he disliked her.

She considered too what Morag had said. She had written a novel, this much was true. Morag had also said that it was explosive, presumably a *roman-à-clef*, as it was called, where the characters are all firmly based on real people. And there was Cameron, revealed as a man who had killed his wife and who liked schoolgirls, but not, seemingly, as a man who preyed on his own child.

But was that true? As he had told her, it was the kind of allegation that was credible, the sort of thing that people would be likely to believe. Like killing his wife. That had to have come from Aurora. Morag couldn't have made that up by herself. But was it true? Unpleasant as he was, maybe he was unjustly maligned.

Luke had told her that Morag was not a reliable witness. She had certainly misled her to a certain extent as to Luke. Morag had implied he was a struggling artist, this was manifestly not the case.

Was Griffiths really a monster as she had intimated, and what about his colleague?

Morag's Creative Writing tutor, Paul Wyre, had been mentioned bitterly by her as a kind of MeToo figure, preying on impressionable students. Was that true? Or was that another lie, or, charitably, another half-truth?

Paul Wyre – he was a published author; he had an Internet presence. Did he have previous for exploiting women or sexually harassing them? She searched for him via the Internet on her phone. There he was, forty-three, slightly older than she was; author of *A Tiger Caged* and *Ninety-Six Square*. Born in Manchester, foster homes, served seven out of a twelve stretch for armed robbery in Wakefield and Armley prisons where he got an Open University degree in English Lit. His first novel was published to critical acclaim (presumably this meant low sales) seven years ago. He had been heading the Creative Writing course at Edinburgh University for the past two years.

She found the number for the English department at the university and asked to speak to Julia Swinson, the departmental secretary who had been so helpful before.

'Julia Swinson speaking.' Her voice was low and pleasant.

'Hi, it's Hanlon, we met a couple of days ago when I was looking for Dr Griffiths.'

'Oh, yes.' Her voice was warm, excited. 'Of course, I remember you…'

'Are you free for lunch?' Hanlon asked.

'No, I'm afraid not, but I am free for early dinner, about six.'

'Great,' said Hanlon. 'I'll take you out somewhere, your choice. I'll meet you outside the building you work in.'

'The David Hume Tower, that'd be marvellous. I'd love to.'

'Don't worry about cost. I'm paying,' Hanlon said. Let Cameron foot the bill.

'OK, well, I'll see you then.'

Hanlon hung up.

The next thing she did was look up the address of Grassmarket Books, which was, surprise, surprise, in the Grassmarket. This, it turned out, was an area of Edinburgh close to the castle, probably a half hour's walk from where she was sitting.

She looked again at Morag's last message to her. She had been to her website; the manuscript of her book was not on it. Nor even any excerpts. She would give a lot to read a copy of Morag's novel. She knew that Cameron was in it; she would have liked to have seen exactly what she'd written about him, compare the fictional with the real. Would Griffiths and Wyre be in it and, if so, how would they be depicted? Was it the kind of thing their careers could recover from? But surely they wouldn't kill over it? Would they?

She guessed it depended how much they valued their livelihoods. If indeed it was as shocking and hard-hitting as Morag claimed.

Someone had killed Morag. Was it for the book, was it for another reason or was it simply connected with Aurora? Had whoever was after Aurora turned up at the Howe Street flat to finish the job and been surprised by Morag?

One more thing to do. She sent Murdo Campbell a text, telling him of the death Aurora's flatmate and asking him if he could let her know any of the details.

She put her phone away and finished her coffee. As she stood up she saw a girl walking into the hotel. She looked about fourteen and was wearing what looked like school uniform under an anorak and a beret. Hanlon watched with a sinking heart. The girl took out her phone and spoke briefly into it then nodded and walked over to the area in front of the lifts; the down arrow on one of them lit up. The doors opened and Cameron appeared, a broad smile on his face. He walked over to the girl and spoke to her. She nodded and together they disappeared into a lift, Cameron's hand now resting casually on her shoulder. He leaned his head close to hers and whispered something in her ear.

The lift doors closed behind them and Hanlon shook her head in disgust. It looked as if Morag had got that bit right after all.

* * *

She walked out into George Street. A freezing wind was blowing between the buildings and a fine drizzle accompanied it. It was bitterly cold. She was wearing jeans, Chelsea boots and a black raincoat; it wasn't enough. She jammed a beanie hat over her untidy hair; she guessed that it would be sodden soon. She retrieved Wemyss from her car, put him on his lead and, after a quick glance at a map on her phone, headed off to the Grassmarket.

Walking in Edinburgh was fun, even in this weather. The pavements were broad and there were few tourists about in February, which made walking easy. She could stride along without having to slow down for other people.

She headed upwards under the lowering grey skies towards the impossible-to-miss landmark of the castle; the Grassmarket, she knew, was on the other side. Wemyss trotted along happily next to her, occasionally straining on his leash to smell a particularly interesting lamp post. She reflected again that it was difficult to work with him around. She would have to find some kind of dog-sitting service back in Argyll; that was going to be easier said than done.

The Grassmarket, a street in the lea of the castle that towered above it, she discovered, wasn't big; it was a rectangular area with a road running through it. It must have been built in some sort of dip in the ground – it was like being at the bottom of a dark, narrow valley. She guessed that in the summer there'd be people sitting outside. It was picturesque – the tall buildings that overlooked the market area were old and quaint. She found the narrow, rectangular building that housed Grassmarket Books and went inside. There was a reception desk with a board on the wall behind the girl on duty. The board showed that there were three floors; Grassmarket Books shared the second floor with a company called JMB Windows. The top floor was an accountancy firm and the ground floor a firm of quantity surveyors.

'Can I help you?' asked the receptionist. She was young and attractive with an open, friendly face.

'No, I'm fine, thanks,' Hanlon said. 'I'm meeting a friend of mine from the publishing company for lunch. I just wanted to check I had the right building.'

'Aye, you do,' said the girl. She smiled at Wemyss. 'Nice dog!'

'Thank you,' Hanlon said proudly. She ruffled his wet fur, Wemyss grinned. 'He's a good dog.'

'You can wait here for your friend,' said the receptionist, pointing at a sofa opposite her desk. 'It's dreich outside.' Good word, Hanlon thought, for the cold, rainy weather.

'No, it's fine, thanks,' said Hanlon. 'I'll wait in the pub.'

They smiled at each other and Hanlon crossed the road to the pub. Yes, they allowed dogs in. She sat at a table by a window and looked at the door of the building opposite.

Various people came and went. Hanlon's plan was to try and discover someone from Grassmarket who knew of Morag. Given how pushy Morag had seemed to be, it seemed a reasonable hope, particularly as the publishing company looked to be quite small. As she didn't know anyone who worked there, she was dependent on gut instinct to identify anyone in the publishing world.

Relying purely on stereotypes, she divided the people she saw exiting and entering the building into quantity surveyors, window people, accountants and publishers. QSs, she decided, would look like men who would be at home wandering around a building site, window people would be sharper dressed than QSs and publishers would be predominantly female and wearing boho chic. Accountants would look well dressed and businesslike. It was as good a set of stereotypes as it was going to get.

At twelve twenty she saw a girl with dark hair, the bottom third dyed pale blue, with a short yellow dress despite the weather, a faux-leather biker jacket and Doc Martens customised with the Hello Kitty image. Must be in publishing, she thought. Hanlon dashed out of the pub, caught up with her and had an exquisitely embarrassing two minutes as she learnt that, no, she didn't work in publishing but was the systems manager for JMB Windows. It hadn't occurred to her that the circle of IT in the Venn diagram of employees in the building would overlap the other professions. She also learnt that her name was Mhairi.

Mhairi was into body art. Her neck was a riot of coloured tattoos, as was the back of her left hand. Hanlon knew nothing about tattoos, but she could see that these were of a high quality. They were beautiful.

She wasn't the only one doing the looking. Mhairi Ferguson ran her eyes over Hanlon speculatively. 'I may not be the kind of writer you're after, darling,' she said, 'but I can write code and if you want to get together for a drink, here you go.'

She handed over a business card, Hanlon took it and Mhairi gave her a meaningful wink, blew her a kiss, then headed away down the road towards the area known as the Cowgate.

Back to the pub. The rain beat inexorably down.

Twelve forty-five, a mixed-race woman in heels, thirty-something, jeans and a black leather jacket. Another quick exit.

'Excuse me?'

'Yes?' Polite but slightly wary.

'I'm a friend of Morag McMillan...'

The woman showed a flicker of recognition. 'Morag McMillan...?'

'You do work for Grassmarket?' asked Hanlon.

'Er, yes, I'm the senior fiction editor,' the woman said.

Yesss! Thank you, God! Hanlon thought silently.

'What's this about?'

'Morag sent you a manuscript recently...' Hanlon suggested.

'Oh, God, yes, I remember...' then a suspicious look '... and?'

'Can you give me five minutes of your time?' She handed her a card that the editor took rather gingerly.

'A PI!' Her eyebrows rose. 'Well, OK, five minutes... Like your dog, by the way.'

'Thank you, he's a very intelligent dog.' Wemyss might be a nuisance, timewise, but he was great as an ice-breaker.

They crossed the road, back to the pub. The two of them went to Hanlon's table and she asked what the woman wanted to drink. She went to the bar and returned with a glass of soda water and lime.

'I'm Lorna, by the way...'

'I'm Hanlon. I have a few questions for you.'

'That's fine.'

'First of all,' Hanlon said, 'I'm sorry but I feel I should tell you, Morag McMillan was found dead this morning.'

'Oh my God, that's awful.' Lorna looked concerned. 'How did it happen?'

'It's too early to say. The police are still looking into it.'

'Poor girl. I never actually met her, but I feel like I know her. I did read her manuscript.'

'Did she have an agent?' Hanlon asked.

'No,' said Lorna, shaking her head, 'but she did know a friend of mine. I think they'd been in a relationship. Anyway, my friend badgered me into reading it, an old-fashioned hard copy. I thought it was interesting, baggy, but it had potential, and its themes are quite in the news at the moment.'

'Morag thought that it would be a media sensation,' Hanlon said.

'She may well have done,' replied Lorna drily. 'It's a line I hear a lot. Forgive me for being underwhelmed.'

'Do you have a copy still?' If I can get to read it, she thought, I might get some idea of who else was threatened in Morag's great exposé.

'Unfortunately not,' Lorna said. 'To be honest I just skimmed through it to see if it had any merit. I was kind of surprised it had.'

'Did you get in touch with her about it, by any chance?'

'No, I never got the chance. David, the MD, got wind of it somehow and asked to see it, so he read it. He was aghast, he said it was libellous, he said he clearly recognised at least one of the characters and we'd get sued. That was the guy who owned an art gallery in the book. So he told me to just tell her we weren't interested and shred the manuscript.'

'Did you?'

'No, it seemed unduly harsh. After all, she might want to submit it to someone else, maybe in print form. I posted it back to her.'

It must still be in the flat, thought Hanlon. It should be easy to find. It'll be big enough.

'I see,' Hanlon said. 'Hopefully I can find it when the police have finished their investigations. But that could be some time away – can you recall any other details of the villains in the novel?'

Lorna frowned. 'There were a couple of teachers – one of them seduced the girls in the sixth form.'

'You've got a good memory,' Hanlon said.

Lorna laughed. 'He was memorably nasty, ultra-sleazy. With his shaved head, forever perving over girls. He was putting on a play and he would give parts out for sexual favours, oh, and high grades for coursework.'

That'll be Paul Wyre, thought Hanlon.

'Who else was there?' mused Lorna, frowning as she tried to remember. 'There was a young artist who made quite a lot of money through semi-pornographic paintings that he'd sell in the Middle East. He'd seduce women into posing for him by giving them drugs that he'd get from his contacts in a deprived area of Edinburgh,' she explained. Hanlon nodded. Lorna continued, 'Then he'd sleep with them.'

So, that'll be you, Luke.

'And there was another lecturer, he specialised in blackmail. But he didn't use it for sex or money, but to humiliate people, not just women. He'd get off on that.'

Griffiths?

Lorna looked at her watch. 'I hate to appear rude...'

'I'm sorry, thank you for your time.'

Lorna smiled. 'No, thank you. I'm very sorry to hear the news about Morag. Her story was interesting. I think it could have been published if it hadn't been so libellous and if whoever the art guy is in real life wasn't so litigious.'

She stood up, shook Hanlon's hand in a rather formal way, and disappeared into the Grassmarket.

Hanlon stood up and followed.

As she made her way along Edinburgh's streets she thought about the suspects for Morag's death. Surely it had to be one of the characters in the book? Cameron's business could be fatally compromised if his sexual preference for young girls got out. Possibly jail time too. Morag had certainly nailed that – Hanlon had seen it with her own eyes. Paul Wyre could be dismissed from work if the allegations about him were true. And Luke – that disappointed her, she had to be honest. She had liked Luke.

She wondered if Morag had made a pass at him and been rejected.

Both Paul Wyre and Luke had access to, and influence with, people who could and would certainly injure people professionally, and possibly kill. Wyre, former underworld acquaintances, Luke, his Muirhouse subjects. Cameron had the money to make it happen. She could easily imagine the close-mouthed Gillies being sent to hire someone to shut Morag up. If only she had a copy of her book.

Her thoughts returned to Luke. Surely to God he hadn't had a part in her killing? But she remembered what he had said: 'I'm a genius, seemingly.' Geniuses often considered themselves above the law, special cases not bound by the rules that governed the rest of humanity. What if he believed his own hype?

Hopefully Julia Swinson would be able to shed some light on the character of the two lecturers.

She reached the car, put Wemyss in and drove back out to Cramond and her hotel.

17

Big Dougie was crouching behind a bush, unseen by the three figures chatting to each other and smoking cigarettes in the distance. It was getting dark and the air was hot and heavy. His targets were heavily armed – two of them had sub-machine guns, the other a pump-action shotgun; he was armed only with a Glock pistol. Still, he was a good shot. In two or three seconds he should be able to neutralise them and then he'd be in. He'd be able to pick up their weapons too.

He slipped the safety off and stood up.

'Oi, cock-suckers!' he shouted as he opened fire. The first of his shots took out pump-action guy, a headshot. Dougie saw blood and brains fly, then bam, bam, bam, three body shots into one of the guards before he had had time to react. He saw a muzzle flash from the third and dived to the right, not fast enough though... he was hit. He staggered to his feet and put two shots into the body of the last one standing but then...

A hand on his shoulder.

'Turn that fucking thing off, you big jessy. Millar's here.'

Dougie sighed and saved his game, Hell's Gate 3. It was going badly – he had lost four of his team of five and they had only breached the outer perimeter of the compound. And now he was badly injured. It was all a lot more fun than real life – it didn't have Millar in it.

He joined Ray in looking out of the second-floor window of the flat in the street in Marchmont, very close to the Meadows, the grassy park that separated the area from the university. It was a highly respectable suburb in central Edinburgh.

Millar got out of the taxi.

'He doesn't look very happy,' Dougie said.

'Since when did Millar ever look happy?' Ray pointed out. 'Is he with anyone? I can't see properly, there's a van in the way.'

'Naw. Oh, wait, fuck...' Big Dougie had the advantage of his height and positioning at the window.

'Who is it?' Ray asked.

'Chris.'

'Wee Chris?' Ray wondered.

'I wish. It's fucking Falkirk Chris.' Dougie's voice was dejected.

'Shite, that nitwit,' Ray said with feeling. He and Dougie both detested the short-assed Fife homophobe. He was a fucking moron. And a self-important know-it-all.

He buzzed them up. A couple of minutes later Millar and Falkirk Chris were in the living room.

Falkirk Chris was a wee guy. He reached to below Millar's shoulders. He had sandy brown hair and pale blue eyes that were mean slits that he peered out at the world through. He had a habit of speaking very emphatically with gaps between each word, so that talking to him was like repeatedly being jabbed in the chest by a finger as... each... point... was... forcefully... made.

Ray had told Dougie that Falkirk Chris mistook emphasis for intelligence. He was a nasty piece of work. He was like a sneer made flesh. He was also, in both Dougie and Ray's opinion, very poor at doing his job. You could use Chris to frighten civilians but anyone who could handle themselves could take him on without worry. He was useless in a fight. Chris knew this and it made him even nastier.

There were two sofas in the flat; Millar and Chris sat on one, Dougie and Ray on the other.

Dougie looked around. Millar was not as crimson-faced as he could be. He could see that Ray, who knew him well, had relaxed slightly. He guessed that Millar's temper was under control, although that could change at any second. For now, anyway, he was OK.

Falkirk Chris, dressed in a horrible blue rayon tracksuit that Dougie wouldn't be seen dead in and garish trainers, a gold chain round his neck, was staring at him pugnaciously. Dougie shook his head. They both knew that they could take Chris out without breaking sweat. One day, Dougie prayed, he would get the chance to do so. Chris was not bright – the only reason he was currently Millar's enforcer in East Lothian was his unexpected promotion after Jordan had been killed by McDonald. Before that he had been tucked away in Fife.

Ray was looking uncomfortable.

'What the fuck have you two been up to with regards to finding McDonald?' asked Millar, conversationally.

'Mr Millar is very eager that he should be found,' Falkirk Chris said, jumping in before Ray could answer.

No shit, thought Dougie. He looked at Ray. Ray was staring aggressively at Chris. Who asked you? he was obviously thinking. He allowed his lip to visibly curl with disdain. Chris noticed; Dougie watched in satisfaction as his face reddened with anger.

Ray patiently explained what he'd done.

'We've put word out that there's two K for anyone who gives us his whereabouts. He's well known, someone will call. He's stuck here in Edinburgh – it's all he knows, here and Glasgow, and he can't go to Glasgow, that's our turf.'

'And what about the girl? Morag McMillan? What happened yesterday? She's dead the now.' Falkirk Chris pointed at Ray dramatically.

Christ, who the fuck does he think he is? thought Dougie. The last few times Chris had stood in the dock he must have been taking notes from the prosecutor.

Ray looked at Millar; he wasn't going to be told when to speak by Chris. Millar nodded assent – answer the question.

Ray sighed. 'We went round there. Dougie rang the bell, someone answered, they didnae speak, we both assumed it was her. We went up the stairs, we passed someone coming down...'

'We didnae pay them any heed,' said Dougie. 'Someone in a hoodie.'

'Almost certainly the killer,' Chris said.

Ray gestured with his hands, a kind of 'so what?'. Dougie nodded agreement. Even if they could have known that hoodie had killed Morag – who they'd thought at the time was alive anyway – what did he think they should have done, made a citizen's arrest?

'Go on,' said Millar. 'Were they carrying anything?'

'I don't know,' Ray said. 'We weren't focussed on that. We got to the door, locked. Dougie forced it. We found her inside. She was dead.'

'We didn't want her dead,' Chris said.

What's with the 'we'? thought Dougie, seething with irritation. Ray dealt with the point Chris had raised.

'I know Mr Millar didnae want her dead, Chris,' he said patiently, as though talking to a child, 'or he'd have told me to kill her. Try and keep up.' Chris scowled. 'We were told to get the laptop and a manuscript. Neither of which were there,' Ray replied.

'How did she die?' Millar sounded intrigued.

Ray shrugged. 'Fuck knows. She hadn't been stabbed – there was no blood.'

'There were no marks around her neck either,' said Dougie. 'She hadn't been strangled.'

'Any signs of sex?'

'Her clothes looked pretty intact to me,' said Ray. 'To be honest I wasn't really looking.'

'I don't really care, but we didn't do it,' Millar said, 'so who did?'

'I don't know, boss,' Ray replied. 'Anyway, we looked for the laptop, couldnae find it, we left.'

'Well, I still want that laptop. I don't know how we'll get it now.' He scratched his head. 'We don't even know who's got it, come to that.'

'Could it be McDonald?' asked Dougie.

'Why would McDonald kill a girl he didn't know and steal her laptop?' asked Millar.

'He killed Jordan... so maybe...'

Millar shook his head wearily. 'Just stop havering, Dougie.'

'So what now, boss?' Ray asked quickly, changing the subject.

'I'm going to be staying for a few days in Edinburgh,' Millar said. 'I've got business here. I'm going to be at the Astoria. Chris will be staying with you.' Ray and Dougie exchanged a glance of horror. Millar stood up. 'You three can find McDonald, and remember I want to know where Aurora Cameron is—' he looked at Dougie '—and you can ask him about Morag as well since you've got such a hard-on for him doing that, and then you kill him. Nobody fucks with me or my crew.'

'Yes, boss,' said Ray, glumly.

'You can call me any time, but not Saturday night, I'm busy then. I'll be round on Sunday evening. You can update me then. And I'd like some good news this time, got that?'

Millar stood up and left the lounge. They sat in silence like children whose parent had just left the room. They heard the front door slam behind him and then the echoing boom of the street door as the sound echoed up the stairwell.

Ray looked across at Falkirk Chris, who had been staring mournfully at Millar's back as he left the room, like a dog being left behind in the car.

Isn't this cosy? thought Dougie.

'Well, hoo-fucking-ray,' said Ray, speaking for all three of them.

18

Hanlon met Julia Swinson at the restaurant at six p.m. It was at the top of the Royal Mile, the thoroughfare that ran from the castle, at its head, to Holyrood Palace, the Queen's Edinburgh residence, at its bottom. As the castle was built on a hill, at night, standing at the top end of the Royal Mile, looking out to the New Town, you could see Edinburgh stretched out below, the lights like jewels scattered on dark velvet. It was achingly beautiful.

Julia was already there. Hanlon joined her at the small table. The menu was French modern, which suited Hanlon. It was expensive, but not outrageously so.

'I've got to go at seven,' Julia said apologetically in between generic chatter. 'It's my Friday-night language class.' That suited Hanlon, who was keen to get down to business.

'Can you tell me about Dr Griffiths?' she said. 'His name has come up a few times. You know I'm looking into Aurora's disappearance...'

Hanlon appraised her. Julia Swinson would have been good-looking when she was younger; she was still attractive in early middle age.

'Dr Griffiths is great,' Julia said, 'he's a pleasure to work with, which not all lecturers are, let me tell you... and Aurora is really nice too...' she frowned thoughtfully and then went off on a tangent, 'My kids are about Aurora's age...'

'How many do you have?' asked Hanlon, going through the motions out of politeness rather than interest. She had never wanted children.

'Oh, four,' was the surprising answer, 'all boys. They've all left home now, flown the coop. One lives with my ex, he's down in London, one in America and two still in Scotland, but they've got their own places now, so I rattle around in my house. I should downsize.'

Hanlon nodded sympathetically, then brought the conversation back to Aurora. 'What was she like?' Hanlon asked, to forestall Julia talking more about her sons, which could easily fill up the hour, she didn't doubt, especially with a phone doubling as a handy photo album.

'A lot of students these days are quite arrogant,' Julia said. 'They seem to think they know it all. Anyway, I have to deal with quite a lot of snotty kids.' She drank some wine. 'I get sick of it at times, but Aurora was really polite. She was nice.'

Well, this was more or less what Hanlon had been hearing all along, about how wonderful Aurora was. Apart from her temper, and her history of addiction.

'Did you know her flatmate, Morag?'

'Oh, God, yes.' Julia pulled a face – that seemed a universal reaction when her name was mentioned. 'For five years. Four years of her doing her MA in English and then this post-grad creative writing thing. If you wanted to define the word "ambitious" I'd just point to Morag – you didn't need a dictionary. Unfortunately, it impinged on my life. I've lost count of the number of various grant applications that I've been involved with for her.'

'How come?' asked Hanlon.

'Well, usually whatever you apply for, and, boy, did Morag apply for a lot of things—' she started to count them off on her fingers '—this bursary, that bursary, application for a Genius grant, even though she was ineligible, application for a hardship grant, application to be taken in as a poet in a writers' colony, application to be taken in as a writer in a poets' colony, you name it, Gifted Young Scot award, whatever, a hell of a lot of whatevers, you need some form of official accreditation, and this always landed on my desk and not a word of bloody thanks.' She shook her head in irritation. 'If anything, the reverse, she'd take it out on me when she was turned down. As she always was. And then her bloody book!'

'Have you read it?'

'No, well, kind of – I skimmed through it, out of politeness. She gave me the manuscript to read through. She'd had a couple bound.' She shook her head and indicated a brick-sized gap with her thumb and index finger. 'It was that thick. I heard about it often enough over the last couple of years, about how everyone who read it had thought it was fab, how it was going to make her famous, oh, yes, and lately how it was in the hands of an editor at Grassmarket who was really, really excited by it.'

That'll be Lorna, thought Hanlon, who certainly wasn't overly impressed.

'Was it just you who she told?' she asked. Cameron knew he was in it; how many of the others were aware of their presence in Morag's book?

'God, no, everyone. We were all informed how talented she was, how clever. I think it was a bitter moment for her when she only got a 2.1.'

'So I take it she wasn't popular with her fellow students?'

'No. Egocentric people rarely are,' said Julia, 'but when I heard that she'd died I rather doubted any of them killed her.'

'Why did Aurora like her?' wondered Hanlon. 'She must have done to share a flat with her.'

Julia drank some more wine. 'Because Morag kind of seduced her – she flattered her and cajoled her. Well, that's the impression I got, anyway. And don't forget, Hanlon, that Morag was good-looking and from a poor background made good, from some nasty estate in Dundee. I'm sure she was kind of exotic to Aurora. And I bet Aurora paid for that fancy flat in the New Town – rents cost an arm and a leg down there.'

Their starters came, pâté for Hanlon, a kind of ox-cheek rissole for Julia. Silence fell, Hanlon digested the information about Morag. Pushy, talented, with a knack of getting what she wanted. Unpopular, and author of a book that reputedly could blight the lives of four powerful men.

A book whose existence she had shouted from the rooftops and whose influence she had also doubtless much magnified. The hype wasn't true, but had someone believed it and acted before their career was destroyed? It would be ironic if she had died because the killer had believed her claims that the book was going to be published when it wasn't.

The waiter cleared their plates.

She moved the conversation back to the suspects for both Morag's death and, by implication, Aurora's disappearance. They had to be linked.

'What about Paul Wyre?' Morag's creative writing teacher, the ex-con. 'What's he like?'

'Oh, well, he's OK, I suppose...' Hanlon could detect the lack of enthusiasm. The waiter refilled Julia's wine glass and she took a big drink. 'No, he's not, sod it, pardon my French, I think he's hitting on the students.'

'Really?' Again, it looked as if Morag had been right. She might lie, exaggerate, about herself, but she seemed to be getting things right about others. First Cameron and under-age girls, now Wyre and sexual misconduct.

'Yes, well, you know his background?'

Hanlon nodded: prison for armed robbery, the Eng Lit degree taken whilst inside at Her Majesty's pleasure, the novel, then the teaching job.

'He really plays up on this "prisoner redeemed" schtick. Do you know what he looks like?'

Hanlon shook her head. Julia hunted on her phone and turned the screen to Hanlon. 'There he is.'

Wyre was tall and gaunt, his head was shaved and he had piercing eyes set under craggy brows. He was wearing a long leather overcoat, white shirt and trousers. His ears were pierced, discreetly. He looked like an elderly rock star on the comeback trail. Hanlon knew he was in his forties, old enough to know better. His whole appearance screamed, 'I am anti-establishment.'

'And he tries to seduce his students?' Hanlon was faintly incredulous. He was very cliché.

'That's rumour for you.' Julia's face was faintly flushed, whether from booze or anger it was hard to know. 'But I believe it.'

'So did Morag, seemingly,' Hanlon said. Julia laughed. Hanlon looked at her questioningly.

'I know I shouldn't speak ill of the dead, but one of the rumours, which I do believe—' her eyes met Hanlon's as she emphasised the word 'do' '—is that Morag seduced Wyre to influence him into bumping her up to a first. I told you she would do anything to get ahead, but she miscalculated. Wyre has nothing to do with that side of things, not in the Eng Lit degree system. But he didn't let on to her, so she screwed him for nothing.'

'So she was complicit?' Hanlon said.

'Morag will do whatever, or whoever, it takes to get somewhere,' said Julia decisively. 'Would have done, I should say.'

Their mains arrived: lamb for Hanlon, fish for Julia. She was one of these deceptively slender people who could eat a lot and not show it. She finished another glass of wine. She also had a head like a rock. The flushed face must have been anger, decided Hanlon. No slurring, no signs of tipsiness.

'What would happen to Wyre if it got out that he had been sleeping with students?' Hanlon asked.

'Oh, the sack.' Julia nodded emphatically. 'He'd deny it but these days, if it were true and Morag opened the floodgates, someone else would probably come forward and, even if they didn't, we live in febrile times; the uni would rather contest unfair dismissal than risk some kind of student protest that might reflect badly on them. We're a business, Hanlon, we know what side of the loaf our bread is buttered. Besides, nobody would stick up for Paul Wyre.'

'And Griffiths?' she asked. Julia smiled affectionately at the mention of his name.

'Dr Griffiths is lovely, a lovely man. No student has ever complained about him. He doesn't talk about it, but I know he does a lot of pastoral work with troubled students. And of course, rather unfortunately in my view, he was instrumental in bringing Wyre to the uni.'

'Someone told me that he isn't as nice as he makes out,' Hanlon said. She didn't want to say that it had come from Morag. Julia would have dismissed it out of hand.

'Well, they're wrong,' Julia said flatly, dismissively, 'end of.'

'What kind of pastoral work does he do?' wondered Hanlon.

'I'm not quite sure – he doesn't like to talk about it.' Julia thought about the question. 'If you're interested, though, I would have a word with Peter Reiss – he's in charge of student counselling. Tell him I told you to talk to him. He's a nice guy and I'm sure he'll have come across Aurora too, although I would imagine that stuff like that would be privileged.'

Julia looked at her watch. 'Oh, dear, is that the time? I'll have to go.' She leaned over the table. 'I've really enjoyed talking to you – you're a breath of fresh air. University life is terribly dull. If ever you need a place in Edinburgh to stay, just call me. Here's my number... that's it, and here's my address. It's in Morningside. It's quite central.'

She declined a dessert and thanked Hanlon for her meal. She stood up. 'Thanks for a lovely evening. I'll doubtless see you around the department.'

'Oh, you can bet on that,' said Hanlon.

19

The following day, Saturday, Hanlon decided to pay a visit to the village where Cameron had grown up. She had been meaning to do this for a while. There was something deeply suspect about him. Aurora's belief that he had killed her mother. Griffiths' concerns about abuse. Aurora's drink and drug abuse could well have been triggered by a traumatic childhood. Hanlon very much wanted to see where everything had begun all those many years ago. The past cast a long shadow.

She got in her car and headed west.

As she drove past the huge police station by the A82 in Dumbarton she thought of Murdo Campbell again. She both liked and respected Campbell – he had certainly helped her land her current job. She wondered if he might be around for a drink since she was passing so close to where he worked. What do I make of him? she wondered. It was a question she found herself thinking about quite a lot. On the plus side he was intelligent, good-looking, had a great body and a reasonably pleasant personality. He could also do various country things that she couldn't. He could stalk, he knew a lot about the local flora and fauna and he could certainly skin a rabbit.

On the negative side, he seemed too quiet. Hanlon had heard he had a reputation as a ladies man, but she wondered how true that really was. He seemed more the kind of man you married, rather than had a fling with, and Hanlon was not the marrying kind. She kind of suspected that Campbell was. Then she laughed at herself, maybe Campbell just didn't fancy her.

She pulled her attention back to the here and now. She was driving around Loch Lomond, the huge hills that surrounded the long wide body of water grey and black and forbidding under the winter sun, reaching up into the sky. There was still snow on their peaks. She smiled to herself; she liked being back in the highlands. Edinburgh was fun, but it felt crowded and polluted. Out here was where she wanted to be.

Hamish Cameron, she thought as she turned right at the head of the loch at a village called Tarbet and headed north, what about Cameron?

At first she was inclined to think that he had driven Aurora away simply by his controlling personality. She guessed it would never be easy being the only child of a highly successful, driven man, but then the spectre of child abuse had reared its head. Let's not get too carried away, she thought. We only have Griffiths' opinion for that. Hanlon frowned angrily. She had her own memories of an intensely unhappy childhood, memories that she was aware that she had repressed and locked away. Now Dr Elspeth Morgan, her self-appointed therapist, was rattling at that door. Hanlon controlled the key, but she wasn't sure if she wanted to let her in.

She hadn't spoken to the therapist for months. There was always something else to do. She was quite aware of the fact she was putting off the inevitable. Some nights as she lay alone staring at the ceiling, she was aware of the terrible burden of regrets and self-imposed unhappiness that she was dragging around with her, but her pride and arrogance and fear of letting her guard down prevented her from talking to her.

She could understand white-hot rage and black crippling shame when it came to childhood memories. But this wasn't about her.

She remembered what the lecturer had said about Aurora breaking down when incest had been mentioned. And there did seem something more than a little creepy about a father who had an oil painting of his naked daughter on the wall of his study. She certainly couldn't remember anyone else she'd met having that as decoration.

Or maybe not. Sometimes a cigar was just a cigar. Maybe it was just art, or business; everything in that room was for sale, after all. Did that include Aurora?

To understand the present, we have to revisit the past. Those had been her therapist's words. That was what she was doing now, hoping to get a better handle on the present by delving into Cameron's and, by implication, Aurora's history.

She drove along the winding road through beautiful hilly countryside. The predominant colours at this time of year were muted, the omnipresent grey of the rock, the brown geometric forms of the dead bracken. The sky seemed huge after Edinburgh. She felt she was in the middle of nowhere. Her spirits began to rise.

North of Oban, she drove over a bridge to the far side of the loch and hung a right until she saw the white sign streaked with rust that said, 'Lochdubsliabh'. The place where Cameron had grown up.

She drove past some houses into the village centre. It wasn't a big place or very pleasant to look at. It wasn't picturesque, no danger of it being overrun by tourists. There was a scattering of sizeable granite houses, a village shop still managing to hang onto a living somehow, a small new executive estate, a fifties council estate, four or five startlingly ugly two-storey small blocks of flats, brown pebble-dashing, a public area with scuffed grass and dog turds and a couple of swings, one broken. There also wasn't a soul in sight. It was a depressing place. No wonder Cameron had left.

She went down to the harbour, for want of a better word, a concrete slipway, a jetty, a few boats on moorings attached to buoys, a stack of plastic fishing boxes. That smell of old fish that lingers around working quays. The water looked cold, dark and ominous.

The wind ruffled her thick dark hair; the sea was the same colour grey as her eyes and about as warm. On the other side of the loch she could see Kinnachan House, a faraway dark geometric shape below the treeline on the far side. She wondered if Hamish Cameron had grown up in the council houses; they seemed of more or less the right vintage.

She glanced at her watch: eleven fifty. There was a hotel on the road above where she was standing, the Etive Hotel. She looked up at it; it had a front bar and a back bar. Standing patiently, staring down at her by the door to the back bar – the locals' bar – were three small old men, identically dressed in long dark coats and flat caps, two smoking, one not. The regulars, she guessed.

She started walking up to them. The pub opened early; she heard two loud clicks as bolts were drawn from inside and the three men disappeared inside. Hanlon walked up to the door and followed them in.

They were lined up by the bar as she went in; they stared at her curiously, as did the barman.

'Guid morning,' one of them said, politely.

'Good morning,' Hanlon said. 'I was wondering if you might be able to help me.' They were younger than she had first thought, maybe they were of the right vintage to know Cameron.

'We'll do oor best,' said one of the others.

She explained that she was a journalist writing a piece on Hamish Cameron, the famous art dealer, and asked did they know anything about his family? They heard her out suspiciously.

The three of them conferred in a huddle and then, 'Aye, we knew the family. I'm afraid you'll no get a positive comment out of us concerning them… I was at school with Hamish Cameron.'

'Really?' said Hanlon. Close up he looked a good decade older than Cameron. That's what poverty and booze can do for you.

'Aye,' said another, 'and I used to work with his younger brother. Graham.'

Well, that was news – she didn't know he had any family. 'What were they like…? Can I buy you a drink by the way?'

She could; she bought them all halves of bitter and a double Scotch each. The four of them moved to a table in the corner.

'Hamish Cameron was a wee shite,' the old man who had spoken first said. 'I'm Tommy, by the way. His parents lived up the brae. His dad was a fisherman, like we are.'

'Were,' corrected one of the others.

'Anyway,' Tommy said, ignoring the interruption, 'if he shook your hand you had to count your fingers afterwards – isn't that so, Dugald?'

'Aye, that's true,' Dugald said. 'He was a wee chiseller. Anyway, his dad, Hamish's dad, died at sea – he was drowned. He left the boy some money.

Hamish would have been aboot what, fourteen, I guess and he went aff tae London as soon as he was sixteen, as soon as he could.'

'And his brother, Graham?'

'Aye, a different father. His mother was a bit of a hoor, she'd go with anyone,' Dugald remarked.

'I did her,' said the third fisherman, who had hitherto been silent.

'Aye, well, that kinda proves Dugald's point, Eck does it not?' Tommy pointed out. The three of them laughed.

'True,' the old guy, Eck agreed. 'Aye, very true.'

There was some more conversation; it pretty much echoed what Cameron had told her. That his family were indeed from there, that he had grown up poor and that his story about staring wistfully across the water at Kinnachan House, the mansion on the hill, was completely plausible.

'How did he get on with his brother?' she asked.

A shrug. 'He was fifteen or so years younger, hen. He'd have been one or two when Hamish left, a wee bit young to have formed an opinion one way or another, I would have thought.'

'Does he still live here?' she asked out of idle curiosity. It would be nice to talk to him about Cameron.

A headshake. 'Naw, the last anyone heard he was in prison. His dad had a hell of a temper, so did the boy. He beat someone up and went down for it. That came as no surprise to me, well, to any of us from the village. He was always a nasty wee kid, and, Jesus, he could really go aff on one, especially if he'd had a drink. I think we were all kind of relieved when he disappeared.'

And that was more or less that. No one missed the Camerons and the mention of the name hadn't brought any revelations of child abuse. Hanlon had a nose for the concealed; she didn't feel that anyone was holding anything back.

She got back into her car and checked her phone for messages. There was one from Griffiths asking how she was getting on. She texted him to say that she'd be available to see him in Edinburgh on Monday. There was one from Paul Wyre to say that Julia Swinson had said she was interested in talking to him – he would be free at eleven a.m. the following day, Sunday, if she wanted to swing by. More importantly, there was one from Luke to say that he had some potentially very important information on Aurora, if she would care to come round in the evening on Monday. She thought for a moment and called the Student Advice Centre and made an appointment to see Peter Reiss.

Another incoming message on her phone, Murdo Campbell replying to her text. Would she care to meet up for a drink at Tarbert, Loch Fyne later that afternoon? She messaged Campbell straight back, yes, she'd like that.

* * *

'Jesus, Hanlon, what happened to your face?'

She frowned; she kept forgetting about it, until she saw her reflection in bathroom mirrors or when people mentioned it. Like now.

'I got beaten up, someone trying to scare me.'

Campbell said, drily, 'I take it that didn't work.'

'No,' Hanlon said.

'Do you want to talk about it?' Campbell asked. Now he looked and sounded worried. She felt a flash of annoyance – she hated people fussing over her affairs. Just a hint of someone trying to tell her what to do and she felt immediate anger, and the desire to do the opposite, just to spite them, no matter how intelligent or caring the advice. What she got up to was her own business, and if that included being beaten up, so be it.

'Not really,' she said. 'I'm just at the start of things. It's getting complicated.'

Campbell sighed. 'When I put your name forward for this I thought it would be fairly straightforward, or at least not dangerous, and now look at what's happened.' He shook his head sadly. 'You've been beaten up and a girl's been murdered.' He smiled. 'Can't you just find a normal job? Get a job in the Co-operative?'

She laughed. 'Say that again.'

'What?' He was puzzled. 'Co-operative?'

'I love the way you say that word, Murdo, Cope-erative. It's so sweet.'

He shook his head. 'Changing the subject's not helping, Hanlon.'

She looked at him hard in the eyes. 'It's my life, Murdo.' Her voice was serious – don't push me.

He held her gaze. 'It'll be your death, Hanlon.' His voice equally serious.

'Here's your coffee.' It was the waitress. The spell was broken. They thanked her and Hanlon looked out of the window at the view. It was a sight she knew well. The picturesque fishing village was the nearest thing to a town from where she currently lived. It was a half-hour drive or, if she was feeling energetic, a two-hour walk or so from her village.

The hotel whose bar they were in was one of several built along the road that ran besides the picturesque harbour. There was a quay below them with fishing boats moored up to it and a pontoon on the far side of the harbour where yachts were berthed. Across Loch Fyne she could see lights going on in the houses on the other side of the water. It was a pretty, almost idyllic scene. Certainly nothing like the bleak desolation of Cameron's home village.

Campbell looked tired and careworn.

'How is your investigation going, your Godfather-style murder?' she asked.

He shook his head. 'It's not. Nobody's going to talk, not on the record anyway. Everyone's scared of Millar. He's an evil bastard.' He looked out at the harbour. 'We found a body in the Clyde last year, an informant. His tongue had been cut out. Millar let it be known that he'd done it himself. The guy's crazy, but unfortunately far from stupid. You don't want to mess with him.'

'That's unfortunate.' She wasn't really interested in Millar. Psychotic gangsters were not her concern. Then, 'Did you find out anything on Morag McMillan for me?'

Campbell nodded. 'Yes, I did. She died of asphyxia – we suspect that something like a bag was put over her head when she was unconscious. She'd been drugged. Diazepam.' He shrugged. 'It certainly wasn't Millar's handiwork. It was far too gentle – he doesn't go in for subtlety. If he'd killed her we'd be scraping bits of her off the ceiling.'

Hanlon nodded, drank some coffee. There was a family of swans on the water; she had never realised that they went anywhere near the sea before.

'And how is the search for Aurora going?' asked Campbell.

'I'm not really getting anywhere. I was at the village today where her father grew up. I learnt that her uncle is some kind of black sheep. Have you come across a Graham Cameron?'

'Who's he?' Campbell asked.

'Hamish Cameron's brother.'

'No, I can't say I have. It doesn't ring any bells. I'll look into it.'

* * *

Hanlon sat back in her seat. It was hot in the upstairs bar and she had taken off the sweater she was wearing. Underneath she had a tailored blouse with a dark T-shirt underneath. She looked good. Campbell was a man who prided himself on the ability to be decisive. He had meant to ask Hanlon out for quite some time now, but he never did; he kept fluffing his lines. Or failing to deliver them.

Just do it, he told himself, just do it. Hanlon's very grey eyes were looking at him questioningly. He felt himself getting angry with his reticence. Ask her out. She can only say no, for heaven's sake – as worst-case scenarios go, surely that's liveable with. OK, but where to? Certainly there's nowhere around here. What even would she like to do?

He decided to take the plunge. 'There's a Picasso exhibition in Glasgow,' he said, desperately. Did she like art? Who knew? It was as good a thing as any to suggest.

'Really?' Her dark eyebrows rose interrogatively. God, that black eye of hers was spectacular.

'Would you like to go?' he asked hopefully.

'I hate Picasso,' she said. She frowned; she suddenly looked furious.

She's got a good face for anger, thought Campbell sadly. He felt himself turning red with embarrassment; he was pale-skinned and he blushed easily. It made things even worse. God, I wish I'd never opened my mouth.

Hanlon continued, remorselessly, 'All that Cubist shit.'

'Oh.' Campbell stared at his highly polished shoes. That went well.

Hanlon nudged him lightly with her foot. He looked up, to see a broad grin on her face.

'I'd love to go. I was only kidding.'

Halleluiah! thought Campbell. There is a God.

20

Falkirk Chris stormed off down the main road that ran parallel to the Meadows. It was dark and raining; the traffic was heavy. He felt the gun, weighty, threatening, in his raincoat pocket. He was very tempted to return and put a few bullets into Ray and Dougie. God, how he hated them. Particularly Ray. He hated Ray more than Dougie. The way he looked down his nose at him, all those snide remarks about his clothes.

He'd like to hold Ray down and beat his face until it was a bloody pulp. But deep down Chris knew that he was no match for Ray in a fight and that made him even more furious.

But what he could do was find McDonald before Ray did, and make Ray look incompetent. Millar wanted McDonald punished for killing Jordan, that meant dead.

Millar had turned to him in the car on the way over and said to him, 'Let me get one thing straight with you, Chris, I want McDonald six foot under. In an ideal world I'd like some information from him, but right now, I'll settle for dead. I'm not sure if Ray's up to it, Chris... If you sort it out...'

The conversation had ended there. But he knew what success would mean: everything.

There was no doubt in Chris's mind that destiny was calling. A call that had been a long time coming, a call that was, not to put too fine a point upon it, long overdue. Millar had picked him; he wouldn't let him down. He'd been waiting for a moment like this for a long time, a moment where he could prove himself, show Millar his true worth.

Chris was heading for a part of Edinburgh called Gorgie. Gorgie was not going to feature highly on any tourist agenda; it was run-down, blue collar. There was a bar there, the Park Bar, that was one of those pubs where you could buy drugs real easy. He'd heard that McDonald was back to his five-hundred-pounds-a-day habit. McDonald had to be struggling for money; since his falling out with Millar, nobody would be brave enough to employ him and face Millar's wrath. There weren't many people in Edinburgh who would be prepared to give McDonald a line of credit as opposed to just a line, but the ones that were would be found in the Park Bar. It was that kind of place.

He was feeling a bit calmer now. He'd got it all worked out. He'd get the credit for finding McDonald, Ray and Dougie would fuck off back to their Glasgow gay bars and he could go back to Fife. Edinburgh was all well and good, but the people were just too up their own arses. He pulled his phone out of his pocket and ordered an Uber. Even if McDonald never showed up at the bar he'd ask around after him. Gorgie was his part of the city; just about all the people who drank in the Park Bar knew him. And Millar's reward money was very generous, a big incentive for people who'd sell their granny for a quick fix or fifty quid. At least he could put the word out. Also he'd score some Charlie and spend the evening getting pleasantly hammered on Guinness, maybe go home with one of the Lothian Road whores for a couple of hours.

The Uber stopped, he got in.

'Where to, chief?'

'Park Bar, aff the Gorgie Road.'

The driver put the car in gear and they drove off into the night.

* * *

Back in the Marchmont flat, Dougie's phone rang. They were in bed together, making the most of Falkirk Chris's unexplained absence. Dougie's body language as he took the call showed something important was happening. Ray watched intently as Dougie sat bolt upright, the covers falling away from his naked body, his voice tense.

'You're sure about that, the Park Bar...? He's still there... alone? With some girl, aye, but not mob-handed... Look, that's great, aye, the money's yours, we'll be straight over... If he goes, follow him, OK... twenty minutes.'

Ray started pulling on his clothes quickly, as did Dougie.

'You got that, Ray?'

'Aye, the Park Bar – it is McDonald, yes?'

'Yes,' confirmed Dougie.

'OK, you take the gun.' Ray thought a moment. 'I'll use this. Maybe we'll need something a wee bit more discreet.' He picked up a hunting knife with a six-inch blade in a leather sheath and put it in his pocket. Thank God there were two of them, he thought. McDonald was a daunting prospect.

'Who was that on the phone?' he asked as they left the flat.

'Davie Jessop, Junkie Dave, he was in that crack house in Muirhouse – do you not remember?'

Ray shrugged. 'No.'

'He's reliable,' Dougie said.

'C'mon, then, let's go. I'll drive.'

21

Chris got out of the Uber, walked into the Park Bar, weaved through the crowd and bought himself a pint of Guinness, shouting and gesticulating to make himself heard. The pub on a Saturday night was packed; hard-faced men of all ages, from raw-faced twenty-year-olds fresh from juvenile detention and youth prisons in tracksuits and hoodies, to lined, balding guys, heavy with muscle and middle-age spread, favouring leather jackets or bomber jackets. Sexual equality was not getting much of a look-in – the women in there were very much either criminal groupies or there because they were being paid and the meter was running.

He saw McDonald almost immediately. He was sitting in a corner with a girl. She had short dark hair and heavy Goth-style make-up; she was very good-looking. Chris felt a stab of jealousy. He disliked women in general, apart from his mother. They usually treated him with disdain, stuck-up bitches all of them. What was wrong with him? He felt the familiar seething rage of envy rise within him when he saw a guy with a pretty girl. He also simultaneously felt the strong grasp of fear now he'd seen McDonald. He swallowed nervously. The guy was a killer. He'd put three bullets in Jordan, or so the rumour said, but he could have killed Jordan with his bare hands if he'd wanted. Chris knew he was out of his league. But what could he do? He was committed.

McDonald was drinking lager and staring pointedly away from the girl, the way you do if you've had an argument. His eyes were starting out of his head – he was Charlied to fuck, thought Chris. His coat was folded on the bench seat they were sitting on that ran the length of the wall. He was wearing jeans, trainers and a blue Guernsey jumper. When he moved his arm to pick up the pint Chris could see the biceps in his upper arms ripple under the knotted, heavy wool.

He also noted how the other customers kept a respectful distance from McDonald's corner as if there some sort of invisible fence between them. McDonald was a well-known face and he scared people.

Chris stood in a corner near a pillar that had a shelf built around it at shoulder height so you could rest your drinks on it. From here he could keep an eye on his quarry. The gun in his pocket felt reassuringly heavy. Your muscles won't do much against that McDonald, he thought. Or your street smarts. He weighed his options. The most attractive of which, almost overwhelmingly so, was to finish his drink and go, pretend he hadn't seen him. No one knew he was here; nobody would know he'd chickened out. He knew he would stand no chance against McDonald in a fight, none whatsoever. Chris liked to pretend otherwise but in general, all he did was sell Millar's coke to a network of small-time dealers and intimidate students from the Forth Valley College in Falkirk.

This was all much harder than he had anticipated. When he'd left the flat in Marchmont, so angry he could hardly think straight, what with Ray and Dougie's shenanigans, he'd had this fantasy of marching into the bar with his scarf covering his face and shooting McDonald in the head. Then he would call Millar, who would reward him handsomely with coke, women, cash...

Nobody would try and stop him. If a fight breaks out in a pub, it's amazing how your friends suddenly disappear, how much more so if the other guy's got a gun. Nobody would lift a finger to stop him, or to try and apprehend him. And even if someone recognised him, this was the Park Bar, nobody would be talking to the police.

But in his imagination the pub had been virtually empty. McDonald had been sitting alone with his back to the door. In his imagination he was

a brave, fearless killer; people said, 'You don't mess with Chris.' The reality was very different.

For one thing, the bar was far from empty. There were nigh on, well, Christ alone knew how many people in the bar – you had to force your way through them. If he started shooting, there'd be mass panic, people running out of the door, bar staff maybe becoming have-a-go heroes, screaming, people throwing themselves on the floor to get out of the line of fire. Chaos.

Also, a big also, Chris had never shot anyone. It was unknown territory. He wasn't sure this was the ideal place to start.

Killing time, searching for inspiration, he looked around the bar again, checking to see if he knew anyone, people he'd maybe done time with or worked with or been introduced to. The only person he knew was a dealer called Davie J and he looked really out of it, smacked out of his head, gauching away, head nodding, in a world of his own. He probably only had a very hazy idea of where he was, much less that Chris was there.

He tried not to stare too much at McDonald. McDonald appeared to be having a bad evening with his girlfriend. Chris knew a lot about arguing with women; he could recognise the signs. She was glaring at him furiously – he couldn't hear what she was saying but you could tell by the way that her mouth was moving that it wasn't friendly. McDonald would occasionally look at her in a kind of sneering way. He saw him roll his eyes theatrically. The girl had had enough. She suddenly stood up. She was in full indie-rock regalia, studded denim jacket, Slipknot T-shirt, short leather skirt, torn tights and Doc Martens. Pretty as she was, she was housing-estate trash, thought Chris, hanging around McDonald for his coke and his hard-man cachet. She said something to him. McDonald shrugged and she grabbed her jacket and stormed out.

Chris saw his chance as she brushed by him, her features furious under the mask of heavy make-up. She left the pub and he followed.

This was his opportunity. He'd never intimidated a man like McDonald, but he'd threatened a fair few women; he knew what he was doing with them. This one was prettier, but she'd be a pushover, they always were, particularly after he gave her a back-hander to show her who was boss, see the pain and fear in her eyes.

He felt exultant triumph rise within him. There was a park – park was putting it a bit strongly, a grassy area with swings for kids – more or less opposite. If it weren't raining and so cold, it was the kind of place where the local Neds, non-educated delinquents as the acronym went – it was how more than one teacher had referred to him when he was a kid – would congregate to neck cider, smoke weed and harass the neighbours. As it was, at half nine in a chilly downpour in early February, it was deserted.

Chris had a small pocketknife on him as well as the gun. He opened the blade, ten centimetres of razor-sharp steel. He had a plan now. He'd slap her face, one, two, back and forth, get her attention, show her who was boss, drag her over there, make her phone McDonald, when he came running to rescue her, he would shoot him, simple as.

She stopped outside and lit a cigarette; he stopped too. Then she moved forward, slowly. He followed, invisible in the shadows. Now she was almost opposite the park. He stared at her. She was tall, taller than him – he'd hit her hard in the kidneys, that would knock the fight out of her, then pull her up by her hair, knife to throat, a wee jab just so she knew it was there, what it would do to her, 'dinnae struggle or I'll kill you,' then into the park, behind the bushes. Aye, that's the way it would be.

Then he smiled with delight – she was only crossing the road to the park. Sweet Jesus, this was going so well it was not true. He wouldn't even need to force her into the park; she was there already. One less thing to go wrong. He followed her. The rain was heavy now, running down his face, cold, Edinburgh rain and a vicious northerly wind. She didn't look back, probably pissed. She reached the park and walked in; there was only a low fence around it, an unlocked gate. He followed, left the gate open behind him, two steps down the path, closing on her, bushes to the left of him... then JESUS!

It felt as if he'd been hit with a baseball bat in the small of the back, like an explosion, then an agony of pain. As if he were on fire. He was too shocked to be frightened, didn't really understand what was happening. He turned and the second punch smashed into the side of his face, like being hit by a rock, breaking his cheekbone and loosening a few back teeth, then another as his nose this time exploded in blood. His legs went and he collapsed to the floor, felt the sudden warmth as he pissed himself in terror and looked up.

Standing over him was McDonald. Looking down. Eyes and expression hard and pitiless. No mercy. It was the last thing he saw.

22

Ray and Dougie walked into the Park Bar. Heavy house music boomed around them. They exchanged glances and grimaced. Ray hated places like this, no style, full of sweaty, no-hoper low-lifes. He recognised half a dozen faces from half a dozen prisons. What a shithole. And the clothes, sweet Jesus! A couple of people nodded hello to him.

'Christ, this place is full of fucking criminals,' he breathed into Dougie's ear.

'No shit, Sherlock,' Dougie shouted.

He glanced around the bar; he couldn't see McDonald. The lights in the pub were dim, it was packed, noisy, the music thundered, you had to yell in each other's ear to be heard. Ray wasn't particularly worried about being seen, he and Dougie would be invisible in this crowd.

'There's Junkie Dave,' said Dougie, heading over to a table. Ray followed and stood looking at him. He didn't recognise him as the guy who had been on the sofa at the crack house a few days previously. Dave was thin, very thin, with long salt and pepper hair and a lined face. He was wearing supermarket-dad jeans that fell away in folds of material from his spindly thighs. Dave was with some old sad sack with white hair, a crimson face, and, as they sat down and he opened his mouth to protest, no bottom front teeth. Dave said something to the guy and he stood up, shaking his head, then disappeared into the crowd by the bar.

'Where's McDonald?' yelled Dougie into Dave's ear.

'Gone.'

'Oh, fucking brilliant.' Ray glared at Junkie Dave, who looked back, his eyes pinned, mind relaxed and floating on a tide of opiates.

'Why didn't you call?' shouted Dougie.

'He's only just left... His girl left, then some guy followed her, then he followed the guy.'

'Did you ken who it was?' asked Dougie.

'Who?'

'The guy.' Jesus, it was like pulling teeth. 'The guy following them?'

'Aye, I ken him, some wee shite called Falkirk Chris.'

'Shit,' said Ray, standing up. 'Come on, Dougie.'

They left the bar and stood uncertainly in the street outside looking around. It seemed amazingly quiet and cold after the bar. Nobody was in sight. The dark wet pavements offered no clue. Dougie shivered in the remorseless drizzle.

'Which way do you reckon they went?' Ray said, looking hopelessly around.

'There's a couple of bars down that way,' said Dougie, pointing across the street. Ray shrugged, might as well.

They crossed the road and cut through the park. There wasn't a great deal of light in it but enough to make out a dark shape lying face down in the muddy grass by some scrubby bushes. They looked at each other.

'Fuck...' They approached the body lying face down on the grass. It wasn't a nice place to be. There were patches of mud, the occasional dog turd and bits and pieces of litter, empty cans and cider bottles, cigarette ends. It was unmistakeably Falkirk Chris lying in this debris and he was also unmistakeably dead. Ray poked him with the toe of his shoe to make sure. Chris's eyes were still open; his body didn't move. It was good enough for Ray.

He took his phone out and took a picture, just in case Millar wanted proof, then turned to Dougie.

'Come on, let's go.'

They walked back to where they had left the car. After they rounded the corner Dougie took a huge lungful of air, as if he'd been holding his breath. Ray put his arm round him to comfort him. 'Shit, did McDonald do that?' he asked.

Ray shrugged. 'It wasnae mice.'

They got in the car and he started the engine.

McDonald two – Millar nil. First Jordan, now Chris. The Big Man was not going to be happy. Ray smiled. On the plus side, they need never see Falkirk Chris again.

23

The following day Hanlon saw the killing on the newsfeed on her phone: *Man Dies in Gorgie Park*, but the story meant nothing to her. It was there with other news items such as *Queensferry Road Smash, Two Held after Leith Incident, Woman Racially Abused on Bus* and *Hearts Manager Reveals New Plan to Beat Hibs.*

She'd been to the gym and had gone for a five-mile run with the dog, who was now resting at the foot of her bed in her room at the hotel. It was Sunday and the roads were quiet. She reviewed what she knew so far.

Aurora had gone missing on Monday 24 January after returning visibly upset from a Narcotics Anonymous meeting. She was a troubled girl with a history of drugs and rehab behind her; Dr John Griffiths, her lecturer, claimed that Aurora had possibly been abused by her father; her father, Hamish Cameron, appeared to enjoy relationships with young girls; Hanlon herself had been attacked in the car park of her hotel and warned off looking into Aurora's disappearance; Aurora's flatmate, Morag, had claimed that she suspected Griffiths of being involved in Aurora's disappearance, she had also made other allegations about people close to Aurora, including her father; Morag had been murdered and some of her accusations seemed to be true but some were of doubtful veracity.

But whatever had or hadn't happened, Hanlon was growing increasingly concerned as to Aurora's safety.

Her phone went.

'Hello, is that Hanlon, the detective?'

It was a girl's voice, young with a faint Newcastle accent. 'Yes, how can I help?'

'It's about the missing girl, Aurora Cameron... I think you ought to know that she was having an affair with her professor...'

'Dr Griffiths?'

'Yes, she wanted to break it off, but she was frightened... Griffiths looks nice, but he's violent towards women...'

'I see,' Hanlon said, frowning. 'Look, could I meet you to discuss this?'

'No, it's too dangerous.' The girl sounded panicked. 'This is off the record. I don't want to be involved. It's just a warning, and you should be careful too – he knows people.'

The call ended. Hanlon looked at Recents; caller ID had been blocked.

She sighed and added another question mark to the name of Dr Griffiths. Well, maybe his colleague could throw some light on the issue.

* * *

A couple of hours later she was in the café that had been nominated by Paul Wyre for their meeting. He was late. While she was waiting, she texted Murdo Campbell.

Could you get some background as to what Paul Wyre, writer in residence Edinburgh Uni, was in prison for?

She knew it was armed robbery but that could cover various scenarios; she wanted detail.

The café was a hipster place – Bean and Gone, it was called. It was full of mismatched furniture and exposed brickwork. It was busy; middle-class customers eating eggs Benedict, smashed avocado and reading Sunday newspapers. It was more or less her idea of hell. At the back of her mind she could imagine Dr Morgan shaking her head at her intolerance. There's nothing wrong with drinking different kinds of coffee, and if you want oat milk is that such a terrible thing? She pushed these thoughts away. Now wasn't the time for self-analysis. She forced herself to concentrate on her surroundings. The waiter had an elaborate beard with a curly waxed moustache. Still, the coffee was good so Hanlon forgave him.

Half an hour later than they'd agreed, Paul Wyre arrived. He was tall and thin, his shaven head glinting in the sun that shone through the café's front window, heavy silver earrings shining. He had chunky silver rings on each finger and was wearing his long black leather trench-coat. The eighties revival starts here, thought Hanlon.

'Hello!' She waved cheerily at him as he came in. She instinctively knew it would antagonise him. I must stop doing this, she thought to herself. But it was hard not to want to prick the bubble of pomposity that surrounded the writer – 'Look, I am an Artist!' his dress proclaimed. Hanlon thought it also proclaimed, 'Look, I'm an arsehole' but for now she would keep that to herself.

'Good morning,' he said as he came over and sat opposite her. He smelt of weed, Lynx and self-satisfaction.

'You wanted to see me?' He sat back in a wicker chair in a theatrical way, flinging his arms onto the rests on the chair and tilting his head at a dramatic angle. She could see the waiter talking to the barista behind the counter; she glanced over at Wyre and rolled her eyes. She suspected they shared her opinion of him. The waiter came over and he ordered a tall, skinny latte.

'They know me here,' Wyre said confidingly to Hanlon. Oh, I bet they do, she thought.

She nodded. 'I'm looking for Aurora Cameron.'

Paul Wyre said, 'I heard she'd disappeared.' He had a northern English accent – she must have read that he was from the North, but for some reason it hadn't stuck. 'Well, I certainly knew her, mainly through her friend and flatmate, the late, unlamented Morag.'

'You didn't get on with Morag?' Hanlon wanted to hear his version of things.

Wyre laughed bitterly. 'That's the understatement of the year. She's been a thorn in my side for a while. Nothing but trouble. I am not that surprised she's dead.'

'Really?' Hanlon said. 'Why's that?'

Wyre's eyes were quite glazed; Hanlon realised he was stoned. 'She was always banging on about her bloody book, all the powerful people she was going to blow the whistle on. Sometimes I'd wonder if I was in it.' He laughed. 'But that's probably just my ego talking... I guess one of them might have done it.'

Like you? thought Hanlon.

'Did she ever show you the book?' she asked.

Wyre shook his head then abruptly changed the subject. 'She tried to seduce me, you know...'

'Tried?' queried Hanlon. She had guessed he would bring sex into the conversation; he was that kind of guy. Here we are, straight into it. The subtext, I'm irresistible to women.

'OK,' said Wyre, with an annoying mix of boasting and complaint, 'I admit it, she seduced me.'

'She was half your age,' pointed out Hanlon.

'Exactly,' said Wyre, irritably. 'That's why it was so bloody easy for her.' He shook his head in exasperation at Hanlon being so slow on the uptake. 'I thought, stupidly, it was because she admired my work, found me sexy, whatever, then I discovered she wanted me to boost her grades so that she could get a first – she was doing an Eng Lit degree at the time.'

'And you had no control over the marking?'

'Exactly...' He looked at her suspiciously. 'You seem very well informed.'

Hanlon shrugged. 'I hear stuff.'

'Well, hear this.' The coffee came and he made a kind of prayerful, namaste gesture to the bearded waiter to signal his thanks.

'That looks amazing, Dominic.'

'Enjoy,' said the waiter with a sour look, as if he hoped Wyre would do anything but.

Wyre resumed his story. 'I got a very nasty shock at the beginning of the year when I saw her name down on my Creative Writing MA. It was like she was stalking me. She said if I objected she'd cause trouble, and I believed her.'

'So it wasn't you abusing your position of power...'

'Quite the reverse,' agreed Wyre, not hearing, or choosing not to hear, the sarcasm in Hanlon's voice. 'And, meantime, my fiancée had found out about the fact I'd been sleeping with Morag, so she dumped me, and I lost my home.'

'I don't understand.'

'My fiancée owned the flat.' He scowled. 'It was a lovely flat, and she booted me out. Now I'm renting a room in a shared flat in a scrotty basement in Marchmont, like a student.'

'Well, you're the one who had the affair,' said Hanlon. 'You can hardly blame her.'

'OK, maybe that's so.' His tone of voice suggested it was far from reasonable. 'I think it's a childish overreaction personally. I'm an artist... I have needs...' he shook his head in annoyance at his ex's selfish refusal to accommodate his literary dalliances '... but I've got a pretty good idea that Morag told her. She was a vindictive cow, one of these people who increases her self-esteem by putting other people down... Anyway, enough about her, you wanted to talk to me about Aurora.'

'Yes, did you know her well?'

'Not really, mainly through Morag. I saw quite a bit of her when I was having my fling—' he checked himself '—when Morag was having her fling with me. We used her flat a lot and I saw quite a bit of Aurora. She was doing a lot of drugs at the time, and I mean a lot.' He emphasised the words 'a lot'. 'She was a sorry state. I know about these things... You've read my books?'

'I'm afraid not.'

Wyre looked wounded.

'They're on my to-read list, alongside Shakespeare,' she said.

Wyre shook his head pityingly.

'Anyway, back to Aurora,' he said. 'Her grades were suffering – well, how could they not? I told Griffiths. He started helping her.'

'Helping her?' Griffiths hadn't told her this. Modesty on his part?

'Yes, he got her into the student counselling programme and I think he badgered her into going to NA and CA, that's the same but specifically for cocaine.' He smiled. 'Just the traditional stuff for Aurora, she left spice and ket well alone.'

'And it worked?' asked Hanon.

Wyre nodded. 'Yeah, it worked. That was a year ago. She quit coke, concentrated on her studies, started helping other people with coke problems. It was a remarkable transformation. I'll give her that.'

'And, of course, you would know about transformations.'

He nodded. 'Yeah, you probably know my history. I was in prison for armed robbery, pretty hard-core stuff. I was involved with a lot of violence – it wasn't nice. I was regarded as one of the hard men of Wakefield.' That was said as a kind of boast: look at my prison credentials.

'Why do you think she's disappeared?' asked Hanlon.

Wyre looked thoughtful.

'If you'd asked me that last year, I'd have guessed to evade her coke debts. She was spending about three hundred a day, nose hard down to the mirror, a couple of grand a week. That's serious money.'

'Did her dad clear her debts?' wondered Hanlon.

'I don't know,' Wyre said. 'I'm not sure he was necessarily aware of how big they'd got. I'm surprised that her dealer allowed it to escalate to that extent. Anyway, the last that I heard her dad was practising tough love and refusing to bail her out any more. He paid her credit card, he could work out what was what on that, but he'd given up advancing her any cash to stop it disappearing up her nose.' He finished his coffee. 'And that is all I really know about Aurora. I've been out of touch with her since Morag and I stopped seeing each other.' He looked at his watch. 'Well, I'd better go, I've got a stack of marking I've got to get through.'

'Before you go,' asked Hanlon, 'what do you think she's doing?'

'I think her debts have maybe finally caught up with her. If they have she could well be dead. Drug dealers can be quite unforgiving, maybe downright psychotic at times. I should know, I met enough inside. I can't think of any other explanation. If I were you, I'd find out who her dealer used to be, see if she owed him any money still. I would guess, yes – a lot.' He stood up. 'Sorry I couldn't be of more help.'

'Thanks for your time.'

He left the café and her phone signalled a message. She looked at it,

Murdo Campbell.

Her face was impassive as she read the text. It was the answer to her earlier question. Paul Wyre was guilty, not of actually lying, but of misrepresentation. His armed robbery was technically that: he had threatened a sixty-year-old woman in a newsagent with a steak knife. In Wakefield prison he'd been on suicide watch because he had been badly bullied by the other inmates.

The 'hard man' persona was just an act.

Wyre was a self-aggrandising fantasist. What a surprise, she thought, profoundly unsurprised. Well, he had that in common with Morag; they were made for each other. How much of what he had told her was just bullshit?

Well, she would have to find out.

Next on her to-do list was Peter Reiss, the student counsellor.

* * *

She found herself back in the Grassmarket, walking past the pub where she'd spent a couple of hours the other day and the eponymous publishing company where Lorna worked. She walked under a bridge that ran high overhead, with the tall buildings rising up on either side – it was like walking through a narrow dark canyon – into a street called the Cowgate. Just off this road she found a scuffed door with a brass plaque next to it, Edinburgh University, Student Advice Centre. It was open seven days a week; addiction and mental illness didn't take weekends off. She opened the door and went in.

There was a tiny reception area with a desk and an enormous, old-fashioned photocopier. On cork boards on the walls were various posters warning against STDs, drugs, alcohol, racism, 'cheap' loans and various other things.

She could hear voices and then a woman with a lined face and dyed red and blue hair appeared through a doorway behind the desk.

'Hello, can I help?'

'Hi,' she said, 'I'm Hanlon, here to see Peter Reiss.'

'Oh, yes, he mentioned you.' She had quite a strong Scottish accent.

'Please, follow me.'

She led Hanlon down a narrow corridor, worn beige carpet, pale blue walls, into a small office. Reiss was tall and stooping, wearing a threadbare suit, with an eager to please face and a beard. As he sat down she noticed that he had a circular bald spot like a monk's tonsure in the centre of his head. This time she recognised the accent easily. Reiss was a Londoner.

Briefly she told him why she had come.

'Ah, yes, Aurora Cameron... I met her a few times. Luckily for you I remember her.'

'Luckily?'

'We've got thirty-three thousand students at Edinburgh University,' he said. 'If we say five to ten per cent of them have mental problems that need addressing... well, you can do the maths, and, as you can guess, we're not over-staffed. I see a lot of students – she stuck in my mind.'

Hanlon digested this; she was interested in Reiss's impressions of Aurora. 'Can you tell me anything about her?'

Reiss scratched his bearded chin thoughtfully. 'Yeah, I can. When I first met her, I didn't believe she wanted to get better. You get a certain amount of time-wasters in rehab. I thought she was one of them. To be honest I considered shopping her to the Old Bill.'

'How so?'

Reiss settled back in his chair. 'Recently there's been a dramatic rise in cocaine usage and therefore addiction amongst the student body. It's very good quality, and it's cheap. It's flooding in. I would say that's a good indication that it's coming from the same source, the same supplier – well, that's my opinion, which, may I tell you, is quite well informed,' Reiss looked at her and she revised her opinion. With his old, cheap suit, dull tie, shoes in need of a polish and pot belly he looked dowdy and unimpressive. But Reiss's eyes were hard and steady – he was, she decided, a bright guy who had sat through a lot of bullshit. If anyone was prone to lying it was an addict, and Reiss had probably seen a lot of people suffer and more than a few die.

'Napier and Heriot-Watt – they are the other big universities here – are also seeing the same coke on their campuses. I think that a new dealer is targeting students, a new supplier, and I thought at the time Aurora

Cameron was one of the conduits that was bringing it in. I thought, and I freely admit I was probably mistaken, that she was maybe recruiting likely student distributors to shift product.'

'Is that why you remember her?'

'To be honest, yes,' he replied. 'A lot of dealers have humongous habits to feed. I was kind of on the lookout for likely candidates, still am.'

'Why did you think that she might be a dealer?' Hanlon asked.

'Two reasons: if you've got a drugs habit like she did and Daddy turns off the taps, which I gather he did, then to fund it, well, it's crime or prostitution. And she wasn't the sort to go on the game. The other reason is, I was tipped off.'

Hanlon was on the point of asking by whom, but he raised his hand to cut off the question. 'I'm not saying who, before you ask. So, believe me, I kept a close eye on her during group therapy work. I saw a lot of her then. It wasn't bullshit, she was genuine...'

'But?' asked Hanlon.

Reiss said, thoughtfully, 'But, I still don't know. If I were a new drug dealer looking to target students, I'd want someone on the inside giving me advice and helping me build up a network. Who better than Aurora Cameron? I thought that's what she was doing. She's very well connected socially, she'd add glamour to parties, people wanted her there...' He laughed. 'I may not look like it but, believe me, I know a hell of a lot about Edinburgh Uni night life, and then her glamorous boyfriend, the artist guy, with his Muirhouse mates, I kind of wondered about them as the main supply, although, maybe this is snobbery on my part, in their tracksuits, "jobby catchers" as they call those horrible tracksuit bottoms, I didn't think they had the class. But I might be wrong...'

Reiss's confident manner belied his words. 'I'm not wrong,' his look said.

'And let's not forget that her father is a very successful salesman. OK, he peddles art, not drugs, but hey, selling is selling. Blood is blood. A lot of things seem to me to be inherited: drug addiction, alcoholism, success.' He sighed. 'But anyway, it looks like I was probably wrong about her.'

'She got better.'

'Well, she's not currently using. John Griffiths, her tutor who was instrumental in bringing her in, has seen her a lot at various drug and alcohol rehab meetings and she's helping others too. That shows commitment, so I guess she wasn't dealing and was just a heavy user. Any more questions?' He looked up at the clock on his wall. 'I can give you three minutes.'

'What's Griffiths like?' she asked.

Reiss considered the question. 'He does a lot of good, steering students towards help. I see him occasionally at NA or CA meetings. He gets a kick out of it, but I suppose that's no bad thing.' She nodded; hardly a ringing endorsement, but reasonable. Now for his colleague.

'Oh, one last question, do you know Paul Wyre?'

Reiss threw his head back and laughed heartily. 'That knobhead! Mr "I'm so tough"... Give me strength. He couldn't fight his way out of a damp paper bag. Seriously, I think he's a wanker.' He laughed again. 'I hope I haven't been too evasive there. That should answer your question.'

She stood up. 'Yes, it does. Well, thank you very much for your help, Peter.'

* * *

She drove back to the hotel, collected the dog and headed off in the car to the village of Cramond. She parked and walked the dog down to the seashore. The rocky beach was deserted. Sunday afternoon, grey and depressing. She stared awhile at the water and the seabirds; it made her feel homesick for Argyll. It was a peculiar sensation. She had never really felt that before about anywhere, including London, where she had lived for four decades.

She wasn't sure she liked the feeling. In her mind she heard Dr Morgan saying, 'It's because you're beginning to heal – you're beginning to feel emotions like most people do instead of burying or denying them.'

I know, I know, she thought. She knew it was her mind, be it guilty conscience or subconscious that made her think so much of Dr Morgan, but it was getting so strong she couldn't ignore its prompting much longer. Yes, I'll make an appointment to see you. Back at your chi-chi Hampstead practice. We do have a lot to discuss.

She sat on a rock overlooking the Firth of Forth and threw a stick into the water for Wemyss. The dog was a strong swimmer and loved the water; he would retrieve the stick, bring it back to Hanlon, who would throw it back, seemingly endlessly.

To take her mind off herself she hunted around on the shore and then she sat the three stones she had chosen up on a flat rock to represent her suspects in the missing Aurora case.

First: Griffiths.

The evidence surrounding him: Morag McMillan's book, which damned him as 'an evil bastard' and manipulative. Then the unknown girl from Newcastle claiming that Aurora was having an affair with him and that he was violent to women.

The motive? Frightening Aurora off in case he lost his job for sleeping with her? Had he killed McMillan for the same reason?

The evidence against him being involved: Swinson and Reiss both thought he was a stand-up guy. Quite frankly, she valued their opinions a lot more than Morag's or this unknown girl. He genuinely seemed to care about student welfare. He did not appear to be violent, despite the anonymous tip-off. Could he be a wolf in sheep's clothing or simply the sheep he appeared to be?

She looked at the next stone. Tall and slender. This represented Wyre.

The evidence against him: he slept with students – that wasn't rumour, that was fact. He could lose his job over it. Definitely would, according to Swinson. He also had a track record of violence – he'd been in prison. Even though he had bigged his crime up, he was still a man who was prepared to threaten a woman with a knife. Reiss didn't find him intimidating but Reiss, despite outward appearances, was a lot tougher than he looked, and from what she was beginning to learn of Aurora, she was a lot weaker than she seemed.

His motive? He didn't seem to have one. If he had been having a relationship with Aurora, Hanlon would have bet that he would have discreetly boasted about it. She was beautiful; Wyre would have wanted everyone to know he had had her. She could see why he might have wanted to kill Morag, but Aurora?

And the argument for the defence? Lack of motive and deep down she didn't believe that Wyre would have the balls to hurt anyone. He could look scary, he was capable of waving a knife about, but, deep down, it was bluster.

The third stone represented the unknown. Wyre had said that he wondered if Aurora had been threatened by drug dealers to whom she owed money. Hanlon thought that was plausible. The stone could be a drug dealer; equally it could be Luke. He had the Muirhouse crime connections; Reiss could easily be wrong about the drug source. And artists were notoriously devoid of sympathy or empathy for others; their selfishness, particularly with women, was notorious. She hoped Luke was nothing to do with anything bad happening to Aurora, but she certainly wasn't ruling it out.

And how did any of the above relate to the attack on her?

Well, everyone agreed that Aurora had connections with drug dealers, either as a customer or, possibly, as a dealer herself. Her supplier could well panic, might have had nothing to do with her disappearance but feared being dragged into an investigation. Part of Hanlon almost hoped they would try again. For her it was unfinished business. She wanted to be handing out violence rather than receiving it.

Well, for now she had achieved as much as she felt she could chasing the university end of things. Time to chase the drugs angle. That, as both Reiss and Wyre had suggested, was the most likely explanation for Aurora's panic-stricken disappearance. Her ex was the person most likely to provide a name.

She picked up her phone and called Luke.

'Hi, it's Hanlon. You said you had some info for me on Aurora. When can I come round tomorrow?'

'Umm, let me think.' There was a pause. 'Have you thought about me painting you?'

'No, Luke.' She let him hear the exasperation in her voice; she hoped he hadn't been lying about Aurora. 'I'm busy trying to find your ex. What time tomorrow?'

'Let me check my diary.' There was a pause. 'Let me see... five p.m. suit you?'

'Perfect, see you then.'

You'd better not be lying to me, Luke, she thought as she walked back up to where she'd parked her car. I'm not in the mood.

24

'This is a real, fucking, nuisance.' Millar was furious. 'Are you sure he's dead?'

'Absolutely, look at him!' Ray showed Millar the picture on his phone.

'He looks pretty dead,' Millar admitted. Ray looked at him nervously. Millar was shaking with anger and he could see the tell-tale vein beating in his forehead.

'Well, boss, we're sorry,' said Ray, 'but it was that shit-head's Chris's fault. If he'd told us what he was up to, rather than try and take McDonald on his own...'

'Aye, he was asking for trouble,' put in Dougie.

They looked at Millar beseechingly. Millar pushed a huge hand through his thick black hair. Ray stared at it appraisingly; he wondered if he dyed it. It was suspiciously free of grey. But Millar was a law unto himself. There was a kind of electric force that surrounded the man; powerful, violent people often had it. An animal magnetism.

However, Millar was ageing now. Ray watched as Millar chopped a fat line of coke out on the glass top of the coffee table and then leaned forward and snorted it. Then he took a big mouthful of Scotch and reached into his coat and took out a small pill bottle and shook out a small tablet. Ray wondered how much more Millar's body could take. As if to prove the point, Millar lit a cigarette.

The devil looks after his own, Ray thought. Millar would probably live to be a hundred.

'Clonazepam,' Millar said as he put the small, brown bottle away. 'I'm under a lot of stress and do you know why I get so stressed?' He glared at Dougie and Ray. Dougie dropped his gaze and looked at the floor. Ray met the look with a certain amount of equanimity. He'd known Millar for most of his life; Millar had worked for Ray's dad, Gordon, when he was a fresh-faced sixteen-year-old, newly arrived in Glasgow.

'The reason I get so stressed is because I am surrounded by fucking idiots.' Millar glared at them. He stood up, Ray did too. He hoped this conversation was over and Millar would be leaving now.

'Christ knows what Jordan was doing with McDonald in the first place, but he was the one in charge of moving product in Edinburgh, and after he died I told Chris to handle it. Well, needs must, and now he's fucking gone.'

He took a deep drag on his cigarette and glared at Ray.

'Do you know what?' Millar continued, as if the thought had just struck him. 'I just want McDonald dead. Is that such a big ask?' He glared at them angrily. 'It seems such a simple request.'

'We're sorry,' said Ray, tactfully.

'Anyway,' Millar said, 'you'll have to pick up the slack, now that Chris isn't around.'

'So you'll want us to stay around in Edinburgh?' Ray asked.

Millar nodded. 'I've got a good person who runs the dealers,' he said. 'They make sure that stock control is handled and they're bright. I'll introduce you once all this shit has settled.

'Meanwhile, you can do something useful.' He fiddled with his phone. 'This is the warehouse of a shipping company out near Balerno. They've got five kilos of coke of mine. I want you to pick it up and take it round to the safe house where we keep the stock. I'll send you the address.'

'Sure, when do you want us to do that?'

Millar looked at his watch. 'Right now would be fine.' He frowned. 'Oh, and one other thing...'

Ray nodded. 'Yes, boss.'

There was nothing in Millar's face to indicate what was coming next. Moving with incredible speed for such a big man, Millar slapped Ray across the cheek, hard, the weight of his upper body in it. Ray staggered with the force of the blow and Millar slammed a punch, which he didn't see coming, into his gut. Ray doubled up in agony and slowly straightened up, supporting himself against the back of the sofa. Dougie sat completely motionless. Ray glanced over at him. Dougie was obviously wondering what the fuck was going on. If it had been someone else attacking him, Dougie would have waded in instantly. Their eyes met and Ray shook his head imperceptibly. He was terrified of Dougie trying to stop Millar. Millar would kill him.

The same thing but concerning himself was running through Ray's mind too. He somehow knew that if Millar hit him just once more, he wouldn't stop. But there was nothing he could do. He was too afraid of Millar to defend himself. Obedience to Millar was too ingrained.

'You two...' Millar's face was scarlet with anger '... are seriously pissing me off. All you've done over the last few days is fuck things up... ARE YOU FUCKING LISTENING?'

'Yes, boss,' said Dougie. Ray nodded.

'I told you scare that woman off, you didn't. I told you to kill McDonald, you let him escape. I told you to find him, you let him escape again and this time... this time he killed Falkirk Chris. When's this fuckery going to end, Ray?'

'I'm sorry—'

'YOU'RE sorry! You're sorry – I'm beginning to be sorry I employed you two cretins to begin with.' He shook his head angrily. 'You used to be good, Ray, but look at you now, fucking useless. You got early onset dementia or something?'

'We didn't...' Dougie tried to say something.

Oh, Jesus, Dougie, don't say anything, thought Ray.

'Did I ask you to speak?' shouted Millar at Dougie. 'And what were you doing, eh? Too busy sucking his fucking dick to do any work.' His attention swung back to Ray. He lashed out with his foot into the glass coffee table. The reinforced glass surface, not designed for this punishment, shattered. The noise was like a gun going off.

'That can be fucking remedied, Ray Downie, as well you fucking know!' Millar's arm was outstretched and he pointed an accusing finger at Ray. A vein throbbed ominously in Millar's forehead.

'Now,' he said, his voice calmer, but dangerously so, as if he were restraining himself with a superhuman effort. 'I'm going to give you, and numb-nuts over there, another chance.'

'Thank you, boss,' said Ray, breathing a heartfelt sigh of relief. He was well aware that Millar had come within a whisker of losing it and killing either him or Dougie and leaving the survivor to clean up the mess.

It was then that a thought that must have been growing for some time in his subconscious finally surfaced.

I've got to get out of this, a part of his brain cried out. I can't take this any more.

'That woman you beat up the other day,' Millar said.

'Aye. Hanlon.'

'She didn't listen.'

'Yes...?'

'Deal with her,' Millar said sternly. 'If she's with anyone, deal with them too. People are beginning to think they can fuck with me, including you, it would seem. Time some lessons were learnt, Ray.'

'Yes, boss – do you want me to hurt her?'

'No, Ray.' He shook his head, visibly counting to ten. 'I don't want you to hurt Hanlon. I want you to kill her...' he stopped by the door and then turned and looked at them '... and you'd better not fuck up, Ray. I'm a patient man, but no more excuses, OK.'

Ray nodded. 'Consider it done.'

Millar stood up and left the room; not long after they heard the front door slam behind him.

'What are we going to do, Ray?'

Ray looked at Dougie.

'Well, better do as he says.' He looked at the broken coffee table. 'You know something, Dougie?'

'What?'

'I don't think the clonazepam's working.'

25

The following day, Hanlon pulled into Luke's reserved parking space in Dean Village. Wemyss looked at her hopefully from the back seat. 'OK, you can come...' The dog leapt gracefully out of his basket in the rear of the car onto the pavement.

'Come on, then...' She clipped his lead onto his collar and they walked up to the door of Luke's studio. There was a café opposite; she could make out the shapes of two people sitting inside, looking out of the window, who had a perfect view of her and the dog as she rang the bell. Luke buzzed them up and they walked up the stairs to the studio, Wemyss's claws clicking on the granite of the steps.

Luke opened the door. He was wearing a shirt several sizes too big for him and a blue T-shirt and jeans, all spattered in paint. His longish hair was tied up in a rudimentary man-bun. He looked very young.

'Come in... nice dog.'

'Thank you,' she said, 'his name's Wemyss'

'Like the castle?'

'It's where he was found, he's a rescue dog.'

Luke smiled and they walked into the small hall. 'So the dog's OK?' Hanlon suddenly thought of wet paint. 'I should have asked.'

'Sure.' Luke scratched Wemyss gently on the head. 'But not in the studio – I don't want dog hairs sticking to my canvases... Do you mind leaving him here a moment while we go through? I'm just in the middle of something.'

'No, not at all. Sit, boy, stay.'

The dog sat, then lay down on a rug by the door to the living room and looked at Hanlon with mournful eyes as she disappeared with Luke into his studio. He closed the door behind them.

She looked around the large, high-ceilinged room. Outside it was completely dark, lights were on in the houses on the other side of the river. It was as she remembered: the long trestle table, the paints, the general mess and clutter you find in a studio.

'How can I help?' he said.

'Who was Aurora's dealer? Do you know?' she asked.

Luke was standing with his back to her, adding some detail to a picture of Arthur's Seat. It sounded an unpromising choice of subject, dull, the kind of tourist kitsch that you could see in shops on the Royal Mile, but in Luke's hands the iconic hill was a brooding, powerful menace under an elemental, pagan sky. It somehow sent a shiver down her spine. Although his back was to her she could see his face reflected in a mirror opposite; it was totally absorbed in what he was doing.

'Her dealer?' he asked, surprised. 'Aurora hasn't been using for months.'

'Yeah, so people keep telling me.' Despite that, she couldn't get Wyre's point out of her mind, that Aurora might have had a huge drug debt to pay. Even if drug dealers weren't looking to kill her they might be wanting to give her a good beating to force Aurora to pay up. Was she hiding from that?

If that were the case, that was something she could help Aurora with. Cameron wouldn't be able to scare off a dealer, but she could. She knew which buttons to press, what threats would work, and she was more than capable of inflicting a beating herself if need be. In fact, it was the kind of job she would relish.

'I met her at the tail-end of her addiction,' Luke said, his eyes not leaving the painting. 'She was really fucked up...' He turned round and looked at Hanlon as though evaluating her. 'I'll show you something. I've never shown these to anyone before – they're private.' He put his brush down, 'it's why I wanted you to come over, I think they'll help you understand her better.'

He walked over to a tall cupboard in the corner, the kind of thing you might find in an old-fashioned primary school to store books and materials. Like everything else in the studio, it was paint-splattered. He opened it. On the floor of the cupboard, several unframed canvases were stacked upright. Luke took out a couple at the back and put them down on the big trestle table.

'Come and have a look.'

She did so. If she had thought that the Arthur's Seat picture was good, then, Jesus, these took her breath away.

They were shockingly, gut-wrenchingly brilliant. Aurora slumped across a table, glassy eyed, clutching a goblet half full of red wine. In her mouth was a half-smoked joint that had gone out; you could see a light frosting of coke on her nostrils. There was a clock on the wall that read two-thirty. Her eyes were dead, devoid of any expression or light.

There was no hope, no life, no joy, no animation, just a dull, mechanical, slave-like addiction.

In the other, Aurora had passed out in the corner of what was recognisably this studio. She was wearing a short strappy dress that had ridden up so you could see her pants. You could also see that she had wet herself. Her long blonde hair was matted. Hanlon got the impression that she had thrown up and her hair was slick with vomit.

'This was her, what, a year and a half ago maybe. We'd started going out, she was new in recovery, and then something happened, she relapsed.' He sighed. 'She never told me what it was about and I never asked, must have been painful though... Anyway, after that, she put the past behind her. She's been clean ever since.'

Her eyes went from these to the Aurora on the wall, the pictures which had previously been on easels. She was beautiful, intelligent but with a challenging, guarded expression in her lovely eyes, saying, 'You don't really know me. You can never know me.'

But Luke did. It was a chilling talent. Hanlon wondered what he would make of her, should she accede to his request to paint her. Part of her felt she would be afraid to find out. She looked at Luke; those eyes were so young, but they saw so much. His talent was frightening, almost freakish. It wasn't surprising that Hamish Cameron wanted to add him to his roster of artists.

Luke waved a hand at the paintings on the table. 'Aurora's past.'

'They're very moving, Luke—' she pressed the point '—but who was her dealer?'

'A guy called Jordan.'

'Jordan, any surname?'

Luke shook his head. 'I don't know. I asked the Muirhouse boys when I was doing some pictures of them. I had some crazy idea of confronting him...'

Hanlon hid a grin at the idea of this nice, middle-class kid confronting an Edinburgh gangster. Jordan would hardly be shaking in his boots.

'They laughed, they said he was big-time, he works for some Glaswegian psycho called Millar, seemingly.'

Millar, thought Hanlon. I know that name. She remembered what Campbell had told her.

Everyone's scared of Millar. He's an evil bastard. We found a body in the Clyde last year, an informant. His tongue had been cut out. Millar let it be known that he'd done it himself. The guy's crazy, but unfortunately far from stupid.

She doubted Aurora would run from Wyre or Griffiths, but Millar, now that made sense. Now we're getting somewhere.

Luke's voice jolted her back into the present. 'Anyway, I had nothing to do with her getting better – she'd just had enough. She said she wants those two pictures framed, just to remind her of the bad old days. I wonder where she'd put them. Over the fireplace, do you think? In her bedroom? Something to show the kids.'

There was a note of finality in his voice; he'd moved on.

'And what happened between you?' Hanlon asked.

Luke stepped back from his picture, evaluating it. 'When she got clean she wanted her own space. We grew apart. We're still good friends. But art comes first, Hanlon. Artists are like that – you've got a relationship with the muse, everything else is secondary.'

'Even Aurora?' she asked.

'Even Aurora,' he said firmly.

The intercom buzzed and Luke went over to it.

'Police,' said the disembodied voice.

He looked at Hanlon questioningly. She shrugged.

'Better let them in, then,' Luke said.

26

Campbell sat at his desk staring into space, thinking of Hanlon. Her face was strong rather than beautiful; she had full lips and very straight eyebrows. And those cold, cold grey eyes. But it was that strength of personality that made her so compelling.

Compelling, that was the word.

'Sir?'

He focussed on the reality of the here and now, told himself to stop daydreaming and glanced across the office.

It was Patterson, looking up from his screen. 'Edinburgh has just been in touch. There's been a guy called Frank Leitch admitted to the casualty at the Royal Infirmary, broken jaw, broken nose, shattered cheekbones, fractured skull, and, more interestingly, he's now missing a thumb and a forefinger on his right hand. He's quite a big dealer, refusing to talk. Do we know of anyone from Glasgow who might be responsible?'

Campbell immediately said, 'If it's any one of our villains it sounds very much like Millar.'

'That's what I thought, sir,' Patterson said.

Campbell asked him, 'Do you remember Penisgate?'

That was an incident from a couple of years previously featuring Millar, who had inflicted some punishment on a rival drug dealer, Hugh McFarlane. They had been tipped off that it was him but hadn't had enough evidence to prosecute, including, of course, McFarlane's denial that Millar had even been involved.

'No, sir, I've heard of it – kitchen scissors?'

'Aye. They managed to reconnect it though…' Both men winced.

'Did it work, afterwards? Could he…?'

'I'm not au fait with Shuggie McFarlane's sex life, Sergeant. But if anyone's getting bits cut off them in Edinburgh, my money would be on Millar.'

He remembered now: McFarlane, when he was interviewed, had said it was a sex game that had gone too far. Nobody wanted to testify against Millar. People were so frightened of him that even after genital mutilation they wouldn't talk. He called over to Patterson.

'Did they say what kind of an explanation Leitch gave?'

'Gardening accident, sir.'

I'll bet it was Millar.

'Call Edinburgh for me, Sergeant. I think you'd better set up a meeting. If Millar's moving in, they should be briefed on what they might be encountering.'

'Right away, sir. Shall I put together an information pack?'

'Yes, do, someone's going to want a hard copy. The older generation. Include photos and notes on Ray Downie and Dougie MacCrossan – they're his two lieutenants. Oh, and there's someone called Chris Harvey, Falkirk Chris, he works for Millar out on the east coast. They'll probably know him, but include him anyway.'

'Yes, sir.'

'And don't forget Jordan McKenna, the guy they found in Edinburgh – he was one of Millar's associates – and mention Drew Lennox while you're at it.'

'Will do, sir.'

Ray Downie. Millar's right-hand man. Campbell put in Ray's name on his PC to remind him and stared at his mugshot. He was a very good-looking man, thought Campbell. He didn't look like his record would suggest. He idly scanned his police history. Ray, in trouble from the word go, from the age of sixteen. Mainly convictions for GBH and affray, a seven-year stretch for armed robbery. Nothing for the past five years. A violent, capable man.

Ray's dad had been a criminal too – Gordon Downie, dead now. Before his time. Campbell seemed to recall he'd left his wife for another man; 'Gay Gordon', he'd been known as afterwards. Ancient history, old even when he'd joined up.

If Millar was in Edinburgh, cutting pieces off people, Ray would be there, that was for sure. Wherever Millar was, he wasn't far behind.

He felt a twinge of worry for Hanlon. Given her almost magnetic attraction for trouble, he couldn't help wondering if she and Millar might somehow meet. Then he suppressed it. She'll be fine, he told himself. It wasn't as if her path and Millar's were likely to interconnect, not over an art dealer's missing daughter. Millar was presumably in Edinburgh because of drugs, not over some girl in her twenties.

Edinburgh. Only an hour's drive down the M8. Campbell had been to see Jamie McDonald's probation officer in connection with the murder of Drew Lennox. It had been a long shot, that Calla Lennox's brother, Drew's brother-in-law, might have somehow played a part in his death, but it had been worth checking out. It had brought one surprise. McDonald wasn't staying where he'd said he would be. The address in Port Glasgow belonged to an aunt. She'd said that Jamie had just popped out to the shops; Campbell wasn't fooled.

This was a serious breach of his release conditions. He began to wonder if maybe McDonald was hiding from someone, i.e. Millar.

He'd rung around informants. Eventually one of them had given him an address in Musselburgh. He was beginning to get interested in McDonald.

Campbell looked at the clock. He was nearly finished for the day anyway; he felt like a drive. He stood up and put his coat on.

'I'm off for the rest of the day now, chasing a lead on the Lennox killing,' he said to Patterson. 'Call me if you need me.'

27

Hanlon took a last look at the pictures of Aurora. Even in the state she was in, she was still beautiful, but these pictures, unlike the ones of her on Luke's wall, or hanging in her father's study, were private, personal, not for public consumption. She picked up the paintings, put them back inside the cupboard and closed the door. She heard Wemyss give a bark as Luke let the police in. Glancing at herself in the mirror that hung on the studio wall, she grimaced at her reflection. With her black eye, she looked nearly as bad as Aurora after a night out.

* * *

Luke opened the front door and ushered the policemen in. He looked at them with a painterly eye. They were unlikely-looking police to his way of thinking, but then again, he reflected, he hadn't met many. Perhaps this was how things were nowadays.

The one who was obviously in charge was good-looking in a silver fox kind of way. He had grey hair that was cut close to the scalp. He was powerfully built and wearing good quality jeans with a really fly pair of trainers. Silver fox was also wearing some kind of expensive cologne and his shapely eyebrows were dark. Luke reflected that you knew male grooming had become a thing when the police started using male beauty products like scent and eyebrow pencil.

His colleague could have done with taking a tip from him. His eyes were badly bruised – he could have done with some foundation to cover that up. He had obviously been roughed up fairly recently in a fight.

Luke looked at them wonderingly, suspiciously. There was something about them that didn't quite ring true to him, but what could he do? The younger one was holding out his warrant card. He was much bigger than the older guy – straw-coloured hair, blue eyes, big-boned. Luke glanced at his ID. It was meaningless to him – who even knew what a warrant card should look like?

The blond guy's phone rang and he glanced at it. Wemyss sniffed him suspiciously.

'Sorry,' Luke said apologetically. 'He's not my dog, he belongs to my friend.'

'Ms Hanlon?' said Silver Fox. He'd given their names, but Luke hadn't been listening.

'Yes, but how did you know?'

Silver Fox smiled reassuringly.

'I'll explain in a minute...'

Luke shrugged. 'Come through. Stay, Wemyss...'

Blond guy said, 'I'll be through in a minute, just got to take this.'

Silver Fox sighed in irritation at his colleague and followed Luke into the studio, closing the door behind him as he did so.

Hanlon was standing with her back to them looking out of the huge picture window over Dean Village. She turned and looked at them. Ever observant, Luke noticed her nose wrinkled slightly as if there were a bad smell in the room and she frowned. Then she smiled at Silver Fox. She looked hard at his trainers. So she's noticed them too, thought Luke, they are pretty cool. It suddenly occurred to Luke that her smile looked slightly strained. She walked over to them, her right hand outstretched as if to shake.

'Oh, hello, you must be...' she started to say, then suddenly—

What the hell?

Luke's mouth fell open; he gaped in shock. He had never seen anyone move quite so quickly. Her fist slammed into the policeman's head and Silver Fox staggered back, then a combination of punches, he could barely follow them they were so fast, stomach, face, side of the head, Hanlon's body twisting as she put the explosive power of her hips into her fists. He had never seen anyone being hit in real life, only on TV or in films, and he was amazed at how brutal it was and the unexpected noise, the sound of fist hitting flesh and the explosive grunts of effort.

What the hell was she doing? What was going on?

It was all over in a couple of seconds. The policeman was totally unprepared and went down. There was a hell of a crash and an ominous thud as his head hit the floor.

What the fuck, Hanlon? he thought to himself, but no sound came out of his mouth. What the actual fuck?

Now Hanlon was down beside the fallen man, her hands frantically going through pockets and as the other cop flung the door open she had a knife in her hand that she must have found in Silver Fox's pockets. She dragged him in front of her; she was crouched on the floor using him like a shield. She pressed a knife to his throat as Blondie pointed the gun in his hand at her.

He's got a gun, thought Luke, increasingly panic-stricken. He's not a policeman – what's going on?

'Drop it or I'll kill him...' she shouted.

'Fuck you!' said Blondie, the gun in his hand unwavering.

Luke stood there silently, motionless, not knowing what to do. He was terrified.

He obviously wasn't the only one. Luke, naturally highly observant despite his terror, noticed that Dougie, staring at the unexpected scene in front of him was looking far from calm. Shit, Luke thought. Shit, shit, shit. Hanlon, crouched on the floor, looking up at Dougie, from behind the shelter of the semi-conscious Ray. This was like a scene from a nightmare, thought Luke.

He stared at the figures motionless as waxworks in front of him,

He had never used a gun; but he had heard that hand-guns were inaccurate. The blond guy might miss her; he might shoot his accomplice by mistake. If he did miss, Hanlon could well cut his throat – God knows she looked capable of it.

For a couple of heartbeats they stood there staring at each other. Stand-off. Now, Hanlon pressed the tip of the knife she'd found in the guy's pocket into the skin under his chin and twisted it. Hard. No pussyfooting around. His eyes fluttered and opened; he craned his head back to try and avoid the blade and Hanlon dug the knife tip in. A very red stream of blood ran out, down the metal and over her fingers. Her eyes didn't leave those of the man with the gun.

Ray was now fully conscious. His head was tilted back as far as he could make it go in an obvious but futile attempt to escape the knife. His eyes bulged with the effort. Luke stared at him, he couldn't tear his eyes away. He didn't speak; he probably didn't want to provoke her. The knife in the flesh under his chin must have been agonisingly painful. Hanlon's left hand was hooked into his hair, pulling his head back.

'Drop the gun, throw it in the corner over there!' She jerked her head in the direction of the far corner. The blond guy didn't move. She pushed the knife upwards; blood was now flowing freely.

'If you don't do it... I'll just keep pushing up until this goes into his brain,' Hanlon snarled.

Jesus, she means it, thought Luke, who was standing stock-still.

'Do it, Dougie,' gasped the guy from between his teeth. It sounded to Luke as if he were auditioning for a ventriloquist act; he obviously didn't want to move his jaw when he spoke.

The other guy's hand didn't waver; he didn't trust her.

Luke noticed the door to the studio open and Hanlon's dog, Wemyss, appeared. He surveyed the room, puzzled and then went over to the blond guy, moving slowly, slightly crouched, his hackles up. Luke glanced over at Hanlon, she must have been aware of Wemyss but equally he guessed she didn't want to take her eyes off the guy with the gun – Dougie, that was his name.

'Wemyss!' called Hanlon, desperately.

Dougie looked down. Hanlon's dog was by his side, growling at him.

'Wemyss!' called Hanlon again. There was no mistaking the urgency in her voice. She wasn't the only one in the room who could think or move fast. Dougie's hand shot out and grabbed the dog's collar.

'Throw me the knife—' he pressed the muzzle of the gun against the collie's head '—or I'll kill the dog!'

Luke saw the anguish in Hanlon's face, then he saw her let go of Ray's hair and she tossed the knife to Dougie. Both she and Ray stood up. Ray walked over to Dougie, the front of his shirt soaked in his blood, Hanlon over to Luke.

Ray picked his knife up with his right hand and found some tissues in his pocket, which he wadded up and pressed to the wound under his jaw. Although the cut was bleeding heavily, it wasn't a serious injury.

'Take the dog next door,' he said to Dougie quietly. No drama, no shouting, just quietly taking charge. He stood there looking at Hanlon. His eyes flickered to the unmoving Luke. No threat there.

'Sure,' Dougie said. He tugged on the dog's collar and he went with him, surprisingly docile.

He led Wemyss into the entrance room. The door closed behind him.

'We just want some information,' said Ray, reassuringly. 'We're not going to hurt you.'

Then, suddenly, unexpectedly, there was the unmistakeable sound of a shot from next door. A single shot. They all heard it. Luke flinched, terrified. Hanlon didn't move. Then a single tear rolled out of the corner of her eye and Luke saw her body sag.

Wemyss was dead.

28

The door opened. They all stared. Dougie appeared. His hands were placed on top of his head; behind him, prodding him forward with a gun, was a big, muscular guy with very dark hair.

A unified reaction. What the hell was going on?

For Ray, this was like something from a nightmare. Him of all people. God alone knew what McDonald was doing here, but here he was, larger than life, and with a gun in Dougie's back. He'd killed Jordan, he'd killed Chris, he wouldn't hesitate to add another couple of Millar employees to the tally. Ray had no more fight in him. He knew when he was beaten. His shoulders slumped and he bent forward, put the knife on the ground and kicked it across the floor into a corner as a sign of surrender.

All he could do was hope for mercy and that maybe McDonald wouldn't want to execute them in front of witnesses.

Wemyss put his head round the door and looked at Hanlon slightly sheepishly.

'Wemyss!' she called out in delight. The dog was alive. He barked and ran over to her. She crouched down and put her arms around him; he wagged his tail furiously.

'Over there, with your friend,' said McDonald to Dougie. He walked over to Ray as instructed.

The man looked at Hanlon and Luke. 'I'm Jamie McDonald,' he said.

'Pleased to meet you,' Hanlon said, 'and who are these two arseholes?' pointing to Ray and Dougie.

'That's Ray,' said McDonald. 'I don't know his name though,' he said, pointing at Dougie. 'You gonna tell us, then, Big Man?'

'Dougal,' said Dougie sulkily. 'Can I put my hands down now?'

'Aye.'

Dougie did so.

'Now, you two,' said McDonald, waving the gun at them, 'can fuck off. You can do something useful.' Ray and Dougie looked at each other in astonished surprise. 'Go back to Glasgow and when you find Millar, tell him he's a cunt. Off you go...' he said.

Ray and Dougie left hurriedly without a backward glance, before McDonald could change his mind. McDonald followed and watched as they exited the apartment and the door closed behind them.

Hanlon glanced over at Luke. Relief was written all over his face. She noticed that he was trembling.

'I don't know about anyone else,' Luke said, shakily, 'but I need a drink.'

* * *

Ray and Dougie walked in silence to the street below. Ray was both grateful to be alive and equally terrified of what Millar was going to do to them. However, there was no way on earth they were going to return and try and rectify the situation.

'How's my chin looking?' he asked as they stood outside in the street in the cold rain of the night, illuminated by the security light.

Dougie stared. 'There's blood all down your throat. Hang on a minute...'

They reached their car and there was a bottle of water in the foot-well of the back seat. Ray tilted his head upwards while Dougie wet his scarf and gently cleaned the blood off.

'That looks fine now, apart from the shirt... at least it's stopped bleeding.'

Ray zipped his black Moschino jacket up.

'That's better, you look presentable. What the fuck are we going to do, Ray?'

Ray leaned forward and kissed him. He didn't want Dougie to know he was equally confused. 'First of all, Dougie, we're going to have a drink at that pub over there.'

They walked over to the bar. The place was empty except for them. While Dougie was at the bar, Ray thought, God, what just happened?

He felt exhausted and sick. Shock, he guessed. Then, to his surprise, an overwhelming sense of relief. At least I haven't had to kill two people, he thought. It was an epiphany of sorts. He remembered looking at the two faces, the woman staring at him with hatred, the boy – he guessed he was some kind of artist, that much was obvious; he couldn't have been more than about twenty – with worry.

He was so beautiful and so young. If McDonald hadn't appeared he would have been forced to put a bullet in their heads. There would have been no choice. Those had been his orders. God knows, he hadn't wanted to, but he had been thinking of Millar. It was either those two or him and Dougie. He would have made it quick. Hopefully it would all have been over before they could work out what was happening.

He'd have shot the woman first, she was the dangerous one.

He exhaled. I'm no killer, he thought. Whatever else I am, I'm not that. What a nightmare.

Fucking Millar.

What are we going to do?

Dougie returned from the bar. They sat in a corner with their drinks and Dougie quietly repeated his question from earlier.

'What are we going to do?'

They both knew the trouble they were in. Millar would kill them. They'd been warned not to fail, they'd had the cost of failure explained to them, and, boy, had they failed! And it was a spectacular failure. They hadn't killed Hanlon and they'd been humiliated by McDonald, of all people, someone else they had previously failed to kill. McDonald hadn't even bothered to kill them. Ray guessed it was because he didn't want to do it in front of witnesses. He thought things would probably have turned out a lot differently if he'd surprised them in a deserted park. They'd be face-down dead now, like Falkirk Chris.

But here they were, alive. Millar would take it as a personal insult. Ray knew how his mind worked – he might even think that they were in league with McDonald.

He saw Dougie looking at him hopefully. Dougie's thought processes transparently clear. Ray was a bright guy. He would know what to do.

He drank his pint of lager in two long swallows. Ray wasn't far behind him and sent him back to get another couple of pints.

When Dougie returned from the bar with the drinks, Ray had formulated a plan. Of sorts.

'Well... do you think it's likely that McDonald or that kid or Hanlon are going to get in touch with Millar?' asked Ray.

'No, of course not,' Dougie said.

'OK, this is what we're going to do,' Ray said decisively, numbering the points he was making on his fingers, 'We're going back to the flat, we're going to pack a bag, we're going to go and stay somewhere out of Edinburgh... somewhere hard to find. We're going to have a nice meal, and we're going to tell Millar that the job is done, that Hanlon's dead, and then we're going to hide somewhere and we're going to hope that McDonald kills Millar.'

'Is that likely?' Dougie said, dubiously. As plans went, it sounded sketchy to say the least.

'Dougie, I haven't got a clue,' Ray said, sighing, 'but McDonald's doing bloody well so far. Jordan, dead, Chris, dead, us... well, he could have killed us, and, the way I see it, he hasn't got much choice. Millar wants him dead. It's kill or be killed. But whether or not he succeeds in killing him, one thing is beyond any reasonable doubt.' He took a drink of lager. 'Millar will kill us. We've really fucked it up, of that there's no doubt.'

'No,' said Dougie with a wry smile, 'no doubt at all.'

29

'So who are you and what the hell are you doing here?' Hanlon asked McDonald. They were sitting in the living room drinking, McDonald beer, she and Luke, wine. She looked him up and down slowly from his head to his feet. Hanlon spent a lot of time in gyms; she could tell McDonald did too. He looked as if he could run through brick walls. His face was brutal but friendly and open, yet there had been no doubt in her mind that he would have been perfectly prepared to have shot Dougie if he'd needed to. Or them, come to that. She had met a lot of violent people; she had met more than a few McDonalds. It also wasn't lost on her that Ray had meekly given up when McDonald had appeared, and Ray was not the kind of guy to just roll over. Whoever McDonald was – he was special.

She added, 'I know your name but what are you doing here and how did you know those two bell-ends?'

He gave her an evaluating look, as if deciding how much he was going to tell her. 'I'm wanted by those two's boss, a guy called Graeme Millar. And what am I doing here? Following them.' He smiled at her. 'Just as well that I did, for your sakes. I didn't think they were paying a social call. I thought I'd fuck up whatever they were up to, mainly to piss Millar off. I'm certainly pissed off with him – he's trying to have me killed.' He looked her up and down in an evaluating way. 'It just so happened it was your lucky day.'

Hanlon looked at him, her eyes narrowed. Really? she thought. Your arrival seemed more than lucky, it was miraculous. Although he had saved them from, she suspected, being killed, she was far from trusting him.

McDonald asked, 'And who might you be?'

'My name's Hanlon. I'm a private investigator. I was hired by a man called Hamish Cameron to find his daughter, Aurora – she's disappeared.'

'I see.' He looked at Luke. 'And you?'

'This is his place,' Hanlon said.

Luke nodded. 'I'm Luke Bastien. I'm an artist. I'm a friend of Aurora's.'

McDonald drank some more of Luke's Japanese lager; he seemed perfectly relaxed for a man with Millar's bounty on his head.

'Right, well, now we all know each other, what happened out there?' Hanlon asked, gesturing to the door. She was still suspicious of their rescuer. His arrival seemed maybe overly fortuitous. 'How did you get in?' she asked.

McDonald shrugged. 'I used to do it professionally, good job I've still got the knack. I got in while you were all in that studio, took numb nuts' gun away from him – that's when it went off.' He stood up and walked over to the wall near the door, where he pointed to a mark she hadn't noticed on the painted surface.

'Bullet will be in there.'

Hanlon took another sip of wine. On the face of things she was just being paranoid, but then she had been beaten up once and the same men had returned and threatened her with a gun. And then by chance they were rescued. She felt she was maybe justified in feeling a tad suspicious. Maybe he broke in, maybe not. The past few days, she felt, things were not what they seemed.

'I wonder how those two men knew you were here?' Luke said to her.

'That's a very good question,' Hanlon acknowledged.

'They weren't following you, that's for sure,' said McDonald to Hanlon. 'I followed them here. They've got a flat in Edinburgh. I've been watching it. They knew you were here from the moment they left.'

'No one knew I was coming,' she said.

McDonald looked at Hanlon. 'Really?' he said. 'They did. So either they're psychic or someone tipped them off...'

'No one could have tipped them off,' she said.

'Well, then,' McDonald suggested, 'let's go and have a look at your car.'

The two of them stood up. 'I'll come too,' said Luke, quickly, eagerly. Hanlon looked at him in surprise – why would he want to come?

'I don't want to stay here alone,' he confessed.

'Bring a torch,' Hanlon told him, 'and an old towel.'

The three of them, accompanied by the dog, went outside to Hanlon's car. It was dark and cloudy and starting to drizzle. The car was parked by a street light so there was plenty of illumination.

McDonald stared at the ancient Corsa and a small smile appeared on his face.

'Business must be doing well, Hanlon,' he said.

'It's a classic,' she replied, irritably.

'It's a heap of shit,' he said equably.

She glared at McDonald as Luke handed her the old bath towel and she spread it on the road, lay down on her back under the nearside of the car and ran her hands along the underside of the body.

'Ha!' She shone the torch on something.

'Have you got it?' asked McDonald.

Hanlon wriggled out from under the car, stood up and held out her hand. In it was a plastic case about the size of a mobile phone but deeper. She opened it up and inside was a small black box.

'What is it?' asked Luke.

'GPS tracker,' McDonald said. 'You attach that to the vehicle and can connect it to your phone, easy. Then it will show you exactly where this vehicle is. Works with the maps on your mobile. And they're dirt cheap.'

Luke stared at it wide-eyed. McDonald gave a kind of annoying know-it-all grin as if he wasn't the sort of guy who would have allowed such a thing to happen. Hanlon shook her head with annoyance. She put the tracker down on the cobbles of the street and stamped on it a couple of times and then picked up the shattered device and put it in a waste bin by the side of the road.

'How long have you been driving around like that?' McDonald asked.

'Nearly a week now,' she said. They must have attached it there when they attacked her in the car park, she thought.

She felt sick knowing that Millar had known exactly where she had been for the past few days. Everywhere. He could have had her taken out any time he wanted.

'A week,' said McDonald, shaking his head. 'I'll leave you two now.' He looked at Hanlon. 'You do know that Millar wants you dead?'

'Why?' Hanlon asked. They stood in the drizzle; you could see it in the orange glow of the street lights as it fell around them. Nobody was around on this cold Monday evening.

McDonald shrugged. 'Because of Aurora, I guess.'

It was these words that triggered something in Hanlon; maybe it was the casual use of her name that implied he knew her. McDonald's appearance had been too fortuitous – how had he turned up at just the right time? How had he known which flat they were in?

McDonald turned away. Hanlon put her hand on his shoulder; he spun round, he was obviously irritated at his space being invaded.

'What?' he snapped.

'You know her, don't you?' Hanlon said, menacingly. 'Where is she, Jamie?'

He shook himself free. McDonald looked thoroughly angry now. He pointed a threatening finger at Hanlon.

'Take my advice, Hanlon, fuck off back to wherever you came from and take the kid with you.'

He started to walk away then turned back to her. 'He'll kill you, Hanlon. Final warning.' He pointed an admonitory finger at her and repeated, '... final warning!'

He disappeared into the darkness of the village.

30

Campbell pulled up outside the run-down tenement in the dark side-street in Musselburgh. He got out of his car and walked up to number eight. There was a minimal strip of path between the pavement and the building, enough space for a couple of bins and a scrawny bush. He stood by the large, heavy communal door and looked at the buzzers. He pressed number four and listened at the intercom.

'Who is it?' A woman's voice.

'Police.'

'The door's no locked, come on up.'

He noticed then that the front door was slightly ajar. He pushed it open, walked inside and looked around. The hall lights came on, bathing everything in harsh white neon. Grey stone floor, grey stone stairs zigzagging upwards. Someone's pram at the bottom of the stairs, the two doors of the ground-floor flats. He walked upwards, the sound of his footsteps, greatly magnified, echoing up the stairwell. That smell that tenement staircases have, a mix of concrete, stone, floor cleaner – institutional, like a school or a prison.

He reached the first floor; a door was open and a tall woman with grey hair holding a cigarette stood there.

'And what do you want?' Her voice was unfriendly.

Campbell walked up to her, showed his warrant card and he pointed across the hall at the other flat's door. 'Do you know if he's in?'

'So that's what this is about.' She didn't seem at all surprised. 'No, he's not in, but I saw a woman on the stairs a while ago going inside.'

Campbell frowned. 'How do you know that?' Had she been peering out of the peephole all the while?

'He's supposed to clean up any mess that's not normal wear and tear – well, last Thursday there was some kind of stooshie outside his door, and afterwards there was a pool of blood on the floor... What folk get up to is their own business but I've got a bairn. I don't want her seeing that kind of thing.'

Blood on the floor after an argument. Millar's men and McDonald.

'What time was this?'

'Och, early, seven a.m. Anyways, an hour ago, I saw this girl go in. I heard the key so I went out. "Hey you," I said. She just ran in and slammed the door.'

'So she's still in there?'

'To the best of my knowledge. Timid wee thing.'

Calla, he thought, has to be.

'Well, thank you...' he took out a notebook '... and your name, please?'

'McGillivray, Carole-Anne, both with an 'e'.'

'Thank you for your help.'

She closed the door behind her. Campbell walked across the hall and knocked on the door. No answer.

He knocked again. 'Calla, let me in... it's DI Campbell,' he said.

There was a pause and then he heard the sound of a key being turned and a bolt being pulled back. The door opened and a frightened face peered up at him.

'Let me in, Calla. We've got things we need to talk about.'

'OK.' She sounded as terrified as she looked.

She led him into a small sitting room. Shabby furniture. They sat opposite each other. Calla was wearing jeans and a sweater. She sat on the sofa and drew her knees up in front of her and wrapped her arms around them.

'You remember me, Calla? I spoke to you after your husband...'

'Aye,' she said, 'I remember you well. How can I help you?'

She looked even smaller than he remembered her. Her short dark hair needed washing and was sticking up in places. Her face had a broad mouth that he could imagine was normally in a good-natured smile, but there were bags under her eyes and she wasn't smiling now.

'Your brother?'

She shook her head. 'I don't know anything about Jamie, where he is, what he's up to... Please, DI Campbell, leave me alone.'

'I know you're afraid of Millar.'

At his name she started violently and her eyes widened.

'No...' she said. He guessed she meant she didn't want to hear his name, certainly not discuss him. You don't name the bogeyman. He might come.

'I know Millar killed Drew,' Campbell said. He watched her reaction. Calla's eyes moistened and she shook her head.

He continued, 'Millar's after your brother, that much I know, Calla. We both know that if he finds him, he'll kill him. Now I want to know why.' He held up a hand to forestall her saying anything. 'I want to find Jamie, Calla.'

'I don't know where he is, DI Campbell, I swear to God...'

Her hands were clutching each other and the fingers of her right hand were playing with her wedding ring, twisting it this way and that.

'Jamie's out on licence, Calla. If he breaks the terms of his parole, then he goes back inside, you know that.'

She nodded.

'He'll be back, for another what? Four years or so...' he said.

She was beginning to look alarmed; she could see which way the conversation was headed.

'If Jamie goes back inside, then Millar has got the kind of clout to reach him, I'm sure you know that.'

She nodded again; remorselessly Campbell continued, 'Jamie isn't residing where he told the parole board. He's in breach of his terms.'

'Please, DI Campbell, don't do this...'

'I'm here unofficially – anything you tell me will be off the record. I want to know why Millar wants Jamie dead.'

'Oh, Christ,' Calla said, 'I can't say...'

'One word from me and Jamie goes back to prison.' Campbell twisted the knife ruthlessly. He could see the pain and indecision on Calla's face. He felt sick at what he was doing but he had very little choice.

'OK,' said Calla. She took a deep breath. 'A man called Jordan McKenna, he's from Edinburgh and works—' she paused and corrected herself '—worked, for Millar. Anyway, Millar wanted him to kill someone and Jordan hired Jamie to help him. I don't know who or why, but something happened and he killed Jordan.'

Campbell took a deep breath. 'You're telling me that your brother killed Jordan McKenna.'

She suddenly realised what she'd said. 'No... aye, but in self-defence.' Calla started crying. 'Oh, God, what have I done...?'

Oh my God, thought Campbell. Various options flickered through his consciousness, but first and foremost was the unswerving desire to get Millar.

'He said he'd throw Palmer out of the window...' Calla whispered, half talking to Campbell, half talking to herself.

Campbell nodded. 'I kind of guessed, Calla...' he looked around, 'where is she by the way?'

'At my auntie Pam's in Greenock,' she replied.

Campbell looked her in the eye. 'Look, I'll be frank – to be honest, I am far more interested in Millar than your brother. If I can get him to testify against Millar then I'm sure we can do something about this alleged incident with McKenna.'

'Thank you,' she whispered.

'For now, I'll keep what you said to myself. But I need to meet your brother.'

'I don't know where he is, that's the God's honest truth.'

He nodded. 'I know, Calla, I know.' He took his wallet out and handed her a card. 'This is my personal mobile number. Give it to Jamie. He's got Millar on his back – you're obviously not the only one that knows Jamie did McKenna. Edinburgh CID are looking for him. He'll need someone on his side.'

'Thank you.'

He stood up. 'Well, the sooner he gets the message, the better. He's in deep, deep trouble. Take care, Calla.'

She nodded and he left her there, staring into space.

31

Hanlon was sitting at the wheel with the engine idling when Luke threw open the back door and put a sports bag down on the seat next to Wemyss. He jumped into the front passenger seat.

'OK, I'm ready.' She suppressed a smile. Luke looked at her with absolute confidence, as if she knew exactly what she was doing. Hanlon had decided that she couldn't leave him behind at his flat. Millar might well come looking for him, maybe to find Aurora as she had. Only Millar wouldn't be asking politely. She liked Luke. In some ways he reminded her of Wemyss – they were both quite sweet and they both needed looking after. And they both trusted her implicitly.

'Where are we going?' he asked.

'I'll tell you in a minute.' She drove for a while to put a few streets between them and Luke's house and then pulled over to the side of the road. She got her phone out.

'Hi, Julia? It's me... yeah, look, something's happened, I'm in trouble, could I stay at your place for a couple of nights? Thanks... Oh, Julia, I'm not alone. I've got someone with me... No... not exactly... I'm more of a babysitter really... Great. See you in about ten minutes.'

She put her phone away and Luke looked at her reproachfully.

'Babysitter! Thanks very much.' He sounded disappointed in her, as if she had let him down. Luke was used to success, it had come early in his life, but what had just happened had made him realise how powerless he was outside his own narrow sphere, the world of art and culture – where pain was a nasty review and violence was a cutting word.

'I'm sorry,' Hanlon said. 'It was an unfortunate choice of expression...'

'Never mind,' said Luke, sadly. 'It is kind of true. I felt so helpless back there. I didn't know what to do. I'm sorry.'

'Look, don't be,' Hanlon said. She turned the engine off. She could see how miserable Luke was. He was obviously traumatised by what had happened at his flat. All the worse that it had happened in his home. He had been helpless and terrified and now he felt guilty. 'Look at me, Luke...'

He did so; he looked as if he was going to cry. Hanlon said, 'Luke, those guys are hardened criminals. They're used to violence, intimidation, all that kind of shit. For all I know, they've killed people.'

'I know but—' he objected.

'You're not a Hollywood action hero, you're not the Rock or Tom Cruise, Luke, and this isn't a film, this is real life. And if you were some violent nut job, like McDonald say, Aurora wouldn't have been going out with you in the first place.'

He sighed. 'I know, I just felt, well, inadequate.'

'Well, don't,' Hanlon said firmly. She started the car and drove off. 'Just thank God that we're still alive. Their job is hurting people and they've got a certain amount of expertise in it, and you haven't. Don't beat yourself up over it. Face it, they'd be equally clueless if you gave them some oil paints and told them to do you a portrait.'

Luke fell silent. As she drove through the dark streets of Edinburgh she was aware of him looking at her. She was concerned that he was replaying the scene again in his mind's eye – her driving her fists into Ray's head, the defiance in her face as she stared down Dougie, the knife at Ray's throat.

'I hear what you're saying,' he said, sounding unconvinced, 'but...' She could almost hear the self-reproach, the self-contempt in his voice as he carried on.

'It's just... what could I have done against them if you hadn't been there?' He fell silent, then, 'Begged them not to hurt me? Offered to do a quick sketch if they'd leave? Cried?'

'That's enough, Luke,' Hanlon said, firmly. 'It's my job to deal with people like them, it's kind of what I'm paid for.'

He nodded, then asked, 'Where did you learn to fight like that?'

She smiled grimly. 'Mainly in a boxing ring, there's quite a skill to hitting people, Luke. You can be taught it.'

'If I'd hit Ray, he would have laughed,' Luke said.

'Well, like I said, practice helps.'

'Would you have shoved that knife up into his head?' wondered Luke.

Hanlon considered the question. 'Well... Luke, the thing is, like I said, I learnt to fight in a ring, but...' Oh well, I may as well be honest, she thought. 'I quite like hurting people, I like violence.' Her voice was very soft as she glanced at him and their eyes met. 'So, yes, yes I would.'

* * *

They pulled up outside a sizeable family house in a leafy, quiet road in Morningside. It was fairly central, affluent. They were in wealthy middle-class land, solicitors, accountants, directors of small firms – it was where the comfortably off and respectable lived.

They walked up a path to a large blue-painted front door and Hanlon rang the bell.

Julia answered. She stood, haloed in the light from the hall, wearing jeans and a T-shirt under an unbuttoned blue Paisley shirt. Her red-brown hair was tied back, her large eyes round with delight.

'Hi, do come in...' She leaned forward, showed Wemyss her hand, let him sniff her and scratched him behind the ears. Wemyss panted enthusiastically.

'What a lovely dog.'

'He is.' Hanlon said proudly. Even if he'd nearly got her killed.

She ushered them through a spacious black-and-white-floor-tiled hall. An old-fashioned bike with a basket was propped against the wall. She led them into the lounge. The living room was large, well-proportioned with a high ceiling and old-fashioned moulded cornices. Hanlon noticed Luke studying the art on the wall with interest: some well-executed impressionist-style views of Edinburgh and some hills, maybe the Lammermuirs.

There were some framed posters for various plays and events and a few photographs. It was low-key assured taste, original and eclectic.

'Can I get you a drink?'

'Have you got a red wine?' Luke asked. 'A large one.'

'Tea, please,' said Hanlon.

'Come and help me in the kitchen,' Julia said to Hanlon. 'You can choose your tea.'

They went through into Julia's large kitchen/dining room. There was a huge scrubbed pine table and ten chairs around it; the room was heated by a large modern Aga cooker. It was a warm, friendly place; a casserole (in a Le Creuset, of course) ticked gently away on the corner of the flat-top stove. It was like stepping into an advert from a quality Sunday newspaper magazine, *The Observer* – she did work in a university, it would have to be *The Observer* – selling the good life. Hanlon watched Julia as she filled the kettle and switched it on. If it was a cliché it was a very comforting one.

'What happened?' Julia asked with concern.

Hanlon gave Julia a brief summary of what had happened at Luke's. Julia opened a bottle of wine and poured a large glass and said, 'I'll just go and give it to… what was his name again?'

'Luke, he's Aurora's ex.'

'Very nice too,' Julia said. She disappeared momentarily.

'So someone's after you?' she said when she reappeared.

'I certainly know that much,' Hanlon said, with feeling.

'Well, look, you can stay as long as you want, OK,' Julia reassured her.

'It'll just be a few days,' Hanlon said. 'I think things with Aurora are coming to a head.'

'Well,' said Julia, 'that'll be just fine.'

She filled a pan with water and put it on the centre of the stove where the heat was fiercest. Hanlon watched with interest. She didn't know how to cook well – she hardly knew how to cook at all; she was getting a bit fed up of her own monotonous meals. But could she be bothered to learn? No, was the answer to that. She suddenly thought of the rabbits in the fridge back in her cottage. How long would they keep? Were they going off? Well, that was how she was at keeping a house together: terrible.

'What tea do you want?' Julia asked.

'Darjeeling, if you have it.'

'Good choice, I think I'll join you.' Julia made the tea and put a bowl of water down for Wemyss, who lapped at it enthusiastically.

'Is there a shop round here? I need to get him some food,' Hanlon said.

'Don't worry.' Julia smiled. 'There'll be boeuf bourguignon left. He'll eat that, I'm sure.'

'I'm sure he will, thanks.'

'So what's it all about?' Julia asked. 'All this drama?'

Hanlon sat down at the table. Her legs suddenly felt a bit shaky – shock, she guessed. 'Money. I think behind all this there's a gangster, Millar, who wants to sell drugs in the uni, and I think Aurora used to be one of his major dealers, probably running a network of sub-dealers.'

'Really? Aurora?' Julia looked highly unconvinced. 'Surely not!'

'I could be wrong – it's a working hypothesis,' Hanlon said, omitting the original source of the idea, Reiss. 'And either because she's stopped using, and so stopped working for him and has become a loose end, a loose end that needs tidying up, or maybe because Morag knew and put it into her novel, like she seems to have done everything else, and Millar's afraid of it becoming public knowledge... for whatever reason, she's fallen foul of Millar and so have I.' Hanlon sipped her tea. 'You've read Morag's book – can you remember if there was anything about organised crime in it?'

'Well, I sort of read it. I didn't want to,' Julia said with an apologetic look. 'I just kind of flicked through it really.'

The water was boiling in the pan on the stove now, she added green beans to it.

'Was there much about drugs?' Hanlon asked.

Julia blew her cheeks out. 'I don't recall. Like I said, I didn't want to read it. It was only because she pressured me into it... There could well have been. I got a mention, that much I know.' She laughed. 'I was like a frumpy, little oppressed mouse.'

'You!' Hanlon said, amused and outraged at the same time. This tall, elegant woman reduced to some ludicrous caricature.

'Yes,' laughed Julia. 'It made me furious at the time, me, an old, unattractive, prudish doormat.' She spoke light-heartedly but Hanlon could sense a feeling of hurt behind it. Morag did have a knack of making enemies.

Once again it made her question the veracity of Morag's statements. So many untruths – truth seemed to be whatever Morag wanted it to be.

Julia pointed to the pan where the beans were cooking. Julia said, 'Go and get Luke in. These vegetables won't take long. just another minute, the cabbage and the mash are in the oven keeping warm, I take it you haven't eaten?'

Hanlon shook her head. 'No, it's very good of you to go to all this trouble.'

'It's no trouble. I batch cook and freeze for when a son turns up, so you've got boeuf bourguignon and spiced red cabbage, haricots verts – the only thing I did was make mash.'

'It's much appreciated.'

'Sleeping arrangements,' Julia said briskly. 'I've got two spare rooms. You can have the nice one with the en-suite, Luke can have the one I use as a junk room.'

'That's great, he won't mind.'

Julia smiled. 'I didn't think he would.'

***

After dinner Luke went upstairs for a shower and Julia poured herself a glass of wine and propped herself up on the sofa, looking at Hanlon.

Now Luke had gone the two women went back to discussing the case. It was almost like 'not in front of the children'.

'So, you think that Aurora was dealing,' said Julia.

'Not necessarily. As I said, it's a hypothesis. I also think there is the possibility that either Wyre or Griffiths were involved too.'

Julia snorted disbelievingly. 'And the evidence for this is, what? More testament from Morag?'

'Not just that. Someone must have told Millar that I was looking into Aurora's disappearance – he'd never have known otherwise. That's when the trouble started, and Wyre has criminal connections. And I'm obviously getting somewhere. The first time that guy, Ray, was told to scare me off.

The second time, to kill me. Then there's Griffiths – you think he's great, Peter Reiss wasn't so sure.'

She had the feeling that Reiss had implied Griffiths rather got off on helping others, but maybe she had misjudged what he'd said.

'Do you think Aurora's OK? I mean, do you think she's still alive?' Julia asked.

'I do – if nothing else, her body would probably have turned up. Millar and his men are violent but they're not criminal masterminds. And they seem quite incompetent, thank God, otherwise I wouldn't be here. Neither would McDonald, come to that.'

'So what's the plan?' Julia asked.

Hanlon yawned. 'Sorry, it's been a long day. I think I'll go and see Reiss tomorrow, ask a few more questions about Griffiths, see what Reiss's reservations were.'

'And you're not going to the police?' asked Julia.

'No, I'll handle it myself.' They'll just tell me to go home, she thought angrily. Like Campbell, like Jamie McDonald. And nobody will be looking to find and help Aurora. Sod them.

'Are you sure that's wise?' Julia asked.

'Maybe not, but it's what I'm going to do,' Hanlon said firmly.

Julia shrugged, and shook her head doubtfully.

Wemyss nudged Hanlon. 'I'll just walk Wemyss for a bit. I think he may need a toilet break.'

Julia let her out of the house and she walked Wemyss around the block, the safe, slightly smug streets of Morningside with their Audis and Yummy Mummy 4 x 4s, most of them with 'Baby on Board' stickers in the back. Her own car looked desperately out of place. Good, she thought, so was she. She undid the boot and took out a small sports bag in which she kept emergency travel supplies: a change of T-shirt and underwear, toothbrush and emergency pre-paid debit card.

Luke was finished upstairs. She found her room and showered and changed out of her clothes into a pair of shorts she had in her sports bag, the tee, and borrowed a dressing gown from Julia. She curled up with her dog on the sofa and the three of them talked some more.

It was a pleasantly relaxed evening. Julia had a wood-burning stove, which threw out quite a lot of heat and a pleasing glow. The lights were dim. Hanlon felt warm and safe for the first time in a while. It was cosy; she hadn't lived anywhere that could have been remotely described as that for what seemed like forever. Her cottage was cold and draughty. Christmas had been amusingly bleak. She'd always hated Christmas.

She suddenly thought as she lay on Julia's sofa, safe and warm, that this was the first time in months she had been able to relax with people that she liked. And in her ear, the spectral presence of Dr Morgan whispered, 'And whose fault is that? Who refuses to let anyone near them? Who runs away whenever someone gets close to you?'

Julia was tidying the kitchen. Luke had a sketch pad that he was playing with and he showed her a couple of drawings he had done of Wemyss. Hanlon thought they were startlingly good; he had exactly captured Wemyss's roguish charm and intelligence. She said nothing but raised an eyebrow enquiringly. Luke shrugged. 'I draw what there is – it's what I do. That's the essence of your dog. I don't use my imagination. I never need to. That's him. I didn't add anything.'

'Can I see the ones you've done of Julia?' she asked. He'd been looking at her and sketching.

He shook his head. 'No, it's not very good. It's come out a bit weird.' He laughed. 'I've got a high strike rate – I'm pleased with the dog, but I'm only human, not everything's a success.'

It got to ten o'clock. Wemyss was stretched out on a rug in front of the stove asleep and snoring gently.

'I'm going to bed,' Julia said. 'I'll be leaving about half seven tomorrow morning. Here's a key.' She handed Hanlon a fob with a Yale and a Chubb. 'Just leave the alarm, don't bother with it.'

'When's your lunch?' Hanlon asked. 'I'll buy.'

Julia smiled. 'Thanks, one o'clock tomorrow afternoon. I'll see you then.' She stood up, tall and elegant. 'Goodnight.' She left the room and closed the door softly behind her.

Hanlon checked her phone, nothing of interest, then, a sudden idea. 'Was Morag a friend of yours on Facebook?' she asked.

Luke nodded. 'Why?'

'Could you find her on your phone? I'd like to see her last posts.'

Luke nodded and came and sat beside Hanlon on the sofa. He was wearing a worn faded blue denim shirt that would have looked awful on an older man, but which somehow suited his youthful body. The proximity to an attractive man must have triggered something deep in her. She suddenly thought, and it was a thought that took her by surprise, I miss Murdo Campbell. She wished it were him sitting next to her.

She cleared her throat, collected her thoughts. 'Let's have a look.'

There was Morag, a selfie taken just before she died – Morag was a keen selfie taker, judging by her timeline. Surprise, surprise. This one was outside the Gallery of Modern Art. Its grassy lawns ran away into the distance. In the background there was the scaffolding framework with the huge neon sign that read, 'THERE WILL BE NO MIRACLES HERE'.

Various posts from friends on her timeline; one of them, captioned 'rorschachstudios', posted by BJ, was of a tattooed arm, a girl's arm. She heard Luke catch his breath.

'Oh my God!' he whispered.

'What?' said Hanlon.

'That's Aurora!' said Luke excitedly.

'What? Are you sure?' She looked at the date, it was the day of Morag's death. Thirteen likes, no comments. She looked questioningly at Luke.

'That arm, that's Aurora… Look at the tattoos. I know all of them… that rose, that geometric shape, that rabbit, but this – this is new.'

'What, since her disappearance?'

Luke nodded excitedly. 'Look, Hanlon, I know every inch of that girl's body, and if anyone's going to remember artwork I can assure you it's me.'

He enlarged the image. They stared at the tattoo. It was four small fish, colourful, lithe; you could feel the movement in them as they almost swam up her arm.

'God, it's good,' breathed Luke. 'It's like they're alive.'

As is Aurora, alive, Hanlon thought, alive and very much functioning if she's having artwork done – that's not the action of a girl that's given up on life. She had obviously never met Aurora, but she felt as if a weight had been lifted from her.

'What is Rorschach Studios?' she asked.

Luke had put his phone down and hunted on his iPad.

'Nothing,' he said. 'At least, nothing tattoo-wise. It's obviously some sort of fake name or avatar for someone or something.'

'Where might she have had it done?' she asked.

Luke shook his head. 'Not necessarily where – she didn't patronise a shop. The question is, who by? If you find the artist, you'll probably find her. Or at least they might have some idea of where to find her. It's quite a tight-knit community. They tend to know each other, the ones who are serious like she is, about ink art.'

Hanlon nodded. She stared at the flickering flame of the stove. She suddenly felt exhausted; the events of the day had hit her like a freight train.

She stood up. 'I'm off to bed now. I'll see you in the morning.'

'What are you doing tomorrow?' he asked. He was looking at her eagerly. She was reminded of her dog. My God, I've got two of them to look after now, she thought. Her earlier thoughts about Luke being as needy as the collie looked like they may be unfortunately accurate. He even had slightly soulful eyes that reminded her of Wemyss. And like Wemyss she felt protective of Luke; she wasn't going to leave him to the mercies of Millar.

'I'm going to find Aurora,' she said. 'Goodnight, Luke.'

32

The following day Hanlon was back in the Grassmarket, the castle looming over the open space, grey and monolithic in the cold drizzle. Luke couldn't go home, not with Millar after them – it was far too dangerous. She'd driven him to go and look at some artists' studios that were for rent in Leith. He'd taken one and then they'd returned to his place to collect paints, easels, brushes, as much stuff as they could fit in her car. At least he'd have somewhere to work while he hunted for a new place to live.

'How long do you think this is going to take?' he'd asked as they drove back to Leith. It was a question to which she didn't really have an answer. As long as Millar is around, she thought. It wasn't a conclusion she wanted to share with Luke.

'Not long,' Hanlon said. 'It should be over soon.' One way or another, she thought, but didn't say.

'Shouldn't we go to the police?' asked Luke, echoing Julia's question from the night before.

'They can't protect us from Millar,' she said. 'We're going to have to handle this ourselves.'

She parked outside the studio.

'How are we going to do that?' he asked.

'I'll think of something,' she promised. Luke looked at her in a trusting way that she found both touching and slightly irritating. Once again it reminded her of Wemyss. They both had implicit faith in her, which was a burden she could well do without.

* * *

Now she was in the pub where she'd been four days previously. She drank a coffee and waited for Mhairi Ferguson.

At quarter past twelve she arrived. She was wearing a trouser suit and a slightly hard-faced expression. There were silver rings on all of her fingers and her thumbs too. The tattoos that were visible, at the top of her sternum where her blouse was unbuttoned, on her wrists, neck, left hand and a couple on her fingers, glowed in the sunlight – for once it wasn't raining.

Hanlon got her a coffee and they sat looking at each other.

'How are you?' asked Hanlon.

'Overworked,' Mhairi said. 'I've been debugging a program I've written. It's taking forever.'

'Oh,' said Hanlon politely. She hadn't got a clue what Mhairi was on about – computers were a mystery to her.

'Luckily, I like puzzles... So, how can I help you?' Mhairi asked. She waved a ringed hand questioningly. 'Come on, it must be important to text me so early.'

Mhairi was certainly larger than life, Hanlon decided. Heads had turned in the pub when Mhairi strode in, and that was how she moved. A stride, not a walk. Her whole personality was a very 'look at me' performance, from her clothes, to her make-up, to her tattoos, to her gait. She was attractive in a slightly in-your-face way, Hanlon thought, and she certainly didn't lack self-confidence. She also had a great figure and dressed accordingly. As half the pub had noticed, judging by the surreptitious looks from the customers. She smiled.

'It is important. I wanted to ask you about tattoos.'

'Did you?' Mhairi grinned. 'It is important, then – you came to the right place, hen.'

Hanlon took her phone out and showed Mhairi the screenshotted picture of Aurora's arm.

'Good taste,' Mhairi said approvingly. 'Very good taste, actually! What are we looking at?'

'The arm belongs to the girl I'm looking for,' Hanlon said. She indicated the tattoo that Aurora had had done recently. 'This was done a few days ago. I wondered if you had any ideas where she might have had it done.'

They fell silent as she looked at the tattoo. The fish swimming up Aurora's arm.

'They're Koi,' Mhairi said. 'They're Japanese. You see how the tattoo looks almost like a water colour, how delicately it's been done? It's fucking superb.'

'So are we looking for a Japanese tattoo artist?' asked Hanlon.

Mhairi looked at her with scorn. 'No, we are not looking for a Japanese tattoo artist at all. We're looking for a Korean tattoo artist.'

'Korean?'

Mhairi pushed her two-toned blue-black hair away from her head and tilted it to one side so Hanlon could see her ear; it was a surprisingly intimate gesture.

'Look at that,' she said. Hanlon's eyes widened. On the earlobe two flowers had been inked. They were red, with a yellow centre; they looked like the blooms on an ornamental quince. The colours were vivid. Then, running up the side of Mhairi's ear was an incredibly delicate tracery of foliage. It was stunningly beautiful. Hanlon wanted to touch the design, to feel it with her fingertips; she knew it was stupid, it wouldn't be raised, but she wanted to actually experience it in a tactile way.

'I got this done in Seoul,' Mhairi said. 'It's typical Korean work.' She put her hair back. 'You're privileged. I only let women I like see my ear-work. It's private.' She smiled complicitly at Hanlon. 'Anyway, Korean tattoo work, as you may have gathered by now, is characterised by its intricacy. It's very distinct, usually very dainty, lots of designs from nature... It's actually illegal to be a tattoo artist in Korea, you know.'

'Really?' Hanlon said.

'Really,' Mhairi said, 'and it's quite controversial. I'm assuming it's like Japan where they think it's like yakuza, like organised crime. Seemingly they won't let you into a bathhouse if you're tattooed. And I also heard that, in Korea, if you've got a big tattoo you can't do your military service, and that's a crime.'

Hanlon waited, a polite look on her face. She actually had zero interest in Korea or their customs, but she didn't want to antagonise the girl opposite.

Mhairi drank some of her coffee. 'Anyway, there just so happens to be a Korean artist who's opened a pop-up parlour here in Edinburgh.' She looked at Hanlon. 'And that's where your girl will have got her work done.'

'Rorschach studios?' Hanlon hazarded a guess.

Mhairi smiled. 'If you have to ask, you'll never know. It's that kind of place.'

'Where exactly?' Hanlon asked.

Mhairi smiled and shook her head. 'I'll take you after work,' she said. 'It's only for those in the know – I wasn't joking. He hasn't got a work permit. They won't let you in if I'm not with you. They'd assume you were Border Force or HMRC or police or something, out to deport him.'

'That's really good of you,' Hanlon said.

Mhairi stood up. 'I'll meet you here at six.'

She left the pub and Hanlon saw her cross the road back to her office. She didn't wait for a break in the traffic, she just strode confidently out, halting the cars with the palm of her hand. Hanlon smiled and shook her head. She wondered what her evening with Mhairi would be like – well, it wouldn't be conventional, that was for sure.

Hanlon called Reiss, the student counsellor, who said he had a drop-in clinic that afternoon and if she turned up he'd see her.

One of the things she was learning to appreciate about the centre of Edinburgh was just how walkable everything was. She had left Wemyss with Luke, who had agreed to take him out, and so she felt remarkably free with this unexpected dog care. From the pub to the student help centre only took her a ten-minute walk.

Reiss was having a quiet day. There was only one student waiting, some kid with a heroin problem, judging by the junkie-style head-nodding and three-quarters-closed hooded eyes.

Inside his cramped, untidy office, Reiss confirmed this.

'Yeah, Olly out there, he says he hasn't got a problem... says he's clean.

How often have I heard that?' He rolled his eyes. 'Just look at him.' He shook his head and mimicked someone out of their head on heroin. 'Clean he most definitely is not. Anyway, how can I help?'

'It's Griffiths again,' she said.

'What about him?'

'You said that he likes to attend twelve-step meetings. I thought it was only addicts who came?'

'It depends on the meeting,' Reiss explained. 'Some are open to non-addicts so, for example, addicts can be brought, maybe dragged in, by family or friends. That's why Griffiths often comes. Olly, for example, who's out there, is one of his students. Griffiths brought him into the meetings and counselling.'

'Doesn't seem to be doing much good,' she said cuttingly, and then immediately regretted it.

'You can lead a horse to water, Hanlon...' Reiss said coldly.

'I'm sorry,' she said. She didn't want to alienate Reiss. It wasn't just because he was helping her; she genuinely liked him.

'It was Griffiths who originally brought Aurora in,' Reiss said. 'I told you that the other day, so there are successes.'

She nodded, thoughtfully. Griffiths did seem a genuinely caring person, but it's not hard to pretend to care. Not if you have an ulterior motive.

'Well,' she said, 'thanks for your time.'

As she walked up to the university to meet Julia she wondered about Griffiths bringing Aurora into rehab. Could that have been mistaken as an affair, the two of them maybe being seen together out of university hours, or was it actually an affair? Someone strung out on drugs, hating themselves, hating their lives, easy prey for someone pretending to care for them. Morag had claimed he was a master manipulator – was she telling the truth? Was that Griffiths' guilty secret, hunting down the weak and the vulnerable, pretending to help them and then insidiously working his way into their lives and bodies?

* * *

Hanlon bought Julia lunch at a vegetarian restaurant near the university.

'My concession to health,' said Julia. There was a self-service salad bar and she had loaded her plate with three different types of innovative food, as had Hanlon. It was such a pleasant change from her monotonous Argyll diet. The chilly voice of Dr Morgan, 'And whose fault is that? That's your own inability and disinclination to cook – not circumstances forcing themselves on you. Stop blaming others.'

Yes, I know, Hanlon told the voice of her conscience. I'll be in touch. Soon.

'So, how's your morning been?' Julia asked.

'Quite good,' Hanlon said, judiciously. 'I think I might have a line on how to find Aurora. I should know more by this evening, but I won't be home until late. Not until at least eleven.'

'Are you tailing someone?' asked Julia, her eyes wide with excitement.

'Probably,' Hanlon said.

'Gosh, how exciting!' She grimaced. 'Your life is so much more interesting than mine.'

Hanlon looked sceptical; it had been somewhat over-interesting lately. If you called being beaten up and threatened with a gun interesting, then the past few days had indeed been fascinating.

'I am going to spend the evening checking staff rostering levels and holiday bookings to make sure that we're fully staffed. That's not going to be much fun.'

Hanlon smiled. She thought back to her time in the police, how many hours she'd spent doing administrative chores or necessary paperwork. She'd been very bad at it. She looked at Julia; she just knew that she would be excellent at her job.

'I had an anonymous tip-off that Griffiths was having an affair with Aurora – does that sound credible to you?'

Julia's demeanour changed; she looked sad. 'I really don't know... I would like to say it was nonsense, but...'

'But?'

Julia looked at her. 'Aurora was/is, gorgeous. If she set out to seduce a man, well, I can't see him putting up much resistance – the flesh is weak. Equally, Dr Griffiths is an attractive man.' She laughed. 'I don't mean that he's Brad Pitt, or whoever's hot these days, but he's highly intelligent, he does have a position of power – admittedly only in uni circles, but power in itself is an aphrodisiac – and Aurora does have a screw loose. So, fan of Griffiths as I am, all bets are off.'

Hanlon nodded. It was an interesting take on it. She'd automatically thought that if Griffiths were sleeping with Aurora, it'd be on him; Griffiths chasing the beautiful young student. Julia had reversed that, casting Aurora as the potential seducer. And Aurora was gorgeous – if she steamed towards you, all guns blazing, it would be very hard to put up much of a fight. Maybe a token, 'We shouldn't be doing this,' as clothes and morals fell to the floor.

'Do you know if any of Griffiths' students are from Newcastle?' She was thinking of the anonymous phone call she had received.

'Yes, there's Jenny, Jenny Evans, red-headed girl, why?'

'Oh, just something someone said...'

They finished their salads.

'I shouldn't say this, but I'm thoroughly enjoying your investigation,' Julia said, 'and the free food.'

'Don't worry,' Hanlon said, 'I'm not paying. Aurora's dad is.'

'Well, I'll still be up when you get back. This is better than Netflix.'

'Oh, one last thing, *Othello*, the play by Shakespeare?'

'What about it?' Julia asked.

'There's a character, Iago, what's he like?'

Julia thought. 'Iago, well. He's the baddie. He's "honest Iago", tells it like it is, except he doesn't. He's an arch-manipulator, and when he can't get others to do his dirty work, he's a killer. Kills his own wife, I seem to remember, to hush her up. Why?'

Hanlon laughed. 'I'm not sure it's important, but you never know.' Morag's description of Griffiths, but was that Morag the liar or Morag, accurate depicter of life? 'Could you e-mail me a copy of Griffiths' timetable?'

'I can and I will, but I can tell you now, you're wasting your time on him.'

Hanlon shrugged. We'll see, her body language said.

Julia looked at her watch. 'Oh my God... I'll be late.' She got up. 'Look, I'll see you tonight. I hope you find Aurora...'

She walked out of the restaurant and Hanlon went to pay the bill.

* * *

She returned to the house at Morningside, Wemyss greeted her enthusiastically and she took him out for a walk. She knew he'd already been out once, but the dog would miss her and, being honest, she missed his company. The moment she'd thought he had been shot had brought it home just how much the collie meant to her. She had known people close to her who had died and she had been much less upset, perfectly dry-eyed, their demise met with a shrug.

While they walked she thought some more about Griffiths. She could understand a student being attracted to him. He was a sympathetic guy and, as Julia had pointed out, in the hand of cards he held in the poker game of life, he had some winners. He was highly successful and respected, he had several books to his name of an academic nature, he was in demand on the inter-university lecture circuit. He did good works by stealth but was not too secretive that no one knew about them. He could easily become a father figure for girls who had issues with their real fathers. Much better than the real thing.

Morag's view of Griffiths as an Iago figure, someone who got others to do his dirty work, was a compelling one. Hanlon also reviewed her own theory that Millar, the psychotic Glaswegian gangster, was seeking to carve out a new niche empire in Edinburgh supplying drugs to the student population, which, if you added up the various universities and colleges, could be a pool of nearly a hundred thousand potential users, maybe more. He would need a network to offload the merchandise and who better than a university lecturer to supervise what was going on? Intelligent, centrally situated and not paid very much, probably alarmingly easy to recruit. In her view, Griffiths was the ideal candidate.

When Aurora had gone straight, if she had been dealing to fund her habit, there was possibly a worry she might talk. There was also a very real worry that she had talked, talked to Morag, and that Griffiths had made a thinly disguised appearance in her novel – one that would be immediately obvious to anyone that knew him.

So, the girls had to go. Morag was dead, but Aurora, like Hanlon herself, had managed to slip through the net. So far.

So far. Millar's men hadn't managed to kill her the day before, but that was by the grace of God, and they were still out there, still looking.

If she could bring down Griffiths, she could bring down Millar, and that would bring the nightmare of being someone's target, someone's quarry, to an end, both for her and for Aurora. The fact they were both in hiding because of one man was intolerable. Millar might be evil incarnate, but he wasn't superhuman and he wasn't invulnerable.

Her plan for the rest of the day was to try to discover something about Jenny Evans, who she suspected was the girl who claimed Griffiths was having an affair with Aurora. Was it true? If so, what was the evidence? The girl had a three p.m. tutorial with Griffiths the following day; Hanlon would see if she could learn anything from her then.

The other thing to do was to try to see if she could learn anything from tomorrow's NA meeting that she knew Griffiths was due to attend.

Her phone went; she looked at it. It was Murdo Campbell. He was due to meet colleagues for a meeting at half four – would she be free at three p.m.?

She thought that, aside from the welcome chance to talk some more about Millar, it would be good to see him.

Yes, she texted, where?

33

'I thought you might like this.'

Campbell handed her an A4 manila envelope.

They were in a grotty pub in Clerk Street, not far from the university. Campbell was drinking an orange juice.

'Your eye is healing up nicely,' he said.

'Thanks, you look nice too,' she replied. She ran her eyes approvingly over him. Campbell always looked smart. Today was no exception. He was wearing a light grey suit and highly polished black shoes. He was tall and lean. She had seen him swimming once; she knew he was in good shape, muscular and toned, a gymnast's build.

'What are you thinking about?' he asked.

'Your body,' she said, matter-of-factly.

Campbell coughed and spluttered as some orange juice went down the wrong way. He was very pale-skinned, and Hanlon watched with interest as the blush rose up his face like mercury in a thermometer.

'Are you OK?' she asked with concern.

'I'm fine.'

'What's in here?' she asked, changing the subject.

'It's information about Millar and his associates,' he said, calming down, now that he was on safer ground. 'A prominent Edinburgh drug dealer was beaten up and tortured the other day – we think it's Millar's work. Prior to that, Millar's man in Edinburgh, Jordan McKenna, was found dead. Last Tuesday in fact, shot three times. He'd been dead a while. And a couple of nights ago the body of a man called Chris Harvey, also known as Falkirk Chris, Millar's man on the east coast, was found shot in an Edinburgh park. The same gun was used that had killed McKenna.'

She remembered a snatch of her conversation with Luke. *They're very moving, Luke, but who was her dealer?*

A guy called Jordan.

Millar's man, known to Aurora. Had she had a part in Jordan's downfall? Was this why Millar wanted her so much? She looked at Murdo and debated sharing what she knew, then decided against it. Hanlon instinctively hoarded information and only shared it reluctantly. She was a very poor team player.

Campbell watched her reactions closely. Thanks to Calla, he knew a certain amount of what had been going on, but it was information he had no intention of divulging, at least not for the moment.

'So, a turf war is going on,' Hanlon said.

'That's what it would look like,' he said, cagily.

'Just what you feared?'

He nodded. 'Yep.'

She touched her eye. 'I think Millar did this, or rather his men did.'

For a moment Campbell was speechless. It was the worst possible thing he could have heard. He knew the kind of man that Millar was.

'Then you're bloody lucky to still have an eye, lucky to be alive.' Campbell felt himself getting angry. He cared about Hanlon and felt she was way out of her depth dealing with Millar. 'Do you know why they hurt you?' he asked.

She felt reluctant to share her ideas about the student drug scene and Millar having a man at the university. She thought it was the kind of tip-off that would probably lead to heavy-handed detective work and scare Griffiths (or whoever) into going underground and she'd never get any evidence. That would mean the whole Millar thing would drag on for ever.

She was a hunted woman as long as Millar was free to operate and the police had failed for years to bring him to justice. She had more confidence in herself than she did in them.

'They told me to go home.'

'Well, quite frankly, you should,' said Campbell, frowning.

Hanlon felt herself bristle. This was another reason why she hadn't gone to the police: she knew they would tell her to back off, go home, leave it to the professionals. Sod that. She thought of Ray's fists laying into her. Well, she'd kind of evened the score, but she wanted more, she wanted to hurt Millar.

Campbell said, 'You're not in the police any more. You're very much on your own.'

She shook her head. 'When I find Aurora, then I'll go home, not before.'

She had been wondering whether to tell him of the incident at Luke's. Campbell's attitude decided her against this. God knew what his reaction would be if he knew she'd been threatened at gunpoint.

Campbell could see the set of her jaw, that look in her eyes. He knew enough of Hanlon not to argue; he decided not to pick a pointless fight. He changed tack.

'And Millar's looking for Aurora, why?' he asked. He wondered if this might have some bearing on his own investigation, but he was focussed on the McDonald angle and unwilling to be distracted from this potentially fruitful avenue of attacking Millar.

'That's the million-dollar question. But I think someone at the university is involved. I want to know who, and I should know soon.'

'Well, I suppose that's all I'm going to get from you for now,' Campbell said. There was a silence as they met each other's gaze. Both knew that the other was holding something back; it was like a game of poker, but neither was going to fold.

'More or less. What are your plans for the day?' she asked.

'I've got this meeting at St Leonard's to discuss Millar, then we'll have dinner somewhere, then back to Glasgow some time tonight.' She nodded. A moment's silence, then he asked, 'Where are you staying, by the way?'

'Morningside,' she said. 'I'm sleeping over at a friend's.'

'Can I have the address?' he asked.

Hanlon frowned. 'Why do you want that?'

'Because,' said Campbell simply, 'I worry about you.'

* * *

Hanlon had some time to kill before she met Mhairi. She walked back in the direction of the castle and down the hill called the Mound, which, with its steep but pleasingly uniform shape, was well named. She went into the Scottish National Gallery which was at the foot of the mound, a brownish oblong building with pillars, and killed an hour looking at the paintings. It would give her something to talk about with Luke.

She wandered around the gallery, which was quiet. She looked at several pictures of some fat Greek goddesses by Poussin; in her opinion they should have joined the Olympian equivalent of Weight Watchers. She looked at some very big pictures of long-dead aristocrats and military figures fighting forgotten battles for an empire that no longer existed. Then she got bored and went to the café and opened the manila envelope that Campbell had given her.

It was quite a contrast to the gods and goddesses and figures from Scottish society and literature she'd been looking at in the quiet, slightly musty-smelling corridors and rooms of the gallery.

Here was the face of real violence in the form of Ray Downie, aged fifty-five, and Dougal MacCrossan, aged twenty-eight. The faces remembered from Luke's. She was surprised at Ray's age – he looked a good ten years younger. Ray with his silver hair and body-builder physique, he looked almost amiable. Dougie, straw-blond, slightly crazy blue eyes. They didn't look like killers, but then not all killers did.

And now here was the face of true evil. She looked at the photo of Millar. A brutal, slab-like face, hard eyes, scowling into the camera. There was no humanity in those eyes, no mercy. It was a compelling face and she felt that she had seen it before but couldn't quite place it. It was infuriating, like having someone's name on the tip of your tongue. Well, nothing to do but hope that it came to her, which it surely would in time.

Their police records, all the expected crimes. The same dreary old list she had seen time after time in her past career in the force. Multiple offences, multiple jail terms. One surprise, though: soliciting for the purposes of prostitution – that was Dougie aged seventeen. Well, that was unexpected. He'd been a rent boy, available on wherever Edinburgh's meat rack was. He'd obviously moved into a more robust area of crime.

And here were photos of the dead. Jordan McKenna and Chris Harvey; dead as those generals on their horses in their gorgeous uniforms, but these two were not nearly as glamorous. Jordan, short, good-looking in a way, droopy moustache, tattoos, not the artistic ones she'd been seeing a lot of. She couldn't imagine Mhairi Ferguson having Love and Hate tattooed in blue ink across her knuckles, or a swallow on her neck. And Chris Harvey, also short, not remotely attractive, bad-tempered-looking, his mouth in a kind of sneer for the camera. The sneer didn't look forced; she guessed it was always there. The kind of face to make you shudder. She imagined you wouldn't get very far from those two begging for mercy. The milk of human kindness had very much curdled there, a kind of ricotta of hate.

There was a short description, a briefing note about Millar's Dumbarton and north-west Glasgow operations. It was mainly drugs, but he also owned several bars and some fast-food outlets and, it was suspected, several upmarket flats that he let out on short-term leases.

It detailed other known information about Millar's contacts in the Edinburgh area, information on the late Jordan McKenna, his girlfriend Catriona Menzies and the (also late) Chris Harvey, aka Falkirk Chris. No girlfriend. The deaths of two men so prominent in his organisation raised the possibility that he was involved in a gang war with a rival.

Both men, as Campbell had mentioned, had been shot with the same 9 mm handgun. There was no usable forensic evidence from either death. McKenna had been shot elsewhere and his body left in his van in his yard, Harvey in the park where his body had been discovered.

No immediate suspects.

I've got one for you, Hanlon thought. She saw again in her mind's eye the hulking dark-haired figure who had rescued her and Luke.

My name's Jamie McDonald. I'm wanted by those two's boss, a guy called Graeme Millar.

Millar wanted him dead because he'd killed two of his employees; it all made sense. She was not going to inform the police though. She'd be in the city morgue if he hadn't showed up, that much she knew. She owed him. The Edinburgh CID could do what they wanted without her help.

She put the photos and the information sheets away.

Well, that was enough for now. It was nice to be able to put a face to the name of the man who had ordered her to be beaten up and then maybe murdered. She couldn't imagine what else Ray and Dougie had been there to achieve, and their uncovered faces suggested that they had not been intending Luke to live either.

Seeing Millar humanised him. She could see he was gigantic; the figures in centimetres put him at about six four or five as she understood height. But she could still visualise beating him to a pulp nevertheless. She'd dealt with Ray; she was more than capable of it. The harder they came, the harder they fell.

Where had she seen that face before?

You shouldn't have picked a fight with me, Millar. You'll live to regret it.

* * *

At quarter to six she walked back into the Grassmarket pub. The barman was beginning to recognise her and put a Diet Coke on the counter for her. She smiled her thanks as she paid him.

At six o'clock, Mhairi arrived. She'd changed out of her work suit into a red tartan miniskirt, black tights and brightly coloured Doc Martens. She was wearing a faux-leather biker jacket and a scowl. She brightened up when she saw Hanlon.

'Hi, how are you?'

She kissed Hanlon on both cheeks; she was wearing a heavy, sensual perfume and pressed her body close as they embraced.

'Would you like a drink?' Hanlon asked.

'No, you can get me one where we're going.'

They left the pub and she led the way down into the gloomy night-shrouded cavern of the Grassmarket. To Hanlon's irritation, Mhairi lit a small joint, the strong smell of the weed billowing around them. A couple of passers-by turned their heads and glared at them.

She offered Hanlon the joint.

'No, I don't smoke.'

Mhairi shrugged. 'More fool you.'

They walked on in silence and crossed under a bridge. The streets were deserted and a cold wind was blowing this cold February night. They walked under a road bridge and then Mhairi turned into a darkened close. Nobody was around. The buildings surrounding them, looming up into the night sky, into the darkness, were shuttered and closed. Commercial properties. The close was a cul-de-sac between two warehouse-style buildings, no lights, nothing in the alley except a couple of gigantic wheelie bins.

Hanlon's eyes narrowed. This didn't look like a place for a pop-up tattoo parlour; this looked like somewhere you would lure a victim. Surely Mhairi wasn't going to try and mug her, or attack her? Well, if she did she was in for a nasty surprise. Mhairi laughed as if she'd read her mind. Behind one of the wheelie bins was a door. Mhairi pounded on it with the edge of her fist.

It opened, a shaft of cold blue light spilling out into the alleyway, the sound of loud music, more cannabis-laden air, a guy with a leather jerkin, a ragged kilt and a T-shirt showing muscular arms appeared. He had the sides of his head shaved to create a kind of Mohican, a beard and multiple piercings. He looked at them.

'Aye?'

'Mhairi Ferguson and guest.'

He picked up a clipboard that was resting on a ledge on the wall, started searching for the name.

'It's OK, she's an old friend…' said a voice.

'Hiya, Giles!' Mhairi waved.

A short, slim, elegant man, fifties, hipster trousers, leopard-skin-print brothel creepers and a silk shirt was standing behind the bouncer. His accent was an upper-class English drawl.

'Mhairi, darling.' They kissed and he turned to Hanlon. 'And who are you?'

'Hanlon,' she said.

Giles ran his eyes over her and arched his eyebrows slightly. 'Welcome to my club... Hanlon dear,' he said, a trace of disapproval obvious in his voice. 'The Black Velvet... do go through...'

Mhairi led her down a short dark corridor draped with black velvet – 'See what we're doing here!' it proclaimed – to another door, which she opened.

The Black Velvet club. The noise was deafening. There was a small stage, unoccupied, but it was set up for a band. On a raised platform was a DJ behind a deck. There must have been about thirty people sitting around at mismatched tables on a variety of chairs. In one corner was an improvised bar made from small pallets and timber. There was a smell of food from an open kitchen: burgers, falafel, noodles.

Mhairi led her to the bar. The clientele were a mix of the alternative Edinburgh art scene, students, elder statesmen of the counter culture who had not aged terribly well, young hipsters, a sprinkling of drag queens on vertiginous heels, some old hippies sporting the balding head and ponytail look, a few haggard women looking daggers at much younger versions of themselves dancing or chatting animatedly amongst themselves. Some people, mainly the older generation, the baby boomers, were smoking weed or doing coke. The decoration was flags, tribal banners, Extinction Rebellion insignia, rainbow nation colours. There were disco balls and lasers.

Hard to believe it was only six-thirty.

'This place gets heaving about ten,' Mhairi said. She inspected the blackboard with wines and beer chalked up on it. The prices were steep. The drink Black Velvet – Guinness and champagne – was available, fifteen pounds a pint.

'I'll have a bottle of Sancerre,' Mhairi said judiciously.

The barman – eyeliner, Daisy Duke shorts, no shirt, leather waistcoat, feather boa, motorcycle boots – opened a fridge and the bottle, gave her two glasses and a wine cooler with ice.

'And a Diet Coke,' Hanlon said.

They took their drinks to a table. Mhairi poured a glass of wine and practically downed it in one. She refilled her glass.

'What is this place?' she asked.

'It's a warehouse. Giles, the short guy you just met, got a six-month lease. He's running it as a club, coolest place in town... Mind you, that's not saying much – this is Edinburgh, not Berlin.'

Mhairi drank some more of her fifty-pound wine and topped her glass up; Hanlon sipped her five-pound Coke. The level in the Sancerre bottle was down a third.

'I hate to remind you why we're here...' The music changed from a kind of trance Arab dance with a heavy beat to be-bop jazz. That really got the table of boomers next to her going.

Mhairi laughed. 'OK, then, come on...'

She took her jacket off and draped it over the back of her chair to reserve her place.

'Come on.'

Mhairi led Hanlon across the dance floor to a staircase that she hadn't noticed in the gloom. They walked up the zigzag metal stairs, and Hanlon looked out over the scene below. More people were arriving now. A girl fire-eater was on the stage, smoke filtering up and floating hazily in the lights. The metal stairs ended in a glass-panelled door with a Hell's-Angel-looking guy in leathers with a cut-off, a big gut and beard guarding it. There were a couple of kids sitting in front of it, waiting patiently for admittance.

'Oi, don't queue jump!' said the girl.

'It's social, darling, not business,' said Mhairi, leaning forward and giving her a menacing look.

She stepped past the girl and her much-inked boyfriend showing off his artwork in a sleeveless vest. 'Evening, Spider,' she said to the biker, who nodded and opened the door for them.

Hanlon and Mhairi walked into a very large room overlooking the space below. She guessed it would have been the offices when the place had been a warehouse, with a view over the shop floor. Now part of it was fitted out as a tattoo parlour with couch and tattoo instruments. At the other end there was a small bar and seats, sofas and armchairs with a velvet rope separating the dozen or so people smoking in the shadows from the ink action. A VIP area.

There was a girl, naked except for her pants, lying face down on the black padded bench. Standing over her with a tattoo gun in his hand was a small man with short wavy grey hair and a surgical mask. He was wearing a black T-shirt and hipster trousers. He looked up, oriental eyes.

'Hi, Mhairi… just finishing off here.' He had a slight American accent.

'There,' he told the girl, 'all done for now.' He wiped her shoulder, she sat up and walked over to a full-length mirror, she watched Mhairi's frank gaze evaluating the girl presumably in terms of attractiveness and the tattoo in terms of skill. The tattooist held up a mirror behind her so she could see the work he'd done.

The image was breath-taking. It was a circular version of Hokusai's wave, the water curving up, full of life and energy as if about to burst from her skin. So much energy and movement, and the colour, the water was an amazing cerulean blue. The small group who'd been watching in the dark shadows burst into spontaneous applause. Hanlon joined in. She wasn't a great tattoo fan, but she recognised genius when she saw it.

'Come back tomorrow,' said the tattoo artist. 'There's a couple of things I need to finish off.

'Now…' he removed his mask '… how are you, Mhairi?'

They kissed. He was a small man, his thick salt and pepper hair atop a lively, humorous face. He had a pair of tortoiseshell glasses through which his brown, intelligent eyes evaluated Hanlon, who was standing next to Mhairi.

'Hi,' he said. 'I'm Joon Woo Lee, Busan Jon, but you can call me Jon.'

They shook hands. 'So you're a friend of Mhairi's – are you here for some work? There's a bit of a waiting list, I'm afraid, but for a friend of Mhairi…'

Hanlon shook her head, took out her phone and showed him the screenshotted image of Aurora's arm.

'My name is Hanlon and I'm looking for this girl,' she said.

Busan Jon looked at the phone. She watched his reaction; immediately the shutters came down. His expression changed from friendly to blank. He knows her, she thought. He's trying not to react. The blonde girl with the tattoo was putting her clothes back on; Mhairi was talking to her and examining one of her breasts that had a delicate tracery of flowers and leaves snaking over its surface.

Hanlon turned back to Jon, who handed her the phone back. He was stony-faced.

'Sorry, excuse me.' A dark-haired girl with heavy Goth make-up and a Korn tee-shirt emerged from the dark shadows of the VIP area and pushed past Hanlon, making for the door. Her head was down; she was staring at the floor. Hanlon looked at her as she brushed by, wondering if she was maybe feeling sick or having some sort of drug-induced bad time. As she reached the door, her back now to Hanlon, she straightened up. She was very tall. There was something about her that seemed familiar. A new song came on the sound system; it was deafeningly loud, even up here, high above the dance floor. Mhairi was deep in conversation with the blonde girl. Goth girl opened the door that led to the stairs; the music crashed through, like Hokusai's wave, louder than ever.

Hanlon looked at Jon enquiringly. 'Sorry, I can't help you,' he said.

'But this is your work?' insisted Hanlon.

Jon shrugged and turned his back on her. That was it, she'd been dismissed. He obviously knew the girl. She glared at him in rage, felt the old-familiar desire to smash something up when she was thwarted. She looked around the VIP platform in the half-darkness, the tattoo couch an island of brightness, the knot of people in the shadows at the end of the room that was the bar, cigarettes and joints glowing in the darkness, the music thundering up from below, strobes and coloured lights flashing from the stage and dance floor. It was a dead end.

'Come on.' Mhairi came up to her and put an arm over her shoulders. 'Time to go.'

'But...' she struggled to find the right words '... but he knows...'

A couple of Jon's entourage approached them, more Hell's Angel biker types, Jon's security obviously. 'Time to go, Mhairi, you and your friend.' The voice and demeanour quietly menacing. Nothing to be gained by starting a fight.

Hanlon marched away angrily, leaving the room and pointlessly slamming the door behind her, its sound drowned out in the heavy disco music now playing. She recognised it – Sister Sledge. She squeezed past the couple still waiting patiently outside and started clattering down the metal stairs.

The Goth girl was at the bottom; she looked up at Hanlon and their eyes met.

IT'S AURORA! flashed into her mind.

The girl disappeared into the crowd below, swallowed up by the dancers. Hanlon ran down the stairs after her. She could see the girl crossing the dance floor. Hanlon strode across it in pursuit – she wasn't going to lose her now – forcing her way through the crowd on the dance floor. Lost in drugs and music, Sister Sledge had pulled quite a few customers to their feet.

Aurora disappeared into the darkness through a doorway at the far side. Hanlon followed. It led into a short corridor painted dark green, lit by a single low-wattage light bulb hanging from the ceiling. There was the Gents toilet on the left, a Ladies on the right, a door marked Private at the end. Nobody around. Which door? Aurora wouldn't hide in the Ladies, no style. Hanlon made for the door marked Private and opened it. The room was a bottle store, crates of beer, wine racks, several metal kegs. And there was Aurora, her back to her, lighting a cigarette.

'Aurora!' Hanlon said.

Simultaneously the door was kicked shut and Hanlon's arms were pinned to her sides by immensely powerful hands. She struggled and writhed, trying to slip out of their grasp, but the grip was like iron.

'Stop struggling or I'll hurt you,' said McDonald. Hanlon did as he asked. God, that man was strong.

'Better,' he grunted as he felt her relax. 'I'm going to let you go. Don't do anything stupid or I'll knock your head off.'

He released her and she shook herself down. She turned around and glared at him. McDonald smiled his unconcern.

Aurora turned around, walked up to her and looked her in the eyes. Her gaze was hostile.

'Who are you and why are you trying to find me?' she demanded.

'My name's Hanlon. Your father hired me to track you down.'

She looked at Aurora. She had done an excellent job of camouflaging herself. Her long blonde hair was now a short jet-black spiked punk crop, her brown eyes were now green, coloured contacts staring angrily out at Hanlon from under heavy liner and mascara.

'He's worried about you.'

'Is he really?' Her voice was sarcastic. 'My father's a total bastard.'

'I know.'

Aurora stared at her in surprise.

'I'm not going to try to defend him,' Hanlon said. 'He's not a nice guy. But he is concerned about you, nevertheless. I said that if I found you, I'd tell you he was worried and maybe take a picture of you to show him I wasn't lying, but there the matter would finish.'

Aurora said, 'Give me your phone.'

She did so and Aurora moved next to her, lifted the phone up, the flash dazzled Hanlon momentarily and Aurora handed her the phone back.

'There, you've got your selfie, satisfied?' she said sarcastically. 'Now fuck off.'

Hanlon shook her head. 'It's not that simple.'

'Oh, yes, it is.' Aurora pointed behind her. 'That's a door – use it or Jamie'll put you through it.' She smiled menacingly. 'Head first. The choice is yours.'

Hanlon folded her arms; she wasn't going anywhere just yet. The music from outside and the smell of weed filtered through the fire door.

'Someone tried to kill me, and I want to know why,' she said. 'Was it because I was looking for you? Or was it because I'm close to finding out something else? And—' she looked accusingly at Aurora '—don't you want to find out who killed Morag? Or have you forgotten about her?'

Aurora flushed angrily. 'Get out!'

There was a noise from behind Hanlon. She turned – McDonald had drawn a bolt on the inside of the door, locking them in. Aurora glared at him furiously.

'Jamie, what are you playing at?' she said irritably.

Hanlon balled her fists and raised them, head height.

'Relax, Hanlon,' McDonald said. He folded his formidable arms and leaned against the locked door. 'She's got a point, Aurora. I think you owe her,' he said mildly. 'Millar's men were going to shoot her.'

'Yes, they were,' Hanlon said, 'and your ex, come to that.'

'OK, OK.' Aurora accepted defeat and sat down on a crate of Budweiser

Budvar. 'I guess I do owe you an explanation.' She stared at the floor. 'You start, then, Jamie.'

McDonald spoke. 'About three weeks ago I got a call from a guy called Jordan McKenna. He worked for Graeme Millar. And you know who he is, don't you?' he asked Hanlon.

'Yeah, I do.' Only too well, she thought. And when I get my hands on him, he'll wish he'd never heard of me, that's a promise, she thought grimly to herself.

McDonald nodded and continued. 'Anyway, Jordan offered me fifteen K for a contract hit, no questions asked, killing plus body disposal. I needed the money. I said sure.'

Hanlon looked at McDonald. About forty, good-looking, those huge arm-muscles and pecs to match, straining his jumper, his glossy dark hair. He could have been a personal trainer rather than a hardened criminal. The way he had accepted the offer, just another job. He'd done it in the past, he'd do it in the future. McDonald was not as nice as he looked.

'I assumed it was a job for Millar, taking out some Edinburgh hard man, probably a dealer, it didn't matter. Then, as we waited in the van, Jordan told me it was a lassie.'

'Does it make a difference?' Hanlon asked.

'Oh, aye.' McDonald nodded. 'I'd have been upset. I'd have charged more. But anyway, I'd said yes. I don't back out of things. So, we're all set to go, Jordan's got the van running, I get out, the target approaches, then I see it's Aurora.'

Aurora took up the story. 'I'd known Jamie for six months from NA. We were helping each other stay clean...'

'No,' he said, shaking his head, 'you were helping me... I'd have died without you, dead or in the loony bin, you've got a year.'

'You stay clean by helping others...' she said.

'Can we stick to the point, please?' asked Hanlon. 'Interesting and moving as your recovery is.'

McDonald laughed. 'Sure, well, so now I wasn't going to kill her, but Millar's a fucking headcase. There was a wee bit of a stooshie in the van.'

'Stooshie?' asked Hanlon, confused.

'Argument, row,' Aurora clarified.

McDonald resumed his story. 'And, well, long story short, I killed that cunt Jordan.'

'Can you please not use the c word?' said Hanlon, irritably. 'It's really annoying, and, quite frankly, offensive.'

'OK, sorry,' McDonald said apologetically. 'Anyway, I drove him back to his yard, put him in his other vehicle, drove out to Craigmillar, torched the van. Then Millar sent Ray and his pal after me.'

'Oh,' said Hanlon.

'Millar knew where I was living – he'd killed my brother-in-law and threatened to throw my niece out the window to find out. Calla, my sister, gave me up. I cannae blame her – she really had no choice.'

Aurora took up the story. 'That night Jamie told me someone wanted me dead, there was a price on my head. I had to act fast. I went home, packed. I had to go somewhere so I got in touch with Busan Jon. I'd helped organise this gig for him, the whole nine yards. I've admired his work for years. He's been putting me up in the flat I'd rented for him. Cut and dyed my hair. Worked perfectly.'

'And why not tell Morag?' Hanlon asked.

'Morag?' You could have cut the amount of contempt that Aurora invested in those two syllables with a knife. She pulled a face. 'I couldn't trust her. If she could get something out of it, she'd have either put me in that fucking book of hers or shopped me. I wondered for ages if it wasn't her who was keeping an eye on me for Dad – someone close to me was. Sometimes I'd suspect Luke. I can't trust anyone.' She smiled. 'Except Jamie.'

'And what happened at Luke's?' Hanlon asked McDonald. 'When you rescued me?'

'She—' McDonald nodded at Aurora '—wanted us to go and visit Luke, make sure he was OK. We were in the café opposite, we saw you arrive, then when I saw those other two get there, I used her key – she still had it – to get in.'

'I thought your story about following them and breaking in was bullshit,' Hanlon said, pleased to be right.

'Anyway, the rest you know,' McDonald said.

'So,' Hanlon said to Aurora, 'Millar wants me dead because he thinks

I'm close to finding his contact at the university and too close to finding you, probably. But why does he want you dead?' That had more or less been Campbell's question, a good one.

'He doesn't,' Aurora said simply.

'What?' Hanlon said. McDonald looked at her in surprise.

'He's my uncle,' said Aurora.

34

Millar sat in the car with two of his rapidly depleting work force. He'd had to bring them in from Glasgow. He was currently four men down. He was furious. He wasn't used to things going wrong, and right now, things were seriously falling apart. He was being betrayed on all fronts. That bitch niece of his! That was when things had started to go awry. And when he'd tried to get rid of her, all this shit had started. Then the revelation that her flatmate might be making waves with some book she'd written. Jordan screwing up, hiring McDonald. Ray... It was a long list. He stared at the door of the building opposite. Under his seat he had a meat cleaver, the sort that Chinese chefs liked to use, very effective at slicing through bone.

'There's someone coming,' Robbo said. He was the driver. The three of them watched the slim youth with the curly hair and the dog on the lead open the gate and walk up the path.

'Fucking wee poof,' said Calum from the back seat.

The youth opened the door and went inside.

'The dog's Hanlon's,' said Millar. 'Don't kill it straight away. I'll do that.'

He'd hold it by its collar, lift the cleaver up, threaten to sever its spine, then she'd give up the girl's whereabouts, he knew she would. People were crazy about their pets. What was it with pets and babies? Both fucking annoying in his view.

He'd had it on good authority that the woman detective knew where to find Aurora. That's why he was here personally, to take care of things himself, to ensure that there were no more cock-ups.

Then he'd deal with Aurora. He was sick of betrayal. Ray letting him down had hurt him badly. He couldn't believe it. It had been like finding out your girl had been seeing another man. Stabbed in the back. Traitor! He was seething.

More time passed. Robbo and Calum talked about football, both Partick Thistle fans, both hating Rangers with a passion.

'Is this her?'

Millar angled the mirror to look at the woman walking down the street, tall, leggy, slender.

'No, that's not her.'

They watched as she opened the door to her house and heard the welcoming bark from the dog inside.

'Come on... come on...' said Millar, drumming his fingers on the dashboard. He was getting bored. Fucking Ray Downie, metaphorically fucking him up the arse like that. After all he'd done for him. He was speechless!

He remembered Ray calling him the night before, confirming that Hanlon was dead. How pleased he'd been. Well, more fool him. And then another call shortly afterwards from another employee to say that, no, she was very much alive and kicking. He'd called Ray to demand an explanation; Ray wasn't picking up. That wasn't Ray's phone malfunctioning. That was Ray. No point even trying Goldilocks. If Ray was hiding, he'd be with him.

Well, he'd deal with Ray at some other time. Downie was a dead man walking.

People letting him down, people taking fucking liberties. Who did they think they were fucking with?

'Car coming...' Robbo said. They slid down in their seats as an Audi 4 x 4 drove slowly down the street and passed them. Not Hanlon's car – she was driving some shitty old Vauxhall Corsa. Millar frowned as the vehicle went by. It was driving as if looking for something; maybe that was his imagination.

They sat and waited, then headlights again, the same vehicle, which had turned and was now driving past them, some guy at the wheel. It stopped near where they were parked and a man got out. He walked along the street, checking the houses, lingering at the one where the youth with the dog and the woman had entered. There was a street light nearby and they could see him clearly: tall, Barbour jacket, red hair.

'Fuck,' said Calum.

'What?' asked Millar, annoyed at having his train of thought interrupted.

'That's DI Campbell, from Glasgow CID. Used to work out of Dumbarton.'

'You recognise him?'

'He fucking interviewed me on a breaking and entering last year,' Calum said. 'Yes, I recognise him. He's a nasty cunt. What's he doing here?'

'Christ knows,' Millar said.

Campbell got back into the Audi.

'Shall we go?' Robbo said. He was uneasy now that the police were parked just three or four cars down the road. It wasn't the issue with the police that worried him, it was Millar. You never knew what Millar might do. He'd been acting weird lately, even for Millar. He might attack Campbell if he got in his way. Or if he looked at him. Kill him even. Then they'd all be in the shit. Joint enterprise.

'No, we wait,' Millar said ominously.

***

Hanlon drove back towards Morningside. She was still processing the bombshell news that Graeme Millar was Aurora's uncle.

He's my uncle...

They had both just stared at her in disbelief. Then Hanlon had remembered the sense of déjà vu she'd had on seeing the police photo of Millar. He had been in the funeral photo. The photo from Giulia Cameron's funeral, glaring at Hamish Cameron. The two half-brothers.

The full story. It confirmed what the old men in the village had told her. Ronnie Cameron, Hamish's father, had drowned. Several years later, Hamish's mother had got pregnant, to a man called George Millar. She had a son, Graham. She kept the Cameron surname. George Millar was a petty Glaswegian criminal; Graeme left Argyll and moved to Glasgow to live with him when he was sixteen. That's when he changed his surname to Millar and, while he was at it, the spelling of his forename. It was as if he had reinvented himself, as people often do.

According to Aurora, Uncle Graeme, although undeniably the possessor of an evil temper, wouldn't harm her. He had been tolerated by Hamish; in later years, he would come and stay at Kinnachan House and Giulia had liked him. Millar had been devastated by her death; he had blamed Hamish. He had claimed, noisily, including at the funeral, that Hamish had neglected her in favour of his business, had encouraged her drug-taking to get her off his back, had even maybe killed her by giving her uncut heroin of a purity she wasn't used to. There had been a furious row; since then the half-brothers hadn't spoken.

Even before Giulia's death, he would visit Aurora occasionally at school, take her up to London, fancy restaurants, buy her clothes. She couldn't believe that Millar would want to hurt her, much less want her dead.

It was impossible, she said.

'Aye, well,' McDonald said, dubiously, 'in fairness, Jordan said he was working for some guy, but he wouldn't say who.'

For what it was worth, Hanlon guessed it had to be Millar's university connection who had sanctioned it. Why? Well, that could wait for the time being.

Technically her job was done. She could just leave Edinburgh now. She had her proof that Aurora was well, she had spoken to her, she had passed on his parental concern, Cameron would be happy. Luke would probably be OK now if she was gone. Julia certainly would be. And ultimately did it really matter who supplied the youth of Edinburgh with drugs? Put Millar away and someone else would take his place. It wasn't as if she were still in the police force anyway. It wasn't her business.

But she knew she couldn't rest until she had dealt with Millar.

'You're addicted to danger, still,' she heard Dr Morgan's voice. 'You're forever trying to prove yourself. You'd be much better off finding out why you're doing this. One day, you're going to run out of luck. If McDonald hadn't turned up when he did, you'd be lying on Luke's floor with several bullets in you.'

She ignored the inner voice. Millar had tried to hurt her and he would have to pay. She would at least track down Morag's killer if possible – that had to be down to Millar, even though the method most certainly wasn't. Millar would not have gone in for gentle asphyxiation while the victim was unconscious, he'd have used an axe if possible.

She parked her car in the quiet street. The truth of the matter was, she wanted Millar; she wanted revenge. Ideally she wanted to beat him to a bloody pulp with her bare hands.

* * *

'Here she is,' Millar said as Hanlon got out of the car and walked towards the house.

Inside the BMW estate with the tinted windows Robbo stiffened with excitement. 'Here she comes – do you want to grab her now, boss?'

Millar shook his head – not with the policeman there. Too many things had been going wrong of late to risk it. They'd deal with her in the woman's house, later.

They watched as she walked along the street; she seemed lost in thought, staring at the pavement. Millar thought how easy it would be just to wind the window down and shoot her as she went past. Low down, so it would take her time to die. But he wanted to find Aurora and he needed her alive. She seemed far more competent, intelligent and trustworthy than anyone he employed. And she was quite foxy. Shame she'd never work for him.

He expected Campbell would get out and speak to her. He had no other reason to be waiting in this street. She turned and walked up the path. No sign of Campbell doing anything. Millar frowned.

They watched as she rang, and the door opened and then closed behind her.

'What now?' Calum asked Millar.

'We wait.'

Half an hour went by. The policeman sat in the Audi. They sat in the

BMW. Millar thought, he must be staking the house out. This could last for hours.

'That's enough,' he told Robbo. 'Let's go.'

Robbo started the engine and they pulled away. Millar stared ahead; there was no rush to deal with Hanlon, not now they knew where she was.

* * *

Campbell watched them go and noted down the registration number and make of car. His face was like stone.

35

Six a.m. Hanlon, dressed in running clothes and a cagoule, walked out of the house accompanied by Wemyss. At the end of Julia's path she closed the gate behind her, clipped the dog onto his lead and started off at a slow jog. She'd do this until her muscles were warm, a few hundred metres, then later she'd open up. It usually took her about ten minutes to properly warm up, to find that effortless stride that would eat the miles.

Fifty metres down the road, Wemyss started pulling on the lead, swerving in front of her. 'Is it something you want on the other side of the road?'

God, I must stop talking to the animal like he's human, she thought. Wemyss gave her an excited look and she let him pull her towards a dark blue Audi estate. It had an SB number plate. That was Argyll. Immediately she thought of Gillies; this was the kind of car she imagined he would drive. Now Wemyss had led her up to the driver's door. She could see a man inside; she rapped on the window. It wound down.

'Hello, Hanlon.' She did a double take and looked at him in astonishment. She really had not expected this. At the same time she felt a surge of pride and affection for Wemyss. What a clever dog, she thought, what a nose.

'Murdo, what are you doing here?'

'Keeping an eye on you,' he said. He looked tired; he was unshaven and hollow-eyed. He was never what you might call a naturally happy man, but he always looked cool and collected. This morning he didn't look his usual confident self.

'How long have you been here?' she asked, half suspiciously, half wonderingly.

'Since last night.'

She nodded. 'Oh, really.' She frowned. Who the hell did he think he was, deciding that she needed a nanny, then keeping watch over her?

'There was no need to have bothered,' she said stiffly.

He said wearily, 'There was a black BMW 4 x 4 here last night. It's registered to a property agency Millar owns in Glasgow.' He paused, letting the implications of what he had just told her sink in. Millar could have killed her last night as she was walking back to the house lost in thought. Who had tipped him off as to where she was staying?

'I'd find somewhere else to stay, Hanlon, if not for your safety, then for whoever owns that house. If you're here, they won't be safe.'

'Millar!' She was incredulous. She asked him the question that was tormenting her suddenly. 'But how?'

'The how isn't important. Go back to Argyll. Edinburgh is not the place for you at the moment.'

He wound the window up, started the car. She watched him drive down the street. Reluctantly she walked back to the house.

When Julia and Luke got up at seven, Hanlon was waiting for them with the news that Millar knew she was here and that she and Luke were leaving.

'But where will you go?' Julia asked, her face a mask of worry.

'I don't know,' Hanlon said, 'some hotel or other. I'm going to leave my car at the Dunedin since it's paid for until I've resolved this. Luke, I'd like you to leave Edinburgh – go and stay with friends in London.'

'What about me?' asked Julia.

'I'm afraid it would be better if you stayed elsewhere,' Hanlon said. 'Maybe with one of your sons, or a friend.'

Julia nodded. 'I suppose so, but surely, if you're not here...'

'Yeah, theoretically,' Hanlon said, 'but Millar is a violent nutcase – he might just torch your house for the hell of it, or hurt you out of frustration. I'd go if I were you.'

Julia looked at her as if she were crazy. Hanlon could see that her naturally sunny disposition and lack of experience in the criminal side of life made her totally ill equipped to appreciate how dangerous Millar was.

'I'll be fine,' Julia said. 'He won't bother me if you're not here. Why would he bother? It'd be too risky, surely. Besides, he's got better things to do.'

'Well, I'd much rather you went,' Hanlon said. She wasn't going to waste breath arguing.

'And what will you be doing?' Luke asked her.

'I'm going to try and take Millar down, if I can,' Hanlon said.

'What about Aurora?' asked Julia.

'I'm not sure,' Hanlon said. 'Priorities have changed, but I'll get there in the end.'

* * *

Later in the day, Hanlon was back at the university talking to Julia in her office. At least she didn't need to worry about her when she was at work. Julia didn't seem to have any conception of the kind of monster that Millar was. Hanlon supposed she had never had the misfortune to meet anyone remotely like him – most people, in fairness, hadn't. If she'd sat down with her and described the kind of things she'd heard about him, Julia probably wouldn't have believed them, or found them so outlandish as to be incomprehensible.

Through the window she could see the reception area for the English department. They both saw Griffiths arrive; he waved at Julia but didn't see Hanlon, who was standing out of sight.

She wasn't quite sure why she hadn't told Julia and Luke the night before that she had found Aurora. She had told them that it had been a wild goose chase. Partly she guessed Luke might try to get in touch with Aurora and right now she didn't think that would be a good idea. She wanted Luke out of harm's way. And Julia, fond of her as she was, did like to talk. She didn't want Julia inadvertently shooting her mouth off to someone, particularly Griffiths, whom she felt Julia was still too fond of. I suppose I've got trust issues, Hanlon thought. Then again, who can blame me?

'So, you'll let me know when Jenny Evans arrives,' she said, checking again that Julia was on point.

'I will.'

'And have you found somewhere to stay, Julia?'

'I'm working on it,' she said and grinned.

Hanlon gave an exasperated sigh; Julia's tone of voice had suggested she was humouring her. She tried again. 'For God's sake, this is serious, Julia. Millar is not a nice man. He kills people!'

'Oh, I'll sort something out,' she said, giving Hanlon a sunny smile. It didn't reassure Hanlon at all, but what more could she do?

A few minutes passed then, 'Look,' Julia hissed, 'there she is... that's Jenny Evans!'

A short girl with bobbed red hair and slightly protuberant blue eyes walked past. She was wearing a short dark coat and jeans. Her skin was very pale. She had a tote bag with a laptop and a pink file poking out. So this was the girl who had tipped her off that Griffiths and Aurora were having an affair. Hanlon thought of Aurora's fierce face, her determined character. She thought of Griffiths' slightly hangdog air. It seemed an unlikely match.

'What time does the tutorial finish?' Hanlon asked.

'Four p.m.,' said Julia.

'Is it the same tutorial group that Aurora's in?' she asked.

'No, it's different.'

Thanks,' Hanlon said. She was relieved. That meant that Jenny probably didn't know what she looked like.

She turned to go.

'Can we have lunch tomorrow?' Julia asked. 'I'd like to know what you're up to, and that you're safe.'

Hanlon smiled. It was the least she could do, after all that Julia had done for her. Besides, she was probably more concerned for Julia than Julia was for her.

'Sure, I'll text.'

* * *

Hanlon went down to the ground floor of the building that they were in, the David Hume Tower. There was a seating area near the door; she sat down to wait, got her phone out and stared some more at Morag's website. She really wanted to read Morag's novel. She felt there had to be a clue there, admittedly, a potentially misleading one maybe, but the sooner she found Millar's man at the university, the better. Aurora was convinced her uncle meant her no harm. If that were true then whoever had organised the attempt on Aurora's life was going behind Millar's back. Millar would be furious. That would surely give some leverage when she found him. *Do you want me to tell Millar you tried to have Aurora killed?* Something like that.

Millar, I'm coming for you, she thought. She wanted him so much it hurt.

She looked again at Morag's message to her.

If I fall under a bus, you can find where I've put my manuscript in Poem for Aurora on my website. Speak soon.

She had studied these lines over and over again like a cryptic crossword clue that she simply couldn't understand. She felt a sudden stab of sorrow for the dead girl, the jokey reference to death, 'if I fall under a bus', never expecting that shortly after this she would die. All those plans and dreams, all that plotting and networking and boasting, all for nothing. I'll find out who did it, Morag, she promised. She looked again at the poem with its peculiar layout and its cryptic dedication.

'Poem for Aurora – Grace a Jean Lescure'

Who were these women, Grace A and Jean Lescure?

The poem itself was of no earthly use to her – there was obviously a clue there, but God knew what it was.

Incoming text.

Are you free tonight for a quick drink? x Mhairi.

Hanlon texted back.

Seven p.m. Grassmarket pub.

Mhairi texted back, a gif of a woman smiling and licking her lips. Hanlon rolled her eyes. She wasn't subtle but she was persistent.

At ten past four the lift opened, and half a dozen students got out, Jenny amongst them. Hanlon followed.

Jenny walked out of the building and into the cafeteria that was next door in the basement of another building. It was a large, soulless, refectory-style place, long rectangular wipe-clean tables and plastic chairs. Hanlon sat in a corner. Jenny was joined by several friends; they were too far away for her to overhear. Hanlon bought herself an unpleasant cup of coffee.

After about half an hour Jenny stood up, said goodbye to her friends and left. Hanlon followed. It was dark and drizzling. Hanlon tailed Jenny through the campus and then across the park known as the Meadows to the houses opposite the university in Marchmont.

The student walked along a couple of streets and then stopped and went down the stairs to a basement flat. Hanlon peered over the railings. The door opened and a man appeared. She watched the bald head of Paul Wyre glinting in the street light as his mouth locked onto the mouth of Jenny Evans below. Wyre said something and she disappeared inside.

Hanlon turned and walked back towards the university lost in thought.

So, Jenny Evans was Wyre's girlfriend. It didn't make her claim that Griffiths was sleeping with Aurora credible – if anything it looked like an attempt by Wyre to get his girlfriend to shift Hanlon's focus away from him and onto his colleague. It also made his assertion that he was the victim of student seduction look a little unbelievable – far more likely that, as Morag had said, he was using his power as a lecturer to seduce his students. He'd done it before; he was doing it now.

Right again, Morag, she thought.

Well, whatever else, it had been a productive afternoon. Hopefully the evening would be equally rewarding.

* * *

It was a hot, sticky, tropical afternoon. The skies above him were an ominous grey and the palms swayed in a sudden gust of wind. A typhoon was on the way. He'd just experienced an exhausting walk in the torrid, humid hell of the jungle. Through the rubble of a demolished brick arch Dougie could see a shape moving. He lifted the heavy semi-automatic to his shoulder, loosed off around twenty rounds. There was a huge explosion and his vision was obscured by a cloud of dust and smoke; shrapnel fell around him like rain. The guy he shot reappeared; he was staggering, injured but still armed; he turned towards Dougie, who shot him in the face. Dougie broke into a run down the street, dropping a couple of mines as he ran. He rounded a corner and ran into three of the enemy – shit... he was so low on ammo. They lifted their weapons, their leader shouted something, he was frantically reloading...

Dougie felt the bed give under Ray's weight and his lips nuzzle his neck.

'Will you get off me? This is important...' He turned his attention back to the game.

* * *

Ray watched uncomprehending as Dougie slammed the new magazine into his gun and lifted it to his shoulder. He shook his head and left him to it.

The younger generation, the things they did for fun. If only it were that simple to get rid of Millar, he thought, as Dougie blew the heads off another couple of Viet Cong. What would Millar be up to? he wondered. He wouldn't be playing computer games, that was for sure.

'Shit,' he heard Dougie say, 'I'm dead.'

Ray thought to himself, We'll both be dead for real, soon. Millar wouldn't be looking for gooks in a virtual 'Nam. He'd be looking for Hanlon, looking for Aurora, looking for them. And it wouldn't be virtual bullets that would be coming their way.

He considered Hanlon some more, turning the memories of their last encounter this way and that in his mind. I must be getting old, he thought ruefully. Well, he was, fifty-five, too old to do strong-arm stuff. He felt the plaster under his chin. Beaten up by a lassie, then stabbed, well, that was a first. That would look good on his CV. I'm too old for this.

When he thought back to the knife pushing up into his flesh, he reflected, I've seen the future. This is what working for Millar will bring. If I keep this up, one day soon, maybe tomorrow, I'll be staggering down an alley gouting blood and I'll die bleeding out behind some bins. Or there'll be a knock on the door, I'll open it, and I'll get a bullet between the eyes.

I've got no more illusions any more and coke and booze can't drown it out. I'm tired and getting old and I'm afraid.

And I don't want to kill anyone.

He was secretly glad, he had decided, that McDonald's intervention had stopped him killing Hanlon and the boy artist. It was like fate, or God, had decided that he shouldn't take their lives. It was time to get out.

What could he do instead? He wasn't qualified for anything except criminality. There weren't too many viable options for an elderly ex-con. Run a bar? No, the hours were too extreme. A B&B? That was actually possible. He owned three houses; he could sell them and consolidate, buy something spectacular. Ray was canny with money; he'd stashed a lot away over the years.

Christ, Hanlon had hit him hard. Respect. He was slow now – a couple of years ago she wouldn't have stood a chance.

He thought some more about Millar. What would he do when he realised what was going on, that they had done a runner? He would bring in Robbo and Wee Dougie from Hamilton, probably. He wouldn't use Calum; he was useless in a fight. Old as Ray was, he could take Calum with one hand tied behind his back. Ray was good at his job, he was a tough old bastard and he knew it.

Millar would know he was hiding; he'd concentrate on the two women, Hanlon first. Millar thought she was getting too close to his university contact, the one who was running five of his main dealers. And making a good job of it – he'd seen the figures, and so far the uni connection had successfully kept a low profile. But Hanlon was getting close.

And Aurora.

Why did he want her dead? Who the hell could fathom what was going on in that psycho's head?

There really was only one way out, and that was to get rid of Millar. He thought of his crazy eyes, his violent paranoia, his uncontrollable violence. They had reached the end of the line together. Time to think the unthinkable: Millar had to die.

That was going to be hard – he laughed softly, without any humour. Hard, that was an understatement, but there was no choice. He couldn't rely on anyone else; they'd have to do it themselves.

No choice any more.

He'd run out of road long ago. The difference being now, he finally knew it.

36

Campbell stood under the street light near the car park for Arthur's Seat. He'd had a text from an unknown number to tell him the time and place; he was assuming it had to be McDonald. Calla had passed on his message.

He looked at his watch: seven p.m. McDonald was late. He looked around. In front of him was the imposing bulk of Arthur's Seat, the huge rocky hill dominating the dark sky. Above him, the sandstone cliffs of Salisbury Crags. It had stopped raining for once and there was a moon. Ragged clouds were scudding overhead. The road at the base of the hill was lit by street lights. There were hardly any cars cutting down Queen's Drive, the road that led from the east of the city, Portobello way, through the park at this time of night.

The car park was empty except for Campbell's Audi. He shivered; it was bitterly cold. He ran over what he'd learned of McDonald's activities in his mind. The bullets from Chris Harvey's body had been fired from the same gun that had killed Jordan McKenna. So McDonald had probably (assuming Calla was telling the truth, and why shouldn't she be?) killed two people.

He knew he should have reported what he had discovered, but what he had told Calla was true: it was Millar that he wanted. He suspected that McDonald, with no previous form for murder, was acting out of duress. If he could get him to testify against Millar, or at the very least provide information that could lead to Millar's arrest, he'd be a very happy man. Seeing Millar's car outside where Hanlon was staying had shaken him. She'd get herself killed if she came up against Millar. He knew that she was tough, and he also knew that she would not back down if he told her to. The longer whatever she was involved in dragged on, the more chance of her winding up dead.

McDonald was his best chance of taking Millar down. And a neutralised Millar meant a safe Hanlon. He was very worried indeed that she wasn't going to survive. Millar was formidable.

He could hear the sound of a motorbike; he watched as it approached, slowing down as it did so. It was a trail bike. Campbell smiled to himself. Clever bastard. If this meet had been some sort of trap, McDonald would have been off, cross country – they wouldn't have been able to follow him – emerging at Duddingston or Craigmillar the other side of the park. Doubtless he'd have a car waiting so he could change vehicle.

The bike, its rider encased in leather, slowed and circuited the car park, checking there was no one about, before pulling up beside Campbell. The rider switched the engine off, dismounted and walked up to him, taking his helmet off.

He had seen photos of McDonald – in the flesh he was shorter than he'd expected, but he projected an aura of great physical strength. He had longish black hair and a largish curved beak of a nose. He looked tremendously self-assured.

'DI Campbell, I presume.'

He nodded. 'And you'll be Jamie McDonald.'

'Aye.' He scratched his nose and pushed some hair away from his eyes. 'And what do you want, Detective Inspector?'

'We know you killed Jordan McKenna and Chris Harvey,' Campbell said.

'Then why is there no arrest warrant out for me?' asked McDonald. His tone was light, but Campbell could see his eyes narrow, calculating what the policeman knew. He took a packet of cigarettes out of a pocket and lit one, turning his body to shield the lighter's flame from the wind. Campbell knew he was checking behind him that nobody was moving in towards them.

'Because we want you to testify against Millar,' Campbell said, 'that he hired you via his intermediary McKenna to kill someone – that's what interests me.'

'So it's the Big Man you're wanting?' He took a drag on his cigarette and looked appraisingly at Campbell through narrowed eyes.

'Yes, in a nutshell. I know he wants you dead.'

McDonald laughed. 'Are you psychic?'

'No,' Campbell said. 'I do know there was a fight outside your flat in Musselburgh last Thursday, a fight with men who were sent to kill you. I do know you've been on the run ever since. On the run from Millar. You are in serious trouble, Jamie. You're between a rock and a hard place. One word from me and for a start you'll be back in prison for parole violation, then Edinburgh CID will be all over you. They'll have such a hard-on for you for those murders that you won't believe it.'

'There's no evidence,' McDonald said, emphatically shaking his head.

'No?' Campbell said. 'Are you so sure? Really?' he put an incredulous inflection on the last word. He saw McDonald frown. 'Are you so sure that you're not on some CCTV somewhere placing you near the crimes? Are you so sure you haven't left some trace behind that might link you to the scene? Are you so sure that Jordan McKenna's ex might not drop you in it? Or Ray Downie…' He saw McDonald stiffen, saw the shadow of doubt fall across his face. 'You've got a record, quite a long one. You'll have no alibi for when the killings happened. All a jury needs is some strong circumstantial evidence and you're probably going down. Thirty years, Jamie, that's if you survive that long.'

'This is all speculation, Campbell. It's not Edinburgh that's got a hard-on for me, it's you.' McDonald's words were defiant, but Campbell could tell that he was badly shaken.

'Millar's a psycho, Jamie. He belongs behind bars. You know that, your sister certainly does. Help me…' he looked at the other man, tried to read the expression in his eyes '… then I can try and help you.'

Campbell felt he had done enough groundwork tonight. He'd leave McDonald to stew for a couple of days. He was between a rock and a hard place. On the one hand, a definite return to prison for parole violation and a possible thirty-year stretch probably on top of the time he had yet to serve of his original tariff. Or outside, hunted by Millar and his men.

He looked hard at McDonald.

'It's Wednesday night, Jamie. I'll give you until Sunday to come up with something. Then I'm going official with everything I know. You've got my number.'

Jamie McDonald laughed, a laugh of sheer bravado and defiance. Campbell, despite himself, was impressed. You had to hand it to him, the guy had balls.

'I'm an innocent man, DI Campbell.'

'And I'm the Moderator of the Church of Scotland,' Campbell replied.

He watched as McDonald pulled his helmet back on, got on his bike and drove off in the direction of Duddingston. He just hoped to God he could get Millar before Millar got Hanlon.

37

The pub in the Grassmarket was quiet. The barman recognised Hanlon; he was a bald guy with glasses and a friendly, world-weary face.

'Diet Coke?'

'Please.'

'No dog this evening?'

'He's staying in tonight.'

Wemyss was in the new hotel that Hanlon had found, just off the Royal Mile. Her car was still out in Cramond; she didn't trust it any more.

At seven, Mhairi came in. Heads turned. A kind of Goth look tonight, a black strappy dress with a black lace top over it, displaying the tattoos that covered her shoulders and upper arms through the filigreed material. The dress was low-cut; she had a great figure. But what interested Hanlon in Mhairi tonight wasn't so much her personality as her problem-solving abilities. Mhairi's IT abilities in Hanlon's mind equated to almost magical powers when it came to dealing with puzzles. Particularly if they were located on a computer. Besides, she couldn't think of anyone else likely to help her.

'Hi,' she said to Hanlon. 'So you found what you wanted last night?'

'I found the woman I was looking for, yes,' Hanlon said.

'Maybe,' Mhairi said, 'or maybe the girl of your dreams, who you're really looking for, is sitting right here – all you need do is ask. You're not exactly quick off the mark, are you?'

Hanlon smiled.

'How are you at puzzles?' she asked.

'Puzzles? How do you mean?' Hanlon saw the perplexity on the other woman's face. Mhairi obviously wasn't quite sure what she was getting at.

'This is what I mean.' Hanlon pulled a tablet out of her backpack and showed Mhairi Morag's website and the poem that was so confusing her. Mhairi was intrigued. 'So you think that there's some sort of coded reference to where she's hidden her manuscript?'

'Exactly.' Hanlon nodded. 'Her laptop's missing, there's no paper manuscript, no hard copy in the flat – the police won't have missed that. I checked via a contact I have. Seemingly there was no external hard drive.'

'Memory stick?'

Hanlon shrugged. 'Sure, but it would be a needle in a haystack – where would you begin? She could well have a whole drawer full. Besides, even if you found the right one, who knows what she labelled the MS as? This—' she pointed at the message '—is definitive. Could you have a look for me?'

'OK, I like a challenge. It'll cost you though.'

'Meaning?' Hanlon asked.

'You'll have to take me out for dinner.'

Hanlon nodded. 'OK, then. Deal...' They shook hands.

* * *

At twenty to nine Hanlon was standing, concealed in a doorway, near the Student Advice Centre watching the recovering addicts turn up for the meeting. Reiss was on the door, greeting the arrivals. At ten to nine Griffiths arrived with the boy she'd seen the last time she was here – Olly, she remembered his name was. Olly didn't look high tonight, he looked pale, ill and shivery. Depressed. She counted about twenty people arriving for the meeting.

At five to nine the smokers – there were quite a few, possibly unsurprisingly – disappeared inside. She had an hour to kill. She walked back to her hotel to check on Wemyss. At ten to ten she was back outside.

At ten the addicts started to emerge. Hanlon stood in the shadows watching. Griffiths and Olly appeared; they spoke and Griffiths shook Olly's hand and Olly disappeared up the road. Griffiths had a word with Peter Reiss then he too started to walk away towards the Royal Mile. Hanlon followed at a discreet distance.

Griffiths had his phone out and then he started walking faster; he was now more purposeful. There seemed to be a spring in his step. He was easy enough to keep up with though. They turned into the Royal Mile and Griffiths started to walk up towards the castle and then at the Lawnmarket, where the cobbled street broadened out into a large square, he disappeared into a sizeable pub that overlooked the high street.

Hanlon slipped in after him. The pub was crowded; the air smelled of people, beer, bonhomie. The place was absolutely packed. Griffiths made his way to the bar and bought a drink, a glass of red wine by the look of it; he moved away from the counter and stood there irresolutely, stroking his beard and looking around. He was obviously there to meet somebody.

A man brushed past Hanlon and muttered an apology. Then she saw his back and froze. He was tall, rangy; he had short straw-coloured hair – Christ, she thought, it's Dougie. She hid behind a couple of large men who were arguing amiably about rugby. She peered round them. There was no mistaking him. She had stared at him at Luke's flat for what had felt like an eternity two days previously.

Thank God, he hadn't noticed her.

He had, however, noticed Griffiths. He walked up to him, spoke to him, the lecturer smiled, nodded and followed him up a broad flight of stairs to an upstairs bar. It was an air-punching moment! So, she thought, savouring her victory. I've been right all along – you're Millar's man at the university.

Hanlon gave them a minute then pulled the hood of her jacket over her head and followed slowly. From the top of the stairs she could see a corner table. There was Griffiths, talking animatedly with Dougie and Ray. She risked a quick photo of the three of them on her phone – they didn't look in her direction; they seemed engrossed in whatever they were talking about – and then she retreated down the stairs and into the comforting darkness of the night.

Outside, sheltering from the icy wind blowing up the Royal Mile, she checked the photo that she had just taken. It was perfect. There they were, the three of them. Her two would-be killers and Griffiths. She thought of Morag's description of Griffiths as an Iago figure, getting other people to do his dirty work. Well, she had been right. She suspected he had got Ray and Dougie to murder for him; he spent time hanging out with the addicts, pretending to be their friend while doubtless on the look-out for potential dealers to help move Millar's product. Spreading ugly rumours about people who might endanger his position, like Cameron abusing Aurora. And had it been he who had silenced Morag, the gentle killer, drugging her and then asphyxiating her? Almost certainly. He had been so pitch perfect. He had fooled her initially; he had fooled Julia Swinson. Oddly, Morag had seen through him. She had been right all along, and she had paid the price.

She felt a cold rage well up inside her. Well, I've got you, you bastard, and I'll use you to bring down Millar.

Every step back to her hotel was a step of elation.

Gotcha, she thought. Millar, I'm coming for you!

* * *

Millar himself was standing in the darkness of the street opposite the house in Morningside. The expensive curtains to the living room, long pale and linen, were three quarters closed but there was enough of a gap to see into the comfortable, cosy room.

The woman appeared, the one who had walked past their car the night before, tall and slim. She wasn't dressed now though; a towel was wrapped around her head and she was wearing a peach-coloured dressing gown. Straight out of the shower. Millar felt himself growing hard. He tipped some coke onto the back of his hand and sniffed it. He felt his heart change up a few gears. Millar felt himself stiffen. He was horny, invincible and super-confident.

Nobody could stop him getting what he wanted. Nobody.

Now, oblivious of his presence, the woman went to the window and grasped the curtains with both hands. He could see into the room behind her. The kind of place that people like her lived in, framed pictures on the wall, bookcases. How he despised them. They were the sheep and he was the wolf that would fall upon their fold. Before she closed the drapes he could see her face, thoughtful, attractive.

Millar felt another sharp stab of lust. He liked attractive, upper-class women; he found them very desirable. He had a small black leather satchel under his arm; it contained the cleaver that had been under the seat of the BMW the night before.

He had been there a while, looking at the house, watching her. Hanlon and the kid were gone but he had no doubt that the woman in the house would tell him where they were. Of that he could be sure.

He looked down at his big hands and flexed his powerful fingers. His fingers were cold and he pulled his gloves on. The drugs coursed through his veins. He felt strong and powerful. No, he had no doubt whatsoever that she would give him exactly what he wanted, do exactly what he wanted.

Time to act. Millar walked forward towards the house and his gloved fingers opened the gate.

38

Hanlon lay on her bed, stroking the dog. She looked at her phone, two missed calls from Julia. It was late, nearly eleven. She felt a sudden urge to tell her, 'I told you so,' about Griffiths being Millar's drug connection.

She called Julia.

Julia answered the phone almost immediately. 'Hi, are you OK? I get so worried about you. At least Luke will be safe. He's gone to stay with his art dealer.'

She chatted on some more; Hanlon interrupted her. 'I'm fine... I just wanted to tell you that I know who Millar's man is.'

'Sorry?' Julia sounded puzzled.

'Millar's contact at the university, it's—'

'Oh shit, that's the doorbell – look, can I call you back?' she asked.

'Who is it at this time of night?' Hanlon was puzzled. It was so late.

'It's Ocado. I got the last slot available, 11–12 p.m. God, where did I put those old bags?' she muttered to herself, sounding flustered. 'I'll call you soon, bye.'

Julia hung up.

So, it was that nice Mr Griffiths all along. Hanlon looked again at the picture she'd taken on her phone. There was Griffiths. He was looking intently at Ray; they were deep in conversation. Dougie was smiling; he looked very happy. What were they discussing? What were they plotting together?

I'll check his teaching schedule tomorrow with Julia. It would be nice to know where Griffiths had been on the morning that Morag McMillan had died. The way she had been killed, drugged, then asphyxiated, that was how Hanlon could imagine Griffiths doing it, gently, almost regretfully. Tying the plastic bag around her sleeping neck, checking his watch, checking her pulse. Putting her laptop in the rucksack he would have thoughtfully brought along to the flat, dropping her manuscript in the bag along with it.

She looked at her phone; still nothing from Julia. Surely her grocery delivery would have finished by now? What was she doing? Putting stuff away probably. She called Julia; she heard the phone ring and then go to voicemail.

She shrugged. Julia must have gone to bed. Or turned her phone to silent. Hanlon felt a bit annoyed that Julia was so unconcerned about which member of her department was facilitating the selling of drugs to the student body – surely that was worth staying up to hear. Oh well.

She changed into a T-shirt for bed, washed and lay there staring at the ceiling, formulating a plan for the following day.

Millar was the man she wanted. He was the one who had ordered her execution. She was chasing two killers: Griffiths for Morag – although that could possibly be Ray – and possibly for ordering the hit on Aurora. If that wasn't Millar, as seemed likely, then it had to be Griffiths. God knows why. But that could wait.

The problem was that she didn't have any proof. She could hope that Griffiths would crumble when he was interviewed by the police; she suspected he would, but that was wishful thinking. He would almost certainly lawyer up and unless there was compelling evidence, all they would get, courtesy of his brief's advice, would be a string of 'no comments'.

Well, if he was the major player in Millar's drug operation, there was a very good chance that there would be some evidence of it at his house. It was even quite possible that he was storing drugs there; they had to be kept somewhere. The police would never think of looking for drugs in a pillar of the community's house. Maybe even firearms.

If she found something, some proof of Griffiths' guilt in his house, she could tip Campbell off. Then he would be able to get a search warrant executed. But first she needed to make sure that there was something to find. She didn't want to make Campbell look stupid by raiding a house and finding nothing. She texted Julia to ask for Griffiths' address – she'd want that first thing in the morning – she also asked for details of Griffiths' working hours for the following day. She closed her eyes; time to carry the fight to the enemy. Time to pay nice Mr Griffiths a visit.

39

The next morning there was still no reply from Julia. Hanlon frowned. She was getting slightly concerned. She would go round to check on her later; she texted her to that effect.

She took Wemyss for a run around Holyrood Park, a quick 5 km, then breakfast, more stolen sausage to appease her conscience at leaving him alone in the room until lunchtime. She stroked his head and looked into his mournful eyes.

'This should all be over fairly soon,' she reassured him. Then she set off at a brisk pace to Marchmont, a couple of miles away. She wanted to have words with Paul Wyre, student abuser.

At quarter to nine she was outside the door of the basement flat where she had seen him embracing Jenny Evans. She remembered how indignant he had been that he had been kicked out by his girlfriend. This must be the shared flat he had complained about being studenty. *Now I'm renting a room in a shared flat in a scrotty basement in Marchmont, like a student.*

She hammered on the door; a bleary-looking Wyre wearing a dressing gown opened it.

'Hello, oh, it's you...' he said.

He was unshaven and smelt quite strongly of whisky fumes. There was a faint odour of stale weed and a sweet smell of rotting food coming from the flat. If Wyre was slumming it as he claimed, following the split from his fiancée, he had certainly embraced the student lifestyle wholeheartedly.

'Can I come in?' asked Hanlon, not waiting for an answer, pushing her way past him.

The flat – a living room, kitchen through an arch, and, she guessed, a couple of bedrooms and a bathroom through another door, which was closed – was a mess. It looked as bad as it smelled. There were books and magazines lying around, a laptop and an iPad on the sofa. On a coffee table a bag of weed and some cigarette papers. The ashtray was overflowing with cigarette butts and roaches from smoked joints. A couple of unwashed coffee cups and a nearly empty bottle of Bell's.

'Haven't you heard of Marie Kondo?' asked Hanlon, casting a withering eye over the mess.

'Why don't you fuck off out of my flat?' asked Wyre, pleasantly enough.

Quite why she did it she couldn't really say; one moment she was perfectly composed, the next she had driven her fist into his stomach. An uppercut, not a punch she used very often, hard to do well. A short, brutal blow, her fist driven by the power of her hips and shoulder into Wyre's flabby gut. Twisting in and upwards to put her bodyweight behind the punch. He doubled over in pain and shock and collapsed back on the sofa, his dressing gown opening, revealing an unexpected big roll of flab and a pair of torn grey boxer shorts.

It looked as though Wakefield would be needing a new hard man, she thought contemptuously, as Wyre groaned and swore.

Almost immediately she heard Dr Morgan's voice in her head, the voice of her conscience. 'That's why they made you leave the police force, Hanlon. Brutality. And you can't even claim that this was justified. He's an open door, all you need to do is push, not kick it in.'

'What the fuck...?' gasped Wyre, hunching forward, fighting for breath.

'Now I've got your attention,' Hanlon said menacingly, 'what were you thinking when you told Jenny Evans to call me and lie about Griffiths having an affair with Aurora?'

'I don't know what you mean... Jesus...' He straightened up painfully.

Hanlon took a step towards him and he put up his hands in protest. 'OK, OK, I did tell her to call you and say that.'

'Why?' Her voice was hard, but nowhere near as hard as her expression.

'To get you off my back,' confessed Wyre. 'I didn't want you snooping around and causing trouble for me.'

'Well, you should maybe stop abusing your position of power,' Hanlon said.

The voice in her head. Who is abusing power right now? This is the way Millar acts, terrorising people. You shouldn't be doing it. You know that.

'We all do,' said Wyre, testily. 'Besides, it was consensual. She's a grown woman.' Well, that was arguable, thought Hanlon, but I'm not here for a debate.

'I'm not interested in that,' Hanlon said. 'Is Griffiths at work today?'

'Yes, I happen to know he is.' Wyre was eager to change the subject away from himself.

'And do you know his address?' she asked.

'Yeah, I've been to his house often enough. Why do you want to know?' he wondered.

'Because I want to go round and snoop and cause trouble for him, that's why,' she said, deliberately parodying the words he'd just used to her.

'Well, I've got a key, if you want it,' Wyre offered. Anything to get this nightmare woman out of his flat. Now that he could see it was Griffiths she was interested in, he was almost falling over himself to be helpful. In a moment he'd be offering to drive her there.

'Yes, I do – how come you've got keys?' she asked suspiciously.

Wyre said, 'Because I feed his cat when he goes away, which is quite often.'

'Right, I'll take the key, then.'

Wyre stood up and returned with two keys and a circular disc on a key ring.

'Just touch this to the alarm when you're inside – it disables it.'

'Thank you,' Hanlon said.

'Post the keys through my letterbox when you've finished, please,' Wyre said. 'I don't want to see you again.'

'The feeling's mutual,' Hanlon said.

And it was that simple.

***

The Dalkeith Road where Griffiths lived was long and wide. She walked past a hall of residence for Edinburgh University and the Commonwealth Pool. The English literature lecturer had a respectable-looking house about five minutes' walk down from where they were situated. He looked to be doing well for himself; Millar would be paying him handsomely, Hanlon guessed.

She rang the bell to check that nobody was in, then unlocked the door and let herself in. A swipe of the fob on the spare set of keys silenced the burglar alarm that was making its bleeping sound, just as Wyre had said. She was in.

She sighed with relief and looked around.

It was always an odd sensation, breaking into someone's house. The utter silence. The total strangeness of the surroundings. The adrenaline rush of knowing that you could be caught. The heightened awareness that came with that, and the feeling of power, almost exultation, that you could take anything, break anything, destroy anything you wanted. She liked it; she liked it more than she cared to admit.

What she wanted to find more than anything else was cocaine or weed, and lots of it, not just a bit for personal use – not that anyone had suggested that Griffiths might have ever used drugs. The drugs had to be cached somewhere, why not here?

Griffiths house was exactly as one might expect from a lecturer in English literature at a university. It was modestly furnished, comfortable. There were potted plants, ferns, a lot of greenery, quite a few bookshelves, arranged by subject and in alphabetical order. Everything was neat and tidy. There were framed prints, some of them posters for movies. Arthouse films, *Querelle*, *Death in Venice*, a Pasolini movie. Others quality reproductions of paintings by artists Hanlon didn't know. There was a large, expensive-looking hi-fi with a record deck and a selection of vinyl, predominantly jazz. Quite a few CDs, jazz and classical.

She moved to the kitchen. It had been knocked through to the dining room. A large stove, more plants, a cat flap in the door and a food and water bowl. She opened cupboards: crockery, herbs and spices, cups. More or less everything was where you might expect it to be; there was no sign of anything out of the ordinary.

She opened some of the drawers; one had flour and sugar in it, stuff for baking. It was probably where she would have put the coke; it wasn't there.

She tried another room at the front. Griffiths' study: a computer, printer, reference books, some framed awards from foreign universities, some framed schedules featuring his name as guest lecturer from foreign universities, framed photos, Griffiths with people she didn't know, presumably academics or writers. None of Griffiths with Pablo Escobar and a mound of coke. None of Griffiths with Millar.

This was all a waste of time.

Then she froze as she heard a sudden noise, magnified by the adrenaline that was suddenly coursing through her veins. It was the sound of a key being inserted into a lock, then a click as the Yale sprang open, footsteps, a cough, a man's cough and a thud as a bag was dropped on the tiles of the hall, and then the sound of the door closing.

She was trapped in Griffiths' house.

40

Hanlon stood stock-still for a heartbeat. Flight was impossible; she thought she might as well try and own the situation. She had no choice.

She walked out of the study. Griffiths was standing in the hall. He looked round, saw Hanlon and started violently.

'Jesus Christ, what are you doing in my house?'

He was more frightened than anything. Well, that's a good start, she thought. Let's build on that.

'There are things we need to discuss, Griffiths.' Her voice was level but menacing, her eyes hard.

'How did you get in here?' His voice was ostentatiously angry, but she could detect a current of fear underneath. 'You can't just break into people's houses...'

'Get in the lounge.' Hanlon's voice was like a whip-crack; she saw him flinch. 'I know what you've been up to, Dr Griffiths.'

He shook his head disbelievingly but obediently went into the living room. She pointed at a sofa.

'Sit down.'

'No,' he protested, but weakly; he seemed to accept that she was in charge. 'This is my house. I want you to get out.'

'What you want no longer matters, Dr Griffiths,' Hanlon said matter-of-factly.

She had her phone in her hand; she unlocked it and showed Griffiths the picture that she had taken the night before.

'Explain that, then.' Her voice was a mix of anger and triumph.

Griffiths did sit down now, looking at the image of himself with Ray and Dougie.

He stared up at Hanlon with perplexity.

'What's my private life got to do with you? We're all consenting adults.'

Now it was Hanlon's turn to feel puzzled. 'What do you mean, "consenting adults"?'

'Are you some sort of homophobe?' He shook his head angrily. 'What's this all about?'

Hanlon hadn't got the faintest idea what he was on about. She said, 'Look, Griffiths, these two men are career criminals. They are implicated in drug dealing to your student body and, three days ago, they tried to kill me. So cut the crap, OK. This is your last chance to explain yourself, to put your side of the story, before I go to the police.'

Griffiths looked bewildered. 'They're criminals? That's not what they told me... What on earth are you on about?' It was now her turn to look unsure; he carried on. 'I met them on a dating app for professionals...'

'I'm sorry?' Hanlon thought incredulously, he met them for sex? And they said they were, 'Professionals?'

'Yes, professionals,' explained Griffiths. 'Uranian, that's the app, is for the older gentleman, no twinks, no time wasters.' He frowned at her. 'Are you sure you haven't got your wires badly crossed, Hanlon? These men are not criminals.'

'They most certainly are!'

Griffiths sighed, as if humouring her. 'Anyway, this is exactly what happened, not that it is any of your business. After the meeting, I hooked up with Ray and Dougie, who I had never met before in my life and, for your information, are perfectly charming. I'll spare you the details, but we spent the night together in a nice cottage in Dalkeith.'

'I've got the picture,' said Hanlon.

Had she got the wrong end of the stick? If he wasn't Millar's contact, then there was only one other possibility.

Wyre! She suddenly felt very alarmed now. He knew where she was going – he'd given her the bloody key. Shit. He'd have contacted Millar.

'Is there a back way out of here?' she asked Griffiths urgently.

'Yes, why?'

Hanlon looked out of the window. A black BMW was parked across the street and as she watched the driver's door opened and a man got out, joined by a second man from the passenger side.

'Fuck!' she said. Griffiths looked puzzled.

'Quick, let's go...' Griffiths looked at her with a resigned 'what now?' kind of expression. 'QUICK, you cretin, they're coming for us!' she shouted.

Griffiths jumped to his feet, alarmed.

'What the hell...?' He looked around, thoroughly bewildered.

'Come on, out the back now!'

She practically pushed the protesting academic into his kitchen and threw the bolts open on the back door. They stumbled into the garden and as she closed it behind her she heard the doorbell ring.

'Come on...'

There was a smashing sound of glass as someone broke the pane by the latch.

'Hurry!' Griffiths didn't need to be told any more. Not now he had heard someone breaking into his house. They ran down the short garden, which ended in a tall stone wall, about two metres high. There was a substantial gate, a wooden door, painted red, set into the wall. Two strands of barbed wire ran along the top of the brickwork above it. Griffiths, thoroughly scared now, lifted a plant pot and picked up a sizeable key hidden beneath it, which he inserted into the keyhole of the garden gate. The lock was stiff and the key turned slowly. They could hear a second pane of glass break. Sweat beaded Griffiths' brow as he frantically tried to move the key, then reluctantly it gave.

They slipped out of the door, closed it behind them and locked it. Hanlon looked around quickly. They were standing in a long grassy lane. On their side was the wall that extended the length of the street that Griffiths' house was in. Opposite an identical wall with gates set into it for the houses in the parallel road.

'Where does it go?' she demanded, staring at the path.

'Up to a crescent—' he pointed to the right '—and down to the cemetery.' He pointed to the left.

'Well, run!' She pointed in the direction of the graveyard.

The two of them sprinted left down the footpath at the back of the houses towards Newington Cemetery. Hanlon stayed behind him, forcing him to run. She knew they didn't have much time. Trapped in the lane between the high walls, they would be sitting ducks. Griffiths was in poor shape, but fear kept him going. He was gasping his chest heaving, taking great lungfuls of air to try and get enough oxygen into his burning muscles. The gate wouldn't detain their pursuers long; she wanted to be out of view before they burst into the lane.

They entered the graveyard via a rusted turnstile. She looked around; the place was mournful and desolate. Her spirits rose. It was huge, there were gravestones everywhere, and plenty of trees and bushes to screen them. There was a lot of stonework, much of it covered with ivy, there were catafalques, stone family chambers and stone angels and obelisks. Griffiths flung himself down on the grave of a sixty-nine-year-old widow, Sarah MacFarlane, who had died in 1902.

'I can't go on,' he groaned.

'Listen, Griffiths,' hissed Hanlon, standing over him, glaring down, 'there are two men who are armed looking for us and I can't think of anywhere better to be murdered than a graveyard. So unless you want to join Sarah MacFarlane in the great beyond, get your fat arse into gear and let's go.'

Whimpering and practically in tears, Griffiths got to his feet and followed Hanlon, her running with an easy muscular jog, he in a staggering, painful, bent-over shuffle as they made their way down a broad avenue flanked by trees and funerary statues.

They exited the graveyard onto the main Dalkeith Road. A black taxi with its light on came by and Hanlon flagged it down.

'Regina Hotel, Royal Mile,' she said. Griffiths lay back in the seat, his chest heaving. Hanlon could see the driver looking at them curiously in his mirror.

'I'm his personal trainer,' she said. 'He's getting in shape for the marathon.'

41

Back in Hanlon's hotel room, Griffiths lay on the bed, still breathing heavily and drinking Scotch from her minibar.

'Now, do you mind telling me what this is all about, please?'

Hanlon made herself some tea and explained to him what had been going on. Griffiths was a good listener. She finished; he looked up at her.

'But why can't we go to the police?' Griffiths wanted to know.

'Because I've got no evidence against Millar and the only way to end this nightmare is to stop him. Do you understand that?'

'I suppose you're right.'

'I am right,' Hanlon said.

'I can't believe that Paul Wyre would have done that to me,' Griffiths complained.

'Several years ago Paul Wyre threatened to slash the face of a woman in a small shop with a knife to get a few hundred quid – that's why he was sent to prison,' Hanlon said. 'He got his girlfriend to lie to me to drop you in the shit, and you find it hard to believe that he's in the pay of a drug dealer. Get real, Griffiths! To be fair to Wyre, he had no idea you were going to turn up. It was just me he wanted rid of. Permanently,' she added bitterly.

Hanlon's phone went. She glanced at it.

'Thank God for that.'

Griffiths looked at her questioningly.

'It's Julia Swinson – she's fine. She apologised for not getting in touch earlier. I was beginning to get worried.' She looked at the prone figure of the lecturer as he poured himself another Scotch. 'She always maintained you were innocent,' she added.

'She's a lovely woman,' said Griffiths. 'So, anyway,' he said, changing the subject, 'Aurora's OK.'

'For now,' Hanlon said. 'There was obviously a contract on her head, presumably from Wyre. Aurora claims that Millar wouldn't harm a hair of her head, but I would beg to differ, as, I suspect, would McDonald. He looked very doubtful when she said he would never hurt her, based on the fact he was her uncle. I find it hard to imagine Millar has any human feelings whatsoever, much less family ones.'

'So what are you going to do about Wyre and Millar?' asked Griffiths. 'What should I do, come to that? Am I a target now?' He looked genuinely frightened. 'It's all right for you – you're presumably used to being chased and attacked by criminals. I'm not. I teach English Literature. My idea of trouble is someone complaining about a grade I've given them.'

'Call in sick for now, take a few days off and go and stay somewhere else,' Hanlon said. 'As to your first question, I don't know. I'm going round to Julia's at one. I'll get her to move too. I don't like the thought of her alone in that house. But she's stubborn. I'm going to put my foot down and insist she get out.'

Griffiths said gloomily, 'Maybe I could go into hiding with her.'

I wouldn't joke about things like that, Hanlon thought, it might come horribly true. She thought of Millar – he wouldn't stop – and then she thought of how they had escaped his men. It had been horribly close, but they had done it. She thought of how furious he would be. She wouldn't like to be in the shoes of the thugs she had got away from. She laughed grimly and Griffiths looked at her questioningly.

'Don't worry,' Hanlon said, 'I'll think of something. Meanwhile, you can help me walk the dog. You need the exercise, that's blindingly obvious.'

42

Back in their Airbnb cottage in Dalkeith, eight or so miles outside Edinburgh, Ray had just finished shaving. He leaned his head back and tweezered out some hair from his nose, his eyes watering with the pain, then he checked his ears for unwanted fuzz. He nodded in satisfaction; he looked great. He had his best clothes laid out on the bed.

Dougie said, 'What's the special occasion?'

I'm dressed for my own funeral, Ray thought, but didn't say. Last night with the bearded guy Griffiths, that had been goodbye sex. If he were still alive this coming evening he'd be surprised. I want to look my best on my big day – that was the thought paramount in his mind. He felt deep down they stood no chance against Millar; the man was invincibly evil. It was like taking on Satan himself. Millar had loomed so large in his life that the thought of challenging him was almost heretical. Ray had worked for him for twenty-five years. It might have been an overstatement to say that he was in awe of him, but not by much. Millar was like a savage divinity, indestructible, and, like the Old Testament God, jealous, vindictive and destructive, raining death and injury on all who crossed him.

They were on a suicide mission.

Ray didn't rate his chances – there was an understatement – but he'd always been a fighter and he was not going to go quietly. Besides, what was the alternative? To skulk away somewhere and live the rest of his life in fear that Millar would track him down. Because he would. Millar never forgot and never forgave.

There was no alternative, then.

He also knew that he would much rather die than fall alive into Millar's hands. He had seen what the man could do. Now came the hard part – Dougie would freak when he told them who they were going up against. Well, if the kid couldn't handle it, he wouldn't blame him, he would handle things himself.

'Dougie,' he said quietly, 'we've got to do something about Millar.'

Dougie sat upright. 'Aye, I know,' he said softly, 'we've got no choice. How are we going to go about it?'

Ray thought he had never loved Dougie as much as when he heard him say that. Dougie knew Ray was probably leading him to his death and he was prepared to go along with him. To die with him.

'How many guys do you think he'll have with him the now?' he asked Dougie. He had his own view, he just wanted it confirmed.

'Here in Edinburgh?' Dougie frowned, thinking. 'Just a couple, Robbo for sure, Wee Dougie, not that fuckwit Calum, Stevie? But he'll need to leave a couple of guys he can trust to mind things in Glasgow.'

'Well, we're going to take them out and then we're going after Millar, so it's just him we've got to worry about.' Ray spoke quietly.

'OK.' Dougie grinned at him. 'This'll be fun…' He stood up and walked over to Ray, bent over and kissed him on the lips. 'I love you, Ray,' he said softly.

Ray turned his head away and pretended to look at his phone. He didn't want Dougie to see the tears in his eyes.

* * *

Millar was at the flat in Marchmont when his phone rang.

'Aye, who's this?'

Robbo and Calum looked at Millar with trepidation. The Big Man had been in a terrible mood. He'd drunk about a third of a bottle of Grouse and done a lot of coke between ranting about how Ray had shafted him and what he was going to do to him. Chop the fucker up. There had been a lot of wild talk like that. He was very volatile, and he was armed. To add to the mix, he was not happy that Hanlon had got away. Robbo couldn't work out who he hated more, Hanlon or Ray. Probably Ray – he seemed to think Hanlon could help him track down some girl he was desperate to find. Millar, Robbo thought, was losing it.

'Dave who? Junkie Dave? Oh aye, I ken you now, what do you want...? Really!' Millar's demeanour changed. 'Text me the address... aye, the money's yours.'

He ended the call and looked at Robbo and Calum.

'That was Junkie Dave, do you know him?'

Calum spoke. 'Aye, tall, lanky guy, he's fae Gorgie, deals smack and Charlie, why?'

'He's just had an order from Ray. Ray needs ten grams of Charlie, and we've got an address. Somewhere in Dalkeith.' He got his phone out and said as his thumbs worked, 'Now, off you go... take this...' He took the gun out of his jacket and handed it over to them. 'I want them dead, nothing fancy, nothing clever.'

'What about you, boss?'

'I'm going to deal with Hanlon. I don't need a gun. I'm going to cut her fucking head off.' He glared at them. 'Something you cunts seem to have been unable to do.'

'Yes, boss.'

'Well, go on, then, go and deal with Ray...' As Robbo reached the door Millar said, 'If you don't kill him and his faggot pal, kill yourselves, it'll save me the bother of doing it.'

43

Hanlon got out of the Uber outside Julia's house at Morningside. The car drove away down the quiet road. How peaceful it was, the solid, expensive houses with their manicured front gardens. It was tranquil, such a contrast to the flight through the cemetery with the panic-stricken Griffiths, running for their lives from Millar's thugs. She suddenly thought of Luke; he was still in Edinburgh too, staying with his art dealer. He wouldn't have to be there long. Now she knew it was Wyre, she felt he would drop Millar in it the moment he was arrested. She guessed he was desperate for money, which was why he'd been working for Millar, but he'd been unable to cope with prison before. He would do anything to avoid going back.

She paused for a moment at the gate as she texted Luke.

At Julia's to make sure she goes into hiding. Keep your head down, Luke, better still, go to London.

Send.

She walked up the path towards the front door. She smiled as she rang the bell. Julia would be amused to hear about the mistakes she'd made, assuming that she'd discovered that Griffiths was the connection to Millar, when all along it was Wyre.

Julia opened the door; her large, beautiful eyes looked unusually worried.

'Hi, Julia. Are you OK?' Hanlon felt a stab of concern. What could have happened? She looked totally unlike her usual self, stricken, almost.

'Come in...' Her voice was shaky, her movements halting. 'No, not really...' she said, pushing a hand through her hair. 'Let me take your coat.'

Hanlon unzipped the puffa and handed it to Julia, who hung it up on a peg in the wide hall.

'Go through, I'll tell you what's been happening,' she said, indicating the lounge door.

Hanlon walked into the lounge, wondering what the matter was with Julia; she didn't seem herself today. As she opened the door she turned her head back to check on Julia, who smiled wanly at her. Hanlon shifted her gaze in front of her and suddenly there he was. She had no time to react.

'Hello, Hanlon,' said Millar and drove his massive fist with all his strength into her face.

44

'I love the hair,' Luke said to Aurora as they sat smoking cigarettes on the rooftop terrace overlooking Arthur's Seat. Aurora looked at Luke. It was great being with him again. Luke seemed changed by his recent experiences. He was now looking happily at the craggy hill in the distance. It was like an old friend. She knew he had painted it innumerable times. The rain had stopped and the sun was out, although it was bitterly cold with a biting breeze. He smiled at her affectionately.

She patted his hand. He had told her how he'd felt he'd been afforded a glimpse into a world that previously he had no real conception of. A terrible, lawless place where people were casually and unimaginably violent. A place where people were hurt and killed. Hanlon was at home there, as was the man wearing the motorbike leathers they could see through the glass of the bi-fold doors.

Luke wasn't and she was very glad of it.

Aurora had texted Luke earlier that morning to come and join her at the flat where she was staying. She had wanted to hear from him what had been happening. Particularly the incident at the studio. She knew what had happened after McDonald had arrived, but not what had been the lead-up to it.

McDonald was inside the flat watching TV. He'd been drug-free for nearly a week now, since the row with Aurora in the Park Bar off the Gorgie Road. She wondered what had happened the night before. He had gone out on his bike early in the evening and had been silent and preoccupied ever since his return, as if he had something on his mind. He was not in the best of moods today either. Something was eating him up. She was worried for him – keeping secrets and drug addiction were always closely allied.

Now she turned her attention to Luke. God, how she'd missed him. After all the crap she'd been through recently it was wonderful to be with someone who was innately good, innately innocent.

'So, where've you been hiding, then, Luke, since those goons that my uncle sent turned up at your place?'

'We were staying at Julia's house,' he said.

'Julia who?' asked Aurora.

'Julia, that woman who works at the university. I think she is the secretary of the English department – you must know her.'

Aurora frowned. There was something about Julia that she had never really liked or trusted. 'What did you make of her, Luke?'

'Why do you ask?' he said.

Aurora looked at Luke. There were three things that Luke could do unbelievably well: he could make genius art, he was an inventive, attentive lover and he was an eerily good judge of character. Maybe all three went together.

'I'm serious, Luke,' she said. She really needed to know what he thought.

'I didn't like her.' He frowned. 'I can't explain it, she's... I don't know, bad inside, like an apple that's turned to mush but still looks good. Rotten to the core.'

Aurora nodded. She had her own suspicions about Julia; she wanted them confirmed.

'You're sure?' she asked.

'It's strange you should ask. It was when I was drawing her...' He took out the small artist's sketchbook he always carried about with him and flipped through the pages. As he did so Aurora glimpsed several pen and ink sketches of Hanlon. Her face in repose, proud, fierce, beautiful. The self-assurance even though she wasn't awake. Aurora was half her age and beautiful, but she envied the other woman's iron determination and self-confidence. Luke had obviously sensed it too. She felt a stab of jealousy.

'Here we are...'

And here was Julia.

The woman that she knew was slim, with large eyes and high cheekbones, very attractive, she had to admit. Here she wasn't. The wide mouth was cruel and voracious, the eyes cold, calculating, dead. It was the face of a monster.

Aurora said, 'That's really what you saw?'

'That's what I saw.' Luke nodded in confirmation. 'I think she's evil. I know it's weird. I didn't understand it myself. I was bloody glad to get out of that house, I can tell you.'

Aurora frowned and thought back. She thought of Morag, of Morag's manuscript. Morag hadn't wanted her to read it, she'd said that she was worried that it wasn't good enough. That, coming from a girl who thought that the sun shone out of her arse, was starkly unbelievable.

Well, she had read it all right. Pinched one of the copies on a memory stick.

Read it with an increasing sense of betrayal, a raging sense of betrayal. Everyone was in it, all ordered according to Morag's Moragcentric world view. Aurora was in it – that was what had sparked the rage. What Morag had written was true, but it was privileged and she had stabbed her in the back. But she remembered now what Morag had written about Julia. It tallied with what Luke had just said.

'Did you tell Hanlon what you thought?' she asked.

Luke shook his head. 'She'd got more than enough on her plate, what with one thing and another.'

Aurora felt cold fingers down her spine. How did Millar know they were in Morningside?

Luke's phone pinged. He looked at it, looked at the message.

'Hanlon's there now.'

Jesus! she thought. She knew instinctively Hanlon was in trouble. Big trouble.

'Stay here, Luke...' She was already on her feet. 'Text me the address,' she called over her shoulder as she yanked open the glass doors to the flat.

'Jamie.'

He looked up, saw the panic in her face, jumped to his feet. She thought he had never looked so good. If what you wanted was a good man in a fight, they didn't come much better than him. Six feet and fifteen stone of hard muscle and violent competence. His dark eyes looked at her steadily.

'What is it, Aurora?'

'Come on, Millar's got Hanlon!'

45

It was a punch that should have knocked her out. But Millar's speed and accuracy were affected, and his vision blurred, by the alcohol and the drugs: he'd had his first drink from the minibar in his hotel room at seven that morning; he'd had a couple of downers, diazepam, as well as the coke, plus his medication, not to be taken with alcohol.

Hanlon had unbelievably fast reactions honed by years of practising in the ring. She was used to people trying to hit her, used to people trying to take her head off. She snapped her head back like a snake and although the punch made contact she was moving backwards away from it.

Millar's knuckles grazed her skin. She ducked under another wild punch aimed at her head. Millar scowled. As well as her own skill, his vision was slightly unfocussed and judging distance was a problem. Millar towered over her; she probably didn't even reach his shoulders. But lack of height could sometimes be an advantage. Hanlon slammed her fist as hard as she could, twisting her body into it, and driving the blow into Millar's balls.

It had been years since anyone had hurt Millar and he had almost forgotten the sensation. Despite the cocktail of drugs and booze, the pain was amazing. He froze and Hanlon hit him hard three times in the face. She was professional-boxer quick. A lesser man would have gone down, not

Millar. He shook his head to clear it. Hanlon picked up a lacquer vase, tall and slim and weighing about a kilo, which she had admired before – a souvenir of Thailand, seemingly – and swung it hard into his temple. Millar crashed to the floor.

Hanlon stood over him breathing heavily. She was elated, wild eyed with triumph, her pupils dilated with excitement. Adrenaline coursed through her veins. She had triumphed over the monster, slain him! Rescued the maiden! His eyes fluttered but didn't open. Julia came into the room; she looked terrible.

'Are you OK?' Hanlon asked. God knew what she'd suffered at his brutal hands, although Hanlon had a pretty good guess.

Julia burst out sobbing. 'He... he grabbed me and he... he made me...'

Hanlon went over to her. 'Shh, Julia,' she said and put her arm around her. Julia buried her head in Hanlon's shoulder and she felt her shoulders jerk as she sobbed against her. 'It's OK,' Hanlon said. 'It's all over now, Julia...'

Julia took a step back. 'I'm sorry,' she said, smiling wanly but bravely at Hanlon. She took the vase from her and held it by the neck in her hand.

'Call the police,' Hanlon said, looking down at Millar, making sure he was still unconscious, and then there was a crack and what sounded like a deafening thunderburst and the sky exploded.

Blackness.

46

Hanlon woke with the most agonising headache. She opened her eyes. Millar was sitting on the sofa staring at her. She was lying on the floor on her side; her hands had been tied behind her at the wrists. Julia was standing behind Millar, her hands resting on his shoulders, looking down at her.

'You!' she said accusingly, staring at Julia. She felt sick. Maybe it was the blow on the head, but maybe it was the betrayal. Julia ruffled Millar's hair and kissed the top of his head.

Millar leaned forward, brought out his wallet and took a small paper wrap from one of the compartments and a credit card. He chopped a generous line out on the glass surface of the coffee table. His phone pinged and he read the message.

'Robbo and Calum have finished. Job done,' he said to Julia. 'Good boys, they're on their way back. Robbo said they'll wait in Marchmont for me to call.' Julia nodded. Millar's thumbs moved quickly. 'See you in an hour,' he muttered to himself as he composed and sent the reply.

'Well, that's Ray and Dougie sorted,' Millar said happily. 'Now for you.'

He snorted the coke and said to Hanlon, 'Not very good at working things out, are you?'

'How could you?' she said to Julia. She could hear the bitterness in her voice, taste it in her mouth.

'My ex left me with no money and a massive mortgage,' she said. 'If those rude, pampered arsehole students want to shove their government loans up their noses, why shouldn't I benefit?' She shrugged. 'Besides, it's fun. Why not?'

God, she played me for a fool, Hanlon thought bitterly. From the word go. She suddenly thought of the tracker in her car. Julia had found out from her the registration and the make when she'd given her the parking permit. It must have been her that installed it – that was how Ray had known where her hotel was. And she'd confided more or less everything to her. How stupid could you get?

She stared at Julia now, her long, slender fingers playing with Millar's hair. Not just working for him, sleeping with him.

Hanlon wondered how much longer Millar would allow her to live. Begging him to spare her wouldn't work, she knew that. It would only gratify him. She knew she was going to die, but she was determined she would go out well. That much she could control.

He sniffed loudly and beamed at her. He seemed to be in a very good mood. Third time lucky. Ray hadn't managed to kill her, neither had whoever had been at Griffiths' house. Presumably Robbo and Calum.

'Got any Scotch?' Millar said to Julia.

She nodded and went into the kitchen. Millar did another line. Julia came back with a glass and a bottle of Macallan.

Millar poured himself a massive tumbler of neat malt. He drank half of it. 'Ahh, that's better,' he said.

'Why did you kill Morag McMillan?' Hanlon asked.

'I didn't,' he said.

Hanlon frowned. 'You didn't? Who did?'

'I honestly don't know, and I honestly don't care.' She could hear that he was telling the truth.

She looked at Julia. 'Did you do it?' Hanlon said.

'Why would I want to do that?' She snorted. 'Of course I didn't kill her.'

Millar sighed. 'Hanlon, no one gives a fuck who killed Morag. You can ask her yourself soon.' Another sip of Scotch. 'Julia, have you got any gloves, and some duct tape and scissors? I think we've both had enough of Hanlon yacking on, don't you?'

Hanlon thought of screaming. She'd get one brief yell out before Millar's hands clamped around her neck – was it worth it? To be honest, she didn't feel up to it. She doubted she could muster a scream, not even a whimper. She didn't feel frightened. She was empty, drained; she just wanted it to be over. She suddenly thought of Wemyss – who would care for him? God, I'll miss him, she thought. I should have made a will. I could have left him to Campbell – he'd have looked after him.

And Campbell would avenge her, of that she had no doubt. He would know who had killed her, or, if she was never found, who was behind her disappearance.

That was something.

Campbell. She wished she'd been nicer to him. She suddenly thought, I think he's in love with me. It was like a revelation.

Julia came back from the kitchen with a pair of yellow rubber gloves and Millar pulled them on. It took a while – they were very tight on his big hands. He flexed his fingers like a piano player. He got off the sofa and knelt down beside Hanlon. Julia leaned forward to watch with interest.

'OK, Hanlon, first things first – where's Aurora?'

'Why would you care?' she spat.

Millar shrugged. 'Unfinished business. Where is she? I know you know.'

'I don't know.'

He shook his head. 'You know I will hurt you until you tell me, and you will tell me, so let's just cut to the chase.'

She shook her head.

He said, 'You do know I enjoy hurting people...' He smiled and leaned forward; she could smell the whisky on his breath. 'Don't talk too soon, this is going to be fun.'

The front doorbell rang.

Millar froze and then clamped his hand over her mouth. She could taste the rubber of the glove and there was a faint smell of bleach.

Another ring. Was it Campbell? she thought. Don't get your hopes up, she told herself. It's probably DHL or Ocado, come to collect their sodding bags.

'Answer it, Julia,' Millar said, adding unnecessarily, 'Get rid of them!'

Julia nodded and left the room, closing the door behind her. Hanlon looked up into Millar's face. He was staring at the door. Hanlon wondered what he was thinking. Could it be the police maybe? Had she told someone where she was going? If it was the police, the charge would be what? Attempted murder, false imprisonment, would he claim it was a sex game gone wrong, a prank even?

They heard the door open, a man's voice saying something and then a very loud thud. Millar strained forward listening intently – what the hell was happening out there? He looked up, puzzled.

The door burst open. Two figures: one was McDonald, in a biker's one-piece and boots, the other was shorter, wearing army trousers and a leather jacket, hands behind their back, face hidden by a motorbike helmet.

There was something familiar about the figure.

'You,' Millar said, glaring angrily at McDonald, his voice snarling, getting to his feet, his hands balling into fists. McDonald looked at Millar's hands, the yellow Marigolds, and he laughed.

'Been doing the dishes, Graeme?'

'You cunt, McDonald, and who's this tosser?' pointing at the figure with the covered face.

McDonald's companion pulled off the helmet with one hand, the other still behind her back, and shook her short dark hair free. The three of them stood stock-still for what felt like an eternity to Hanlon, lying on the floor and looking upwards.

'Aurora!' Millar said, his eyes widening in surprise. 'Aurora, darling...' He smiled at her, and held out his yellow rubber-gloved hands beseechingly as Aurora Cameron pulled the trigger of the gun she was holding in her right hand and fired three times.

47

Hanlon sat on the bed cuddling Wemyss and looking at Aurora. The two of them were back in Hanlon's hotel off the Royal Mile. McDonald had stayed at the house in Morningside, 'cleaning up'.

'Do you want to talk about it?' Hanlon asked.

Aurora nodded. 'I was thirteen.' Her eyes were focussed, not on the wall of Hanlon's hotel room with its anodyne print of Monarch of the Glen, but on events a decade or so previously. 'I'd been at that school for a year. I was lonely – lonely and bored. He came down – he was staying at the Hilton in Park Lane. He took me up to town, bought me lunch, gave me wine, said we should go up to his room to look at the view, you could see all over London, you could see Buckingham Palace...'

Hanlon nodded. Aurora carried on, tonelessly. 'We did some coke – I'd never had coke before – and we smoked a joint, which I had done before, and then he put his arm around me, said I reminded him of my mum how much like her I was... then. Well, I don't need to tell you the rest.'

She stood up; tears were flowing. She paced angrily up and down. Hanlon remembered Griffiths' words.

We were looking at this text by an author who had been sexually abused by a close relation and Aurora, well, she almost literally howled...

Well, you were right, Dr Griffiths.

'It became a regular thing, every couple of months. I tried to say no; he said he'd tell my mum, tell her what a dirty whore her daughter was; that I had done all the running. I told myself it was my fault, that I was bad, that I deserved all this shit... I tried to blot it out, to escape. I took drugs, I fucked around... I felt I was worthless—' she gave a mirthless laugh '—so I acted that way. Give a dog a bad name... Christ...'

'And it stopped?' Hanlon asked.

'Yeah, when I was seventeen, after Mum died and we had the funeral I didn't see him. It was like he'd forgotten about me. And then he got in touch with me about a year ago. I got back to the flat and he was sitting there with Morag. I hadn't seen him for four years or so. He wanted "to resume our relationship".'

Hanlon nodded. Aurora continued, 'I told him to fuck off. I told him I'd rather die.'

'It looked like he took you at your word,' Hanlon said.

She nodded. 'I know that now, but not until a couple of days ago. When Jamie later told me he'd been hired to kill me, I thought it couldn't be him – do you know, I even thought it might have been my dad. That Millar had told him what he'd done to me, or rather he'd have said what we'd done, and that Dad literally wanted to kill me. How fucked up is that?'

She stood up and walked around the small room restlessly. 'Anyway, before Graeme got in touch, I'd been clean about six months. I saw him that one time and I was back to square one. I went out and I got some gear and a bottle of vodka and I got absolutely fucked. For several days.'

Hanlon thought of the paintings hidden in Luke's cupboard, a record of those days, Millar's legacy. Shooting was maybe too merciful a death for him.

Aurora continued. 'Morag looked after me. Then, I pulled myself back together again. I started going to NA, which is where I met Jamie and we became mates. Just mates. I'd had enough of sex with violent criminals. I think that's why I like Luke so much – he wouldn't hurt a fly.' She nodded to herself. 'If you want the opposite of Millar, it's Luke.'

Aurora sighed. 'So now you know my past.'

'But why did he want you dead now?' Hanlon asked.

'I got this weird text from him in January. He said he'd always loved me,

I was the one, he had to have me back in his life. I think he'd really gone off the rails. Anyway, I told him my answer was the same. He texted back, "you've made your bed…" I didn't want to tell you and Jamie in the club – I'd have had to tell you the whole story and at the time I couldn't. It was still my dirty secret, like he owned me. But now he's dead, I'm free of him and I want to be free of the lies too, and free of the shame.'

Hanlon nodded. 'Sure, I understand.' She'd got enough dark secrets and shameful behaviour in her own life. She could sympathise.

Aurora sighed. 'You're only as sick as your secrets, that's what they say, isn't it…? So what happens now?'

Hanlon said, 'McDonald will clean up. Millar won't be found. The police will assume he's been killed by a rival – they already think he's involved in a drugs turf war. I'm not going to tell anyone what happened. Neither will Jamie.'

'And Julia?' Aurora asked.

'I don't know. I don't know what McDonald's plans are for her.' And I really don't care, she thought. 'Whatever happens, she won't be going to the police.'

'What about me?' Aurora asked.

Hanlon took a piece of the hotel stationery from the desk in her room and wrote a name and a phone number.

'This woman is a therapist. I'll be in touch with her so she knows who you are. Dr Morgan is very good. She's based in London. Go and see her – I'll make sure she makes time for you. You need to get out of Edinburgh for a bit. Griffiths will be sympathetic. Take some time off. And when you get back, there's always Skype or Zoom. She's expensive, but your dad's paying.'

'Thank you.'

'You're the one who saved my life.' Hanlon shrugged.

Aurora walked over to her and hugged her. She said, 'You didn't give up on me.' Hanlon could feel the wet warmth of her tears on her neck.

'Neither did your father,' Hanlon said. 'You should speak to him.'

* * *

In the flat in Marchmont, Ray and Dougie were getting increasingly stressed. Robbo's android phone sat on the coffee table while they stared at it. They were waiting for it to ring. For Millar to call. They couldn't open it. Ray had used Robbo's thumb originally after they'd dealt with them, pressing it to open it and send the message to Millar, but Ray didn't want to cut it off and take it with them to try and do it again. That was exactly the kind of thing Millar would have done.

'Where the fuck is he?' wondered Ray. They wanted the waiting to be over. They wanted the much-feared confrontation. Where the hell was he? He said he'd be there within the hour – that was four hours ago. Millar was never late.

'He maybe went back to Glasgow?' Dougie suggested. 'Or he's in his hotel?'

'Well, surely to God he'd still call?'

Another hour went by. Where was he? Why wasn't he calling Robbo?

'Your turn to watch the street,' said Dougie. They'd been taking turns on keeping a watch for Millar's arrival.

'Fuck it,' said Ray. He couldn't take this waiting around for nemesis to call any longer. 'I'm gonna call him.'

'How?' said Dougie.

'On my phone.'

'On your phone?' Dougie looked aghast. 'Are you crazy?'

'I'm sorry, I can't stand the waiting, Dougie.'

Dougie watched as Ray, pulling a face, found and pressed Millar's number.

He listened, then put the phone down.

'Did it go to voicemail?'

'No.' Ray's face was exultant. 'It's completely dead!'

'What, as in not working at all?' Dougie asked.

Ray nodded. 'No ringtone, no voicemail.' The implication sank in. Millar would never go anywhere without his mobile; he was addicted to it, nearly as much as drugs and Scotch. It was unthinkable that he wouldn't pick up. It wasn't as if it were out of charge – something irrevocable had happened to that phone.

Had McDonald added Millar's scalp to those of Jordan McKenna and Chris Harvey?

'Do you think he's...?' Dougie drew a finger across his throat, expressively.

'I don't know, Dougie, but I think we can dare to hope. I think we can do that much.'

Ray and Dougie embraced. Dougie's shoulder rubbed the puncture wound under his chin. I'll bet it was her, he suddenly thought. I'll bet it was Hanlon.

48

The following day, Hanlon was walking Wemyss around the base of Arthur's Seat when her phone rang. It was Mhairi.

'You owe me dinner,' she said.

'You've found the manuscript?' asked Hanlon.

'I've found the manuscript – at least, I know where it is. I've booked a table at a restaurant I like, I'll forward you their address, you're paying, seven p.m. See you then.'

'OK, look forward to it.'

* * *

Getting dressed for dinner that evening at six, she was listening to the local news; police were investigating the discovery of two men found dead in a burnt-out BMW 4 x 4 near Dalkeith. It was believed the men were involved in a feud between drug gangs, victims of gang violence. She thought back to Millar's phone call when she'd been lying on Julia's lounge floor. Calum and Robbo, she thought. It could be Ray and Dougie, but she had a hunch that an old fox like Ray would be smarter than Millar's other men. Either way, it didn't matter. She didn't care. She was free. Free and safe.

Mhairi met her at the restaurant. She was dressed surprisingly conservatively in a tailored jacket and matching skirt with low heels, immaculate understated make-up, severe white blouse.

'I've come from a meeting,' she said. 'This is the business me, the public face.' The waiter came and she ordered a mojito while she was looking at the menu, and a bottle of Chablis for later. Hanlon winced at the prices. She could imagine Cameron paying eventually, but Gillies would almost certainly raise an eyebrow over the receipt.

'So, you found your girl,' Mhairi asked.

'I did,' Hanlon said. 'It's all settled, but there are a couple of details that need sorting out.'

Mhairi nodded. 'Your manuscript.' She leaned back in her chair and nibbled an olive. 'The girl who wrote it had a flat, right?'

Hanlon nodded. 'Yes, in Howe Street, near Stockbridge. So where is it?'

'Not so fast,' said Mhairi and sipped her drink. 'Let's savour the moment, our surroundings, Hanlon, this lovely drink... It's always rush, rush, rush with you, isn't it? You should learn to relax more. You should learn to enjoy yourself.'

Hanlon looked at her sourly; she hated being told what to do. Mhairi smiled sweetly; 'Now, let's look at the poem.' She read it aloud; it was very short. Hanlon practically knew it by heart.

'You and me durable as dried-foods it's easy to say easy to imagine in fact the image is ancient like pulses we kept them like love in a jar.'

'And?' Hanlon said.

'So, the manuscript hard copy was taken, the laptop was taken, but we're looking for a specific memory stick.' Mhairi smiled. 'Let's look at the title of the poem, "Poem for Aurora – apologies to e e cummings – Grace a Jean Lescure". What does that mean?' asked Mhairi, teasingly.

'I don't know,' Hanlon replied.

'Well, I'll tell you. Grace isn't a person like you thought. *Grâce à* means "thanks to" in French and Jean Lescure was a French writer who invented a kind of code for generating text. It's called N+7 – it's easy to crack.'

'I'll take your word for it,' Hanlon said. 'What does it say?'

Mhairi smiled. 'There are various versions but, here, just take every seventh word in the poem and we get "*It's in pulses jar*". She frowned, 'to be precise, Morag miscounted, the last seventh word is 'a' but I think we can safely assume that this indefinite article refers to its adjacent noun, 'jar.' In her kitchen, in Howe Street, there will be a storage jar full of lentils and buried in there will be your memory stick. I'd get round there as quickly as possible before someone makes soup or a dal.'

'I'm impressed,' said Hanlon.

Mhairi said, 'I like puzzles. I like codes. Now you can tell me about yourself... I find you puzzling. So tell me... I know Java, I know HTML, I know Python, what's the Hanlon code?'

They talked, they ate, they laughed. After a fortnight of tension, she could finally relax.

They finished their meal and the bill came; Hanlon paid. They sat for a moment, looking at each other.

'Show me your ear again,' Hanlon said quietly.

Mhairi put her hand up to her hair; Hanlon noticed that her fingers were quite strong-looking, the nails cut short and clear varnished. Mhairi tilted her head slowly to the left and pushed her two-toned hair, black with the bottom dyed a deep blue, to one side. Hanlon stared in fascination at the two red flowers with yellow centres tattooed on the shapely lobe and the pattern of leaves running up the edge of her ear. It was even more beautiful than she remembered.

Hanlon's foot moved to stroke Mhairi's calf, felt the returning pressure.

'So,' Hanlon said, her grey eyes meeting Mhairi's brown ones, 'are you going to show me how to enjoy myself?'

'I thought you'd never ask,' Mhairi said.

Hanlon thought back to the day before, lying on the floor of Julia's house, Millar crouching over her. 'I nearly didn't,' she said softly. 'I very nearly didn't.'

49

A week later Hanlon was sitting in Cameron's suite at the hotel in George Street. She showed him her selfie with Aurora; he smiled.

'So that's what she looks like now. I'm glad. She looks well – not sure about the hair though...' He drank some coffee. 'She's been in touch with me. Thank you.'

'I did my job,' she said. He shook his head.

'You've done far more than I could have hoped, Hanlon,' he said. 'You found Aurora and we're talking again, thanks to you.' He paused, drank some more coffee and looked out of the window. It was raining again. Then he turned his attention back to her. 'I'm going to tell you this because I think I owe it to you...' He took a deep breath. 'I'm not Aurora's father.'

'I'm sorry?' Had she misunderstood something, misheard?

'I'm not Aurora's father,' Cameron said.

'Who is?' She suddenly felt very cold; she knew what he was going to say.

Cameron looked at her, his eyes sad. 'My half-brother, Graeme Millar, is.'

'Millar had an affair with your wife?' she repeated, stupidly.

He nodded. Oh my God, she thought. 'Did he know... about Aurora?'

Cameron nodded. 'Oh, yes, he knew he was her father all right. That's why we quarrelled all those years ago, after Giulia died – he wanted custody of Aurora. There was no way I was going to give her up to him and luckily even our courts were not likely to grant custody to someone with his criminal background.'

'And you never told her?'

'No. I don't know if I did the right thing, given his record.'

Christ, yes, you did the right thing, thought Hanlon, but I'm not going to betray Aurora's confidence. It's not for me to tell Cameron what Millar was up to.

'Was I playing God?' said Cameron. 'Probably. There's no obviously right answer... I wasn't going to let Graeme have her. And now he seems to have disappeared, hopefully for good. I was interviewed by the police, asking if I knew his whereabouts. Good riddance. He was a nasty piece of work.'

He was far worse than even you could ever have imagined, Hanlon thought. Far worse.

'I love Aurora like a daughter. I just want her to be happy...' They sat in silence for a while. Cameron stared into space, then he looked her in the eye. 'I saw you in the lobby that day, when I took that girl up to my room.'

'Oh,' Hanlon said.

'She's twenty-six. She'd dressed as a schoolgirl because it excites me, not because she is one. I saw your face, Hanlon. I'm a lot of things I would rather not be, but paedophile is not one of them.' He stood up; the meeting was obviously terminated.

'Well, that's it, then. Your money is in the bank, and a bonus. Aurora tells me that she's going into therapy with someone you recommended.'

'She's good,' Hanlon said.

'If you need money, call me. If you need legal help, call me – I'll lend you Gillies.'

'Or if I just fancy a chat. I'll miss the banter with Gillies,' she said, smiling. She stood up.

Cameron smiled. 'Oh, one last thing, who killed Morag?'

'I don't know.' Hanlon shrugged. 'I guess I never will. Goodbye, Hamish. Good luck with Aurora.'

She left the suite.

50

Waiting outside the hotel was McDonald. For some reason she wasn't surprised to see him. It was a day of closures. He fell into step with Hanlon.

'Fancy a drink?' he said. 'There's a quiet pub in Rose Street, the Crown.'

She nodded. They walked down the road to the bar. It was empty; it had only just gone twelve.

'Were you following me?' she asked.

'No, Aurora told me you were seeing her dad.' He raised his glass to hers. Lager clinked against Coke. 'So that's that, then.'

'Yeah,' she said. 'Griffiths told me that Julia Swinson's resigned. Her house is on the market.'

He nodded. 'I told her to get out of Edinburgh or I'd kill her. Which I meant. She knows she's lucky I let her live... I wanted to say thanks to you for protecting Aurora.'

'That's OK.'

McDonald looked relaxed and content with life – well, maybe that was not surprising now there was no longer a price on his head.

'Dr Morgan's a good therapist.'

'That's not what I meant, Hanlon,' he said.

'What did you mean?' asked Hanlon quietly.

'We both know she killed Morag,' McDonald said. 'How did you know?'

'I knew it wasn't Millar or Julia,' Hanlon said. 'They told me so. I read Morag's book.'

'So you found it, then?' McDonald said.

'Yes, I found it.' In the jar of lentils, where Mhairi had said it would be. 'Aurora was in it, sex scenes with her uncle, very graphic. Aurora told me she went into blackout after seeing Millar, and Morag looked after her. I guess it all came out when she was out of her mind on vodka, smack and coke, and that bitch took it all down verbatim, put it in her book and Aurora found out.'

She thought of the pictures in Luke's cupboard that she'd seen, the dead-eyed girl, her eyes the reflection of her dead soul; and it was that view of Aurora that Morag wanted to release to the world for her own greater glory. No wonder Aurora had acted the way she had done.

McDonald nodded. 'When I first met Aurora she told me about Morag's book. She told me Morag hadn't let her read it. She took a copy when she went into hiding, read it then. All her dirty secrets as she saw them, all her private stuff laid out for everyone to see: Millar raping her, Millar fucking her, fucking her mum, all her war stories from the booze and the drugs, all laid out for anyone to read, all in the name of entertainment. Unbelievable.'

'Morag would have done anything to further her career,' Hanlon said. 'She paid the price.'

Millar, thought Hanlon. You're dead but part of you lives on. Aurora's inherited your temper, your violence. Hopefully, Dr Morgan would teach her how to harness it, to channel that destructive energy for good. She smiled grimly. You're a chip off the old block, Aurora. You killed Morag and you killed Millar. Dad would have been so proud.

'What are you up to these days, Jamie?' she asked McDonald.

He laughed. 'I'm retraining as a drug and alcohol counsellor. The pay is unbelievably shite. Cheers, Hanlon.' They clinked glasses. 'Oh, this will amuse you. I went to see Ray and Dougie.'

'And what are they up to?'

It was hard to believe that it was only a week or so since Aurora had killed Millar. It was as if he had exerted a spell that had bent everyone, Ray and Dougie, Aurora, McDonald and her, to his iron will. Now he was dead, the bonds were broken. People could live their own lives free of his tyranny.

'They're planning on running a very upmarket B&B for like-minded gentlemen in Bearsden, which is a very genteel part of Glasgow. I wanted to tell them that Millar was dead so they wouldn't be looking over their shoulders for the rest of their days.' He laughed. 'They think you did it. I didn't enlighten them. They're delighted.'

Hanlon laughed. McDonald continued, 'Do you know a DI Campbell?'

Hanlon nodded. 'Vaguely,' she said warily. 'Why do you ask?'

'Oh, there were some parole irregularities and a couple of other things he could have pulled me up over.' McDonald was being studiously vague; she could see there was a lot more to this than he was letting on. 'He called me to say no action was going to be taken… I wondered…'

'Nothing to do with me, Jamie.'

He smiled, a smile of polite disbelief.

Hanlon winced and swore under her breath.

'You OK?' he said, concerned.

'No, I'm fine, sore back.' She shook her head. 'It's nothing.'

They said their goodbyes. He left the pub. She gingerly rubbed the top of her right buttock. A present that Aurora had paid for. The work was so beautiful: a stem with six flowers growing from it, dark and velvety, mysterious – and, looping around the stalk, an intricately drawn white snake, dangerous and beautiful. Busan Jon had excelled himself.

Thank you, Joon Woo Lee, she thought.

Time to think of the future, not the past.

She got her phone out, got his answerphone. 'Hi, Murdo, it's me, Hanlon, when are you going to take me to that Picasso exhibition you promised me ages ago? Call me.'

Maybe she'd let him see her tattoo.

Then one last call. *To understand the present, we have to revisit the past.*

'Hi, Dr Morgan, yes, it's Hanlon. We need to talk.'

MORE FROM ALEX COOMBS

We hope you enjoyed reading *Missing For Good*. If you did, please leave a review.

If you'd like to gift a copy, this book is also available as an ebook, digital audio download and audiobook CD.

Sign up to Alex Coombs' mailing list below for news, competitions and updates on future books.

http://bit.ly/AlexCoombsNewsletter

Silenced for Good, another gripping case for Hanlon, is available to buy now.

ABOUT THE AUTHOR

Alex Coombs studied Arabic at Oxford and Edinburgh Universities and went on to work in adult education and then retrained to be a chef. He has written four well reviewed crime novels as Alex Howard.

Visit Alex's website: www.alexcoombs.co.uk

Follow Alex on social media:

facebook.com/AlexCoombsCrime
twitter.com/AlexHowardCrime
bookbub.com/authors/alex-coombs

ABOUT BOLDWOOD BOOKS

Boldwood Books is a fiction publishing company seeking out the best stories from around the world.

Find out more at www.boldwoodbooks.com

Sign up to the Book and Tonic newsletter for news, offers and competitions from Boldwood Books!

http://www.bit.ly/bookandtonic

We'd love to hear from you, follow us on social media:

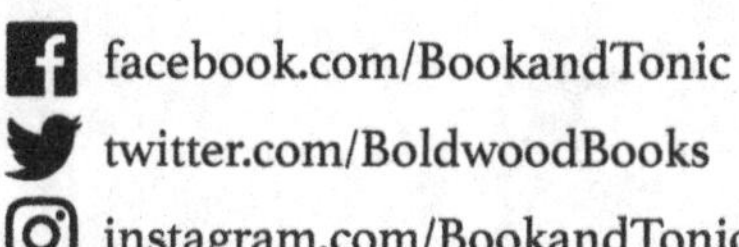

facebook.com/BookandTonic

twitter.com/BoldwoodBooks

instagram.com/BookandTonic

ABOUT BOLDWOOD BOOKS

Boldwood Books is a fiction publishing company seeking out the best stories from around the world.

Find out more at www.boldwoodbooks.com

Sign up to the Book and Tonic newsletter for news, offers and competitions from Boldwood Books!

http://www.bit.ly/bookandtonic

We'd love to hear from you, follow us on social media:

www.ingramcontent.com/pod-product-compliance
Lightning Source LLC
Chambersburg PA
CBHW010746310726
48980CB00004B/383

* 9 7 8 1 8 0 4 2 6 1 8 5 9 *